ONE FOR SORROW

A Wild Fens Murder Mystery

JACK CARTWRIGHT

ONE FOR SORROW

JACK CARTWRIGHT

PROLOGUE

THERE WAS A FINALITY TO THE DOOR SLAMMING BEHIND HER. The closing of a dark chapter. It was as if the house itself mirrored her husband's sentiment with the clear message – *and don't come back*.

The whites of Daniel's eyes had been red with rage and his pupils had been dark and wide enough for her to see the furious corners of his mind, or so she had thought during those moments when his words seemed distant, overridden by the uneasy sense of abandonment.

She loitered for a moment. At least the neighbours couldn't see her. Even if they had heard the argument and the front door slam, the house was tucked way back from the road and tall Leylandii lined the front garden. They wouldn't have seen.

It had been her pocket of paradise. A south-facing haven in which she had whiled away many a week. The garden had been her pride and joy. It made her smile every time she came home and each time she ventured out.

At the end of the driveway, perched on the brick wall, was a single magpie, its glossy feathers lit by the moonlight. It stared at her, head cocked, inquisitive. Taunting her.

A sign, maybe?

"One for sorrow," she whispered to herself, and then skipped a few lines to the last line of the poem. "A secret never to be told."

A small part of her thought to search for a second magpie so that she might announce, "Two for joy," if only to find some comfort in the fabled rhyme.

But she didn't look. She knew the magpie would be alone.

Bright as the moon was that night, a shadow swept its cloak over the fruits of her labour so that only the front door could be seen. The door to hell. It was as if nothing else existed. The light from inside shone through the square pane of glass. A portal into another world. Her world. The world she would be leaving behind. As desperately cruel as that lonely world was, leaving it wasn't something she was quite ready to do. She could accept her marriage had suffered and was likely over. But leaving the home they had built together was a different story.

The square of light showed him approaching, a lean shape moving fast toward her. The door snatched open and, for a moment, she saw his features – his square jaw, his deep-set eyes and broad forehead. She had always loved how trim he kept. His cheekbones were pronounced and his eyes glistened, not with sadness but with that rage she had cowered from time and time again.

A small suitcase, the type that fit into overhead lockers on planes, landed at her feet and bumped her shin. But she didn't feel it. Not really. He tossed her heavy coat after it.

He paused, one hand on the door handle, and for a fleeting moment, their eyes met. He was going to say something. He was going to make everything alright. He was going to say he was sorry for all the times he had hurt her.

But the door began to close and his face slipped from view, until it was obscured by the frosted glass, featureless.

"I'll tell everyone," she said, yet she didn't know why.

The closing door slowed to a stop. Seconds passed like

minutes as her words permeated his arrogant mind. Then, slowly, he pushed it open.

Another chance.

"If you throw me out, that's it. I'll tell everyone what you do. I'll tell the world who you really are."

He said nothing. Instead, he stared at her, a silhouette in the door frame lit from behind.

"It's not just me that loses, Daniel. We both lose."

Considering her words with evident scorn, the shape of his face altered as he smiled. He stepped forward from the doorway and she stepped back, eyeing the case on the ground. With a light kick, he moved the case to one side and took a step closer.

There was no use in running. He would catch her. There was no use in shouting. The neighbours had heard it all before.

But there was something about the way he was standing.

"No, Jane," he grumbled, tired of it all as much as she was. "No, you won't tell anybody. You have nobody to tell."

He paused, offering her the chance to argue his words, but he was right. She had nobody to tell and nowhere to go. For a moment, she thought he might say something else, but instead, he seemed to look up at the sky, then at the trees, and then, finally, he gave her a contemptuous look before closing the door on her.

The square of light seemed to shimmer in Jane's watery eyes. Then that portal of hers to a world she had loathed closed as he switched off the hallway light.

She stopped a horrified gasp from escaping her lips with her hand clamped over her mouth.

It was happening. It had happened. It had really happened this time. Dragging her small case behind her to the road and pulling on her coat as she walked, she gave a cursory glance back over her shoulder. Not at the house, and not at the door in the hope that he might have changed his mind, but at her garden, hoping to catch a glimpse of the roses she had nurtured. It was the dead of winter, and they had all been deadheaded, but in her mind, their flowerless skeletons remained noble and majestic. The king of the flowers.

But the kings remained in shadow, their lifeless limbs bowed as she passed.

With her options amounting to a single phone number that she dared not call, she walked. The wheels of her carry-on were loud in the night, loud enough that the neighbours would hear. She imagined them in the dark confines of their bedrooms, tugging at curtains to see who was making such a row, then letting the drapes fall back and saying to their partners, "It's okay. It's just the weak girl from up the road."

Turning from Acacia Drive onto the main road brought with it a sense of relief. A confidence grew in her. She would be okay. She wasn't the only guilty party here. A shadow beneath a tree seemed a suitable place to stop and tug her phone from her pocket. The messaging app on her phone contained a number with no name, a number she had never once called but had messaged frequently. Her hands trembled as she typed a text blurred by tears, and twice she thought she had heard Daniel following her, his footsteps approaching from Acacia Drive.

Then she heard it. The angry growl of his diesel van. Stepping into the shadow of a tree, she took a final glance at her message, and with her teeth biting down on her lower lip and Daniel's headlights approaching, she hit send and watched the message go.

I need to see you. You know where. Please.

CHAPTER ONE

The Witham and Fens surgery on the outskirts of Woodhall Spa, as per its name, boasted glorious views across the fields and fens beyond. A bird hung in the sky searching the ground below for the tiniest of movements. The cold wind brushed over the land so that the crops seemed to dance in unison, swaying back and forth.

Detective Constable Jackie Gold was mesmerised. She didn't know what the bird was, or what crops were growing, but still, she thought the view to be spectacular. She stared through the floor-to-ceiling glass in the surgery reception thinking about everything and nothing in particular, all at the same time.

"Are you even listening to me?" her mother asked, her voice snapping her back to reality.

"Eh?"

"I said, are you listening to what I'm saying?"

Although they had left Edinburgh when Jackie had been a small child, a hint of the accent still clung to her words. Her mother, however, had been born and bred there and her accent was still prominent. It suited her, Jackie thought, when she was being lovely, as was most often the case. But during those moments when her feisty Celtic heritage shone though, she could be a right old dragon.

"Yes, of course I am. Christ, Mum. I'm not fifteen anymore."

"So?"

"So, what?"

"What are you going to do?"

"When?" Jackie asked, frantically trying to remember what her mother had been saying to add some context to the conversation. The woman sitting opposite them gave her a disapproving look. She could go stuff herself. She shouldn't even be listening to other people's conversations.

"Not *when*. If."

"If what?" Jackie asked. "Sorry, Mum, look, I've got a lot on."

"*If* Charlie needs to see a specialist, dear. It could be serious, you know? You'll have to take care of him. There's a limit to what I can do. I'm not getting any younger."

"I know, Mum. I know," Jackie said. "I think about it every day."

"Why don't you try and get a transfer? You know, back to uniform. Regular shifts. I know it's not what you want, but at least you could make plans."

"I'm here, aren't I? I'm doing what I can. We'll muddle on through, like we always do."

"Aye, you're here. But you only just got here on time. If it wasn't for me, you would have had to go all the way home to get him."

Him. Charlie. Her son. Her pride and joy. He wasn't even listening. He ran a toy digger over the back of the seat and somehow, in his childish imagination, it managed to drive down the vertical drop and onto her leg. His chest rattled as he inhaled, just as it had done for weeks, despite the antibiotics, despite the humidifier, and despite him being kept away from his friends. As if to add a little weight to her mother's argument, he coughed, a sickly, wet cough that sounded painful.

"If he gets really sick, then I'll think about it, Mum. I know you help–"

"I don't mind helping–"

"And I know you don't mind. But please. I'm doing the best I can. If I go back to uniform, I'll never get this chance again. And I told you, we've got a new DI now. A woman. I really think I can learn a lot from her."

"I thought you said Ben was all over her."

"I didn't say he was all over her. I said they work closely. He's a DS. That's what he does."

"I sense a bit of jealousy," her mother said with a smile. "I had a fancy man once. Before your dad, of course. Oh, I could have stared at him all day and night. Bright eyes. Clean shaven. They were back then, you know. Clean shaven. The good ones anyway."

"Mum, Ben is not my fancy man," Jackie hissed, as quietly as she could. "Besides, he's got a date."

"Oh, a date. Sounds lovely. Still, he told you about her. Sounds like he's trying to make you jealous."

"He told me about her because he needed help with what to wear. Ben isn't really clued up about that type of thing. He's..."

"He's what, dear?"

"Simple, Mum," she explained. "Not in the head. You know? He's intelligent. He just lives a simple life. He's not into fashion."

"And where did he meet this other woman, then? Maybe you can get down there."

"He met her in his local doctor's surgery, as it happens, Mum. Which is lucky because I always seem to be here. Maybe I'll meet someone," Jackie said, then nodded at a man out in the car park helping an elderly woman from his car. "How about him? Shall I go and ask him if he's single?"

"Oh, stop it," her mother said, with one of her classic eye rolls. "I just don't want to see you end up struggling. It creeps up on you, you know?"

"What does?"

"Depression."

"I am not..." She paused and lowered her tone, all too aware of the other patients in the waiting room. "I'm not depressed, Mum."

"Not yet. But carry on, and–"

"Can we do this another time?" Jackie asked, just as the girl behind the desk leaned from behind her screen.

"Charlie Gold," she announced.

Jackie waved as if to confirm she had heard, then peered across at her mother. "Are you coming in?"

"I suppose I should, seeing as I'll be the one looking after him."

Taking a deep breath, Jackie stood, collected her bag, then leaned down to reach for Charlie's hand. But her mother had beaten her to it, and she marched him off toward Doctor Harris' door. The woman opposite her pulled another of those disapproving expressions, but rather than cause a scene, Jackie ignored it and followed her mother.

"Ah, if it isn't young Charlie," the doctor said, as Jackie entered the room. Her mother had taken one of the guest seats and Charlie hopped up onto the other then began to swing his legs back and forth, biting down on his lower lip. The doctor looked across at Jackie's mother, then up at Jackie. "I see you've brought the family. How lovely."

"Sorry, Doctor. This is my mum. She's–"

"I'm the day-care," her mother explained, closing Jackie down. "I thought my opinion might be useful. I'm with him most days."

"I see," the doctor said politely.

They were interrupted by a knock at the door, and the receptionist walked in. "Sorry it's late," she said, carrying a cup of coffee on a tray. "Don't mind me."

"Not there," the doctor snapped, as the woman tried to put the tray down on his desk. He cleared a space without even looking at her. "It's been back-to-back all day. Haven't even had time to stop for lunch. I hope you don't mind."

"Not at all, Doctor," Jackie's mother said, before Jackie could offer her own response.

"Now, where were we?" he continued, as the receptionist left the room, her face a little redder than when she had entered. He searched through Charlie's file, glancing up at Jackie's boy every so often. "The antibiotics haven't done anything?"

"No," Jackie said, leading the conversation from the Gold side. "It's not so bad during the day. It's the night time when he's worst."

"I said he should sleep on his side," her mother interrupted. "A few blankets and a hot drink. That should loosen it up."

"Yes, unfortunately that's not a permanent fix."

"He struggles to breathe, you see," Jackie said, trying to regain control. "It's horrible to see. It's like he's fighting for air sometimes."

"Yes, as I thought. I'll give him something stronger for a few days. If that doesn't work, then I'm afraid I'm going to have to refer him."

Slowly, Jackie's mother turned to look up at her with her best *I told you so* expression.

"Refer him?" Jackie said. "To where?"

"To Lincoln. The hospital. He'll need to be admitted. He'll need more X-rays and possibly an inhaler. But let's take one step at a time. I'm writing him a five-day prescription. Three per day with food."

"An inhaler?"

"It wouldn't be permanent, don't worry. But if the higher dosage doesn't work, he will need to go in. It usually takes a few days to a week to clear."

"What does?"

"Bronchiolitis," the doctor stated, closing the file and resting his elbows on the desk. "That's my opinion."

He stood, collected his stethoscope from a drawer, and then spent a few minutes listening to Charlie's breathing, telling him to take a deep breath every now and then.

"Yes. I'm quite sure. It's not an emergency, but it won't go away without treatment. If the antibiotics don't help, then the hospital will be the best place for him. I'll refer him, obviously."

"So, what do we do?" Jackie said. "Should I take him there now?"

"God, no. Come back and see me after five days. If need be, I'll ask Cheryl to make the arrangements. They'll call you with an appointment," he said with a smile. "He'll be fine in no time at all. He's a happy lad. If it was very serious, he would have a very different disposition, I can assure you."

He did that thing that all doctors seemed to do when they were finished talking. He set his hands down on the desk and looked between them. It was a demonstration of patience, and a subtle hint that the session was over.

"Thank you, Doctor," Jackie's mother said. "Do you have many more to see?"

"At least three more," he said, checking his watch. "Five o'clock. Busiest time. Have you had your jab?"

"My jab?"

"The flu jab," he said. "There's a lot of it about right now. You can get it for free you know?"

Jackie smiled inwardly. It was a very discreet way of telling her mother that she was old enough to receive the free flu jab, and that she should consider it if she hadn't done so already. But knowing her mother, Jackie guessed the comment would have been taken off-kilter and seen as a dig at her age.

"You too," he said, looking at Jackie. "Eighty per cent of my patients this week have been children or pensioners. The flu vaccination helps. You should all consider it. Especially with young Charlie the way he is. A bout of the flu on top of this could be quite serious."

"Thank you, Doctor," Jackie said, leading Charlie out of the door. Her mother followed, buttoning her coat as she walked, but she made a point of taking Charlie's other hand.

At the reception desk, Jackie stopped, waited for Cheryl to stop what she was doing, and then repeated what the doctor had said.

"Doctor Harris has given us another prescription. He said if it doesn't help, then he would ask you to book an appointment at the hospital for Charlie."

"Okay," Cheryl said. "He'll pass me the file when he's ready."

"Can I just ask if you could call me on my mobile, please? I'm not at home much and I don't want to burden my mum too much."

"I'm perfectly able to answer a telephone," her mother began, to which Jackie didn't reply.

"My mobile," she repeated to Cheryl.

"Of course," Cheryl replied. "I'll just make a note of that."

"Thank you," Jackie said, leading them through the waiting room and out of the door.

"I suppose you have to get back to work, do you?" her mother asked, although, to her credit, her tone was softer than it had been before, with nobody listening in.

"Yeah, I'm on call," Jackie replied, fishing her car keys from her pocket. "There's some oven chips in the freezer, and some fish fingers—"

"I'll do him some vegetables," her mother replied. "He needs some vitamins. None of that frozen rubbish you feed him."

"Thanks, Mum," Jackie said. "I mean it. I do appreciate what you do."

"Aye, I know, sweetheart. I just don't want to see you working yourself to the bone, that's all."

———

"Total disregard for protocol and process," said DCI Granger, the man who had been making Freya Bloom's life difficult ever since she had been seconded into his department. "And then during a debrief, I find you daydreaming."

"I wasn't daydreaming—"

"I don't know how you did things in London, and quite frankly, I don't care. You don't have fifty officers around you anymore, Bloom. You have nine, and only three of them are in your team."

"I'm aware of the limitations, guv."

"Limitations? Is that what you think this is?" he said, his face augmenting into a sneer. "Two Detective Constables, A Detective Sergeant, and you. I'd love to meet the man that awarded you a DI badge and no doubt gave you a nice pat on the back to go with it."

"I earned my rank, guv. Much the same way you did."

"We've held that number for as long as I care to remember. In fact, if you recall, I was going to make the team smaller before you turned up."

Knowing that he was about to begin a difficult conversation, Freya put the brakes on and played to his ego. It was no secret that DS Savage was due to be moved up to DI before her arrival – a gap in the team formed by the death of the previous DI.

"I can never replace DI Foster, guv. I know that."

"No. No, you bloody well can't."

"I also know he was a close friend of yours. I'm not here to taint his memory. Everyone here speaks highly of him."

"He was a good man and a bloody good detective."

"I'm also well aware that DS Savage was stepping up to DI when I arrived. Again, it was never my intention to cause disruption. If you want me to go, then let's make arrangements. I came here looking for a fresh start, not to change the world."

"You've got a smart mouth," he said, then seemed to ease off a little. He didn't want her to go. "Sit down, Bloom, please."

Being told to sit was a contradiction in Freya's mind. It was a polite gesture in the form of an instruction. Ordinarily, Freya would have remained standing, but DCI Will Granger was clearly not in the mood for Freya's games.

"Most of the team like you," he began. "But you haven't won *me* over. Not yet."

"Is that a challenge?" she asked, and regretted it the moment she said it.

"No, Bloom, it is not a challenge. You have an attitude and I don't bloody well like it. If your career is to flourish here in Lincolnshire, then I suggest you up your game. You're a DI for crying out loud. You're supposed to set an example to the team. Maybe not DS Savage, but DC Gold and DC Chapman will be looking to you. You're a strong, successful female detective. You're everything they want to be."

"Well, I'd better set them straight then, hadn't I?"

"If you're going to lead, then damn well lead. If you're going to stare into space like a zombie, then do it in your own time, and if you're going to destroy a crime scene, then go somewhere else and destroy someone else's crime scene. Do I make myself clear?"

Freya remained silent. She sat upright in her chair, fingers interlaced.

"Well?"

"Guv?"

"What happened last night?"

"The investigation was going nowhere," said Freya, loud and clear, just as if she were leading a briefing. "We had a tip-off that Andrew Summers was involved in the stolen red diesel CID are looking into. I was helping out, unless of course you want us to sit around waiting for something more important to happen. A major investigation, that is."

"What about the hit and run incident? Where are we with that?"

"You assigned that to Standing."

"Can't you help him?"

"He's a lost cause, guv."

"Excuse me?"

Freya inhaled, long and loud. "He doesn't want any help. Says he can manage just fine without us," she said, shrugging. "We got a tip-off, and we acted on it."

"A tip-off was all it was. You requested a warrant and I denied the request. So why did you go there?"

"I needed a warrant to search the place. I don't need a warrant to go and ask questions."

"So you disobeyed a direct order?"

"I disagree, guv. Respectfully, you didn't tell me not to pursue the matter. In fact, you told me, and I quote, 'Do your job, get some bloody evidence, and I'll get you a bloody search warrant'. So that's what I was doing."

"The entire bloody barn went up in flames."

"It was on fire when we arrived, guv. In fact, it was DC Gold who called the fire service," said Freya. "But it was too far gone. The barn was pretty much just a smouldering ruin by the time we got there."

"And Andrew Summers?"

He stared into Freya's eyes and she held his gaze, swallowing the stench of charred flesh that lingered in her throat.

"There was almost nothing left of him when I found him," she said quietly. "I dragged him free of the fire and covered him in an old blanket to…"

She paused, hoping that the context of the conversation would give Granger enough for him to complete the image.

"To what?" he asked.

Clearly, he wanted her to verbalise it. She sucked in a breath and stared at him.

"To put him out, guv."

Granger nodded, studying Freya for any indication of weakness.

"How did DC Gold handle it?"

"She didn't see him. I made sure of that. It wasn't pretty."

"So what now?" he asked. His voice was calmer, indicating that he must have at least some understanding of the trauma involved in witnessing a charred body.

She sighed.

"Case closed, guv. Summers was using his old RAF buddies to steal red diesel then selling it on at pure profit."

"Can we prove that?"

"Not anymore. The evidence has gone up in flames and, funnily enough, nobody seems to know a thing about it. Summers went out to the barn, sparked up a cigarette, and, well, the rest is history. Death by misadventure, guv."

"Death by misadventure? Is that the best we can do?"

"He left behind a wife and child. Do we really want to drag them through the legal process? It's bad enough they had to see him like that. Death by misadventure is taming it down so the family can move on."

"But what actually caused the fire?"

"The cigarette."

"Diesel isn't flammable."

"It is under extreme heat or pressure. For example, if say the old wooden barn where the stolen diesel was being stored was accidentally doused in petrol and set on fire."

"Arson?"

She nodded. "He knew we were onto him. He would have lost his military pension if he'd been found guilty."

"Are you suggesting he was disposing of the evidence and accidentally killed himself in the process?"

"No. At least, not publicly. There was nothing left at all, apart from four empty fifty-gallon drums, a burned-out, old car, and the smoking remains of Andrew Summers. The story I'm going with saves his family some dignity, at least. The heat would have been incredible. Andrew Summers was trying to put a fire out. I don't see any reason to mention the diesel. Not to the press anyway."

"So what do we do? How do we move forward?"

"We can still go after whoever stole the diesel in the first place. They won't stop. There will also be an inquiry–"

"Not with Summers. With you. How do we move forward with you?"

"I'll do my best to lead by example, I guess," said Freya. "What do you want me to say?"

"I want to know what happened. I want to know why you dropped a high-flying career in London and came here."

There it was. The question Freya had been avoiding even answering to herself was laid out in the open.

"I came here for a fresh start, guv."

"Your last case in London was James Marley. Am I right?"

Freya said nothing.

"He killed five women." Granger cocked his head as if waiting for Freya to make a comment, but there was nothing to say. "You caught him, then you disappeared off the face of the earth."

"I didn't catch him."

"You were instrumental in his capture."

"Only because I let him catch me," she said flatly. "But that was never the plan."

"You vanished soon after. You left everybody to pick up the pieces."

"I took leave, guv. I'm entitled, the last I checked."

"You took six months. Good detectives don't take six months' leave without good reason. Good detectives don't leave their team wondering how they are, then pick up the first secondment that comes along. What happened, Bloom? No lies. No games. Tell me what happened. He caught you, didn't he? He held you captive for three days. I know that much."

She stared across at him, searching for a hint of smugness in his tone. But there was only compassion.

"He caught you, Freya. I've read the report. I've read the account of the officer that untied you and removed the hood from your face. Don't worry. Your secret is safe with me. But if you want to stay, then I need to know that you're stable. What I've seen so far suggests otherwise. If I know what happened to you, then maybe I can help."

"Help? You can *help* by not mentioning it, guv. I came here for a fresh start. I came here to forget about James Marley. If you want to know what happened, then I'm sorry but you'll be sorely disappointed."

"You won't ever be stable until you can move on, Freya. You have to try."

"Try?" she said. "I saw six different therapists, guv. Every one of them tried to find out what happened to me. Every one of them failed. Every one of them marked me down with dissociative amnesia. Nothing they can do. Strike me off. Throw me away. Worthless."

"I'm trying to help you–"

"I don't know what happened, guv. I don't know. I was in the forest. I found his cabin. And I heard a scream."

Granger leaned forward onto the desk, eager to hear more.

"I have snippets. I was tied up. That's all I can remember. The next thing I remember was waking up in the house."

He stared at her, confused.

"A big, blank space, guv. Three days apparently. Three days of my life are missing. Is that what you want to know?"

"You don't remember anything?"

"Like I said, snippets. But none of it makes sense," she said, and before he could push for details, added, "and it's nothing I ever want to repeat. Not to you. Not to anybody."

"Have you seen anybody? A professional?"

"Harley Street, London. The best. Half a dozen of them. Not one of them could help. The truth is, guv, I don't *want* to remember it. The Metropolitan Police spent a fortune trying to bring those memories back, and I don't even want them. I don't want to relive those three days."

"You have to," he said, not as an instruction or an order. His tone was almost fatherly. Like he was letting go of his daughter so she could ride her bicycle unaided for the first time. "It's going to hurt. But it's something you have to do to move forward."

"I told you I don't want them," she snapped, then calmed. She closed her eyes, fully aware that her reaction had been unacceptable.

"You are what they call in the business, DI Bloom, a loose cannon," he said, leaning back in his chair again. He was going to make a deal. She'd seen the combination of expression and posture before. "I knew you were trouble when you first came here. But I was told you're good. And you are. Could be, at least."

"Guv," she said, by way of appreciation, but with little else to add.

"I seem to recall when you closed your first investigation here. The girl on the beach," he said, clicking his fingers, trying to recall the victim's name.

"Jessica Hudson," she said.

"That's it. I seem to recall speaking to you afterwards. Right here in my office."

"You did, guv, yes."

"Do you remember what I said?"

He clearly remembered. He would know what he said word for banal word.

"Not verbatim."

"The gist, then," he said.

"You said I could stay."

"I said you could stay, yes," he said, as if he'd just stumbled on a revelation. "What else?"

He stared at her across the desk. Daring her to say the words.

"You said I could stay if I bucked my ideas up, guv."

"That's right. Would you call this bucking your ideas up?" he asked. "Daydreaming? Talking back to me? Going against orders? The list goes on, Freya."

There wasn't a positive spin she could put on it. The ball was well and truly in his court. There was nothing Freya could say to argue. He was right.

"You're a bloody good detective. Here's what we're going to do," he said, and he sat back in his seat and announced his plan to either bring Freya Bloom back to the land of the living, or throw her to the wolves. Either way, it would be her choice to stay or go.

CHAPTER TWO

It was late when Freya closed the door of her small, rented cottage and switched on the hallway light. The cottage wasn't much, but it was everything she needed. It would do for the time being. Habitually, she engaged the second lock – a small security chain that wouldn't stop a squirrel, let alone anybody determined to get in. The old cottage was cold with a boiler that took its time to heat the radiators and a wood-burning stove that required both wood and the knowledge of how to build a fire that stayed alight for more than two minutes.

Choosing to keep her coat on, she moved through to her small kitchen. It had been decorated at a time when Artex ceilings were fashionable and muted colours were all the rage. It hadn't been touched since. Filling the kettle on her return from work was another habit she had developed. It was the same every night. By the time the kettle had finished boiling, she had already poured herself a glass of wine, leaving the untouched hot water to cool until the morning.

The cottage, though basic in amenities and seemingly stuck in 1970, was a large step up from the motorhome that was parked outside on the private lane, which she had called home for a while. The first night she had been in the cottage, she had been tempted to creep outside to the camper to sleep in familiar surroundings. Instead, she had selected the old armchair that filled the nook beside the log burner and slept beneath a heavy blanket.

When she thought of what she once had and compared it to her current circumstances, she couldn't help but wince at the pang of failure. It was only natural. She had left a beautiful, four-bedroomed house in the glorious London suburbs, along with her husband and his child, who she had once considered her own, to live in a motorhome on a remote Lincolnshire beach. When she thought of it that way, she could see why Granger had his concerns.

She sipped her wine, as she always did, then, coaxed on by the sweetness and the promise of sleep, she took a larger, very unlady-like mouthful. Wiping her mouth with the back of her hand, she took a breath, her thirst satiated.

She stepped from her boots, clutching her drink, a practised move that would not be possible after her third or fourth glass. The cold, terracotta floor tiles bit at the soles of her feet until she worked her socks into soft slippers. The trouser suit she had been wearing that day needed washing, but it would suffice for the evening. Anything was better than having to strip off in the cold. The lack of TV in the cottage suited her just fine. The lounge, with its log burner and armchair, was also furnished with a dining table, on which Freya ate her meals when she decided to actually cook, and worked, which she rarely stopped doing. She found a place among the paperwork for the glass then plopped into the hard, wooden dining chair to sort the papers into some semblance of order ready for the morning.

The papers were a jumbled mess but could easily be sorted into folders, she told herself, pulling the papers and photographs together into one neat pile. DC Chapman could easily sort them into relevant files in the morning. She enjoyed organisation.

For Freya, police work, if one was to follow the rules, was eighty per cent paperwork, ten per cent waiting, and ten per cent taking action. But if a younger, less experienced officer was following in the ranks and keen to make progress, delegation was her friend. *Paperwork is a rite of passage*, she remembered her first DCI telling her.

This case had been simple to investigate and even easier to catch the suspect. Andrew Summers was already dead when they found him. Like most cases, it would have been difficult to collate enough evidence to form a conviction. But when the suspect was a smouldering pile of bones and singed flesh, a confession was out of the window. All that remained was to tie the stolen diesel to the man that stole it, and Freya knew just the officer to help.

The glass of wine in her hand had been well-earned, though it trembled with her fatigue. More pressing was the single sheet of headed paper on which was printed DCI Granger's formal instruction to seek a local therapist.

She set it down on the top of the disorganised pile.

Life in Lincolnshire was a far cry from the pace of London. Sure, there were less investigations but the reduced workload was welcomed. Her London role had provided a backlog of investigations and reports to work through in a perpetual state of balancing budgets and resources. She no longer had the head space for that kind of pressure. Fresh air and a simple workload was what she needed, and Lincolnshire provided just that. Talking to a stranger about her loss of memory would achieve nothing, but she would have to play Granger's game if she wanted to stay.

She missed London's wine bars, the selection of live music, and the shopping, but she could, she felt, bring a certain refinement to any place she called home. Even her tiny little farmworker's cottage would look different when she had the time to hit the city and bring in a few soft furnishings and maybe some paint. Then all she would have to think about would be heating the damn place.

But her residence in wild and rural Lincolnshire, thanks to Granger's instructions, now had a ticking clock marring the beauty of the place.

The armchair beside the fire afforded very few comfortable positions, one of which was with her legs tucked beneath her, so she could rest her laptop on the arm of the chair and lay the blanket over her. Her wine glass had a space on the floor just within reach, and she had just set it down and closed her eyes when there were three raps on the door, hard and unmistakable.

___

CHAPTER THREE

___

Detective Sergeant Ben Savage stood in the freezing cold, his hands firmly entrenched in his jacket pockets.

"It's midnight," said Freya, before the door had even opened enough for him to see her.

"It's eight p.m.," he replied.

"It feels like midnight."

"I spoke to Jackie. She told me what you did. Are you okay?"

"I would have thought you'd have better things to be doing with your evening."

"Like what?" Ben asked, waving his hand across the pitch-dark landscape behind him.

"Oh, I don't know. A date or something."

He cocked his head to one side, and his eyes narrowed.

"How did you find out about that?"

"Oh, so I was right?"

"Who told you, Freya?"

"Nobody. Must have been a lucky guess," she said with an unconvincing smile.

"I cancelled it, if you must know."

"Oh," Freya said, sounding disinterested, but Ben knew better.

"I was never really interested," he explained. "And neither was she apparently. She didn't seem to mind."

"What is it exactly that you want, Ben? It's been a long day."

"Do you need to talk about it?" he asked. "You know? What happened today?"

"No, I need to forget about it," she replied.

He stared at her, looking her up and down.

"Are you cold?"

Leaning on the door frame, she looked like she hadn't slept for days.

"I haven't been home long. Granger wanted to see me."

"Oh, what did he want?" asked Ben.

"To challenge me. Do you have many of these questions? I was keen to sit down."

"Do you always wear your slippers with your coat? It's a good look. Is that a London thing?"

"Laugh all you want. I'm too tired to care. But can we finish this in the morning?"

"Sure," said Ben. "I've brought you a present. Thought you might appreciate it."

Freya stared at him with a delightful blend of intrigue and fatigue, almost childlike.

"There's no smoke coming from your chimney, Freya," Ben said.

"I haven't lit the burner thing."

"That's because you don't have any wood," said Ben, and gestured at the empty wood store, a small, shed-like structure beside the kitchen window.

"Is that what that is?"

"We lost a tree in the top field last weekend. Dad said you can have some of the off cuts. He'll use the rest himself."

"So your dad rents me a house on his land for next to nothing, and then gives me free wood?"

"I might have persuaded him," Ben said, offering her his finest charming smile. "I can be quite persuasive when I want to be."

She said nothing but nodded, not too tired to be fooled into a scam.

"It's the least I can do," he continued. "Go inside. I'll stack it for you."

Shoving herself off the door frame, Freya pulled her coat around her.

"I might be a city girl, but I can still stack wood, country boy."

"Can you?" he asked, tossing her a log which she caught with little effort. She weighed it in her hands, sized up the mound on the back of the truck, then added two more to create a pile in her arms.

"Can't be that hard. Besides, I prefer to keep a tight hold on favours that come my way."

"Your independence will be the death of you, Freya Bloom."

"My independence has nothing to do with it. I don't like favours, Benjamin Savage," she said. "Because favours have to be paid back, and frankly, I don't have the time or the energy."

"It isn't a favour. It's neighbourly." He leaned into the driver's side of the truck and flicked the switch that lit the pick-up's flat bed. "You'll have to get used to it if you're staying."

"Ah," said Freya. "Digging for information will get you nowhere fast."

"I'm not digging for information," he said, as he formed a pile of six logs on the truck's flat bed, then eased them into his arms. "I'm a detective, remember? If I wanted to find out how long you're staying, I'd do what any good detective would do. I'd exercise patience."

"And what is it you would wait for? For me to leave?"

"No," he said, dropping the logs into the small wood store to form the beginnings of a stack. "I'd wait for Will Granger to call me asking me to step up to DI again. You can't keep a good man down, Freya Bloom."

His reference to the position she held was light-hearted. It seemed like only a few weeks ago that he had been offered a chance to go for the vacant Detective Inspector position that David Foster's death had opened. It had been a sad time, but the team had felt that Ben was ready for the role. That was until the new girl had showed up on secondment from the Met in London, and had shattered his chances.

"You know," she began, leaning against the truck. Her breath clouded around her and she clearly thought he wasn't looking when she wiped her nose on the back of her hand without a handkerchief. "I can't tell if you want me to stay because you enjoy my company, see an opportunity to learn more, and appreciate my leadership, or if you want me to go so you can make DI."

Reaching into the cab of the truck, he retrieved a box of tissues his dad always kept on the dashboard. He tossed them to her and ignored her embarrassment as she blew her nose.

"I can't work it out either. But one thing is for sure."

"What's that?"

"It's a lot more fun around here since you came."

"Fun? Do I make you laugh?" she asked, cradling three logs and balancing a fourth that threatened to fall.

"Not all the time," he replied, as his phone began to vibrate in his pocket. He paused to retrieve it and studied the number on the screen, then gave her a look that he hoped said, 'Brace yourself'. He hit the green button to answer the call.

"DS Savage," he said, and closed his eyes trying to hear above the wind.

"Ben, it's Jackie. Where are you?"

Ben had known DC Jackie Gold for so long that, to him, the cute girl with the soft remnants of an Edinburgh accent had become like a little sister. The fact that she had followed him into the force was testament to their friendship.

"At home. Sort of. What's wrong?"

"I'm sorry, Ben. I'm on duty. I had a call from the desk. I should have called earlier—"

"Slow down, Jackie. What did they say?" Instinctively, Ben raised the tailgate of the truck with his free hand. He knew he would be leaving imminently.

"Someone has found a body in a forest."

———

"You didn't have to drive," said Ben, and to Freya's surprise, he opened the passenger window a few inches, letting the freezing winter air inside.

"Of course I had to drive. We can't turn up in your dad's old pick-up truck, and would you mind closing the window? It *is* winter, you know?"

"Well, you didn't have to come. I can handle it. It's just a body. It's not going to run away." He rolled the window up.

"Oh right, and do you honestly think I could sit at home in the cold while you and Gold enjoy yourselves on a new crime scene?"

"I wouldn't call it enjoying myself. You could have finished your wine. I was actually going to help you with *the burner thing*, as you put it."

She cast a sideways glance at him, which he, of course, noticed.

"Red, if I'm not mistaken," he added, then reached into his pocket and offered her a small packet of gum. "I didn't have a keen sense of smell until I was in uniform. It's the drink drivers that brought it out in me."

"I had half a glass—"

"I'm not doubting how much you had to drink. You're a police officer. I couldn't imagine you would drive while over the limit, let alone attend a crime scene while inebriated. But I am grateful, you know?"

"Grateful?" said Freya, as they came to the end of the long and bumpy farm track to the main road. "For me coming?"

"No," he said. "Turn left here. I'm grateful that you changed out of your fluffy slippers before we left. I'm pretty sure someone would have said something."

He had a wry smile on his face. For a career police officer, Freya found his humour to be dry and his wit sharp. In her experience, those traits were hard to find in a colleague.

She left his comment hanging and returned to the job at hand.

"Are you going to tell me where we're going?"

He pulled his phone from his pocket and a few moments later, she heard a ring tone.

"DC Gold," said the familiar voice through the tinny loudspeaker.

"Jackie, it's Ben. Do you have a location for me? Or should I just drive into the middle of Woodhall Spa and look for a body?"

"Sorry, Ben. I've been a bit preoccupied," Jackie replied, her voice sounding a little frail. "It's a mile or so from Woodhall Spa. I'll drop you a pin. It's not easy to explain."

"Thanks. How's it looking?" He glanced across at Freya as he waited for Gold to reply, and mouthed that she should take the next turning.

"I've got uniforms here to cordon the area off and I've made the calls to CSI and the FME. I'm expecting them within the hour. They're coming in from the city."

They heard her car door close and the sound of her walking through brush, and then a man's voice in the distance, which Freya presumed was a uniform pointing her in the right direction.

"Keep talking to me, Jackie. Tell me what you see."

A few digital clicks came across the call as she enabled the loudspeaker. Jackie's breathing was laboured, and the sound of her pushing through bushes was clear.

"I've sent you the location. You'll see my car when you drive in. We're about one hundred yards away. I'll get uniform to get a light set up so you'll see us."

"What about the body? Tell me what you see. Take your time."

"It's hard to be sure. She's face down, partially buried in leaves and brambles."

Both Ben and Freya startled as a loud scratching issued from the speaker, like somebody was covering the mouthpiece of Jackie's phone. But the sound that followed was unmistakable.

There were a few moments of more heavy breathing, a sniff, and then Jackie returned to the call.

"Feel better?" asked Ben.

"I'm sorry, I–"

"Don't be. It happens to us all. Ask a uniform to mark where you were sick so it doesn't confuse the evidence."

"I'll do it myself," she replied. "Sorry, Ben. It's not pretty."

Freya eyed him again and he felt her eyes boring into him, waiting for him to get a handle on the young DC.

"Are you ready for another look? Or do you want to wait for me to get there?"

"No, I can do it. I want to."

"Good," he said. "Let's try again, shall we? Deep breaths."

The deep breathing was loud, and Jackie's control and determination were commendable.

"Female, thirties or forties judging by the clothes she's wearing. I can't see her face properly. She's fully dressed with an earring in her right ear, and she's wearing a gold necklace with a name engraved on it, but I can't see what it says. I guess that's a sign she wasn't robbed."

"Could be," Ben said.

"Hold on. It looks like it could be a head wound. It's hard to say if it's mud. Oh god, no. It's definitely a head wound."

"Do we need to shut the area down, Jackie? Is the blood still wet?" He glanced up at Freya who was listening to every word, picturing the image Jackie was describing.

"No, Ben. No, she's been here a while. Whoever did this is long gone."

"A while? How long are we talking?"

"I don't know," she replied. "I wouldn't know where to start."

"A day? An hour? Make an educated guess, Jackie. It doesn't matter if you're wrong. You're not a pathologist."

"I know I'm not. You don't need to be a pathologist to know it's longer than a day, though."

"You think she's been there for longer than that?"

"Judging by the bloating and decay–"

"Decay?"

"Yes. This isn't a fresh body, Ben. It could be six months old. Or more."

―――――――

CHAPTER FOUR

―――――――

"We won't have any trouble finding them," said Ben, as Freya switched off the engine and pushed open her door. She breathed in the fresh air and watched her breath form a cloud. A bright halogen light shone in the forest to her right, marking the scene. They had parked behind Jackie's car on a single lane in a deep forest, and aside from the liveried car at the entrance to the trees, there was only one other vehicle. A police van, presumably sent to deliver the lights and uniforms.

"Are you familiar with this place?" she asked.

"I might have come here when I was younger," he said, and smiled at her oddly.

"Why? To walk your dog?"

"I live on my dad's farm with more than a thousand acres, Freya. Why would I drive out here to walk the dog?"

"So why did you come, then?"

He raised his eyebrows, as if the answer was obvious, which it wasn't.

"During the day, this place is popular with dog walkers. There's a few footpaths and routes you can take. I guess it's convenient enough and away from too many people," he said. But then he adopted a more sinister tone. "During the night, however, it is a scene of infidelity and voyeurism."

"Voyeurism? You mean like flashers?"

Ben sighed. "It's a dogger's paradise, Freya. People come here to—"

"Okay, okay, I see," Freya said, not wanting to hear Ben's explanation of dogging.

She faced the source of the light erected a few hundred feet away, and the rumble of men's voices could be heard in the otherwise silent forest.

"Other than the randy and the adventurous, it looks like a nice spot for a walk," said Freya, peering into the gloomy shadows.

"In daylight, maybe."

"You're not afraid of the dark, Ben, are you?" she asked, peering back at him. "I thought you said you came here..." She paused, and something clicked. "Hold on. You said you came here before, when you were younger. You're not into dogging, are you?"

The revelation lit Ben in a whole new light. He was by no means ugly. In fact, there had been several moments during the past couple of months when she could have just reached out and kissed him. He had a way about him. A confidence that stirred something inside her.

"Dogging is when you make yourself available to strangers," he said. "I think it's a modern thing. When I was young, it just used to be a place for young couples to come."

"What for?" she asked, teasing him.

"To be away from prying eyes."

"I don't understand," she said, pulling him further into her trap. "Why would you come all the way out here if, like you said, you had a thousand acres of land to hide in?"

"Ah, for crying out loud, Freya. Do I have to spell it out?" he said. "I used to bring my girlfriend here. You know? We used to get in the back seat."

"Are you saying that, before it became a dogging hot spot, this was a kind of lovers lane?"

"Something like that. But I doubt very much that any loving went on. Come on. If you've finished interrogating me on my teenage sex life, let's see what all the fuss is about."

"For now, DS Savage," she said, smiling to herself. "Maybe you can fill me in on all the lucid details another time. How many?"

"How many what?"

"How many girls did you bring here?"

"For Christ's sake, Freya–"

"I'm just curious," she said, holding her hands up. "More than a dozen?"

"One," he said, stopping and facing her. "One girl. I brought her here a few times. That's it."

"That's disappointing," Freya muttered, enjoying seeing him riled.

"And that's exactly what she said, too," Ben replied. "Now, shall we?"

It was when they had closed the doors that the real silence of the forest struck Freya. Her vision blurred like an out-of-focus photograph; a hint of lost memory revealed itself, then slipped behind a tree. In Freya's mind, she followed it – a shape, a man. Peering around one tree only to find the dark shape slink behind the next.

"This way," said Ben, rousing her, and the memory slipped away.

"You go ahead," said Freya. "I just need a moment."

"Are you okay?"

"I'm fine. Just give me a minute, will you?"

The place was familiar – the trees, the canopy above her, and the silence. Only the sounds of the wild things dared to be heard. But no matter how hard she tried, the memory she had glimpsed was gone, and she was alone.

She sought Ben in the shadows, then followed him towards the bright light that had been set up.

The path to the light wound around trees and bushes. It was less of a path and more of a game trail, free of debris, informal and faint in the dark.

"I'm looking for DC Gold," Ben called out to a uniform who was stationed at the blue and white tape that had been used to cordon off the area. He flashed his warrant card and shielded his eyes from the officer's torch.

The man inspected the ID, shone his torch on the ground, and then gestured with his chin and pointed into the brush toward the light source. "Through the trees, if you please."

"Thank you," Ben replied, then turned to Freya as she caught him up. "Are you ready for this?"

Edging past Ben, Freya moved a low-hanging branch from out of her path and ducked through a narrow gap. A single wispy branch caught her cheek and she hissed a curse to avoid calling out. She emerged from between the bushes at the site and found DC Gold crouched beside the remains of a woman, who was partially covered in leaves, as Gold had described. If the sight of the body wasn't enough, the smell of decaying flesh was a sure sign they were in the right place.

"What's the story?" said Ben, as he pulled himself through the bushes behind her.

Looking from Freya to Ben and back again, DC Gold tried to conceal the look of utter disgust on her face. But it wasn't from the stench. She hadn't been expecting Freya to arrive with Ben, and Freya sensed a pang of jealousy.

"Jackie?"

She shook her head, then sighed. Clearly, she had been looking forward to working with Ben, maybe even impress him with how she was handling the scene.

"A man found her," she said, then referred to her notebook. "A

Lee Charlton. He called us from home. Said he saw the body and ran."

"Is he a dog walker?" said Freya, and she cast a glance in Ben's direction in silent referral to his comment as they were parking the car.

"Yes. Well, his dog found her. He's given a statement over the phone and said we should call his mobile if we need any more from him."

"Right," said Ben.

"Said his dog was digging for something in the bushes. He said he called him to come back, but the dog wouldn't come so he had to drag him out."

"So he was alone?" Freya asked.

"Apparently so," Gold replied.

"And that was when he discovered the body?" asked Ben.

Nodding, Gold shuffled her feet, a sign she was uncomfortable engaging with Ben. Her reaction raised a smile on Freya's face, so broad that she moved behind the bright spotlight to conceal it.

"Do we have a positive ID?" she asked.

Shielding her eyes from the bright light, Gold tried to meet her stare. "I haven't touched her. Forensics—"

"Are on their way, yes, you said," finished Freya. "But still, have you checked her pockets?"

"No, ma'am."

"Are you comfortable checking her pockets, DC Gold?"

The young detective said nothing, and again, she shuffled her feet.

"I'll talk you through it, if you like," said Freya. "There's a knack to doing it without disturbing the evidence."

"If you think I should, ma'am."

Content with Gold's willingness to engage, Freya cast an eye to Ben, who obviously felt something for the girl and was moving closer to help.

"You seemed comfortable crouching down beside her. Have you got used to the smell?" Freya asked.

"I wouldn't say I've got used to it. I had to force myself just to look at her."

"But you've seen a body before?" asked Freya, referring to the first investigation Freya had helped the team with.

"That was different. There wasn't a smell. Not really anyway. The body hadn't had time to..."

She gagged once more, but held herself together.

"It's okay. Take your time."

"I'm sorry. I have to get used to it, I know."

"What were you looking for when we arrived?"

"I don't know really. Anything, I guess. A clue. A mark maybe."

"Did you find anything?"

"No, ma'am."

"Good. How long until CSI arrive?"

"Another thirty minutes or so."

"Then I think it's safe to check her pockets as long as we don't disturb her position."

Gold had frozen to the spot.

"Do you want to do it, Jackie?" Freya urged.

"Freya, come on," said Ben, sticking up for his friend.

"It's okay, Ben. She can do it. She's tougher than you think. Isn't that right?"

But Jackie was unsure. She said nothing, and looked down at the bloated remains of the woman.

"Tell me what you see."

"A body," she replied.

"Okay," said Freya. "Use your imagination. Look at her. Look at how her arm is stretched out. Look at the direction of her body. What happened here?"

"Nothing," said Gold.

"Go on," Freya said, intrigued.

"Nothing happened *here*. I think she crawled here."

"Good," said Freya, encouraging the young woman's efforts, partly to bring her on, but more to repair the damage that she could do if she opened her mouth about Freya and Ben arriving together with the smell of wine on Freya's breath. Especially when Jackie had only called Ben, and there had been no mention of contacting their DI.

"Look at her arms. Her fingers," Jackie continued. "The scratches. It's like she dragged herself across the forest from somewhere."

"Where was she trying to get to?"

"Anywhere. She was just getting away. She was injured. What if it happened at the lane where we parked? What if whoever did it thought she was dead and left her there? But she crawled away and this is how far she got."

"And this is where she's been lying ever since?"

"I think so."

"She's buried in leaves. Who buried her?"

"Nobody, ma'am. She's been here since summer time at least. The leaves must have covered her during autumn."

"Ben, do you agree?"

"It's a possibility. We won't know until daylight when we can search the area."

"But DC Gold's assessment, do you think it's a good assessment?"

He nodded and caught her eye. "It's a fair assumption, yes. At this stage at least."

"Good, so do I. Now we have to find out who she is."

A wince passed across Jackie's young face, creasing her flawless skin for a moment. She took a breath and dropped to a crouch, pulling on a disposable latex glove.

"Easy now," said Freya. "If you can't find anything without moving her, then we'll wait."

"I found something," she said, with her hand in the woman's coat pocket. "Some keys, I think."

Deep in concentration, Jackie eased the keys from the rotting coat, being careful not to disturb anything else. She stood, proud, and breathed a sigh of relief before dropping the keys into a plastic evidence bag that Ben held open for her. He passed Gold the bag. It was her prize for stepping up.

"There's a keyring," she said, holding the bag up to the light.

From where Freya was standing, she could see a little, yellow identifying tag on the keys. It was the type with a small panel for somebody to write on.

"Witham and Fens," Jackie read out loud, then stared up in disbelief.

"What is it, Jackie?" asked Ben.

"That's the surgery. Witham and Fens surgery."

Suddenly, her proximity to the corpse was not an issue, and with the utmost care, Jackie probed a gloved finger to the dead woman's neck.

"Shine the torch," she said. Then she held the gold pendant around the woman's neck into the light, before whispering to herself, "Jane."

Both Ben and Freya exchanged glances, hoping that it wasn't an old friend of Jackie's, which could have been even more traumatic for her.

"Do you think she was a doctor at Witham and Fens surgery?" asked Freya.

"No. Not a doctor," Jackie replied, crouching once more to study the small section of face that was visible. She reached for Ben's torch and shone the light without hesitation. "It's Jane Blythe, ma'am. She used to work in the doctor's surgery."

"Are you sure?" said Ben, joining her in a crouch.

"Positive. I take Charlie there," she said, glancing up at Freya to explain. "Charlie is my son. I take him there. I was there earlier today with him. He's got this cough..."

"It's okay, Gold," said Freya, and stepped closer to put her hand on her shoulder.

"I haven't seen her for months. I thought she had just left to work somewhere else. You know, as people do. She used to work on reception. She was lovely. There's a new girl now."

"Well," Freya began, "we'll need a positive ID on her in the morning. We'll let Doctor Saint and the forensics team do their work tonight. And, Jackie, if you feel up to it, perhaps you can go with Ben to see her family tomorrow? In the meantime, get some rest. Perhaps you could take Ben too, seeing as it's my fault he's here without transport. We need to preserve the site as much as possible."

She looked confused at what Freya had just said, but tried to hide her disappointment.

"DS Savage was delivering firewood to my house when you called," Freya said, by way of an explanation. "I couldn't have him arrive in a beaten-up, old farm truck now, could I?"

"Ma'am," was all Jackie could say, although she glanced at Ben, who smiled, then back at Freya, showing a little relief.

"You did well tonight. There will be a briefing at the station in the morning, so bring your A-game. I'll wait for Doctor Saint. Now go. Get some rest."

But Jackie offered her a scathing look in response, which she shared with Ben, before barging her way out of the little clearing and heading back towards her car.

———

The car ride was mostly silent. The few times Ben tried to make small talk with Jackie, she closed him off with a curt "yes," or "no." Or, if the question was open, she muttered something about being too tired to talk. It was only as they were pulling into the top of the farm track, a half-mile long stretch of gravel and potholes that cut between two of Ben's father's fields, that Jackie opened up.

"Do you like her?" she asked, then sighed as if she had been building up the courage to say it out loud.

"Freya?" he replied. "Yeah, she's okay. She's a little bit funny in her ways, but then aren't we all?"

"No, I mean, do you *like her* like her?"

"Oh," said Ben, and all of a sudden he felt stupid for not recognising Jackie's misinterpretation of the evening.

The way Freya had paid special attention to Jackie, coaxing her through the steps, had been admirable, but now he understood the real reasons behind it. The look Freya had given him when Jackie was standing beside the body had been odd at first. But now, things began to fall into place, although, Jackie drawing the wrong conclusion from them arriving together wouldn't normally have upset Freya. In fact, he imagined that Freya would have played on it to wind Jackie up in any other circumstance. But if Jackie fed her misinterpretation back to Will Granger somehow, there would be questions to answer. Things could get awkward. Now he understood Freya's softly-softly approach, and he smiled to himself.

"No, Jackie. No, I don't. She's nice enough, but honestly, she's not my type at all."

"So why were you with her?" asked Jackie. "You were with her when I called, weren't you?"

"Stop here," said Ben, and Jackie gave him one of her confused looks. "It's okay. Just stop here."

Pulling the car to a stop in the middle of the empty track, Jackie applied the handbrake but kept the engine running for the warmth.

"Do you see my house over there?"

He pointed to the left, where, had there been daylight, Jackie would have looked across two ploughed fields bearing winter crops to three houses that formed a U-shape around a central courtyard. The middle and largest house belonged to Ben's father, the owner of the surrounding farmland that had been in the Savage family for generations. The house on the right was where Ben's brothers lived, unmarried and already following in their father's footsteps. The house on the left had been given to Ben, the first male of the Savage family to break free of the mould for as long as anybody could remember. He was the oldest of the three brothers, and although at first the family had been perturbed at his career choice, they now understood. Profitable farming was becoming harder and harder. Diversifying was only part of the solution. But to be truly safe from the changing world, the family had needed somebody on the outside. A source of income that did not rely on the weather, the landscape, or the government's ever-changing taxes and policies.

In the darkness, all they could see over the black fields were a few lighted windows; the houses themselves were indistinguishable against the night sky, save for a faint cloud of white chimney smoke.

"I see it," she said.

"Now look over there," said Ben, and he pointed to her right, where across another field, a few more buildings were visible only by similar lighted windows. "Farmworkers' cottages. They belong to my father."

"I always wondered who owned them."

"He rents one to Freya. It hasn't been lived in for years, but it's functional and much warmer than her motorhome."

"Why does he do that? Surely he doesn't need the money?"

"It's not about the money, Jackie. It's about being a friend. I asked him to. I figured that if she had somewhere to live, then perhaps she would stay. I don't know how it works, but maybe she could extend her secondment or make a permanent move."

"But then you wouldn't get your promotion. Why would you do that?"

"I don't know. Maybe I'm not ready."

"You are *so* ready, Ben. It was yours for the taking before she came along."

"Then maybe I like having her in the team? Maybe I think she brings a different style to what we do? Maybe we can learn from her experience in the city? Look at what she did tonight. Look at what she brings out in you. Anyway, from my kitchen window, I can see across those fields. I can see when she's home. Not that I look often, mind," he added to prevent her mind from racing away with itself. "But I could also see that she hadn't managed to get her fire working. No smoke from her chimney."

"Does the cottage have heating?"

"It does, but it's old and I'm not sure she's worked it out yet. She's a city girl, remember."

"So what was she doing to keep warm?"

"Fluffy slippers, her coat, and a blanket, from what I can tell."

"What?"

"Like I said. I don't know for sure. But I figured I'd help her out. I took her some wood. I was going to get her wood burner going too, but then you phoned."

"Oh," Jackie murmured, and in the darkness, a sheepish expression emerged on her face. "I jump to conclusions. I'm sorry. I didn't mean to."

"How long have we known each other now?"

"Years. I don't know for sure."

"Do you really think your habit of jumping to conclusions is a surprise to me?"

"Now I feel really stupid. Thanks, Ben. But I was so rude to her. She was trying to help."

He laughed and straightened in his seat. "It's okay. Come on, let's go. I've got an idea of how you can make it up to her."

————

In Freya's opinion, nobody enjoys being the last to a morning briefing. First is okay, if you're the one running the briefing, or if you have a large coffee and some work to be getting on with. Arriving five minutes early is polite for attendees, as long as everyone arrives early. Arriving late for a morning briefing is unacceptable for both attendees and the presenter alike.

Unless your name is Freya Bloom and everything you need to say is memorised and well-versed. In fact, arriving a few minutes late to a briefing, then blowing your team away with a good plan is far more memorable than being on time and referring to notes to give a mumbled and mundane overview of a case that, at this stage, nobody knows anything concrete about.

She was fully aware that all she had to go on were theories.

Freya arrived three minutes late, after waiting in the stairwell for one of those minutes, and didn't offer an apology, not even to DCI Granger, whose furrowed brow resembled the backside of a baboon.

She held that thought while she waited for silence.

Five pairs of eyes stared up at her. DCI Granger, Ben, DC Gold, DC Chapman, and Sergeant Priest, the Duty Sergeant whose team would be conducting the search of the area. Having Priest on board was vital.

From the far end of the room, DI Standing, who led the other Major Investigations Team, looked up from his desk. He glanced at Freya's audience, then grinned before returning his attention to his own team and mumbling something across the desk to DS Gillespie.

It wasn't the first time Freya had encountered a hostile equal. She cleared her throat and began her briefing.

"A woman's body was discovered last night at around seven-thirty p.m. just outside of Woodhall Spa. A call was raised to the desk who in turn called DC Gold, who in turn called DS Savage. DS Savage and I attended the crime scene at eight-fifteen p.m. and found DC Gold, along with several uniformed officers. The area had been cordoned off and I believe is still under uniformed supervision. Is that correct, Sergeant Priest?"

"Ma'am," he replied, his thick Yorkshire accent rumbling through like an old diesel engine.

"DC Gold established a likely scene of events. Before we go on, can I ask you to share your thoughts, Gold?"

Jackie Gold looked horrified. She looked to Ben for some kind of support.

"It's okay," said Freya. "Both DS Savage and I are in agreement."

Gold cleared her throat and shifted her feet.

"My theory is that the victim was attacked on the lane, a few hundred feet from where she was found."

"What makes you think that?" asked DCI Granger. "She could have fallen, or frozen to death or something."

"Too much blood, sir," Gold said with confidence.

"Blood?"

"And scratches, guv. The way she was lying. It was like she had crawled there. She has a head wound. My guess is blunt force trauma. The pathologist will tell us more, I imagine."

"Any other visible signs?"

"It was dark," Gold said. "And I didn't want to move her."

"Forensics agreed with Gold's assessment," Freya added. "But like she said, we won't know for sure until the pathologist sees her. One thing is for certain. It was no accident. It's possible her attacker thought she was dead and left her there."

"Anything else?"

"The man who found her has given a statement saying that his dog disappeared into the trees and he had to go in after it. At this stage we have no reason not to believe him, but we do have his records on file. As for the crime scene, I sent DS Savage and DC Gold home early so they could be sharp for today, while I stayed behind to meet CSI."

"You sent your team home?" asked Granger. "Are you so arrogant that you think you could handle the case alone?"

"The forest crime scene is less than three metres square. As DC Gold said, it's a tiny space between bushes and trees that we were trampling over. Plus, the surrounding area was in pitch darkness, so I couldn't put them to work managing a detailed search. Early examinations by the local Forensic Medical Examiner, Doctor Saint, indicate that death occurred more than six months ago, but no more than eighteen months. We expect more accurate results from the pathologist along with cause of death, and if it does turn out to be suspicious, a potential weapon."

Granger nodded his acceptance of Freya's briefing so far, but as it was with all senior officers, the briefing had to move at his pace. He would ask the next question.

"So, we have a woman who we believe was killed more than six months ago in a dark lane in a forest habituated by dog walkers mostly. But if I'm not mistaken, isn't that a common place for teenagers to meet, DS Savage?"

"It's been a while since I was a teenager, guv," he said with a smile. "But yes. Teenagers and adults alike. It's quite secluded."

"And we believe the victim dragged herself through brambles to a spot a few hundred feet away, where her body gave up and she died?"

"That's correct," Freya confirmed.

"And we have the details of the man who found her with a reason for being there."

"Yes, guv," said Freya.

"Excuse me," Ben said, standing from his chair. He waved his phone at her, indicating an incoming call, and moved toward the door to take it.

"I've also taken the liberty to enlist the help of Sergeant Priest's team to perform a detailed search of the area," Freya continued. "Five hundred yards in all directions." She glanced across to Priest, who in her opinion was one of the most reliable and sincere men she had ever had the pleasure to deal with.

"Ma'am," he responded. "I have twenty uniforms on the scene. Had to pull in a unit from Lincoln HQ. They began as soon as the body was removed at first light. We also have a dog at the scene, as much of the area is covered in undergrowth. Brambles and the like."

"And there are no reports yet?"

"It's early yet. They'll do a thorough job though. Mark my word."

"Thank you, Sergeant."

The initial briefing had gone to plan. It was all the information they had so far, and Freya had delivered it with practised ease. As far as Granger was concerned, there was nothing to complain about. However, given the expectation he had delivered the night before, along with Freya's apparent arrogance, there was every chance he would hand the case to Standing and run Freya through the protocols that she had broken. It would be a power play to remind her who was the boss and that he was serious about her seeing a therapist.

"That just leaves two things," Granger added, and he seemed to sigh at the thought. "Who is our mystery woman?" He glanced around the room at the faces, who in turn looked to Freya to complete her briefing. The final person to turn their attention to Freya was Granger. "And what are you planning to do about it, DI Bloom?"

———

"We think her name was Jane Blythe," said Ben, returning to the briefing and pocketing his phone. He nodded to Jackie, ensuring that Granger saw. "That was Doctor Bell, the pathologist. We can expect an initial report this afternoon. So far, all she can tell us is that the victim does indeed have extensive head injuries, but she needs to do a thorough examination before she can give us the cause of death. All Doctor Bell has been able to do so far is clean her up."

"ID?" Freya asked.

"Not yet. Her pockets were empty. All we have to go on are the keys and the pendant."

"And what are we going to do to obtain a positive ID?" Granger asked.

"DC Gold and I will be paying the husband a visit after this," Ben replied, then nodded for Freya to continue.

"As for what I intend to do about it, sir," Freya said. "Nothing. Until we identity her and inform the next of kin."

"Nothing?"

"When we have a positive ID, we'll build a network and establish what her last days looked like," Freya explained.

"And if she is who we think she is?"

"Technically, this should be treated as a cold case," Freya said, raising her voice so the team were sure to hear her. "Our approach will differ from a standard murder enquiry. Details will be harder to obtain. People will likely be harder to find. However, in light of there being no missing persons report for Jane Blythe, we'll approach everybody with caution. Typically, right about now, we'd be visiting the next of kin to deliver the bad news. We'd arrange a family liaison officer, and we'd begin the enquiry on confirmation of the deceased identity."

Freya stared at them all individually.

"But you're suggesting a different approach?" Granger asked.

"Nobody reported her missing. That makes everyone we talk to, everyone she knew, a potential suspect. Including the husband. Somebody left her there. Perhaps they thought she was dead, perhaps not. Either way, they've had more than six months to learn how to deal with it. A large percentage of domestic murders are accidental. You'd be amazed at how many people surrender themselves and confess, unable to deal with the guilt. But this one has not. Whoever they are, they will have developed coping mechanisms to get them through those dark days. We need to watch every twitch, every habit, and listen to everything people say. There *will* be a sign, and we'll need to spot it."

The team nodded. Even Granger agreed.

"Good," she said, then turned back to Ben. "Did Doctor Bell say anything else?"

"The head injuries occurred prior to death," said Ben. "Lacerations surrounding the wound suggest it was a rock, or an object with a rough surface. She also had scratches on her face, arms, and hands, from which the dried blood indicates that she was indeed alive when the scratches occurred."

"So DC Gold's theory is accurate?"

"Seems to be, yes."

"And the weapon is probably a rock?" Granger repeated, verbalising the facts as if he was imagining the scene.

"Most likely. It's an early analysis, but Doctor Bell is quite sure. She thought it might help us to know what we're looking for while the area is being searched."

"Do you have any concerns right now, Ben?" Granger asked, flicking his eyes across to Freya for a fleeting moment.

"Everything seems to be straight-forward enough. I agree with Jackie's assessment, as does DI Bloom. We'll need to know what the victim's last few days looked like before we can move forward. We need to talk to her family and friends. But a couple of things are puzzling me, guv."

"Go on." DCI Granger shifted his weight. He was sitting on the edge of a desk with his legs outstretched before him. He folded his arms, a sign that he was giving Ben his full attention. "Let's see if our puzzles match."

"Why wasn't she reported missing?" asked Ben. "And why doesn't she have any belongings on her?"

Looking across to Priest, Will Granger only needed to raise his brow.

Priest nodded. "If my boys find anything, you'll be the first to know."

"If she took a direct path from the lane," Ben explained, "she would have had to crawl beneath the brambles. She may have dropped her bag along the way. In which case, it'll be buried beneath eight feet of thorns. If she crawled along the little trail, however, then it's likely that somebody found it."

"Has anything been handed in?" asked Granger.

"I'll check at the desk," Priest confirmed, making a note of the conversation.

"And you have the pleasure of breaking the news to Mr Blythe, do you, Ben?"

"And me, guv," said Jackie. "I knew her. Kind of, anyway."

"You knew her?"

"Well, I spoke to her. She used to work in reception at our local doctor's surgery. Used to dote on my Charlie, she did."

"Ben will accompany her," said Freya. "She'll be fine."

"Good, well, if the husband hasn't filed a missing persons report, you may find he has very little to say."

"Yes, guv," said Jackie, with a confidence Ben rarely saw in her.

"What about you, Bloom? What is it you'll be contributing to the initial fact-finding effort?"

"I'll be going to the doctor's surgery to understand exactly how Jane Blythe's employment ended. We need to know more about her. I think you're right, guv. If the husband didn't report her missing, he might be loath to say much. But we need to know who her friends were, what she did in her spare time, and who she would have seen on a regular basis."

"I can check her social media if you like," said DC Chapman.

"Good idea. We also need to find any family she may have had. Siblings, parents, aunts, uncles. Anybody who may have known her well enough to give an account of her state of mind."

"I'll do some research."

"Thank you, Chapman. Let's meet back here at three p.m.

Sergeant Priest, do you think we could have a list of any findings by that time?"

"It'll be short, but yes."

"Do you have enough resources?"

"The area has been cordoned off. Given the nature of the environment with the dense brambles, if they manage one hundred square meters per day, I'll be impressed."

"It might serve well to get an extra dog in if we can," Granger added. "It's been at least six months. If she made a trail while she crawled through the forest, it'll be gone. If there are footprints, they won't stand up in court. We'll send the dogs into the hard-to-reach areas while the teams search the open spaces."

"I could do with one more, guv," Freya said, and she glanced back at DI Standing's team at the far end of the long, narrow room. Stephen Standing, a seasoned Detective Inspector, looked up once more and made no attempt to hide either his interest or his resentment. "If this case is a year old, I'm going to need experience and bodies. I was hoping we could use DS Gillespie."

Gillespie, a Glaswegian DS, was sitting behind DI Standing, and on hearing his name looked up from his desk.

"Eh?" he said.

"No chance," Standing added defensively. "I need him."

"Take Detective Constable Cruz," Granger said to Freya. "Gillespie is needed on the red diesel investigation, if you remember?"

"I need Cruz too," Standing said.

"Tough," Granger said, pulling rank before the two DIs went head to head. "Cruz, you're on loan to DI Bloom. Get your things. DS Savage will get you up to speed."

Clearly annoyed at the result, Standing threw his pen into the corner of the room.

"First of all, I have to pick up the pieces of her botched investigation, and now you're giving her my team, guv. Give me a break here, will you?"

"You have a hit and run accident that's already a month old, one dead body, and some stolen diesel, DI Standing. You don't need six people for that."

"What a joke," Standing muttered in defeat.

While DC Cruz gathered his belongings, Standing eyed Freya with contempt.

Offering each of his team mates an apologetic nod, Cruz made his way across the room to an audience of shaking heads and tuts. He was the youngest of everyone under Will Granger. His hair looked as if his mother had spat on her hand and flattened it forward before he left for work each day, and he seemed to have that dishevelled look like he was always wearing yesterday's clothes, regardless of the day.

"Can I ask a question?" asked Chapman, bringing them back to the investigation.

"Of course," said Freya, seemingly pleased for the input and distraction.

"Why would she have crawled through brambles?"

The question was valid and the answer required a little empathy.

"That's a great question. I'm pleased you asked it. Right now, it's winter. The brambles and blackberry bushes have thinned. The leaves have been shed and the fruit has either been picked, eaten, or fallen. A dog could certainly get beneath them. A person might also be able to, under the right conditions. But in the summertime, a person stands very little chance of getting in there. Have you ever been blackberry picking?"

"Of course. We do it all the time."

"So you know how thick and dense a tangle of brambles are?"

"Right," said Chapman. "I'm following."

"Close your eyes."

The request caught Chapman off guard. She looked to Jackie for support.

"It's okay," Freya reassured her, and Jackie nodded, conveying that she should trust her.

Chapman closed her eyes.

"It's winter time. You're in the forest. It's pitch dark and you're alone. Or so you think. You hear somebody nearby. Your heart begins to race and you call out. But nobody answers. You turn to see who it is. But you see nothing, and it's so dark you disorient yourself. Can you picture it?"

"I can," she said.

"What is this?" Gillespie called out in his thick Glaswegian accent. "Amateur dramatics?"

"It's called empathy," Freya said quietly, not rising to his off-hand comment. Granger gave him a look that prevented any further distraction, then nodded to Freya to continue.

"Somebody comes at you from behind," she said. "You turn to defend yourself, but it's too late. They're right there in front of you, and you see the attacker raise their hand. You see the weapon. You know what's coming and it's too late to move. Then you're hit. Adrenalin takes over. You drop to the ground, the body's natural instinct. Then flight kicks in, so you crawl. It doesn't matter where. You need safety. Your instincts are in full control now. You slip beneath a bush and hear the footsteps running away above the thumping of your heart in your eyes. You crawl further inside, but the going gets harder. You feel weak. You have to get to somebody, but you're in so deep that it's hard to turn. So you keep going." She paused to let that image settle in the young detective's mind. "Finally, you emerge in a small clearing between some trees. But it's too late. All you can do is hope somebody finds you. But they never do."

A silence fell over the room.

"Open your eyes."

Chapman nodded. "I get it. I can picture her."

"Christ, how did we end up looking for stolen red diesel while she gets the murder enquiry?" Standing said.

But Freya ignored him, as did the team, who were captivated.

"If Jane Blythe crawled through that tangle of thorns, then we can be quite sure the attack happened during winter time, and there's likely something beneath them that might tell us more about her. Something she dropped maybe. Something that nobody has found."

"What difference does that make? Winter or summer? Where are you going with this, Bloom?" asked Granger.

It was as if she expected the question, just not from Will Granger. A few moments passed, during which Ben surmised she was adjusting her response to suit his rank.

"In the summertime, guv, it would be damn near impossible to crawl through the brambles. That means she was murdered before the spring. Which begs the question, why wasn't she wrapped up warm? No hat, no gloves, no scarf, and beneath her jacket, a thin blouse."

He nodded and turned his attention to Cruz, who had settled in beside Chapman and waited for an instruction.

"DC Cruz?" said Freya. "What's your first name? Sorry, I'm still learning everybody."

"Gabriel," he said. Then he offered a little more insight, seeing Freya's reaction to the unusual name. "My parents are Filipino."

"Nice to have you on the team, Gabriel," Freya said. "Show me your hands."

Gabriel appeared a little bemused at the request. He held his hands up, palms out.

"Other way," Freya said, and she held them, turning them over to see the backs. "Good strong hands."

Seeming pleased at the comment, he smiled at the team. "I think so too."

"Ideal for door knocking," Freya said. "See Sergeant Priest after this briefing. He'll assign you a uniform to help you."

"Eh?" he said.

"Ma'am?" Chapman said, with her laptop perched on her knees.

"What is it?"

"Jane Blythe's social media. There's been nothing for months."

"On Facebook?"

"On any of them. I found her Twitter and Instagram too," she explained. "It looks like she used to post quite regularly. She was a painter by the looks of it. She's posted photos of her artwork."

"But nothing since when?"

"October, by the looks of it, ma'am."

"Good work, Chapman," Freya said. Turning to Ben, Freya pushed on, becoming more certain that the victim was Jane Blythe by the second. "Get Cruz up to speed, will you? I want a full door-to-door plan prepared by the time you've seen the husband. One of the neighbours might have seen something. I want full details from all of them."

"Yep," Ben said, taking a breath and nodding for Jackie to get ready. "This is the bit I hate."

"We don't even know it's her yet," Cruz said, clearly hoping for an excuse not to go door knocking.

"I think we all know it's Jane Blythe," Granger said. "We just need to prove it before we can do anything about it."

CHAPTER FIVE

"I love her," Jackie quipped, as she slammed the passenger door of Ben's Ford. She lay her folder on her knees and reached for her seat belt, snapping it into the receiver. "And I hate her at the same time. Is that normal?"

"Perfectly, in my experience with her," replied Ben, amused at her outburst.

"What? I'm just speaking my mind. You haven't exactly found her to be plain sailing."

"No, I haven't."

"And you fancy her."

"I admire her, Jackie."

"I admire her too. I admire her, I love her, and I hate her."

"Do you know what I think it is?" asked Ben, as he pushed the ignition button, and then turned on the heated seats. "I just think she's one of those people who wears various faces. She's been through a lot."

"No wonder she needs to see a therapist," Jackie mumbled.

"Sorry?"

"Nothing."

"Jackie?"

"It's nothing, Ben. Come on, let's get a move on."

But Ben wasn't about to go anywhere without hearing what Jackie had to say. He sat back and folded his arms. "I can wait all day."

"It's nothing, Ben. Just something I saw in her house last night. It's none of my business."

"Jackie?"

She sighed. "You're like a dog with a bone sometimes."

"Says the woman who can't help but stick her nose in where it doesn't belong."

"For crying out loud. Okay, okay. When we were in her house last night, I saw something. A piece of paper on her table."

"Why were you even looking on her table? I asked you to make a fire up for her while I finished unloading the wood."

"I didn't mean to. The headed paper caught my eye. I just thought it was work stuff, you know?"

"So what was it?"

"Now who's being nosey?"

"Jackie."

"It was a formal letter from DCI Granger. Apparently she has some kind of problem she needs to get over. He suggested she sees a therapist if she wants to stay in Lincolnshire. If she doesn't arrange a meeting by the end of this week, he'll take further action which may result in her secondment being withdrawn."

"I don't believe it."

"I do."

"Jackie?"

"Well, let's be honest. We know she has issues. We know she went through some kind of trauma and that's why she left London, and let's face it, the way she behaves in front of DCI Granger, can you blame him for suggesting it?"

Pulling out of the parking spot, Ben crawled the car to the edge of the car park. He waved his thanks at the security camera to the guard who monitored the screens and had raised the barrier, then he nosed onto the road.

"I can't believe we're going through this again. Didn't you get in enough trouble last time?"

"You're the one who was asking me to tell you about it."

"You were snooping in her house. Did you hear the praise she gave you in that briefing? Let me tell you something, praise like that does not come from someone like Freya easily. You've really made an impression on her, and you reward her by going through her stuff?"

"Oh, come on, Ben. You make it sound like I was rifling through her paperwork. The police logo caught my eye, I looked, and I saw a single paragraph of a letter. What's the big deal? I'm not going to tell anyone. If anything, I'd like to help her."

"How do you plan on doing that without letting her know you read her personal letter?"

"I don't know. Maybe you can help? Maybe you could have a word with Will? Tell him how much you enjoy working with her? Tell him the team like her too. I'm sure Chapman will agree after what Bloom just did in there."

"Don't get her involved."

"I'm not getting anybody involved. I just meant that she would agree with you if you told DCI Granger that we liked her. I'm just trying to stop him from giving her a hard time."

"Look, nobody is talking to anybody. It's none of our business. Whatever you saw, forget about it. Let's just let things play out naturally. If she needs our help, she knows where to find it."

"Okay, okay."

They rode in silence for a while, and while Ben drove, he noticed Jackie going through some photos on her phone.

"You okay?" he asked.

"Yep, fine."

"Come on. Is that Charlie you're looking at?"

"Yeah," she said despondently.

"Is everything alright, Jackie?"

"I don't want to talk about it," she replied, which in Ben's experience was Jackie for, 'I really want to talk about it.'

"It's not Freya, is it?" he said. "Is it Charlie?"

"Don't, Ben. Please."

"Tell me. You mentioned he was sick. What is it?"

She turned away, cuffing a tear from her eye.

"Come on, Jackie. If you need time off–"

"I don't need time off," she snapped, then calmed herself with a deep breath, before the flood gates opened. "That's the last thing I need. My job is all I have. I don't have a husband, do I? I've got my mum, but who knows how long she's going to be able to help me for."

"We can work something out though. If you need help, just say–"

"I don't need help, Ben. I just... I just feel like I'm being held back. It's like people feel sorry for me, that's all. I think to myself that maybe if I didn't have Charlie, then things would be different. That somehow I might get opportunities, or that I could work longer hours to really show DCI Granger what I can do."

"Oh, he knows what you can do."

"Yeah, but does he? Really?" she said, turning to face him and shaking her head, her eyes blazing. "I'll always be disadvantaged. I mean, how long do I have to wait to make DS? And if I got a promotion, could I really work the hours while I support Charlie? He'll be at big school soon. I'll have to drop him off and pick him up. Not to mention the after school stuff. Games and sports and that. It feels like I'm stuck here while everyone else is making waves, moving on, and doing well. And then..." She stopped, unable to get the words out.

"Jackie?"

She inhaled long and hard and let her head fall back onto the headrest. "He's poorly. He might need extra care."

"Like what? What's wrong with him?"

"I don't know. It's his breathing. Doctor said it might be bronchiolitis. He might have to go into hospital, Ben. It's getting worse. It might be a long-term thing, and if it is, then what chance does my career stand?"

"We don't know it's a long-term thing yet."

"But that's just it, Ben. You don't get it. You haven't got kids. You don't even have a mortgage. I have to have a plan. My mum's not getting any younger, so I can't rely on her for too much help."

"Do you need some time off? When was the last time you had a holiday?"

"A holiday is not the answer. What I need is a miracle. I need Charlie to be okay so I can focus on my career. When I was a kid, we had nothing. I'm not going to let Charlie go through that. I can't. I promised myself he'd have whatever he needs."

"So let me help you."

"I'm not looking for a handout."

"And I'm not about to give you a handout. It's not about money. You're time poor."

"I'm what?"

"Time poor. You need to work, you need to look after Charlie, and you need to keep an eye on your mum. What that doesn't give you is any time for yourself and any time to deal with problems. Charlie's health being a prime example."

"Right, so you can magic more time, can you?"

"As it happens, no," Ben said. "But leave it with me, will you? Right now, we're going to see a man and it's likely we'll have to tell him his wife is dead. Who would you rather hear that from? Me? A six-foot-something bloke with the compassion of a carrot? Or you? A lovely, empathetic young mother, who might just understand what he's going through?"

"I guess," she said, and there was a spark of enthusiasm in her voice.

"Give me time to work out how to help you," he said, holding up his hand to prevent a barrage of objections. "For the time being, let's just keep our minds on the job. What number is the house?" Ben asked, as he slowed the Ford to a crawl.

"Thirty-three. It's a little further on," she said. "What do you think?"

"About?" asked Ben.

"Daniel Blythe," she replied, clearly looking to stay focused. She was good like that. She was stronger than she gave herself credit for. "Why wouldn't you report your wife missing after a year?"

"Here we are," said Ben, pulling the car to the kerb. "Who knows what goes on in people's minds. I, for one, often wonder."

"Is that meant to be a dig at me?"

Smiling, Ben unfastened his seatbelt.

"Jackie," he began, still smiling. "You're one of my best friends. But I came to the conclusion a long time ago that I'll never understand you. All I can do is stand by your side."

"The feeling's mutual," she replied, as she opened the car door and climbed out.

He met her across the roof of the car, glanced up at the house, and then back at her. "I'm not that complex."

"No?" she said. "So you'll admit you like her."

"What? Are we back on that now? No, I don't."

"Okay, then."

She was toying with him, and he knew it. But that was a thread he just had to pull.

"What makes you so sure of yourself?" he asked.

She gave a disappointed smile, then turned and walked up the drive to thirty-three Acacia Drive.

CHAPTER SIX

"I'd like to speak with Doctor Harris, if I may," Freya announced quietly to the receptionist, an attractive, middle-aged woman who wore an expression of assumed authority. The experience was not the pleasant welcome that Freya would have hoped for in a doctor's surgery.

The Witham and Fens practice was located in a modest yet modern building that, along with its car park, occupied a half-acre plot between two large, detached, residential houses. Set back from the main road to the rear of the plot, the main entrance was a set of double doors at the centre of the L-shaped building. It was only when Freya stepped inside did she realise the reasons for situating the building there. The views to the rear, accessible from the reception desk and waiting room, were astonishing.

The fens, an expanse of wild marshland and farmland, is a wild place where nature thrives and man exists beneath an unpredictable sky. Kites, kestrels, and buzzards hang in the breeze, while wild hare, deer, and livestock thrive in the forests, fields, and fauna as they have for centuries. The scene through the floor-to-ceiling glazing at the rear of the waiting room captured Freya's imagination, so that the receptionist, whose name tag read *Cheryl*, had to ask her the question twice.

"Can I take your name, please?" she said, and Freya, pulled from her imagination, had the feeling that the first time around the question had been asked with a little more politeness.

"Detective Inspector Freya Bloom," she said, revealing her warrant card.

"Oh, do you have an appointment?" Cheryl replied, a little taken aback.

"No, I just need to ask him a few questions."

"Well, I'm afraid you'll need to make an appointment. He's very busy–"

"It's concerning an employee," Freya added, and enjoyed that fleeting moment when Cheryl's eyes widened. "I've been told that this is his surgery. Is that correct?"

"He's the Managing Partner, yes–"

"Then I'm sure you can slot me in between his appointments."

"I see," she said. "Would you take a seat?"

"I'll stand, thank you," said Freya, stepping back from the reception desk and turning to browse a pin board on which local businesses advertised their services.

The board seemed to naturally gravitate toward parental-based services. There were three cards offering day-care, two baby photographers, a dog walker whose tagline alluded to owners not having time to walk their dogs, plus several other random services that, not being a mother herself, Freya didn't even know existed. After day-care, the board was weighted toward home services. Window cleaners and gardeners provided their details for people to obtain a free quote, and a very immature looking A5 poster advertised a builder for whom, no doubt, no job would be too small. Filling the spaces between the cards, as if to prevent two similar services being offered side by side, were cards offering groups and classes. There was a karate class for children and adults, a pottery class, and an art group, as well as piano lessons.

The board, in all its infantile glory, was a picture of suburban life that both sickened Freya at the idea of relying on other people so heavily and created a pang of regret in the pit of her stomach. The family life was one she had once had, and had lost. Though she had no children of her own, she had fallen in love with her ex-husband's child from his previous marriage to the point where she had deemed the boy her own. It was only when she had severed the tie to her family that she had realised how fragile that connection had been. A sad thought hit her. Seeing the parental services on the board had reminded her of Greg and Billy. But it was the first time she had spared them a thought for a full two weeks. Having been so embroiled in her new life – living in her camper van on a beach and then moving to the cottage, plus the two investigations she had worked on – she'd had little time to sit and ponder on what might have been.

She missed them both, Greg and Billy. There was no denying it. But she didn't miss the life. There was an acceptance of single life, an imagined destiny, that steeled her. It was only when Freya glanced at the top corner of the board that a black card caught her eye. It was different to the others in that it was of professional quality. The card had been printed with white, plain text that was easy to read, and left enough negative space to invoke a sense of elegance and class.

Prof. D. Ford.

MSc Int. Psych.

M.BACP.

LLB.

UKCP Registered.

Therapist.

There was no indication if the therapist was male or female, but the credentials were admirable and respectable. Freya knew this from the previous therapists she had seen, who had shared a similar alphabet in their titles.

She snapped a photo of the little, black card using the camera on her phone.

"Detective Inspector Bloom?" A man's voice snapped Freya from her musings.

She turned to find an attractive man in his early fifties with a well-managed flock of grey hair standing in a doorway. A girl in her twenties was wheeling a mature lady in a wheelchair away from the room. The girl eyed Freya as she passed, while the woman in the chair issued a scathing sneer. Combined with the blunt and authoritarian receptionist, Freya's opinion of the quaint market town was plummeting fast.

"I understand you wanted to see me?" said the doctor.

"Yes," she said, glancing back at the card for a moment before giving him her undivided attention. "Yes, I have few questions–"

"I can give you five minutes, but that's all, I'm afraid," he said, cutting her short, but then standing to one side by way of an invitation.

Entering the doctor's room, Freya closed the door behind her and ignored his hand that proffered the visitor seats.

"How can I help?" he asked, leaning back in his chair.

"Doctor Harris, do you know a Jane Blythe?"

His welcoming face paled in tone, and the upturned corners of his mouth fell.

"Jane? Of course."

"When was the last time you saw her, please?"

Shaking his head, he leaned forward from his relaxed pose to rest his arms on the desk. His shoulders hunched to give him a somewhat weighted posture.

"Must be getting on for a year now. If not longer."

"I understand she used to work for you?"

"She did. She worked on reception."

"And was her departure amicable, would you say? Or did she leave under a cloud, perhaps?"

"Jane lives under a cloud, Detective. She's a very unhappy soul."

"Can you answer the question, please?"

"Neither," he said, a little too abruptly. "Her departure from this surgery, as you put it, was neither amicable nor otherwise."

"Can you explain what you mean by that?"

"Yes," he replied, with confidence returning to his posture. He leaned back in his chair once more. "One evening, she left work, and she hasn't been back since."

———

"Mr Blythe?" Jackie called through the letterbox of thirty-three Acacia Drive. They had used the doorbell three times and knocked on the frosted glass window, all to no avail.

Estimating the house to be a mid-seventies build, mimicking the Victorian style with large front rooms, bay windows, and a central front door, Ben guessed the property would be of significant size. The large front garden was dominated by a long driveway to one side which was lined with Leylandii. The other side of the garden was a tangle of weeds and overgrown shrubs, as if somebody had gone to great lengths to brighten the shady space, and then given up.

Parked on the driveway was a white van. The driver, presumably Daniel Blythe, had reversed onto the drive, and the rear doors were ajar.

"Let's try around the back," Ben suggested, making the connection between the open side gate and the van's rear doors.

He didn't wait for an answer; instead, he peered into the alleyway beside the house and entered with caution. Hearing the distinctive sound of a shovel scrape against concrete, he announced his presence.

"Daniel Blythe?"

The shovel stopped.

"Mr Blythe, it's the police."

By the time Ben had reached the back of the house, Jackie was a few steps behind him, peering into the side windows, and a man who Ben presumed to be Daniel Blythe was waist deep in a hole, out of breath and leaning on his shovel.

"Now then," Blythe said, a typical Lincolnshire greeting.

"Daniel Blythe?" Ben asked, to which he nodded and wiped his brow.

Holding his warrant card up for Blythe to see, Ben approached the hole.

"I'm Detective Sergeant Savage. This is DC Gold. I wonder if we could have a few minutes of your time?"

"Is it important?"

"We wouldn't be here if it wasn't, Mr Blythe. Perhaps we could talk inside?"

Noticeably, Daniel was lithe and fit. He hopped out of the hole he had been digging, dug his shovel into a pile of sand, and wiped his hands on the legs of his jeans. He eyed them both with a distrusting look then moved toward the back door.

"What's the hole for?" asked Ben.

"Broken drain," Blythe replied, then turned at the door. "Feel free to have a closer look."

"I'll take your word for it."

The kitchen was large, modern, and free of clutter. After checking there was water inside, Blythe switched on the kettle.

"Brew?" he asked.

"I wouldn't say no."

Pulling three mugs from the cupboard, each with an outline of a farm animal printed on the side, he began to set up the tea bags.

"No sugar for me," said Ben, and Jackie requested just one.

"So what's all this about then?" he asked, while he waited for the kettle to boil. It was noisy, so Ben had to raise his voice above the gurgling of water.

"Perhaps we can sit down?" Jackie said.

"Or perhaps we can stand and you can tell me what all this is about."

"When was the last time you saw your wife, Mr Blythe?" Ben asked, watching his expressions closely.

There was no look of surprise, irritation, or even dismay in his eyes. With an unmoving expression, he considered the question for a few seconds, then answered, as if he had been asked the weather.

"Nearly a year now. Ten or eleven months ago. Give or take."

"And you haven't heard from her at all since then?"

"Not a dickie bird. We split up."

"And when you last saw her, how did you leave it? Did you say goodbye on friendly terms?"

"What is this all about, Detective?" he said, pretending not to remember Ben's name.

The kettle clicked, and he began filling the mugs with water. Waiting for him to finish pouring the hot water, Ben nodded discreetly to Jackie.

"A body was found last night, not far from here," she said. "We believe it's your wife, Mr Blythe. I'm sorry to be the one to deliver the news."

Only when Jackie had finished her sentence did Daniel display the first sign of emotion. Stirring a mug of tea to the point of it becoming stewed, he appeared shocked.

"Are you okay, Mr Blythe?" Ben asked. "We can arrange a family liaison officer, if you feel you'd like to talk to somebody."

"When?" was all he said.

"When was she found? Last night. In some woods not too far from here. A mile or two maybe? But no more than that."

"So she was here all along?"

The questions were just the ramblings of a man digesting a blow.

"Would you like me to help you with that?" suggested Jackie, standing to take over the tea making.

"She died last night? Is that what you're saying?"

"At this stage, Mr Blythe, we're not really in a position to investigate. We were wondering if perhaps you'd provide a formal identification."

"See her?" he said. "Dead?"

"Until we know if it's Jane or not, we can't move forward. I appreciate this is difficult."

"This woman. She died last night then, did she?"

"I'm afraid she's been dead for some months."

"And you think it's Jane?" he said, staring through the window into his garden.

"She was wearing a necklace," Jackie said, and Blythe bit his lower lip.

"Said Jane, did it?" he asked. "Her name?"

"It did. Does it sound like something she—"

"I bought it," he said, cutting Jackie off. "I bought it, she wore it."

"There was also a set of keys," Ben said, and Blythe turned his head to face him.

He shrugged.

"They had a little yellow tag on with the words 'Witham and Fens.'"

"Ah," Blythe said. "The surgery."

"So, perhaps you can see why we were led to believe it might be Jane?"

"When and where?"

Jackie glanced at Ben, who stared directly at Blythe. "Sorry?"

"You want me to see her. When and where? Today?"

"Erm, yeah. I'm sure we can make the—"

"Two o'clock. Where is she? Lincoln hospital?"

"She is, yes—"

"I'll be there," he said, and took a sip of his tea. "Will that be all?"

"No," Ben said, unhappy with the man's attitude. "Tell me about the last time you saw her."

Curling his hands around the warm mug, Blythe turned his head away to stare out of the window again.

"We can do this another time if you prefer," began Jackie.

"No," he said, and returned his attention to Ben. "No, let's talk now. Better to get it out there."

There was a pause, as Blythe sipped at his tea and Ben imagined his mind reeling. He would have so many questions, which he would be putting in some kind of order.

"I won't lie," he said, "we didn't part on friendly terms. We argued. Had been for months. Nothing out of the ordinary. I guess we just grew apart. We had a final argument and that was that."

"So she just left of her own accord?"

He nodded.

"Do you know where she went? She must have had somewhere to go."

"I don't know. I didn't ask."

"Did she have friends nearby? She might have gone to them."

"Not really. We hadn't been here long. Jane was shy. She preferred her own company. I'm stationed at RAF Coningsby a few miles away, and I don't really know what she did during the day, other than painting or working that is."

"RAF? What do you do?"

"I'm an engineer. We service the equipment used to maintain the aircraft. Nothing glamorous."

Remembering the van on the drive and the hole in the patio, Ben made an assumption. "I know a few ex-servicemen who retrained in a trade. They tend to be good too, as far as I can tell anyway. It must be the military grounding and discipline."

"It's not what it used to be," said Blythe. "The RAF. Even if they renew your contract, they make budget cuts to make your job harder."

"You're moving into construction work, I see. How is that going?"

"I've done a few projects. Conservatories and patios mostly. Finished a patio this morning as it happens. Had a few slabs left over, so I figured I'd fix my drain and patio at the same time," he said, nodding at the garden. "You have to make a name for yourself. Put cards through doors and the like. I take what I can, but there's healthy competition out there and not much money being spent."

"You seem to be doing okay."

"The house is paid for. The jobs are pocket money and, to be honest, I'm building a name for myself for when I retire. Besides, it keeps me out of mischief."

"Does it?" Ben said.

Blythe stared back at him, not rising to the comment.

"Yes. Yes, it does."

"Didn't Jane make friends with your colleagues' wives?" Jackie asked, still pondering his wife and their circle of friends. "There's normally little clicks, isn't there? My ex was in the RAF. There was always some kind of gathering."

"I think you'll find that kind of thing is a choice," Blythe suggested. "We chose not to join."

"How come?"

"Because then we would have had to spend evenings with each other playing the happy couple, wouldn't we?"

"Things were that bad, were they?" Ben said. "So she had no-one? What about her painting? Did she meet anyone there?"

"I think she used to talk to the girls at the surgery, but she never spoke of anybody in particular, except one bloke. Doctor Harris. His name was mentioned frequently."

"It's his practice," Jackie said. "She was on reception, wasn't she? She would have reported to him."

Nodding but saying nothing, Blythe looked away again and,

using his cuff, wiped the second sign of emotion he had displayed from his eye.

"Was there anyone in particular? Someone she might have called upon?"

Blythe shrugged. "I don't think so. She preferred not to air her dirty laundry."

"Airing your dirty laundry is one thing," said Ben. "But having no friends at all I find very hard to believe—"

"She had nowhere to go, damn it," Blythe hissed, slamming his hand on the table. "I assumed she went back to her parents, and good bloody riddance to her is what I thought if you must know."

A few seconds passed. Blythe took an audible breath and rested his head in his hands.

"I know it's hard, Mr Blythe, but anything you can tell us will help. What time of day did she leave? What was the date?"

"Evening. It was dark. I remember. It was dark and cold." He seemed to recall the evening and he looked up at Ben to explain. "The door was open. I remember thinking that the heat was getting out."

"And was Jane carrying a handbag?"

"I don't know. No, wait. She had a case. She had one of those little cases with wheels. Her handbag was inside."

"Are you sure of that?"

"Positive. It was me who packed it for her. I wanted to make sure she had no reason to come back. I packed it, and tossed it at her on the driveway."

"You threw the case at her?" Ben asked.

"It was an argument. It could have been worse."

"What about a phone?" Jackie asked. "Did Jane have a mobile?"

"Of course. It was a pay-as-you-go thing. Cheap and cheerful."

"And did she take it with her?"

"I guess so," he said, shrugging. "I haven't come across it."

"I have to say, Mr Blythe, you don't seem to be bothered by

the news in the slightest," Ben said. "We've just told you that we believe your wife is dead, and–"

"And what?" he replied. "What do you want me to do? Cry? You want me to break down? We were over a long time ago. Long before she walked out that door."

"And she did walk, did she?" Jackie asked. "She didn't have a car of her own?"

"She did, but she didn't take it."

"She chose to walk? At night, in winter, with a suitcase?"

He sighed, and guilt spread across his face the way a dark cloud shields the sun.

"I took the key off her bunch. *I* paid for the bloody thing. It was in *my* name. We argued about that, of course. Argued about bloody everything. In the end, I think she just wanted to get away."

Ben leant back against a kitchen counter. "And what did you do after she had left?"

"What do you mean?"

"Well, did you go after her? Did you call a friend?"

"No, neither of those. I closed the door and locked it."

"And you haven't heard from her since?"

He placed his mug on the table, clutching it with both hands and finding Ben's inquisitive stare across the table.

"Like I said before, I haven't heard a thing from Jane since the moment I slammed the door behind her."

CHAPTER SEVEN

"How well did you know Jane, Doctor Harris?" Freya asked, searching his face for a tell that he might be lying. "Would you say that you were friends?"

"No," he replied. "Not friends. She told me a little about herself over the short period she worked here, but you know how it is. I don't like to get too close to my employees. People talk, don't they? They fill in the gaps, as it were."

"*Your* employees. So you own the practice, do you?"

"Majority shareholder. Fifteen years now," he said with a proud sigh.

"Forgive me for saying, but is it common for a man of your experience, with his own surgery, to still be practising?"

"Do you mean to say, what is an old fart like me still practising for?" he said with a smile that lit his entire face. He was a handsome man, groomed and mature. There was something about his pale blue eyes and whiter-than-white smile that caught Freya's attention. "What do you expect me to do? Sit back and watch my staff do all the work? I lead from the front line, Inspector Bloom. I like to keep my finger on the pulse, if you pardon the pun."

That smile again.

"What did Jane tell you about herself?"

"Sorry?"

He had heard her clearly enough, of that Freya was positive. Asking somebody to repeat themselves was a sure way to buy time while a suitable response was prepared.

"What did Jane tell you about herself?" she repeated, and the answer came almost immediately.

"Oh, not a lot really. Husband in the RAF. No children. You know? Just a snippet here and there."

"So you take the time to get to know your staff, do you? But prefer not to get too close? Would you say that was part of your leadership style?"

"Well, I…" he began, a little off guard. "I just asked her a few polite questions when she brought me my coffee. I didn't really get to know her, as such."

"I understand," she said. "Perhaps then you could tell me a little about Jane's last few days at work?"

"I'll do my best, but as I said–"

"You just asked a few polite questions when she brought your coffee," Freya said, finishing the sentence for him.

"That's right."

"Did she bring your coffee every day for you?"

"Well, yes, most days. When she was here anyway."

"Oh? Was Jane sick often?"

"No, no. Nothing like that. Jane worked part time. Three days per week. I would have preferred her to work full time, but she was honest from the start that she wasn't looking for a career. It was just something to keep her busy for a few days. Of course, it meant my wife had to stand in until we found Cheryl to work the remaining two days."

"Was that Cheryl that I just met?" said Freya, pointing back at the reception with her thumb, knowing full well that her name tag had stated the name.

"Yes. She's full time now," he said. "Much neater. It gets a little complex when a role is shared. I would have preferred Jane to be full time, but she was adamant. She wanted her free time for her art classes."

"Art classes?"

"Yes," he said. "She was a keen artist. Quite good too, from what I saw anyway."

"From what you saw? I thought she only told you snippets? You know, while she was bringing your coffee, Doctor Harris?"

"That's right."

"But you've seen her art?"

"She showed me a photograph once. It was on her phone. Facebook or something. It was nothing really."

"But it was a little more than a snippet. I mean, how do you enter into a conversation about somebody's art for long enough to see a photo of their work, when all she was doing was bringing you coffee?"

"What are you insinuating?" he said, his voice sounding bored.

"I'm not insinuating anything. I'm just curious as to what else you might be able to tell me. More snippets, as it were," said Freya. "I'm trying to understand what happened to Jane Blythe during her last few days."

"Her last few days?"

"Oh, didn't I mention it? We think we found her body last night."

The doctor digested the news in silence.

"You think?" he said finally.

"We're having her formally identified. But we're quite sure."

"How sad," he said, from obligation more than sincerity.

"To understand what happened, I need to know who she interacted with, what she did, where she went. So, if you have any more of those snippets, I think it's time you indulged me, Doctor Harris."

Clearly not a man to enjoy being cornered, Harris leaned forward in his seat, resting his arms on the desk. It was a power posture that, had Freya elected to take the offered guest chair, would have placed him in a taller position, looking down at her.

"I've told you all I know about Jane Blythe, Inspector—"

"It's funny. I don't think you've told me half of what you know, Doctor. How long did she work here?"

"Are you always this accusing?"

"Only when the person I'm talking to is defensive."

"Irritated, I believe is the word. Defensive is not in my nature."

"But being irritated is?"

"Two years," he said. "Give or take."

"Thank you. I'm also trying to understand something else here, please bear with me. During those two years of working three days per week, which is…" Freya had already done the math, but she feigned working through a calculation in her mind, watching the doctor's expressions. "Fifty-two times two, times three. Jane made you three hundred and twelve cups of coffee. Give or take—"

"I didn't count them."

"And during those, let's call it three hundred coffees, the only information you know about her life outside of work is that her husband is a serviceman, she had no children, and she was a keen artist."

"That's about right," he said. "Now, if you'll excuse me, it's likely that I have a room of sick people who need my attention."

Freya stood and made her way to the door, stopping to glance back at the doctor where she offered a warning shot.

"Don't go anywhere, Doctor Harris. I may need to ask you some more questions."

"If you don't allow me to get on with my work," the doctor replied, unable to hide his irritation, "I shan't be going anywhere for a very long time, Detective Inspector Bloom. Good day to you."

___

CHAPTER EIGHT

___

"Well, that was unequivocal," Jackie mused, as Ben nosed the car back onto the main road. "What now?"

"Freya wants to meet me at the hospital. I'll drop you off on the way," said Ben, reaching forward to the dashboard. He clicked the reset button on the odometer. "There's something I want to know before we do that."

"What are you doing?" asked Jackie.

"You'll see," he replied, as they crossed a junction.

He drove slowly, heading away from the station. It was only when they were passing the main row of shops in Woodhall Spa that Jackie pushed for a response.

"Where *are* we going, Ben? Bloom said we had a briefing this afternoon, and no doubt I'll need to type up the notes."

"Not far," he replied.

"And what about Blythe? What do you think?"

"Mixed thoughts. I usually get a feeling about somebody when I talk to them."

"You mean, you judge them?"

"No, not really."

"Right."

"My intuition, when we first met him at least, is that he's a cold-hearted bastard."

"I thought the same. Especially when he told us he slammed the door behind her. How could a man do that to his wife? In the middle of winter with nowhere to go? I mean, that was at least a four-bedroom house. Surely she could have slept in a spare room if they wanted to be apart for the night?"

"We don't know that she had nowhere to go."

"Sorry?" she said, sounding confused. "He said that Jane hadn't made any friends around here."

"He said he didn't know. Let's see what Freya comes back with after her visit to the surgery," Ben said, as he pulled the car over to the kerb and peered through the windscreen at the row of shops. The shops were the hub of the small town, and he parked outside a ladies hair and beauty salon, a little gift shop that sold greetings cards, picture frames, and small household goods, and a newsagents. He unclipped his seatbelt and checked the mirror for cars before opening his door. "I'll just be a moment."

"Is this it?" she asked. "Is this where you wanted to go?"

"No. This is a pit stop. This is research," he said.

The door closed, silencing Jackie's questions, and Ben walked over to the newsagents and found what he was looking for. Among the various advertisements for babysitters, day-care, nurseries, and gardeners was a card titled *Blythe Construction*. The design was poor but served a purpose, Ben surmised. Using the camera on his phone, he snapped a photo of the board in its entirety, and one close up of Daniel Blythe's card, then returned to the car.

"Did you find it?" Jackie asked, guessing the purpose of his little stop.

"I did. At least some of what he said holds up."

He indicated and pulled out onto the road, keeping a watchful eye on the odometer. Shuffling in her seat, Jackie's curiosity was clearly getting the better of her patience. But Ben decided to hold out a little longer; he was enjoying watching her mind work as she sought to understand what was going on in his head.

"What about now?" she asked. "What does your intuition tell you?"

"My intuition?" he asked, his mind busy with the board and the odometer.

"You said you thought he was a cold man when we first met him. How about now?"

"Why don't you tell me what *you* think?"

"Honestly? He clearly paid her so little attention that I'm not surprised she left. He has a temper too."

"I caught that."

"Not particularly nice to live with somebody who doesn't care and may lash out once in a while. I can vouch for that."

"We don't know that he lashed out, Jackie."

"No, we don't. But you asked what my impression was of him."

"Do you want to know what I think?"

"Go on," Jackie said.

"He's one to watch. It's not always what they say, it's what they don't say."

"What's that supposed to mean?" Jackie asked.

"What didn't he ask us?"

"Eh?" she said, clearly not enjoying being put on the spot. She was silent for a moment, as she recollected the conversation and processed her thoughts.

"I'm pretty sure the first thing I would ask if somebody told me my wife had been found dead is *how* she died," said Ben.

"Bloody hell. You're right," Jackie said. "Come to think of it, he didn't even appear to be surprised."

"That's not the last we've seen of him. Something tells me there's far more to him than meets the eye."

The town of Woodhall Spa was now in the rear-view mirror, and the road was lined with tall trees. The houses on the edge of the town were set back from the road, detached, and Ben knew the area to be expensive.

"Are we going to the crime scene?" she asked. "I wish you would have told me. I would have brought my boots."

"Correct. But you won't need to get out, Jackie," he replied, watching the odometer click around. "We have everything we need just here."

They navigated the bumpy track that led between two fields, and then turned into the forest access road where he and Freya had parked behind Jackie's car the previous night. A uniformed officer was standing guard by the entrance. Flashing his warrant card to the uniform, Ben passed beneath the police tape while the man held it up.

"And, here we are," he said, stopping the car in the exact same place and checking the odometer for the final time.

"What are we doing here?"

"Well, let's try Freya's method for a moment. Imagine you are Jane Blythe. You've just had an argument with Daniel Blythe, your husband. Arguments are frequent, but this time it's bad. Bad enough that you pack a case with the things you need."

"He said that he packed the case."

"Okay. Whoever packed the case–"

"You're not very good at this."

"Just do it, will you?" he said, losing a little patience. "Close your eyes."

"Right," Jackie said, hands on her lap and eyes squeezed closed.

"You argue with your husband. You take the case and you leave. You're upset, crying probably, and you have nowhere to go. You say your final words to him and he slams the door, leaving you alone. You don't have many friends, because you haven't lived in the area for long."

"Or maybe I do have a friend, but my husband doesn't approve of her."

"Or him," Ben added.

"Or him," Jackie repeated.

"You're carrying the case, or dragging it behind you, but you choose to come *here*. Of all the places you could have gone, you come here."

"A place that lovers come to be away from prying eyes."

"Exactly."

"Do you think she was having an affair?"

"Why else would you walk exactly one mile in the freezing cold with a little suitcase?" Ben said, pointing at the dashboard.

"Because she couldn't go to her friend's house. Because they were lovers," Jackie said, her excitement growing. "And her lover was married."

"It would explain why Daniel Blythe threw her out."

"We need to know who her friend was," said Jackie. "Daniel Blythe knows more than he was letting on."

"And whoever her so-called friend was also hadn't reported her missing. Does that seem odd to you?"

She nodded, but her expression said more. It was a sign she was disappointed in something.

"I'd like to think that if I ever went missing, someone would notice and report it."

"I'm sure they would," Ben said, as he turned the car around. "I'll drop you off. Make sure you're ready for this afternoon."

"What's happening this afternoon?"

"You're meeting Daniel Blythe at the mortuary."

"But you said *you* were going. You said you were meeting DI Bloom."

"I am. We are. But we'll be meeting the pathologist to understand how Jane Blythe died. You, on the other hand, will be meeting Daniel Blythe to work out if it is actually his wife, and to see how he reacts to those head wounds."

"Why me?" Jackie asked. She leaned on her door, waiting for his response.

"Because you're the loveliest person I know, and if I had to formally identify my wife, I'd want you beside me."

"Do you mean that?" she asked, and she stared at him with those big eyes.

"Of course," he replied. "Besides, it was either you or Cruz, and if what we just witnessed was an indication of Blythe's temper, we'd have more than one murder on our hands if we sent Cruz."

CHAPTER NINE

A shrill whistle went straight through Freya as she approached the hospital doors. She winced at the noise, but didn't stop, turn, or even acknowledge the noise.

"Freya?" a voice called, and a pang of disappointment washed through her. She thought he was better than that.

Footsteps grew louder, and as the automatic doors swished open, he slowed to a walk beside her. "Didn't you hear me?" he asked.

"Hear you?"

"I whistled from the car park. Had to bloody run to catch you."

"You whistled?"

"Yeah. Didn't you hear it?"

"I am not a dog, Ben," she said. "I hope you're not expecting me to roll over onto my back."

He raised his eyebrows and a smirk crept onto his face, no doubt reading something else into her statement.

"Not here, Freya. It's a public place."

"Shut up."

"I'm kidding," he said, as he pushed the double doors into the long corridor that led to the mortuary. He pulled his little notepad from his pocket and clicked his pen. "I'll make a note. Freya does not respond to whistles."

She had to admit, he did have a way of lightening a mood, and the grin she thought she had concealed was apparently recognisable enough that he was encouraged.

"What about biscuits?"

"Biscuits?"

"Yeah, you know. Treats," he said. "Or long walks."

"Now you're taking the–"

"Well, well," a voice said from behind them, and they both glanced at each other, instantly noting the deep Welsh accent. They turned in unison to find Doctor Bell strutting down the corridor like she had all the time in the world. Her bright red Crocs slapped on the smooth floor. "I'd recognise that voice anywhere, I would. Thought to myself, well, if that isn't Benjamin Savage, I'll eat my hat."

"You don't wear a hat," Ben called back, grinning as the young doctor approached.

Having only met Doctor Bell once before, Freya offered her a brief smile and an accompanying nod. Not only was she not wearing a hat, but she seemed to have changed her hair colour. This time it was a deep violet. Not that describing her would ever be a problem, Freya thought. The woman had more piercings than she had ever seen in a single human body. It was a surprise she didn't rattle as she walked. There were rings in her nose, eyebrows, lower lips, and even a bar through her chin, which was just plain bizarre. Without her smock, her bare forearms revealed heavy tattoos, and given the ample size of the doctor, there was plenty of skin for the tattoos to tell a story. She wasn't short of space to have them done.

"Detective Inspector Bloom," she said, as she drew nearer, and Freya noted she was slightly out of breath, despite not actually making any attempt whatsoever to hurry up. "Still here then, are you?"

"Apparently," Freya said. "Are you just starting work?"

"Just had my lunch. The big man upstairs doesn't like me eating in the office. Says it's not right."

"The big man upstairs?" Ben asked, his eyes darting to Freya then back to the pathologist.

"Boss man," she replied, her eyes flicking upwards. "Well, if he doesn't want me to eat in there, he can pay for me to walk to the canteen, is what I say. In his time, not my own. Only get an hour, I do, and it takes me ten minutes to get there."

Unsure of how to respond to the doctor's comment, Freya addressed her hair.

"I see you've changed your hair."

"Ah, you noticed, did you?"

"Kind of hard not to," Ben said.

"I was inspired by my living room," she said, as they finally reached the doors to the mortuary and she held a hand up for them to stop so she could swipe her access card. The door beeped then clicked, and she entered the small reception room, holding the door for Freya and Ben to follow.

The mention of Doctor Bell's living room sparked Freya's curiosity. She imagined her home was a cute, one-bedroom flat. There would be brightly-coloured throws on the couches and armchairs, and her bedroom would be Gothic-themed, with candles and joss sticks. She had to have joss sticks.

"Is it violet then?" Freya asked.

"Is what violet?"

"Your living room? You said you were inspired."

"Why would I have a violet living room?"

"I don't know. Maybe you have a feature wall?"

"A feature wall? Do I look like bloody Kevin McCloud? No, I do not have a feature wall."

"Who's Kevin McCloud?" Ben asked.

"You know? That fella," Doctor Bell said, clicking her fingers trying to remember. "From that show. The one with all the houses and whatnot. Tall fella. Snappy dresser."

"Grand Designs?" Freya asked, and even Ben who, like Freya, famously didn't own a TV, raised his eyebrows in surprise.

"So what inspired you?" Freya asked. They had come too far not to get to the bottom of the inspiration now.

"My candle."

"Your candle?" Ben said, in nearly as much disbelief as Freya.

"Yeah. Above my fireplace. Scented. Lavender, it is."

"Lavender?"

"Yeah. Violet? I ask you," Doctor Bell said, pulling a strand of hair forward so she could see it. "It's clearly lavender."

"I don't think lavender is so bright, is it?" Freya said.

"Course it is. Violet is deeper. Like a goth. And before you say, I am not a goth."

"What's a goth?" Ben said, and they both turned to him, wide-eyed. He smiled at them. "Just kidding. How about we go and see our mystery woman? Or we can stand here all day discussing your hair?"

"I thought you'd never ask," Doctor Bell said, and then pointed into the corner, clicking her fingers again, another pet peeve of Freya's. "Masks, hats, gowns in there. Suit up, and I'll see you on the other side."

The door closed with a swish of the insulating brushes, and a blast of cold air washed through the little reception.

"She's mental," Freya said, as Ben passed her a set of PPE. "Honestly, I've never met anybody like her. Well, that's not strictly true. I did meet somebody quite like her once before."

"Oh yeah. Who was she?"

"Some nutcase in London. A druggie. Poured petrol over herself and sat in the middle of the greeting card aisle in Tesco. She's in Broadmoor now, I believe, reciting Bedknobs and Broomsticks word for word, over and over," Freya finished, snapping her mask into place. "Ready?"

Ben tied his gown, clearly a little bemused at Freya's comment.

"And we thought we have it bad up here," he muttered.

They entered the sterile area beyond the doors, feeling the difference in temperature almost immediately. It wasn't cold enough to warrant hats, scarves, and gloves, but it was definitely a few degrees cooler than comfortable.

"Right then," Doctor Bell called out from beside one of the stainless steel benches. Canon in D was playing through a little portable speaker, and Bell, in her white smock, was waiting with her hands folded before her like a priest. Ben and Freya walked side by side across the room like some kind of weird wedding procession.

Unable to hide his amusement, Ben laughed, and the doctor's frown deepened. She rested her hands on the still mound beneath a blue sheet before her.

"I don't," Ben whispered, and Freya glanced up at him. "In case you're wondering."

Had Doctor Bell not already irritated Freya, she may have found the comment amusing. They stopped at the bench, and Ben, in his usual casual manner, pocketed his hands and waited while Doctor Bell studied Freya to the point of being awkward.

"Female. Pretty. Auburn hair. Non-smoker. No tattoos," the doctor said, staccato. It was only when she said, "Late thirties," that Freya was sure she was referring to the woman on the slab, and not her.

"Any distinguishing marks at all?" Freya asked.

"None at all," she replied. "A few moles, but nothing prominent. Only the chain."

"I guess we'll have to see what Daniel Blythe says," said Ben. Then he turned to Doctor Bell. "He's the one coming in at two o'clock."

"Ah, yes. Heard about him, I did. Lucky I gave her a good clean up then, wasn't it?"

"Time of death?" Freya asked. "Do we have an idea of exactly when she died?"

"Hard to say. A year, I'd say, give or take a month either side."

"That's what we thought. Last winter."

"Right," Doctor Bell muttered. "What I find interesting are these scratches on her arms here, see?"

The doctor lifted the edge of the sheet to reveal the woman's torso. Under the bright ring lights, the scratches they had seen by torch light the previous night were clear. Deep gorges covered her forearms, and even her forehead.

Any humour they had found in the doctor's stance and the choice of music had gone the moment the body was revealed. A dead body was not a thing of beauty, especially one that had been exposed to the elements, hidden beneath the thickets.

A Y-section had been cut into the woman's flesh. The arms of the Y ran down from the shoulders and met at the chest, from where a central incision continued down to the pelvis. The cuts allowed the pathologist to examine internal organs, and were usually sutured by the time Freya arrived. Not this time.

The doctor, for all her sins, had done a good job of cleaning her. The woman's facial features on the undamaged side were clear, which was pretty much all Freya could have hoped for.

"Cause of death?" Freya said, feeling slightly uneasy about the open chest cavity in front of her.

"Haematoma," Doctor Bell replied. She removed her pen from her breast pocket and waved a circle around the area. "I mean, the toxicology report will confirm it, but the organs all look healthy. You can see here the slight lacerations I was telling DS Savage about on the telephone. I've since analysed fragments of matter from the wounds."

"And what did you find?"

"Sand. Tiny fragments of rock. Now, whoever hit her is right-handed and taller than her. Of that I'm certain. The rock came down hard, fracturing her skull and causing those lacerations. Beneath the fractured skull, however, the blood vessels were damaged. Blood pooled in the area, filling that space between the skull and this membrane here. This is the dura, the outermost membrane that covers the brain." She looked up at Freya while she spoke, to make sure they were following. "You okay there, are you?"

"I'm fine," Freya said. It wasn't the first time she'd seen inside a skull.

"As I was saying," Bell continued, "this pool of blood is called a haematoma. As more blood pools, it forces the dura down, compressing the brain. Death would be slow. Very painful. The worst migraine you can imagine."

"Anything else?" Freya said, shifting the attention from the head wound.

"Not yet. I'm still working on her. You'll have a full report tomorrow, I expect," the doctor said, then turned the tables onto them. "What are your thoughts so far?"

"It was reactive," Freya said, without hesitation. "They grabbed the rock in anger. It wasn't planned."

"I can see why you earn the big bucks, Detective Inspector Bloom."

Checking her watch, Freya glanced at Ben. "Let's get back and brief the team." Then she turned to Doctor Bell. "We'll leave you to get her ready for the husband."

"Ah, yes. Get all the fun jobs, I do."

"DC Gold will be here to meet him," Ben added. "I spoke to him earlier."

"How did he take the news?" the doctor asked.

"He's a tough character. Hard to read."

"Bastard, you mean?"

"One to watch, I would say," Ben suggested.

"Are you sure it's her?" the doctor asked. She sighed as she sat on her stool and pulled a few files towards her.

"I've never been surer of anything. But then, I'm not always right," said Freya. "Thanks for your time, Doctor Bell. You've been a great help."

———

It was past lunchtime when Freya and Ben returned to the station. Ben had beaten her there and parked in his usual spot, so Freya pulled in beside him.

She entered through the secure rear doors and climbed the fire escape stairwell to the first floor, only to be welcomed by a hum of activity – indistinct noise, a collective melee of printers, conversations, the kettle, and fingers on keyboards. There were always fingers on keyboards, it seemed.

The first door on the right was DSI Harper's office. With the entire area under his command and retirement looming, he was rarely seen. She glanced in through the window as she passed to confirm he wasn't there. It had been Harper who had made Freya's secondment to Lincolnshire happen. With a career spanning three decades, he had rubbed shoulders with his regionally disparate equals, the decision makers. From what Freya had seen, Harper was a fair man, though somewhat behind the times. Somebody higher up had made the call to allow him the decency to see his retirement out, while DCI Granger picked up many of his duties.

Affectionately, Harper was known as Arthur for his uncanny ability to start a project then only complete half of it before delegating completion to one of his command. "Half a job here, half a job there. Keeps me busy," Freya had heard more than one of Standing's team joke affectionately.

On the left was the incident room, which was significantly

larger than the rooms on the right of the corridor and was where the teams worked.

DI Standing's team operated from one end of the large room, while Freya's team occupied the other half. With six desks arranged for maximum collaborative effort and a white board to brainstorm plans, there was plenty of room for them to stand and discuss investigations, while keeping their distance from Standing's jibes and sneers.

The next door along on the right was the small kitchenette, and beyond that was Will Granger's office, who, when Freya looked in as she passed, gruffed a greeting, making a point to break eye contact to focus on the report he was poring over.

Finally, there were two washrooms, which Freya had heard various members of the team refer to using a variety of terms. Arthur had referred to the toilet as the lavatory, while Will Granger used the much simpler and much more British term – bog. Gold, one of the youngest in the team used the term loo, and DS Chapman never referred to the room itself; instead, when the time came, she chose to discreetly inform Gold that she was about to *spend a penny*.

To anybody else, these observations would appear mundane and irrelevant. But to Freya, who considered them as she leaned on the wash basin and peered at herself in the mirror, the terms each individual used were a direct reflection of their characters. Arthur, the seasoned and wizened old man. Granger, the rough and ready senior who had worked his way through the ranks through sheer grit. And then Gold and DC Chapman, who were young and malleable playthings for Granger to mould.

It was odd, she had never heard Ben refer to the washroom at all. She wondered what term he would use. In the past, she had carried out similar analyses of how each of them liked their tea and coffee, and what they did in their spare time. Her opinion of them all was as a collective bunch of misfits with varying degrees of refinement, mostly bordering the lower ranks of society. This was all part of her consideration of Will Granger's request. The decision had been rolling around the perimeter of her mind for over a day now.

Should she go and see Professor Ford, and embrace a future with the misfits? She hated to admit it to herself, but she was beginning to like them all, not just Ben, who seemed to be the most personable and grounded of the team.

Or should she shy away from opening herself to scrutiny from yet another therapist she had never met before in the hope that one day the nightmares and anxiety she carried would be bearable?

Perhaps she could go back to Greg and Billy? If Greg would take her, she could try and repair the damage she had caused. The damage she had run away from. No matter which way she spun the idea, she knew in her heart that returning to her failed marriage was just another excuse to run away again. It was the easier of the two options.

Pulling her phone from her pocket, she opened her photo library and found the image of the advertisement board in the surgery. Upon leaving Doctor Harris' room, she had stopped beside the reception desk to take another photo for two reasons. The first was to incite a dialogue with Cheryl, the brash lady who had taken over from Jane Blythe. She found the second reason in the top right-hand corner of the photo and zoomed in to see the phone number.

Memorising the number, Freya navigated her phone to the dial pad and dialled. Slightly alarmed at her clammy hands, she realised how nervous she was.

"Hello, Professor Ford," a voice said after only a single ring.

But Freya couldn't speak. It was as if a strong hand had clamped around her throat.

"Hello? You're through to Professor Ford. Can I help?"

Freya hit the red button to disconnect the call and leaned on the basin, suddenly able to breathe again. She wanted so much to rinse her face with cold water, but with the team waiting for her to lead the briefing, there was no time for her to redo her makeup.

The professor had sounded nice. She had been soft-spoken, calm yet confident. Freya wondered what the D stood for in Professor D. Ford. She sounded like a Diane, an alarming similarity to her long-dead mother.

A knock at the door roused Freya from her thoughts.

"Ma'am? Are you in there?"

It was Chapman. Clearing her throat, Freya took one more glance in the mirror before speaking.

"Chapman?"

"I was just wondering if you were okay."

How nice. Invasive, but nice. Another confliction to add to the decision she would have to make.

"I'll be out in a moment," she said, as she saved the number she had dialled, creating a new contact in her phone. In the NAME field, she typed *Diane*.

CHAPTER TEN

"It's her, Ben," Jackie said over the phone. Her voice was quiet, but it wasn't quite a whisper. It was more of a respectful hush, like she was in a church or something.

"Is he upset?"

"Hard to say. There's a sadness there for sure, but honestly, I can't tell. He's like a bloody emotional rock."

"Did you go in with him?"

"No way. I waited for him out here in reception. I sat him down after. You know? Just to calm him down a bit."

"Did he need it?"

"No. He's just left. I thought I'd give you a call to let you know. I guess that's what we needed to press on?"

"Brace yourself, Jackie. The next few days will be hard. But remember, it's moments like this where you shine. And honestly, whatever time you need, you tell me, and I'll make sure you get the opportunity to make a difference elsewhere."

"Thanks, Ben. That means a lot."

"No worries," said Ben, with one hand on the incident room door. "I'll see you back here soon."

He pushed open the door, caught Freya's attention, then gave her the nod.

"Jane Blythe?" she asked.

"Confirmed."

"Right, listen up," Freya said, clapping her hands three times.

"All we do is bloody listen," Standing called out from his end of the room. "Can't help but listen with you rattling on every five minutes."

"How's that red diesel investigation going? It's not exactly a hive of activity up there."

"Slowly," he called back. "Someone burned the evidence."

"Well, I'm sure you'll crack it. In the meantime, I'd appreciate it if you didn't interrupt me when I'm preparing to talk to my team."

"You told everyone to listen up. I thought you were talking to us as well. Isn't that right, Jim?"

"Aye, boss. I've got my pen and notebook ready. Even found a clean page," Gillespie added.

"Well, you'll know when I'm talking to you, because I'll look at you."

Freya turned away from them as they began their childish wooing noises. The team's attention was waning.

"We have a confirmed ID," Freya announced from her position beside the white board.

The murmuring stopped. Although Ben knew the softer, more personable side of her, he couldn't help but admire and fear the sterner side of the woman who had taken his opportunity to climb the ladder.

"From this moment on, we're pushing all lines of enquiry. What happened to Jane Blythe? Forty-one years old, married, no children. She moved to Lincolnshire three years ago with her husband, Daniel Blythe, and worked in a doctor's surgery on reception. She worked three days per week, preferring to keep two days to herself to attend art classes. According to Doctor

Harris, one evening Jane left work and she never returned. Ben, do you have anything to add?"

The afternoon briefing consisted of the same individuals who attended the morning briefing, with the addition of a uniform whom Ben knew only as Griffiths, and minus DC Gold who was on her way back from the hospital.

"Yes," Ben said, seeing the opportunity to update the team on his visit to the husband. "DC Gold and I paid a visit to Daniel Blythe. He took the news as well as could be expected. Better, in fact. I have no reason to disbelieve anything he said. He did not try to hide his feelings for his wife, in fact, he made it quite clear that he was glad to be shot of her. He even packed her suitcase so she had no reason to come back."

"I wonder why," Chapman asked.

"According to him, Jane had no friends in the area. They had been arguing for months. Long enough for their marriage to break down. Jane elected to leave. It was late at night, freezing cold, and all she took with her was the small, carry-on suitcase that Daniel Blythe packed for her."

"What was inside?" asked Granger.

"Her purse and some clothing. Daniel Blythe also took her car keys, so we can make an assumption that Jane was on foot. To mirror Freya's account, we know that Jane left home that night and never returned. It's a one-mile walk to where her body was found, so if she walked all that way then she must have had a reason to do so."

"Unless somebody picked her up and took her there, in which case he or she must have selected the place for a reason," added Ben.

"True," Freya replied, then addressed the team. "DS Savage and I paid a visit to Doctor Bell, the pathologist. Jane Blythe bled to death from a haematoma. She was hit with a rock, heavy enough to fracture her skull. Time of death, based on the decomposition of the body, is estimated at eleven months to thirteen months ago. Which makes it last winter. The report goes on to conclude that Jane's clothing supports this time frame, albeit a little light for a winter stroll. That might suggest she hadn't planned on leaving. Further to that, findings from the victim's fingernails, along with swabs, have been sent to the lab."

"Sexual interference?" asked Granger.

"Initial assessments suggest not, guv. The swabs will tell us for sure."

"Ma'am?" said Chapman, using the break in accounts to make an announcement. She looked up from her laptop to ensure she had their attention. "I've got the phone records back for Daniel and Jane Blythe. Jane Blythe's phone was a pay-as-you-go. They've sent me the last twelve months' call history and SMS data for both."

"Anything of interest?"

"Nothing. Jane hasn't used her phone since last October. The twentieth, to be precise."

"Who did she call?" Ben asked.

"Not call. She sent a text. The number matches Michael Harris. The doctor."

"What time was this?"

"Just after eight o'clock in the evening."

"Anything before that?"

"No. Not really. She called Daniel Blythe's phone a few times. But there's really not a lot to report."

"She could have been using WhatsApp," Cruz suggested, and the team turned to him. "What? It's a messaging service."

"He's right," Ben said. "The phone provider wouldn't have records of that."

"So we need her phone," Freya said. "I'll add that to the list of things we don't have, which, for the record, is far longer than the list of things we do have."

She turned to face the white board and drew a horizontal line.

"This is our timeline," she said, marking a spot a few inches in from the left. "This is when she sent the text to Michael Harris. What did it say?"

"We'd need one of the two phones to get that," Chapman said.

Unperturbed, Freya marked another spot in the centre of the timeline.

"This is when she was killed. What happened before she sent the text, and what happened after? Where was Jane last seen – her house or the surgery? If both Doctor Harris and Daniel Blythe said she left and didn't return? We have no conclusive evidence that she didn't go to a friend's house when she left Daniel, and then to work the next day. We need to ascertain accurate dates as to when she was last seen at the house and the surgery. We'll need to bring the husband in for questioning. Ben, can I charge you with developing a list of questions for him? I don't want to spook him, so if you need to go and see him again in a less formal environment, do so. Take Gold with you."

"Will do," he replied. "She's on her way back now."

"Good. Let's have some theories, then," said Freya, turning to face them all. "We have a year-old body with next to no evidence. We've spoken to Jane Blythe's husband and her boss, and pretty soon DC Cruz will be out knocking on doors. Perhaps you can tell us which fact we should begin with?"

Cruz let his head fall back in silent protest.

"Come on, people. Wake up. Let's have some ideas. We can sit here twiddling our thumbs until we get some facts to work with, or we can use our combined experience to suggest reasons why Jane Blythe's last breath was spent lying on the floor of a forest beneath eight feet of brambles on a cold winter night."

"I think we should refrain from hypothesising, and focus on reality," Granger began.

"And I would agree, if the murder took place last night, when we might stand a chance of catching her killer with blood on his clothes, or even acting oddly. But we're not. Whoever did this has had nearly a year to come to terms with their actions. They've lain awake at night thinking about us approaching them one day. They've thought about what they might say a hundred times or more. They are ten steps ahead of us. We need to get creative, and to do that, we need theories. *Theories* allow us to place Jane Blythe in potential situations based on what we know so far. They force us to ask questions that might shed a different light on the situation. And as for judgement, we have a collective career spanning more than fifty years. I think that fortunes us a little room for judgement to have its place. So, with your permission, guv, I'd like to see what comes of it."

Snapping the lid back onto her marker, Freya turned to face Granger, offering him the respect he deserved and nothing more. Ben could see she had a valid argument for pushing for the brainstorming session. It was the only way for them to find new lines of enquiry. But the manner in which she had delivered her argument left Granger little room for manoeuvre, and he wouldn't like that.

"Go on," said Granger, and after a long, uncomfortable pause, he added, "let's see what comes of it."

"Let's start with you, guv," said Freya, offering him a warm smile to bring him into the game. "All you know is what we've reported after going out and talking to Daniel Blythe and Doctor Harris. So your opinion will be quite clear-cut."

"Are you asking me to guess what happened to her?"

"Not guess. You're the most experienced officer in the room. Surely you might have a few theories of your own knocking around? We have at least one day before the lab results are returned and DC Cruz brings us some insight. Let's get some creative juices flowing."

"You won't win me over by feeding my ego, Bloom."

"Perhaps not. But I can try," she said, and smiled once more with that infectious confidence.

CHAPTER ELEVEN

"The art class," Granger started, and Freya smiled inwardly at his engagement. All she'd had to do was prompt him and steer him. "Have we been there yet? Has anybody spoken to whoever runs the class to see if they remember her?"

DCI Granger's question was interrupted by the squealing of the incident room door opening. It slammed shut and the team turned to find DC Gold quietly putting her bag down.

"Doesn't open until tomorrow morning," said Freya in response to Granger.

"Do we know where the classes are held?"

"I saw a card in the surgery. It was on one of those advertising boards. I took a photo of the board and sent it to Gold."

"I've got it here, ma'am," Jackie said, taking her seat and opening her laptop. "Did I miss anything?"

"No, you're just in time. We're working some theories," Freya said. "I'd be keen to hear your input a little later."

"Why did you take a photo of an advertisement board?" asked Granger. "That seems an odd thing to do."

"I was waiting for Doctor Harris to be free. I noticed a yoga class," Freya lied, and felt Ben's penetrating stare. "So, presuming the art class turns out to be nothing, what's your theory? What do you think happened to Jane in those last few hours?"

"Let's say she was last seen at the house," Granger began. "She had an argument with her husband and left with a suitcase never to be seen again. I'd get a date and a time from him. Then I'd be looking at her husband's phone records to see if he tried to call her at all."

Freya glanced across at Chapman, who after a few clicks on her mouse had the answer.

"Daniel Blythe's phone records," she said, by way of buying herself a little time, "suggest he has not called Jane's number since October nineteenth last year. The day before Jane Blythe walked out."

"So he didn't call," said Freya.

"Why not?" Granger asked. "Even the most vicious of break-ups need a phone call or two to tie up loose ends. To decide who gets what. Plus there would be financial impacts on at least one of them."

"Okay," Freya continued. "Let's say she left the house one evening, stayed with a friend her husband didn't tell us about, or maybe he didn't know about. She went to work the next day. To her colleagues, everything was normal. But then she left work, and nobody saw her again."

"Same questions," said Granger. "We need the time and date of the last time she was seen at the surgery. We need to know who spoke to her, and at the very least, we need to know who knew her."

"That's the funny thing," Freya said. "The more I think about it, the more I realise that Jane Blythe existed in a very small world, as far as everyone else was concerned, at least. You might say it was too small."

"What are you saying?" Granger asked.

"I'm saying I think Jane Blythe had a whole other life that nobody knew about, or at least nobody is confessing to knowing."

"Not even her husband?"

"It's a theory. It's possible, and it would explain a few things, like why she left with no apparent place to go."

"An affair," Ben mused out loud. "I thought the same. Daniel Blythe didn't strike me as the controlling type. The opposite, in fact, like he didn't actually care what she did."

"He was also deployed several times," Gold added. "I checked in with his unit."

"So?" said Granger.

"Well, she would have wanted to busy herself," Jackie said. "She was a military wife. So was I. When boredom and loneliness set in, it's hard, especially if you don't have friends to turn to who understand. It strikes me that we need to find out who the real Jane Blythe was. What was she actually like? Daniel Blythe gave us the description he probably wanted us to hear, and no doubt Doctor Harris made no effort to know her."

"What makes you say that?" asked Freya.

"I saw them together," said Jackie. "I told you, I take Charlie to Doctor Harris. I was there yesterday, in fact. He barely even talks to Cheryl," said Jackie, then explained to the team. "She's the new receptionist who took over from Jane. She came into his room while we were being seen."

"To bring him his coffee?" said Freya.

"Yes. How did you know?"

"Just a hunch."

"He barely said a word to her. He didn't even say thank you."

"If he was seeing to Charlie, then I'm sure we can give him a break," Granger suggested.

"No, guv. It's more than that. It's like he makes a point of ignoring her, or belittling her, or something. I don't know."

"I think we need a plan of action," Granger began, and exhaled long and hard. "DI Bloom, it's your investigation."

"Okay, so we've got Daniel Blythe, the uncaring husband, and Doctor Harris, the boss who claims not to take any interest in his employees. Who knows what doors the art classes will open. Ben, I'd like you to pay Daniel Blythe another visit. Find out exactly when Jane left. We need dates and times. If he can't provide them, then we have to assume he's hiding something. Arrange to bring him in."

"No problem. I'll drop by in the morning and catch him."

"Good. Chapman, arrange for Daniel Blythe's phone records to be passed on to us. When you've done that, extract any bank statements you can. I want to know what accounts they have or had, both joint and personal. I want to know if any large sums of money have been sent or received, and I want to know the last time Jane's card was used and where. The same applies for Doctor Harris as well, please."

"Is that necessary at this stage?" DCI Granger questioned. "Is the doctor really a suspect?"

"No more than Daniel Blythe is. One person was the last to see Jane Blythe alive, and right now, they are the only two people we have."

Seeing where Freya was taking the investigation, Granger relented.

"Do you have everything you need, Chapman?"

"Yes, ma'am," she replied, beaming at her long list of research to carry out.

"Cruz, how's the door knocking going?"

"I'm, erm..." he began, stalling for time.

"You're erm?" Freya repeated. "I want you out there. I want to know if the neighbours saw or heard anything that night, or any time, for that matter."

"Yes, boss," he replied sulkily, under the scrutinous gaze of Granger.

"What about me, ma'am?" Gold asked. "Should I go with Ben?"

"No, I have something planned for you, Jackie. I want the

details of the art class from the photo I sent to you, and then I want you to take a trip."

"A trip?"

"Find out if Jane's parents are still alive."

"They are," Ben said. "Daniel Blythe thought she had gone there."

"Good. Jackie, go and see them. I'm sure DCI Granger will allow you the use of a pool car for a day."

Granger nodded his agreement.

"On my own?" Jackie said, her Scottish accent shining in that moment of uncertainty.

"You should have more confidence in yourself, Gold. Last night, you gave an accurate assessment of a murder scene. This morning, you accompanied a man to see his dead wife's body. We can arrange for local uniforms to meet you if you want, but I think your soft skills are exemplary and will appeal to a couple who have just lost their child. It's time you stepped up."

She looked up from her notes, stared at Ben suspiciously, and then nodded.

"How comes she gets to go on a road trip and I'm out knocking on doors?" Cruz said, then immediately hushed when Granger turned in his seat and glared at him.

"Knocking on doors, as you put it, is a fundamental part of police work, DC Cruz," Freya said. "I imagine DI Standing has explained that to you?"

"Eh?" Standing said from the far end of the room. "I heard my name."

"I was just telling your Detective Constable how important the role of going door to door is in an investigation like this. Would you agree, DI Standing?"

"I usually leave that to uniform," he replied. "I prefer to keep my team occupied with more important tasks."

"Such as?"

"Ah, you know? Fetching coffee. Digging up dirt. The gritty stuff."

"Are you telling me that DC Cruz has never been exposed to anything other than making coffee and doing your dirty work?"

Standing sat back in his chair and glanced at the ceiling as if he was deep in thought. Then he nodded. "Yeah, that's about the size of it. Everyone's got to start somewhere, Freya."

She glanced at Granger, who shook his head at the comment and shrugged.

"Right, that's it. From now on, DC Cruz, consider yourself chief door knocker."

"Chief what?" Standing called out.

"Chief door knocker," Freya replied. "If he can't master that, I'll demote him."

"Demote him? To what?" Gillespie called out, his Glaswegian accent adding more than a hint of sarcasm to the comment. "You can't get much lower than Constable."

"Suicide investigator," she finished, and Standing's expression suddenly dropped. "Although, I expect he'll exceed my expectations, so he won't have to sink that low."

She waited a few seconds for Standing to retort, but he turned back to his work, mumbling something under his breath.

"Right now," she said, addressing her team with a renewed smile on her face. "The only potential suspects we have are Daniel Blythe and Doctor Michael Harris. It's time to either eliminate them or process them. Let's talk MMO. Cruz, go."

"Me, boss?"

"Yes, you. I just stood up for you, now show me what you've got."

"MMO?"

"You do know what it means, don't you?"

"Yeah, but—"

"So?" Freya said, hoping the young Constable would step up and not show himself up in front of Granger.

"Well, if we're talking about her being hit by a rock, they both had the means. I'm presuming they both have hands, and have access to a vehicle to get there."

"What about opportunity?" Freya asked.

Scanning the file Chapman had given everybody, Cruz found Gold's report on Daniel Blythe.

"He stayed at home when she left," he said. "It says here he slammed the door and never heard from her again."

"Do we believe him?"

"Well, I don't," he said emphatically. "Sounds like a complete bastard, if you ask me."

"And Harris?"

"We haven't got that information yet, have we?" he said, flipping through the pages in the file.

"Not yet. I intend to find out what he was doing tomorrow."

Cruz seemed a little relieved that he hadn't missed a key piece of information. He sat back in his seat, clearly hoping Freya's focus on him was over. But it wasn't.

"Okay, now the big one. Motive?" Freya said, coaxing him on.

He didn't need the file to answer this. It was good to see how he acted with a little freedom to demonstrate his abilities. Freya was under the distinct impression that Standing had repressed the young detective with benign tasks that would give him absolutely zero chance of success.

"I guess the husband had a motive. He clearly didn't like her."

"Is not liking somebody motive enough to kill them?" Freya asked.

"Well, no. But I thought we agreed the murder was reactive. It wasn't premeditated. He might have hated her enough that she said something, or maybe did something, to tip him over the edge."

"Okay, that's a decent answer. I don't think it's Blythe, personally. He's too honest about his feelings," Freya said, nodding. "What about Harris? Motivation?"

"The doctor? Ah, I have no idea. Maybe she was stealing from him?"

"Chapman?" Freya said, without removing her eyes from Cruz, who seemed to shrink beneath her watchful gaze.

"No large sums of money in or out of her accounts," Chapman replied.

"So no motive for Michael Harris then, Cruz?"

"I can't see why he'd do it, boss."

"Anybody else?" Freya asked, addressing the room.

"Maybe she threatened to introduce him to you?" Standing called out, in a poor attempt to raise a few laughs from his team. Nobody took him up on the offer.

"Nothing, then?" Freya said, ignoring Standing. "I'm not ruling him out. Not yet. Not until we can categorically eliminate him."

"How do you intend on doing that, DI Bloom?" Granger asked.

"By inviting him in to give a statement, guv. Voluntarily, of course," she added. "Ben, do the same with Blythe. Make him feel like he's helping the investigation and not under observation. He might be a flight risk."

"Understood."

"Chapman, I want you to go and see Doctor Bell tomorrow morning. I need her report and toxicology if we're going to present to CPS anytime soon."

"Got it, ma'am," she replied.

"Good. So, DS Savage, you're focusing on Blythe. I'm going to take a deeper look into Harris. I think there's something there. We all have jobs to do. Call me if anybody needs help or has any concerns. By this time tomorrow, we should be in a good position to start bringing people in for questioning. That's all."

CHAPTER TWELVE

Ben sat for a moment considering his second line of questioning for Daniel Blythe, and how he might react after seeing his wife's body.

"DI Bloom?" Will's soft-spoken voice carried through the hum of chatter like a laser-guided stealth missile. "A word, if I may? My office."

Leaning over the pathologist's initial report, Ben caught Jackie's eye and they shared a worried glance.

"I've never seen Will be so difficult before," Jackie commented, despite Ben turning the page in an effort to distract her. She watched as Freya left the room and the squeaky incident room door slammed shut behind her. "What gets me is that he knows what she's been through."

"Jackie," said Ben, and he glanced up at the few uniforms that were dotted around the room, to make sure none of them had heard her. Chapman, whose face was hidden by the lid of her laptop, peered up for a second then returned to her research. "Remind me not to share my darkest secrets with you."

"Sorry," she said, lowering her voice. "It's just infuriating. Why does he give her such a hard time?"

"It wasn't long ago that you were ranting to me about her. Maybe he just needs a little more time to come round?"

"Maybe he needs a little help to see how good she is. Isn't there something we can do?"

"Stay out of it, Jackie. *I'll* talk to her," Ben said, seeing that Jackie was likely to overstep the mark. "Haven't you got a list of things to be getting on with? Like tracking down Jane Blythe's parents?"

Ben considered his friend's mannerisms. There were times when Jackie was an outstanding detective, and then there were times when she could put her nose into places it wasn't necessarily appreciated. Ben often put it down to her almost childlike naivety, which on more than one occasion had paid dividends to an investigation. But there were also times when her immaturity stood in the way of her progress.

"There's something else, Ben. The photo of the advertising board."

"What about it?"

"I know why she took the photo."

"Does this have anything to do with the case?"

Jackie said nothing and looked down at her feet.

"Leave Freya to me," Ben said with a sigh "If I find anything out, I'll let you know."

Disheartened, Jackie stood back and seemed to make a decision.

"Promise?" she said, and her sentiment was from the heart. She truly cared what happened to Freya, that much was clear.

He nodded. "Go on, before Will comes back. Do you need anything before you go?"

"No, I don't think so. But it's a bit weird that I'm being sent down there on my own. Do you think she's trying to get rid of me?"

"Get rid of you?" said Ben. "She's trusting you to deliver the news of Jane Blythe's death to her parents. That's not something I would take lightly. You should be proud that she asked you."

"That's what I thought. I just had this doubt."

"You can handle it, Jackie. If you need to call me, then do so. Otherwise, enjoy the trip. Enjoy the time to yourself," he added with a knowing wink.

"Thanks, Ben. I'd better get on," she said, realising that he must have said something to Freya, and they parted just as Sergeant Priest joined Ben at his desk.

"It's not good news I'm afraid, Ben," he said. "I've had my boys scour every inch of the immediate search area."

"Nothing?"

"It's been nearly a year. We don't know who has been in and out of those woods. If she dropped something–"

"I'm looking for a suitcase, Michael. It won't be hard to miss."

"Then, I'm sorry. It's just not there. In fact, they found nothing but drinks cans, an old sock, and a cigarette lighter."

"Well, she had a case when she left the house. So unless she *did* stay with a friend for a night or two, then somebody must have taken it."

"The killer maybe?" Priest offered. "Perhaps she dropped the case when she was attacked and the killer took it?"

"It doesn't fit the theory."

"Which one?" said Priest, and he rolled his eyes – a silent dig at Freya's briefing. "I thought we were working on pure conjecture?"

"Don't mind her ways, Michael. She might be a bit odd, but I have a feeling she's heading in the right direction. Right now, we have a woman who has been dead for nearly a year, plus a husband and a boss who both know nothing about her going missing."

"Scratching at a hope?"

"A hope would be nice right about now," Ben said. "It boils down to this, though. The evidence doesn't support a scenario where the killer planned the murder. What would you do if you had an argument and killed a man? What would be your first instinct?"

"I'd turn myself in, Ben," Priest said with his charming smile.

"Maybe after a day or two. But at first, you'd run, just like the rest of us would. In which case, I doubt you would stop to pick up the case."

"But if they did? We can't rule it out?"

"They would have dumped the case somewhere. It could be anywhere."

"Unless somebody else found the case a little while after she had been attacked. The killer would have been gone by then. Jane Blythe would be a couple of hundred feet away under the brambles, and the case would have been lying there on its own. Anybody could have taken it."

Picturing the scene, Ben had an idea. He sat up and scanned the room.

"Chapman," he called out, across the near-empty room. She looked up from her research. "Before you go home, get me the moon cycle for last year. Last winter, to be precise. When you've got it, find me the current moon cycle."

"The moon cycle?" She stared up at Priest, who straightened and shrugged back at her, mirroring her confusion.

"Yes, you know, what stage of its cycle the moon is at. Full moon, waning or waxing, crescent or gibbous," said Ben, nodding his goodbye to Priest as he gathered his belongings. "Send it through to me, will you? Goodnight, everybody."

CHAPTER THIRTEEN

"You're pushing your luck with me, Freya," said Granger, as he flopped into his seat.

He moved his computer mouse to wake the screen then entered his password. It had taken years for Freya to learn the art of reading a password upside down as it was typed, but she thought she had it, and made a mental note of the combination of letters and numbers for no real reason. It was just a habit that she knew would land her in trouble if ever she actually used the password.

"I've been as lenient as I can with you. I've offered you advice. I've ensured my team welcome you, and now, when I ask you to do one simple thing, you have the audacity to belittle me in front of them."

"I wasn't belittling you."

"No, but you were trying. Sit down, will you?"

"I'd prefer—"

"I'd prefer if you sat. For once in your life, Freya, do as I say, please."

It was the whine of a man at the end of his tether. Freya obliged, reasonably content to have made such an impact. Maybe he'd grown tired of waiting for her to book the appointment. Maybe he couldn't handle a female leader. She'd seen that before. Maybe she'd be packing her case sooner than anticipated.

His voice was a muted hum while her thoughts seemed to bounce around inside her mind. The idea of her packing her case seemed to float above the rest.

The case.

"What do you think about the case? Jane Blythe had a suitcase. Who do you think took it?"

"What?" Granger was incredulous, almost lost for words at being interrupted.

Almost.

"I haven't brought you in here to talk about Jane Blythe's missing suitcase. I've brought you in here because you need to learn some bloody respect. Your attitude stinks, Freya."

"It wasn't found in the search. Somebody took it," Freya said, then considered the alternatives. "Or she didn't have it with her."

"Listen to yourself. This is your career you're messing with."

"It doesn't make sense, guv."

"I'll tell you what doesn't make sense. Every time I extend a helping hand, you throw it back in my face. You hold a briefing and have me talk about theories. I don't want theories. I want results. I want facts."

"So tell me the facts," said Freya, her tone sharper than expected. "Right now. Tell me where we are."

He paused for a moment, cautious of her ability to lead people down a path of her choosing.

"We'll come back to your attitude," he said.

"I'm sure we will," Freya replied dismissively. "We have a body and we have an attack that took place eleven to thirteen months ago. What else do we have?"

"A set of keys."

"Yes, we followed that trail to the doctor's surgery. She left one night after work and didn't come back."

"There's a lot more to unearth on that trail."

"That's right. I'll be dealing with that tomorrow morning," said Freya. "What else do we have?"

"The art class."

"Chapman is getting me the details, I'll cover that while I'm in Woodhall Spa at the surgery."

Granger frowned. "There seems to be an awful lot of tomorrow happening, and not much now."

"That's by design. Both Daniel Blythe and Doctor Harris have been questioned today already."

"Pursue Blythe, by all means. But Harris is off-limits."

"What? Guv, he's involved."

"Is he? As far as I can tell, all you have are theories. Michael Harris is a well-respected member of the community. I will not have him harassed."

She stared across at the older man in disgust.

"And there's me thinking that the old boys' club was limited to London. Clearly I was wrong."

"There is no old boys' club, Bloom–"

"What are you?" she spat. "Golf buddies?"

"May I remind you who you are talking to, DI Bloom?"

"Doctor Harris is a suspect."

"Not in my book. Not at this stage anyway," he said, and they shared a moment of truce. A single word uttered from either one of them in that moment could have sparked a full-blown argument. But there would be only one outcome, and Freya knew when she was out-ranked. She sighed, in lieu of a verbal apology.

"Look, guv, I don't want either of them to feel like suspects," Freya said. "That's not going to do us any favours at all. I want them to think we have a lead and we're pursuing it with their help. We've got nothing here."

"Jane Blythe had been arguing with her husband. That raises a red flag to me."

"It's not a crime to argue with your wife, guv."

"It's a crime to kill her."

"There you go."

"There I go what?" Granger spat.

Leaning forward in her chair so that her elbow rested on the cheap desk, Freya met him eye to eye. "Daniel Blythe killing his wife over an argument, or a series of arguments, is a theory."

"Well, it's a lot more likely than–"

"It's a theory," she said with a smile to quieten his mood. "And it's a theory we're investigating, but if I might say, it's a theory that is a little far-fetched. When I asked you for theories in the incident room, it wasn't to belittle you. It was to broaden our minds. I hate to use the phrase, but we need to think outside the box, guv."

"Outside the box?"

"You also mentioned Jane leaving the surgery after work and then disappearing," Freya continued. "It's just a theory. Don't you see? In the absence of evidence, we can't limit ourselves to the facts. We don't have enough of them. We have to broaden our minds a little. We have to voice our ideas, no matter how bizarre. I did a year on cold cases. The blue files. Until anything that resembles evidence arises, all you have are theories. You have to work them until they either blossom into reality, or come tumbling down."

Sitting back in his chair, Granger eyed the clock on the wall. It was five forty-five. As far as initial investigations go, they had made poor progress. But what they did have was a solid plan to explore all avenues open to them.

"What's the idea of sending Gold to see Jane Blythe's parents on her own?" asked Granger.

"Idea? There's no idea. She's the best suited to do it. I need Ben here, Cruz is door knocking, and Chapman seems to have a talent for research."

"Don't you think Gold will be useful here?"

"I think that in any other town, in any other part of the country, Jackie Gold would still be uniform."

"Oh now, come on—"

"Hear me out," she said, offering her hand to calm him. "She has the emotional intelligence of a teenager sometimes."

"She's a bloody hard worker—"

"And one day she'll be a fine detective. But right now, she's too soft. She'll never make DS. I honestly don't know how she made DC."

"She made DC through sheer determination."

"And I'm guessing because you had a gap that needed filling," said Freya, "and she was the hungriest of a bad bunch."

"You're crossing the line."

"You asked me why I sent her. I sent her because I truly believe she has what it takes. She read the crime scene exactly as I did. She's memorised the rule book, but she's too soft. She'll be slaughtered if you sent her out to someone like Harris or Blythe alone. What that girl needs is responsibility. She needs something to harden her up. All I'm doing is capitalising on her abilities to give her that confidence. It's like she's everyone's kid sister."

"She's more than that," said Granger.

"I know. That's what I'm trying to draw out of her. She needs to see what she's capable of with her own eyes."

"Why would you do that?"

"Because I happen to like her. She has potential, and when I was green behind the ears, somebody saw something in me too."

"To the untrained eye, sending her to find Jane Blythe's parents might have looked like you were trying to get rid of her."

"Well, thankfully we're all trained then," said Freya.

He considered her words for a moment, then relented, knowing he wasn't going to have the last word.

"Drink?" he said, and he opened the little cupboard door of his desk.

"That's a little cliché, isn't it? I thought people only did that in movies."

He said nothing. Instead, he waited with a raised eyebrow for her response. However, instead of producing a bottle of fine scotch, he unscrewed the lid of a cheap, half-bottle of brandy and sat poised. It was a temporary peace offering.

"Sure," said Freya, and she took the glass Granger offered. "What are we drinking to?"

"We're drinking to you showing a bit more respect, and me being open to your ideas. I'll meet you half-way."

"I'll drink to that."

"I mean what I said, Freya."

Placing the glass down and swishing the brandy around her mouth to savour its heat, she responded with a silence of her own.

"You need help," said Granger. "And if you want to stay here, you'll get it."

"*If* I want to stay here," she said, taking another sip of the terrible brandy. "This meeting wasn't about how I spoke to you in there, was it? And it certainly wasn't about DC Gold."

"I gave you one week, Freya. If you haven't made an appointment by Friday, I'll have no option but to send you on your way. I'll do so with a heavy heart. But in case you're wondering," he said, sinking the remainder of his drink, "I never go back on my word."

———

It was dark by the time Freya left the station. Her car was cold, and had she left an hour later, her windscreen would have needed a hammer and chisel to clear. But as it was, a couple of minutes with the heater on full blast and a few aggressive swipes of the window wipers, and there was just enough of a clear patch for her to drive through. The rest would clear in a few minutes.

She pulled out of the car park, waited for the security guy to open the barrier, but had to lower her window to pull onto the main road. Apparently, the side windows took a lot longer to clear than the windscreen.

Even after a couple of months in Lincolnshire, she was still amazed at how dark it got compared to London. The lack of streetlights didn't help, and as soon as she was out of the town, her headlights carved a tunnel of light into the gloom. It was that time of year when the sky was grey and the whole country seemed to be hanging on for the big freeze. There had been a snow storm a few weeks back, just as she was finishing the last investigation, but that had been freak. Global warming, probably. The real cold weather hadn't hit yet, and Freya was unsure if she was ready for it.

The road cut between two fields with deep dykes on either side. Ben had told her once it had been the Romans who had dug them to drain the fields. Apparently the whole place had been a bog. But she was sure that was one of those facts that probably held a little bit of truth to it, but had been blown way out of proportion. Nearly every bloody country lane had a dyke on either side. The Romans couldn't have dug them all; they were only there for four hundred years.

Typically, it would be a twelve-minute drive from the station to home, but she poodled along lost in her thoughts, and at the junction where she would normally turn right, she turned left.

Less than ten minutes later, she pulled into the track that led to the forest where Jane Blythe was found, and she stopped, letting her headlights light the trees ahead. It was a strange place, she thought. A condensed patch of trees in the middle of fields. But in the mass of wide open farmland, she kind of had an idea of why people went there. The forest offered privacy. Sanctuary maybe. A place to hide, perhaps?

For Freya, the trees offered far more. They offered a glimpse into her past.

She rolled forward slowly, letting the bumpy track roll her

from side to side. There was no hurry. What she sought had been evading her for more than nine months now. A few minutes wouldn't make much difference.

The search had finished, and the single piece of cordon tape that had been tied between two trees to stop people entering slid over her car bonnet, up the windscreen, and then over the roof. She rolled forward, bringing the car to a stop where she and Ben had stopped two nights before. But where there had been several cars parked, halogen lights lighting the forest, and the dull hum of men's voices, there was now peace. Silence. Nothing. The weak moonlight did little more than indicate where the track ended and the trees began.

Turning the engine off, Freya sat still, wondering if she was doing the right thing. But it was the only way. The only way to induce a memory. The only way to have something of any substance to take to somebody like Diane Ford, if that was actually her name. The only way to stay.

The sound of the car door opening was loud in the still of the night. Wishing she had brought a torch, Freya stepped out, braving the cold, the dark, and the unknown.

It was as if she stood on the precipice of worlds. A single step into the trees would take her into that world she had tried so hard to forget, and which half a dozen of Harley Street's top therapists had tried so hard to recover.

She closed the door, extinguishing the car's interior light. To take a step forward off the track felt like committing to something. Committing to reliving something she genuinely feared. An experience that she never wanted to relive. But to move on, she had to face it. She had to understand what happened during those three days.

Three days, she thought. Out of how many? Procrastinating, she ran a quick calculation in her head. Three hundred and sixty-five days in a year. Call it three fifty. Times that by her age rounded down to forty. Three fifty times forty. Fourteen thousand. Fourteen thousand days, give or take, she had been alive. What was three? Why did those three days really matter? She'd had thirteen thousand odd others she could remember.

But they were important. The most important. And if she was to live for another fourteen thousand days, and wanted to sleep at night, wanted to have a relationship, or just live an ordinary life, then she had to understand those three days.

And the only way to understand them was to relive them.

She stepped forward to where the gravelled track gave way to the forest floor. Her eyes darted this way and that, serving for that glimpse of somebody she had seen two nights before, slipping behind a tree, coaxing her forward. Teasing her, even.

Another step.

She could picture him. But not from the memory of that night. Not the night that she had ventured alone into the forest in search of where James Marley was holding a teenage girl hostage. Not the night she had stumbled on his house in the trees and stood watching, waiting for him to leave so she could go in and be the hero. For fame. For glory. For that young girl's life. Not the night she had felt his warm breath on her nape, and had known in that first almighty beat of her heart that it was too late. That running was futile. That she was his now.

The memory she recalled of James Marley was from the photos of him somebody had pinned to the board in the incident room in London. Where more than two dozen officers worked day and night to prove he was the killer. But that was after she'd been through hell. That was after she had gone in alone and her life had changed forever.

"Come on, Marley, you bastard," she said aloud, taking another step forward into the trees. "Come on. Show yourself."

Braver now, she searched each and every tree. Some were lit by the pale moon, some deep in shadow. And she scrutinised each and every one of them. He was there with her. His memory.

"Come on. I'm here now."

But there was nothing. Not a sound. Not even that of a bird, or a creature, or the wind in the canopy above. She strode forward, serving that spot where she had seen him only days before. Where his memory had teased her. But there was nothing. No sign.

"Marley?" she said, daring to call a little louder. Then, in a tone a child might use in a game of hide and seek, she announced, "I'm here."

Nothing.

"Marley?" Sharper now. She was growing impatient.

Maybe it was wrong? Maybe she couldn't just induce the memory at will. Maybe the forest and the dark weren't the triggers. Maybe it was something else.

She pictured Marley's house – a wooden structure, black against the pale lake it sat beside. Maybe that was it. Maybe she had to recall that moment. Maybe she had to think of that exact moment when she was waiting. When she had felt him. And when it had been too late. It was the hardest of all the memories to recall. It was the moment when she knew she would die. Surely she would die. But dying wasn't the reason for her fear. Failing was. There would be no glory for Freya Bloom. She would be just another of Marley's victims. Maybe? Maybe?

Nothing.

She sighed, and reached out to a tree to hold her steady as she caught her breath, searching the darkness around her.

"You coward," she whispered. To Marley. To his memory. To herself. But as she turned her back on the chance to relive that terrible moment, the moment that would light those three days up like Christmas, she felt him.

A warm lick of stale breath on the nape of her neck.

She saw him there in her mind's eye. Behind her. Reaching for her. His cold touch marking her as his own.

And she ran.

CHAPTER FOURTEEN

A brass knocker in the shape of a plough had been fixed to the centre of the front door. Ben hadn't seen it before yet must have passed by it at least thirty times in his lifetime on the farm.

He knocked and stood back, listening for her to shuffle across the old, tiled floor. A stream of light fell through the doorway when it opened, but there was no blast of heat.

He held up a brown bag of takeaway.

"Thought you might like some dinner," he said, and smirked again at Freya still wearing her work clothes and coat, but with the addition of her slippers. He squeezed past her and she joined him in the kitchen, a bemused look on her face.

She looked good, despite the odd combination of clothes.

"Two nights in a row," she said. "I can't keep you away. We'll have to watch out. Jackie might get jealous."

"Oh, don't start that. We're friends," he said. "I swung by earlier, but you weren't home. Where did you get to?"

"When?"

"After work? I didn't see your car here."

"Must I run all of my movements by you, or am I allowed

some free time? Time to myself? Time to think about something other than a dead body in the woods?"

He shrugged, not getting the point she was making. "If you want."

She nodded, seemingly happy with his response, and changed the subject back to Jackie.

"She likes you, Ben. Girls know these things."

"I've known her since we were kids."

"Like a little sister, is she?" said Freya, and there was a meaning behind the phrase that Ben didn't quite get.

He set the bag down on the kitchen side with a look of disgust on his face and approached her, standing tall over her. He could have just reached out and proved her wrong so easily, and she wouldn't have argued. The move was a test of her resilience and confidence, and Freya, as he thought she might be, was unflinching. He leaned in close to whisper in her ear, then reconsidered voicing his lust. The words were on the tip of his tongue. But there they should stay.

"You get the plates and dish that lot up. I'll get the fire going," he said, and slipped past her into the lounge.

"I am capable, you know?" she called. "I don't need you to build my fire every night."

"Is that why you're still wearing your coat?" he said, as he moved into the lounge. He called out as he walked. "Besides, Jackie built your fire last night while I unloaded the truck."

She didn't respond to that comment, and he imagined her irritated that Jackie could do something she couldn't. He could see that she had at least brought some wood inside, but the log burner was cold and the few pieces she had tried to light hadn't taken. He pulled a handful of kindling from the little pail and built a little pile up around a fire lighter. A single match did the job, just as he heard the sound of the takeaway bag being crushed and the lid of the bin slam.

"So?" she said, as she entered the room and handed him a

plate of rice and butter chicken. A naan bread had been laid over the top to keep warm. Taking the plate, he chose the wooden seat at the dining table, pushing her papers to one side to clear a space for his plate.

"So what?"

She eyed him, and then the papers he had pushed to one side, before continuing.

"So, dinner is the *excuse* for being here. What's the real reason?" she said.

"You're good," he said, tearing off a large chunk of bread, collecting some of the butter chicken, and stuffing it into his mouth.

"Too good for you," she replied, and forked a polite mouthful onto her spoon. Her plate held a modest amount of food compared to his, and without the bread.

"One word," said Ben, swallowing the mouthful and wiping his mouth with the back of his hand. "Suitcase."

He said it with pride. Like it was the answer to the world's problems. Yet even he knew that the word alone could only invoke thought. He waited for her response, unable to hide his glee.

"If the killer had acted in haste, he or she would have run and left the case. If Jane had dragged it through the bushes, it would have been found during the detailed search."

"You thought about it already?" said Ben, his glee fading to disappointment.

"Which means one thing. The killer hadn't acted in haste. In fact, the suitcase could have been the reason she was killed in the first place." She forked a small mouthful into her mouth, chewed, and swallowed with no mess. "Either that, or the killer held it together better than most people would have, and just took it and dumped it somewhere."

Ben was speechless enough not to disturb her forking another mouthful.

"Of course," she continued. "That reactive theory also supports the choice of weapon."

"A rock," Ben said. "Wouldn't be my first choice if I was *planning* a murder."

"Exactly. It's the type of weapon somebody picks up in anger. They made a spur of the moment decision."

"It wasn't planned. Jane said something, or did something, to trigger that reaction."

"Yep. What motivates somebody to do that?"

"Someone who holds a grudge," Ben suggested, folding a large piece of naan around a large piece of chicken and taking a bite before it dripped over his shirt.

"Why would they hold a grudge?" Freya asked.

"What if it wasn't a grudge?" said Ben. "What if it was something closer to the heart?"

"Like?"

"Jealousy."

"Explain," Freya said, as she shoved her plate away after only taking a few mouthfuls.

"An affair."

"An affair that Daniel Blythe heard about?"

"He has a temper," Ben explained. "Who's to say he wasn't waiting at the forest? Or maybe he followed her there? And if that's the case, then maybe the reason we can't find the case–"

"Is because there wasn't one," Freya finished, nodding as the scene took place in her mind. "We need to get close to Jane. I'm going to talk to Cheryl tomorrow. Girls talk. She must have known something, and if she doesn't, then maybe somebody at the art class does."

"There's another thing that's bothering me," said Ben, mopping at the curry with the last morsel of bread. "Daniel Blythe said he took her car keys off her. That's why she had to walk."

"So?"

"So, where's the car? He said he scrapped it but I had Chapman check with the DVLA," Ben said. "Nothing. According to them it's still out there somewhere. Untaxed and uninsured, but out there."

"Maybe he sold it?"

"Maybe," said Ben, and he pushed his dinner to one side. "Cover these over. We're going out."

"Out where?"

"I'm thirsty. You can buy me a drink."

CHAPTER FIFTEEN

The Red Lion pub near Timberland looked as old as the world. It was small, and while Ben parked, Freya surmised it would have low ceilings, quaint beams, and a log fire. She also surmised the clientele would be a bunch of boring, old men with nothing better to talk about than the price of bread. If she was lucky, there would be a football match on the TV. Not that she followed the sport, but Greg had, and she had learnt how to enjoy it as best she could.

"Is this where you bring all the girls?" she asked.

"Only the ones that don't want to sleep with me," Ben said, and he winked before climbing from the car.

She followed close behind and inhaled the familiar scent of dirty washrooms and stale beer. A few seconds later, she entered the saloon and smiled inwardly at the low ceilings, quaint beams, and the fireplace. There was a TV too, mounted in the corner of the room. But it was off, and the pub was devoid of all life save for three men at the bar, and a young girl standing behind it.

"Now then," one of the men said when Ben dropped his keys onto the bar. He turned on his stool to smile up at Ben, but was distracted by Freya, who looked away, eyeing the row of taps and feigning interest in the names of the ale selection. "What brings you here, Master Savage?"

"Same as you, Snowy," Ben replied, and he nodded to the remaining two men who were staring at Freya.

"Bad beer and terrible company?" said the first man, and Freya smiled. "Who's your friend?"

Freya hated introductions. Especially to men whose confidence wrote cheques their body couldn't cash.

"This is my friend Freya," said Ben, by way of an introduction. "Freya, this is Snowy, Rob, and Squawk."

She followed Ben's hand as he spoke each of their names, but found it hard to move past the first name.

"Snowy?" she said, eyeing his grey hair. His shoulders were free of dandruff, and he had the type of eyes a child might draw when asked to characterise their father. Big, droopy eyes like the cartoon dog. Judging by his weathered skin, he worked outside. She nodded to him, refusing to enter into a conversation about the origin of his name.

"What will you have?" Ben asked Freya.

"I thought I was buying?"

"You are," he replied. "But I'll order."

"I'll have what you're having then."

"Two pints of Summat Blonde, please," Ben said to the girl behind the bar. Freya thought her attractive enough. She was young, maybe twenty-one, and Freya wondered if she was working part time while she trained to be something else. The bored bartender look didn't suit her.

"You're not trying to get me drunk, are you, Ben?" Freya said quietly, so the other men couldn't hear.

"Like I said outside, if I was trying to get you drunk, I would have taken you somewhere else."

"So why are we here?"

"Thanks, Franky," said Ben, as the bartender slid the first of the still-settling pints toward Freya. She eyed the pint of ale. It wasn't as dark as she had thought it might be, and hoped it wasn't as heavy as the IPA Greg used to enjoy. For a brief moment, she considered venturing to the washroom to bring up the Indian. But then, remembering the smell on their way in, she figured that would probably happen naturally at some point anyway.

"Do you still have that old Triumph, Rob?" Ben asked the tallest and broadest of the men, then turned to Freya to bring her into the conversation. "Rob here has been restoring an old Triumph TR6. How's she doing? Is she finished?"

"Finished? No," the man laughed. "My wife used to accuse me of spending more time working on that car than I did with her."

"Was the accusation true?" Freya asked.

"Damn right it was," Rob said with a laugh. He sipped his pint and beamed.

"What does she say now?"

"Eh?"

"You said that your wife used to accuse you. Which implies she no longer does."

Rob looked serious. His expression dropped to dead-pan.

"She doesn't say anything anymore," said Rob, and he leaned forward conspiratorially. "Not since I killed her."

The four men were silent, and each of them studied Freya in anticipation. It was clear they all knew Ben, and therefore must have known what he did for work, which, by assumption, meant that they had an inclination that she too might work for the force. She sipped her pint, surprised that she actually quite enjoyed it, then leaned forward to meet Rob.

"I hope you did a proper job, then," she said, and winked at him.

Ben, Snowy, and Squawk laughed, and Rob, who was a little taken aback, fell in with the joke.

"I was wondering where you picked up the bits for her, Rob," Ben said, moving the subject on. "I need a new door for my dad's old truck."

"What? That old Toyota?" Snowy said. "About time the old man got himself a new one, ain't it?"

"Leave it, Snowy. The beast is still going strong. Might be a little rough on the outside, but the old dog is reliable as ever."

"What about the truck?" Squawk said.

"Oh, that's knackered, mate," said Ben, triggering a round of raucous laughter. "I thought you were talking about my dad."

The jokes were nothing Freya hadn't heard before, amongst a different class of men, in an altogether different class of establishment. But they were the same jokes.

"In all seriousness though, Rob. Where do you get your parts?"

"You don't need a door, do you?" Rob said.

Ben smiled at his intuition. "I'm looking for an unlicensed scrap merchant."

"You didn't hear it from me."

"Of course," Ben said. He turned to Freya to bring her back into the conversation. "Rob also does a spot of racing at the weekends."

"Oh, is that right? What do you race?"

"Rally cross," Rob said. "It's mix of—"

"Tarmac and gravel, yes. I know it well. If you don't mind me saying, though, aren't you a little on the large side to be a racing driver?"

"It's a hobby, not a job," Rob said, as if stating the obvious.

"I see. And what is it you do?"

"I'm a plumber. You know, bathrooms and kitchens."

"Yes, I've heard of those too," Freya said, smiling at him. She gave him a quick appraisal, noting the jogging bottoms with mastic stains and the loose fitting t-shirt.

"If ever you need a leak plugging," Snowy said with rough hand on Freya's shoulder. "Rob's your man."

Rob winked as if to support the comment, and Freya removed Snowy's hand.

"I'll bear that in mind."

"So?" said Ben.

"So what?"

"Scrap yard? Jacksons used to be the place to go, but ever since he got closed down, the only place I know of is in the city. Bit far to go in a rush. Where would you go to get rid of an old scrapper?"

"Try Fox's down at Horncastle," Rob said, then caught Ben's arm. "Keep me out of it."

"Fox's. Right. Cheers, Rob. Are you lot down here for the duration then, are you?"

"No. I just stopped by to wash the dust from my throat."

Freya glanced at her watch.

"It's nine p.m. Did you work late?"

"No. I finished at four," Rob said, his face retaining that deadpan expression.

"How's the dust going?"

"Still a bit in there," he said, and winked again.

"Right, I'm going to have one more beer," Snowy announced, as he slipped off the stool and reached into his back pocket for his wallet. "Then I'm going to have three more."

A round of low laughter ensued, and Freya marvelled at how men found amusement in such benign statements.

"And what is it you do then, Missy?" Snowy said, as he beckoned Franky the barmaid over from where she leaned on the point of sale device. He waited for her to arrive, then simply nodded for one more round, a gesture he could have done while she was at the other end of the bar. Franky rolled her eyes but saw the amusement in the charade.

"She works with me," Ben said. Then he smirked as he added, "She's my boss."

"So you're a policeman woman, are you?" Snowy said, and wobbled a little on his feet. "I didn't know they made them so pretty."

"A police officer? Yes," she corrected him. "But don't worry. We're all off-duty here."

"I think we're done here," Ben said, as he swallowed the remainder of his pint. "Enjoy your evenings, gents. Catch you next time."

"Are you down for the quiz night, Ben?" Squawk said, which to Freya's recollection was the first thing he had said. He jammed his thumb over his shoulder to a chalkboard stating the date and time of the quiz night. "We could do with a few more, and I reckon your boss can score us a point or two."

"About what?" said Freya.

"I dunno. Stuff, I guess."

"He's saying that you sound educated, and that we're welcome to join them on their quiz team," Ben added.

"What he said," Squawk said, jabbing his thumb at Ben. "Are you up for it? Wednesday night, seven p.m."

"We're pretty busy–" Ben began.

"What's the prize? It doesn't mention anything on the board," Freya said.

"Eh?" Squawk said. His face twisted with confusion and his mouth hung open, dumbfounded.

"The prize. What do we win?"

Squawk shrugged. "I dunno. We've never won."

"Well then, maybe next time," she said, and thankfully Ben caught her glance. "Good night, gentlemen. It's been a pleasure."

The door closed behind them, and the bite of the cold wind found Freya's exposed flesh.

"What the bloody hell was all that about?" she asked.

"What?"

"Bringing me here. It's not exactly swanky, is it?"

"I didn't bring you here for swank, Freya."

"So, you brought me here to meet your friends? A few drinks and a BBQ would have been nicer, even in this weather."

"I didn't bring you here to impress you, and I certainly didn't intend on introducing you to my friends."

"So why then? Why drag me out in the cold? What a complete waste of time."

"Not exactly," Ben said, as they reached his car. He leaned on the door and addressed her over the roof. "But if I were a man whose wife was to have a sudden accident and disappear–"

Freya cocked her head to one side. "You mean a man who would prefer to stop the neighbours from asking too many questions?"

Ben nodded, smiling. "Then I've found the best place to get rid of her car. No questions asked. It's gone the same night she is."

"As far as the neighbours are concerned, she drove off one night and didn't come back," Freya said.

"I'll be interested to see what Cruz finds out from the neighbours when he goes door to door."

Ben climbed into the car and closed the door, leaving Freya pondering the evening. Her window lowered and she bent to peer in, waiting for him to speak.

"And another thing," he said. "Dinner will be cold."

"That's okay," she replied, as she climbed in and raised the window. "I bloody hate curry anyway."

CHAPTER SIXTEEN

There were two cars in the Witham and Fens surgery car park when Freya arrived the next morning. One was a newish Jaguar, light blue with a tan leather interior. The second was a five-year-old Vauxhall, which was tiny in comparison to the Jag.

Choosing a spot nearest the road, Freya dumped her little rental with minimal finesse. According to the sign, the surgery wouldn't be open for another forty-five minutes. She tried the door anyway and, to her surprise, it opened. Before stepping inside, she listened for a few seconds, hoping to hear voices. But there was nothing except the overpowering lavender air-freshener with an underlying aroma of disinfectant lingering beneath it. The automatic device had been positioned above the door, and as if on cue, it hissed once, issuing a spray of perfume.

Closing the door quietly behind her, Freya moved through to the reception desk. It was empty, but the computer was switched on and was unlocked, and another scent caught Freya's attention with equal distaste. Cheap perfume. She walked slowly and softly to prevent her heels from making a premature introduction, then stopped at the door to Doctor Harris' room. She quietened her breathing to hear the murmur of voices from inside.

With her ear as close to the wood as she dared, she closed her eyes and focused on the voices.

"Don't be silly."

It was a man's voice. Arrogant. Freya pictured Harris sitting behind his desk, leaning back in chair, the king of his world.

"I don't know if I can afford it," a female voice said, who Freya was certain was Cheryl Butcher. She had a local accent, which Freya usually enjoyed, finding it far more alluring than many British accents due to it being easy to understand. In her opinion, the local accent gave more life to the English language than her own flat, southern tone.

"If you really want it, I can help you."

"I couldn't. It's really nice of you, but–"

"Look, take your time. Think about it. But honestly, it'll be no trouble. My pleasure, in fact. You work so hard."

"I'll think about it. It's a lot of money."

"I can't very well take it with me when I die, can I?"

Freya rolled her eyes and was about to put a stop to the charade to save them all from embarrassment when the door suddenly opened. On seeing Freya, Cheryl gave off a scream and the tea tray she had been carrying clattered to the floor. A mug broke and coffee splashed up the door. Panicking, Cheryl crouched to gather all the pieces, wiping the door down with a tissue.

"You bloody careless idiot," the doctor exploded, and he moved across to see the damage she had caused. He helped her stand, his hands more familiar with her body than they perhaps should have been. It was then that he saw Freya standing in the doorway. "Detective Inspector Bloom. What on earth are you doing here?"

"Investigating a murder, Doctor Harris. Do you mind if I talk to Cheryl for five minutes?"

"Well–"

"We won't be long. Shall we use one of these rooms?" Freya

asked, with her arm held out, leading the uncertain Cheryl toward the next door.

"Is this really necessary?" Doctor Harris said. "We'll be open in–"

"Thirty-five minutes," Freya finished. "Enough time for you to tidy that up and put the kettle on. This way, Cheryl."

A very wary and uneasy Cheryl followed Freya into the next room, a stark contrast to the brash and abrupt girl who had been borderline rude the previous day.

"I won't bite," said Freya, as she closed the door. "I just need to ask you a few questions about Jane Blythe."

"About Jane? I don't know anything. I'm sure I don't."

"You might know more than you think."

Clutching the collar of her blouse together, Cheryl appeared doubtful and insecure.

"Shall we sit?" Freya asked, and she pulled the visitor chair closer for Cheryl, choosing the desk to lean on for herself.

The girl was timid, out of her comfort zone, and with furtive glances at the door, she waited for Freya to begin. It was a very different Cheryl to the woman who had provided such a cold welcome on Freya's first visit.

"How long have you worked here, Cheryl?"

"Eighteen months or so, I think."

"And do you enjoy working here?"

"It's nice, yes. The doctors are nice, and I know most of the patients now. The regulars, anyway."

"How does Doctor Harris treat you?"

She glanced at the door before answering, a nervous trait.

"Okay, I guess," she said, before announcing the elephant in the room. "Michael told me."

"Michael?" said Freya. "Do you mean Doctor Harris?"
She nodded.

"He said you found Jane's body. How terrible."

"Well, I hope Doctor Harris treats his patients' sensitive

information with a little more discretion. We weren't sure if it was her until last night."

"No, it wasn't gossip or anything. He just thought I should know."

"Why were you in his room this morning? Is that normal?"

"I was just taking his coffee in," she blurted. "I take it every morning."

"Always this early?"

"Well, whenever really. I told him I was coming in early to get a head start on the typing."

"The typing?"

"Yes, I have to type up the doctors' notes into patient records. I'm supposed to do it during the day, but we've been so busy lately. There's been a terrible bug going around."

"Children?" Freya asked, remembering Gold's statement about her boy, Charlie.

"Yes," she said, adopting that soft mothering quality that Freya saw and admired in Jackie Gold. "It's mainly the children anyway. When one gets something, they all seem to get it, don't they?"

"So you came in early to finish typing up the records?"

"Yes, it's out of hours but I don't mind."

"Do you type up all the doctors' notes?"

"No, most of them do it themselves. Doctor Harris has a lot on, though, so... Well, it's no bother to me."

"And, presumably, he pays you extra for doing so?"

She blushed.

"It's okay, Cheryl. There's nothing wrong with working for a living," said Freya, sensing the girl closing down through embar-rassment.

"The extra money helps. My husband..." She paused, and Freya remained silent, inviting her to finish. "He doesn't earn much and he's not very good with money. His salary just about covers the bills. It all helps, doesn't it?"

"Especially with Christmas around the corner," said Freya, steering her back onto the dialogue and sensing that Cheryl's husband wasn't always forthcoming with a full salary. "And Doctor Harris, is he usually in this early?"

"No, not really. He'd rather stay later in the evenings than come in early."

"You're fond of him, are you, Cheryl?" said Freya, watching for the alarm in the girl's eyes. "He takes care of you, I hope?"

"He's a nice man," she said, nodding as if convincing herself of her own words. "He has a hard time with his wife, you know?"

"No, I'm afraid I don't. Are they divorcing?"

"Divorcing? No. She's not a well lady." Leaning forward, Cheryl lowered her voice and checked the door once more. "She had a stroke. She's wheelchair bound."

"That's terrible. What caused it?"

"I'm really not meant to say."

"It's okay. Discretion comes with the job," Freya said. "As much as it pains me sometimes."

"Ah, well," Cheryl began, "it was their daughter. Rita, her name is. Or it was anyway."

"Oh no, don't tell me she died–"

"No, no. Nothing like that. She ran away. They were close, her and Mrs Harris. She'd just got back from university. I can't remember which one. Michael told me once. I guess her running away was the straw that broke the camel's back."

"You hear of these stories," Freya said quietly. "But somehow they never seem real. There always has to be a reason. Something to blame."

"Anyway, she gets on with it. No fussing. She's still as bullish as ever. But please don't say anything."

"So their daughter runs away, and nobody flinches an eyelid?" Freya said.

"They came up with a story," Cheryl said, fiddling with her

hands, as a schoolgirl might. "They told people she'd got some well-paid job in Paris. You know? To pay for her education."

"And I suppose the rest of society lapped up the idea of Mr and Mrs Harris teaching their daughter the value of money?"

"Please," Cheryl begged. "Please don't say anything. Mrs Harris will kill me."

Freya's eyebrows raised at the comment, and a wry grin formed on her lips.

"Oh, you know what I mean," Cheryl said, blushing at her choice of words.

"She can't be very old," Freya said. "Mrs Harris, I mean."

"No. I don't know for sure. In her fifties, I think. But like I said, Doctor Harris is a nice man. He gives her what she needs. She has a full-time carer to take care of her."

"I'm sure," said Freya, and for a moment she was lost in the sadness within Cheryl's expression. Then she recalled seeing Mrs Harris. "When I came here yesterday, there was a lady in a wheel-chair with a young woman pushing her."

"That was her," said Cheryl, her tone deeper and more scathing than before. "She comes in every week and goes through my work. She's the business manager."

"So she's still able?"

"As I understand it she's paralysed from the waist down."

"I see."

"Her tongue still works just fine," said Cheryl, then quietened, leaving a pause for Freya to move the subject on.

"How well did you know Jane Blythe?"

That was when Cheryl's eyes widened briefly, and her nervous-ness returned.

"Not at all, really. She worked Monday to Wednesday. I only did Thursdays and Fridays back then, plus any weekend shifts that came up, but they were rare."

"But you did meet her?" Freya asked.

"Yes, yes, I met her. She had to teach me the ropes. In my first two weeks I came in every day. To show willing, you know? To learn the system on the computer. It's quite complex. And, of course, there was the gala dinner for Doctor Harris' charity."

"That sounds nice," Freya said, tuning into the thought of the sly, old man running a charity.

"He does it for the children, you know? Those less fortunate than ourselves. Everyone was there. Even the mayor turned up with his wife. Black tie. No expense spared. Raised a fortune, he did."

"That must have been a lovely way to meet everybody."

"It was okay, yes. Lots of people I didn't know, except Jane, of course, and Mrs Harris. I just spoke to Jane all night. I'm not very good with those types of occasions. I'm more of a cup of tea and a slice of cake girl, if you know what I mean? Jane was the same."

Freya nodded.

"So you got to know Jane? What was she like?"

"A little. She never said much about herself. I'm not exactly an extrovert, but Jane? Well, she gave nothing away. And I mean nothing. Still, it was a good ice-breaker. A few days later, she took me through the patient software, so it was nice to have that familiarity with her. It's quite difficult, you know? And you have to get it right. Mistakes won't be tolerated. Oh no."

"I'm sure diligence and attention to detail are key requirements," Freya agreed.

"But after that, once I was up to speed, as it were, we'd just leave each other notes."

"Notes?"

"You know? If I didn't manage to finish something, I'd leave a little note for Jane to pick up on Monday, and she'd do the same for me on a Wednesday."

"I see," said Freya. "So you were ships that passed in the night, were you?"

"I guess you could say that, yes."

"It must have been quite challenging to go full time."

"Sorry?"

"You work full time now, is that right?"

"Yes, I–"

"I was just saying, it must have been quite a change for you, but the extra income must have been a godsend?"

"Well, of course, but–"

"And the workload? I can only imagine what it must have been like to suddenly *own* the role, instead of having to share it with Jane."

"Yes, I made it my own. I had to make it work for me, and Jane did things in a way that didn't always make sense to me. The filing, for example."

"So, you didn't exactly see eye to eye? Is that fair statement?"

"I never once said a word out of turn–"

"But you did have your conflicts?"

"I think conflicts is rather a strong word to use–"

"When was the last time you saw Jane Blythe?"

She sighed and gave Freya an apologetic look. "I didn't see her very often. Like you said, we were–"

"Ships that pass in the night, yes," finished Freya. "I'd like you to look into something for me? Can you do that?"

"Well, that depends on what it is," Cheryl replied, with another of those furtive glances at the door.

"It's nothing that will get you into trouble, don't worry. But I need to know the date that Jane was last here at work. Can you do that for me?"

"That's easy," said Cheryl. "It was the twentieth of October. A Wednesday."

"You remember the date?"

"It wasn't difficult. It was my birthday."

"It was a Wednesday, you say?" Freya said, musing on the timeline in her head. "Did she leave you a note that night?"

CHAPTER SEVENTEEN

"I thought I'd find you here," Ben said, calling above the noise of the cement mixer. Daniel Blythe stood up straight from inside the hole in the patio. His shoulders slumped a little when he saw who it was. "Do you mind if I ask you a few questions? We're progressing with your wife's murder investigation, and I just need to understand a few things."

"We can talk while I work," Daniel replied, and gestured at the mixer.

Taking two steps forward, Ben hit the red button to stop the machine. The concrete inside fell to the bottom with a whump, and there was silence.

"That's better. I can hear myself think."

Daniel Blythe, clearly unimpressed, stared up at him.

"You've got less than five minutes before that lot starts to set and my mixer is ruined."

"I've got a list of questions that need answers. Questions about your wife's murder."

"I've got a mixer full of concrete that needs pouring."

"We'd better talk fast then," said Ben. "What car did Jane drive?"

"A blue Toyota."

"Where is it now?"

"Scrapped it," he replied, as his shovel hit concrete with a harsh metallic scrape. "Worthless."

"Who to?"

"Can't remember. Some travellers, I think," Blythe replied, doing a fine job of keeping his poker face.

"What about her other possessions? Do you still have them?"

"Nope. All gone. Gave it all to the charity shop in Woodhall a few days after she left."

"You gave you wife's belongings to charity?" said Ben, incredulous at the remark. "What about her clothes?"

"Charity shop, and all her shoes."

"Her jewellery?"

"Sold it on eBay. It paid for a new drill."

"Her photos? She must have had family photographs, and I can't believe a man like you would have got rid of them."

"I burned them all. Our wedding photos. Her childhood photos. The lot." He nodded toward the end of the garden, where a cylindrical incinerator was standing on a patch of dirt – one of those metal dustbins with holes in the sides.

"Do you mind if I look inside the house?"

"Do you have a warrant?"

"I can get one if I need to."

"So, get a warrant."

"Perhaps I haven't been clear. You're not a suspect, Mr Blythe. I was hoping you'd help us find out what happened to her."

He stopped and leaned on his shovel. "I don't care if I *am* a suspect. I didn't kill her. I have nothing to hide."

"Would you be prepared to give a statement?"

"Would that mean you'd leave me alone?"

"Maybe? That depends on how helpful you are."

"Are we done? My concrete is going off."

"What happened that night, Daniel? You're bitter about something. What happened between you two?"

"Marriage happened," he said, and he hauled a shovel load of gravel and sand from the hole. It formed a small pile that rolled onto Ben's shoes. "Are you married, Sergeant? I'm guessing not judging by those shoes."

Taking a brief glance at his shoes, Ben agreed they were in bad shape. He hadn't really noticed until then.

"Mr Blythe, do you remember what I said about helping us? I meant it. You knew her better than anybody. If we stand a hope in hell of finding who killed her, we're going to need your assistance. You haven't met my boss yet. But believe me, if you don't offer your help, she'll make your life pretty unbearable."

"Is that a threat?" said Blythe, and resumed his position leaning on the shovel.

"It's a fact, Daniel. How long were you married?"

"Long enough."

"Don't you *want* to know? Doesn't a small part of you care about her still? You might not have seen eye to eye, but she's dead, Daniel. Think about that."

"I have thought about it," he replied, and that flash of anger flared once more. He tossed the shovel from the hole and it landed in the pile of dirt he had removed. In a few quick and lithe moves, he was out of the hole and he stood tall. "I've thought about it since the night she left. Do I regret letting her go? Yes, sometimes. Not often, but sometimes. Do I know who killed her? No, I don't. Do I want to know who by or why she was killed?" His voice cracked and his tone softened. "No. The truth is that there were times when I wished she was still here, annoying me, or moaning. There are times when I genuinely think I can smell her perfume in the bathroom. But those times are few and far between. I don't think of her often. But when I do it's usually in a daydream."

"So, you do miss her?" Ben said. "You daydream about her."

"No," he replied, shaking his head. "No, I daydream that it was me."

"That left?"

"No. I daydream that it was me who killed her," he said with a smile.

"You bastard," said Ben, before he could hold his tongue. "I want the date and time that Jane left here, and if you don't want twenty uniforms kicking your door in first thing tomorrow morning, you'll get it to me today."

"Are we done here, Sergeant? I have a patio to finish and the forecast is looking bleak."

CHAPTER EIGHTEEN

"I wondered if I might have a word," said Freya, catching Doctor Harris just as he was entering his room. Cheryl scurried back to the reception desk without so much as a backward glance.

Harris turned in the doorway, failing to hide his irritation, and made a show of holding the door open for her by way of a silent yet reluctant invitation.

"I'm not sure there's much else I can tell you," he said, placing his mobile phone on his desk as Freya closed the door behind her. She noted the damp patch on the floor and presumed that, like any other man, he'd simply picked up the cups and doused the area with a wet rag.

"I don't know about that," she replied. "In fact, I think there's plenty you can tell me. I'd like to know more about your relationship with Jane Blythe."

"There was no relationship. She worked for me."

"Did you look for something more with her?"

"What on earth are you implying?"

"I'm not implying anything, Doctor. I'm merely asking if you used your position here to make an impression on Jane. We're all adults."

"I'm a married man."

"You're a man," she said, then added, "and Jane was a woman. When two people work together, feelings can develop. It's only natural."

"I'm appalled. It might be natural for someone like you, but I happen to be an upstanding member of–"

"What about Cheryl?"

"I don't see what she has to do with your enquiry."

"Does it make you feel powerful?"

"If you have something to say, then I suggest you either just say it, or get out."

"The women you choose to work on your reception all fit your criteria, don't they? Young, good looking, in need of some extra cash."

He opened his mouth to speak but no words followed. Instead, he looked away, red-faced and watery-eyed.

"I thought so," said Freya.

"Listen to me," he said, and for the first time, he lost the smug, untouchable attitude. He leaned across the desk with his index finger outstretched. "I had nothing to do with Jane Blythe disappearing, and I certainly had nothing to do with her dying. Whatever ideas you have in your head about me can damage a man around here. So if you want to make accusations, I suggest you think long and hard about the repercussions."

"How is your wife, Doctor?"

"My wife? What the hell has she got to do with any of this?"

"I was sorry to hear that she was involved in an accident."

"Where are you going with this?"

"Must be hard for you. I mean, running a surgery and caring for her. Has she recovered?"

He stared across the desk, his face pale and his skin shiny.

"My wife will never recover. She has a full-time carer and we get by. I have a good team."

"Clearly. Cheryl speaks very highly of you."

"I'm sure," he muttered beneath his breath before giving an audible sigh.

"I'd like to know what happened when Jane went missing. What can you tell me?"

"It was challenging, of course. Jane was a good worker. My team liked her. *I* liked her."

"But what strikes me is that Jane Blythe was missing for eleven months and nobody reported her missing."

"Report her missing? Why would we report her missing?"

"Well, I like to think that if I didn't show up to work tomorrow, my team would at the very least try to find me. Unless, of course, I left on bad terms."

"I'm sure we called her house."

"You're sure?"

"Yes, Cheryl would have done it. It was so long ago, how the bloody hell should I know? It's not my responsibility to check on my employees' wellbeing outside of this establishment."

"You have a duty of care, Doctor Harris. You of all people should know that."

"She was a miserable old sod. Always bloody complaining that her husband was this and that—"

"There we are," said Freya. "Why haven't you told me this before?"

"There we are nothing. That's it. It was none of my business. What could *I* do?"

"You could have called the police."

"This is a doctor's surgery," he said, "not the Samaritans. I have enough to deal with."

"That's right. I remember now. Your wife?"

"I believe I've answered your questions, so if you don't mind. I'm very busy."

"Would you be willing to make a statement?" asked Freya. "You'll need to come to the station."

Doctor Harris sighed.

"A voluntary statement would be far better for your reputation than the alternative, Doctor Harris."

"Okay, okay. I'll make a statement. Tomorrow is my day off, so I'll be at home. Cheryl will give you my address. But I promise you, Detective Inspector, I don't know what happened to Jane when she left here. All I know is that she was a very unhappy woman. Like I said, she left here one night, and she didn't return, and that's all there is to it."

"Understood, Doctor Harris. Keep your diary free tomorrow. Oh, and I might advise you not go on any sudden holidays until this is over."

Closing the door behind her, Freya digested all he had said. The confliction in events raised a red flag in her mind. She found herself staring at the board, and in the top right-hand corner, a small, black card stared back at her.

Pulling her phone from her pocket, she found the recently dialled numbers on her phone. Diane was halfway down the list.

She stopped at the reception and leaned over to catch Cheryl's attention.

"When Jane Blythe went missing, did you try to call her?"

"Come to think of it, yes. We were all very worried. The whole team were."

"Did you call the police?"

"No. We had no reason to call the police. I called her house. I spoke to her husband."

"You spoke to Daniel Blythe?"

"Yes."

"And what did he say?"

"He just said that she was gone. She wouldn't be coming back."

"I'll be in touch soon," she said to Cheryl, and offered her gratitude by way of a courteous smile from across the reception desk. She stepped outside into the bright daylight and hit dial on Professor Ford's number.

Three bright flashes caught her off-guard and a melee of voices attacked her senses.

"Detective Inspector Bloom, is it correct you're investigating the murder of Jane Blythe?" said the first reporter.

"Can you confirm that it was indeed a murder?" another called out.

"Hello, Professor Ford," the voice said at the other end of the line.

Freya dropped the phone from her ear and held it to her chest, thinking fast of what she might say and who had informed the media. She moved forward, forcing a space between the crowd of seven or eight bodies.

"I don't know what you're talking about," Freya muttered, and she pushed her way through the crowd and ran across the car park.

"How is Doctor Harris involved?" one yelled.

"Do you have any leads?"

Reaching her car, Freya slammed the door, while the photographers took photos that she had no doubt would appear in the paper the following day. She hit the red button to end her second failed call to Diane Ford, and she found another number.

She hit the dial button just as somebody knocked on her window. Looking up, startled, she found the first of the reporters alone.

"Detective Bloom," she began. "Molly Fox, Lincoln Today. Is it true that Jane Blythe was pregnant when she was killed?"

———

Detective Constable Gabriel Cruz watched DS Savage go around the side of number thirty-three Acacia Drive and disappear from view. He'd left strict instructions for Cruz to get statements from as many neighbours as he could, starting with the house closest to the Blythe house.

"Why don't you start with number thirty-one?" Cruz suggested to the uniform who was with him. "I'll start with thirty five. Shall we say five houses down, then work our way back up and meet in the middle?"

"Sounds about right to me," the uniform replied, clearly as enthusiastic about the task as Cruz was. "It's not like anyone six or more houses down would see anything up here anyway."

"That's what I was thinking," Cruz agreed. Then, in a pang of leadership, he clapped his hands and said, "Right, we better get on with it. I'll see you in a bit."

He strode up the driveway of number thirty-five, keeping an ear out for DS Savage on the other side of the fence. He heard nothing.

Why couldn't he be part of the interviews? He'd love to sit in front of somebody he knew was lying and try to get them to slip up or make a mistake. He knew, of course, that police interviews were rarely like that. Most people broke under the pressure from the environment alone. A night in a cell, being woken up by a big, angry uniform, and a soggy sandwich for breakfast was enough of a glimpse of what prison life would be like to make most people just spill the beans.

He rang the doorbell. It was one of those digital bells that had about fifty different pre-programmed tunes. Most people just selected the standard *ding-dong*. But the people at number thirty-five were far more racy. They had selected the William Tell Overture. Only this rendition had not been performed by a fifty-two-piece orchestra. It sounded like it had been recorded by a two-year-old with just one finger and a Casio keyboard.

"Oh Christ," he said, when he heard it, and braced himself to meet the type of person he hated the most. The general public.

A figure appeared behind the frosted glass door, who then spent no less than thirty seconds unlocking no less than five different locks. Some were sliders, some were bolts, and at least two keys, the last of which they had to rattle to get to move.

The old man that peered around the door inquisitively looked Cruz up and down, but said nothing.

"Hello?" Cruz said, and ventured into his first introduction of the day. It would not, he knew, be the last. "I'm Detective Constable Cruz from the Lincolnshire—"

"Not today, thank you," the old man said, and tried to shut the door.

"Hang on," Cruz said. "You haven't heard what I have to say."

"We don't need any."

"Any what?"

"Of whatever it is you're selling," he called out through the frosted glass.

Putting his face up to the door, Cruz peered through, squinting to try and see his face.

"I'm not selling anything."

"Then what do you want?"

"I'm with the police," Cruz said, pressing his warrant card to the glass.

"The police?"

"Yeah. Can I talk to you?"

"Is this one of those scams?"

If it was a scam, Cruz thought, he'd hardly admit to it.

"It's not a scam, sir. I'm investigating a murder."

A second figure came to stand beside the man. His wife, probably.

The door opened in a heartbeat, and they both stood there, looking down at him.

"Detective Constable Gabriel Cruz," he said again, baulking at the fact that he'd just had to introduce himself twice. "I'd like to take just five minutes of your time to answer a few questions, if I may?"

"Why didn't you say?" the old man said. "I thought you were one of those scampers you hear about. You know, they come around knocking on your door with bag full of old toot, and while you go and get your wallet just to get rid of them, they see what you have that's worth stealing."

"Ah yeah," Cruz said. "You should watch out for them. Plenty of them about, I hear."

"Shouldn't you be stopping them?" the old lady asked. She scrunched her nose up to study him through her bifocals. "You're the police, aren't you?"

"Well, yeah, technically. But that's another team."

"Ah, I see," the old man said, nodding to his wife knowingly. At least one of them had some sense. "Somebody else's job, is it? That's the trouble these days, dear. Everything is somebody else's job."

"Well, it kind of is."

"In my day, our local bobby dealt with everything, you know. You name it, he was there. Not that we had much crime then. People had more sense. It was just a few that didn't want to work for a living. Not like these days. Everybody wants something for nothing."

Suddenly, Cruz's feet ached like he'd been standing on them all day, when, in fact, he'd been sat on his backside for most of the morning and this was his first house. The old man's voice droned on and on, and when the urge to yawn overcame him, he held the back of his hand to his mouth to disguise it.

"Isn't that right?" the old man finished, and Cruz realised he hadn't heard a single thing the old man had said since something about people wanting something for nothing.

"Oh, yes," Cruz said, spirited, and hoping that his answer fell in line with the old man's ideology.

It didn't.

"What do you mean, yes?" the man's wife piped up. "You mean you agree with what's happening in this country? The bloody taxes we pay. I suppose it pays for young men like you to come knocking on our door."

"I'm sorry," Cruz said, holding his hand up in defence. "I think we got off on the wrong foot. I'm not responsible for investigating burglaries and petty crime. I'm investigating a murder."

"A murder?"

"Yes," he said, relieved to be finally getting somewhere. "I was wondering if I could have a few minutes of your time to go through a few questions with you?"

"Well, why didn't you say so?" the old man said, for the second time.

"I tried," Cruz replied. He jabbed his thumb in the direction of number thirty-three. "Jane Blythe. Unfortunately, we found her body a few days ago. I was wondering if you maybe heard or saw something?"

"The girl?" the old lady said. "From next door, you mean?"

"Yes," Cruz said, hearing the desperation in his own voice and trying his hardest not to sound like he was ready to break down and cry.

"No. We haven't heard anything from her for months," the lady said.

"S'right," her husband added. "Must be getting on for a year now. More maybe."

"That's fine," Cruz muttered, and he was about to enquire if they had heard or seen anything untoward before that time, when...

"Not since that night anyway."

"What night?" he asked.

"The night she buggered off."

"The night she..." Cruz started. "You mean, you saw her leave?"

"Of course we did. Bloody racket they were making. Half the street must have heard them."

Excited now, Cruz rummaged through his pockets for his notepad and pen.

"We knew she wouldn't be back, didn't we, dear?"

"Yes, dear," the lady replied. "Had a little suitcase, she did. You know, one of those ones with little wheels on. Made a right old noise."

"So she left here with a suitcase? When was this?" Cruz asked.

"I told you. A year or so ago. Don't know the exact date. But it was... What do you reckon?" he said, turning to his wife. "Eightish?"

"Yes, I'd say so. It was after Corrie, I know that much."

"Corrie?" Cruz said.

"Coronation Street. I know it was after because they were arguing while it was on. I remember it clearly. I had a good mind to go round there and tell them to hush it. Half the blooming street must know all their comings and goings."

"I don't suppose you heard what they were arguing about, did you?" Cruz asked hopefully.

"No, dear. Sorry," the old lady said. She leaned in closer to use her discreet voice. "We like to keep ourselves to ourselves, if you know what I mean. Unlike some around here."

"Of course, yeah," Cruz agreed.

"You're not local, are you?" she said, out of the blue.

"No. Can you tell by my accent?" he said. "Came up here years ago. Grew up in London originally."

"London?" she said disbelievingly. "I see."

"Don't remember it much though. I can't seem to shake the southern twang."

"The southern twang?" she said, nodding and holding onto her husband's arm. She stared at him, her eyes wider than they had been.

"Right, that's all I need for now, Mr and Mrs..." he said, hoping they would fill in the blanks so he could complete the report.

They said nothing.

"Erm. Your names, please?" he said.

The question seemed to drag them from a trance.

"Oh, sorry. Yes," the old man bumbled. "I'm Jeffrey. This is my wife, Judith."

"Brilliant, that's great. And can I take your last name, please?"

"How did she go?" the old lady said, suddenly seeing that there were gaps in the gossip that she should familiarise herself with.

"I'm afraid I'm not allowed to discuss that."

"But it's definitely her?"

"Again. We're just making enquiries right now. You know? Going door to door to see if anybody saw anything, Mrs..."

Again, she failed to recognise his prompt.

"And was what we said okay? We didn't say too much, did we?"

"No, no, it was great, Mrs... Erm, what was your last name?"

"You never know, do you? I mean, murdered, you say?"

"That's right," he said, resigning to the fact that he had now had to spend another ten minutes looking up their last names from their utilities. "Anyway. I'd best be off. Got a whole street to do yet."

"You don't want a tea?"

"No. No, you're fine. Thank you, so much. You've been very helpful. Get back inside in the warm. Supposed to rain later, you know," he said, backing away as politely as he could.

"Maybe next time," the old man said with a smile.

"Yeah. Maybe," Cruz agreed, just one step away from being out of sight.

"Then we can tell you about the husband."

"The husband?"

"Up to no good, he is," the old lady said, leaning in conspiratorially. "He went out as soon as she left."

CHAPTER NINETEEN

"Freya?" said Ben. There was a muffled voice, distant and unclear, and Freya's breathing was loud. He heard an engine revving and the screech of car tyres, and then she spoke.

"Ben?"

"I'm here. Are you okay?"

"Where are you?" she asked.

"The charity shop in Woodhall Spa," said Ben. "Daniel Blythe gave all her belongings away. It's a long shot but I'm following up to see if there's any truth in it. What about you? It sounds like you're in a Formula One car."

"I'm heading into Lincoln. Somebody has tipped off the press. I was just lynched outside the surgery."

"Oh, bloody hell, that's the last thing we need. Who would have done that?"

"I don't know but whoever it was knows more than us."

"Go on," said Ben, as he fingered a rack of women's dresses, feeling more than a little bit conspicuous.

"They asked if Jane Blythe was pregnant."

"Pregnant?" he said, realising his voice was a little too loud for the empty shop. The girl at the counter looked his way, eyebrows raised.

"I'm heading to Doctor Bell now to see if there's any truth in it. Do me a favour, talk to Granger, convince him to let us bring Harris in."

"Why me?"

"Because if I ask him, he'll question my motives. And can you cover the art class? I didn't get time to investigate."

"That's two favours."

"No, that's one favour and a dinner."

"People will start to talk," said Ben, and he caught the shop keeper staring at him. Being the only customer in the shop, there was little else to stare at but a man browsing women's summer dresses.

"Let them talk. Shall we say six p.m.? I'll get some food in. You can sort the fire out."

"You only want me for my fire."

But the quip was lost to Freya's mood. She disconnected the call, leaving Ben to ponder the news of Jane Blythe's pregnancy. He let his head roll back and closed his eyes to focus. It was often the case so early on in an investigation, when information came from all angles, that most of the leads were just distractions. He knew that. The trick was to filter out the good from bad. But in this instance, the good information came when he opened his eyes and they rested on a painting that had been hung on the wall beside a few others, the owner seeking to make use of every inch of space.

The painting was powerful, dramatic, and familiar. Too familiar.

"Can I help you?" the girl asked.

"I'm not sure," Ben replied, walking over to the counter, pocketing his phone and retrieving his ID in one move. "Detective Sergeant Savage. I wonder if you could answer a few questions for me?"

"I'll try," the girl replied, a little taken aback by Ben's introduction. "But you should probably talk to my aunt."

At barely an inch over five feet and with skin that resembled the surface of a forest road, Ben placed her at being no more than sixteen. All she lacked were the braces and greasy hair to tick all the 'just out of school' boxes.

"Let's see, shall we? Where does all this come from?" asked Ben, and waved his hand as if presenting the shop.

"The stock? All over, I think." She shifted her weight to one leg and shuffled her free foot. "I don't really know. I just look after the shop when my aunt needs me to."

Whatever the process was, Ben had an inclination that it wouldn't be too challenging. Simple enough for a girl who should have been in college to understand.

"This is your aunt's shop?"

She nodded.

"Do people just walk in with stuff? How does it work?"

"Some people do. Some people just leave boxes on the doorstep at night. We have to go through it all."

"I suppose you get the lovely job of sorting through it to see what's good enough to be sold?"

"Sometimes. But mostly Aunt Pat does that."

"Does your Aunt Pat keep inventory records, do you know?"

"Of the stuff that comes in? I'm not sure. I think she just goes through the boxes and makes a note of what she wants to sell. She has a little notebook."

"I don't suppose you could show me that notebook, could you?"

Her eyes widened. It was a big ask.

"I think you had better talk to my aunt."

"I thought you'd say that. It's okay. When is she back?"

She shrugged. "Sorry. Maybe you could try again tomorrow?"

"Maybe," he said, and moved toward the door. He stopped with his hand on the brass handle and turned back to her. "I could wait. I mean, she can't be gone too long. I'm sure there's a law against people under sixteen being left in charge of a shop."

"It's under eighteen," she said, and silently cursed her own stupidity.

Smiling, Ben dropped his hand from the door and turned to face her.

"I won't tell her you showed me the notebook if you think it will get you into trouble."

———

A familiar figure was walking through the hospital doors when Freya arrived. Her appearance – a smart trouser suit, flats, with a silk blouse – was marred, in Freya's opinion, by the functionally warm yet tasteless parka. A large, faux-fur hood hung off-balance on one shoulder, and her hands were barely visible from within the long, warm sleeves.

"Chapman," Freya called from across the street, and looked for a space between the slow-moving traffic.

In Chapman's arms were several folders, the bulk of which were her case notes comprising of the research that Freya and Ben had asked her to carry out, as well as the full pathologist report.

"Ma'am," said Chapman, a little alarmed at seeing Freya. She held the report up in triumph. "I caught them before they went in the post. It's the full report."

"Good, let's find somewhere to go through them, shall we?" Freya replied, and then settled on using her car. She gave Chapman a gentle tug. "Let's sit in my car out of the cold. Have you been through it yet?"

"I skim read it, ma'am."

"Okay, good. Get ready to read it in detail," she said, knowing that a skim read by Chapman was a detailed analysis by anybody else's standards. The girl had a unique ability for detail.

"I found one thing out that might be interesting," said Chapman, as she waited for Freya to unlock her car. "I spoke to Doctor Bell. She said she only discovered it this morning."

"Jane Blythe was pregnant?" said Freya, and offered her an accompanying smile.

Chapman's elation deflated.

"It's okay. I just found out myself," said Freya, as she climbed into the car. "But it does throw a whole new light onto the investigation."

"If Daniel Blythe knew about the baby, but didn't want it..."

"That's one option. But what if Jane Blythe was having an affair and Daniel found out about it?"

"Surely he would have gone after her lover?" Chapman asked. "Unless he took care of both of them?"

Freya nodded, liking the way Chapman was thinking. They had only worked one investigation together and she had already proved to be a solid researcher.

"According to Ben, Daniel Blythe has a bit of a temper," Chapman continued. "What about if Daniel caught Jane and her lover, you know? He could have killed Jane and left her there, then got rid of the man's body. Ben called me earlier. He said he wanted me to find Daniel Blythe on the DVLA portal and track down a blue Toyota. He said it was the car Jane used to use."

"Prioritise that when you get back to the station. And run a report on missing men around the twentieth of October," said Freya, as she halved the pathology report and passed Chapman the second half where, in her experience, the real detail would lie. "Find me the results of the fingernail scrape."

Knowing that lab results were often formatted in a way that made sense only to the lab technicians that compiled them, Freya was counting on Chapman's scrutinous eye to find the results faster than she could. Meanwhile, she found the results of the pregnancy and shuddered at the thought of an unborn child being a victim.

"Ma'am," said Chapman, rousing Freya from her thoughts. Her

tone signalled that Chapman had found the section Freya needed. She stared across at the young detective. "The fingernail scrape was inconclusive."

"Nothing?"

"Not according to this."

"She didn't fight back. Damn it. I was hoping to nail Daniel Blythe with that."

"Do you really think it was him?"

"Never mind what I think. Tell me *your* theory. I've heard everybody else's. What do you think happened that night?"

"Well, I haven't been to the crime scene, but the way I see it, ma'am, we only have one suspect. Daniel Blythe."

"Yes, that's what I thought. It's too obvious though."

"Sometimes it's the simplest answers. Isn't that what they say, ma'am?"

Freya gave a little laugh. "Yes, it is. But sadly, *they* don't have to deal with death on a daily basis."

"Ma'am?"

"We're no better off, Chapman. If anything, the investigation just took a more complex turn."

"Can I ask a question?"

"Sure," said Freya, peering at the light drizzle that was dotting the windscreen. "Point the way and I'll drive you to your car."

"It's over there," Chapman said, pointing to the far side of the car park. "I was wondering, is it considered a double murder if an unborn baby is killed with the mother?"

"That's the sad thing about it all," Freya began. It was the exact sentiment that she had been considering internally. "For the baby's death to be classed as a murder, the prosecution must prove that the killer intended on killing the baby. Jane Blythe was less than twelve weeks pregnant. It's highly unlikely that anybody knew she was pregnant. She might not have even been sure herself."

"So if it was Daniel Blythe that killed her, he could get away with it. The baby's murder, at least."

"The chances are, yes."

"Who else could have known about it, though? She had no friends, and from what I heard from Jackie, her parents were almost impossible to track down."

It was Chapman's words that lit a fuse in Freya's mind. They brought her thoughts and theories into a single, cohesive idea that would be almost impossible to prove. Almost impossible, but still possible.

CHAPTER TWENTY

"No takeaway this time, I'm afraid," said Ben, raising his voice above the incessant wind. "But I did bring some rain."

A blast of cold wind tugged at Ben's jacket, as if to confirm his statement. The light from the open cottage door spilt onto the little footpath and silhouetted Freya in the doorway. Leaning against the frame, Freya seemed to be enjoying the sight of his suffering. Ben held his jacket closed, squinted against the light, and turned away from the wind.

The flat fens of Lincolnshire bore wild winds with little obstruction. The sparse rural community enjoyed dark, unpolluted night skies and a silence in which to enjoy the relentless breath of wind.

"You should be careful walking around in the dark. There's a killer loose. Didn't you know?"

Smiling at Freya's dark humour, Ben stepped into the lee of the building, just one pace from where she blocked the doorway with her sultry pose.

"If only it was as easy as that. I'd be grateful for him to come and find me."

She slipped from the doorway, fluid and composed. The long,

woollen overcoat that she wore did little to detract from her magnetism. Twice, Ben had to remind himself that she was not only a colleague, but his boss as well. In the space of under five minutes, that was a new record.

"What are we eating?" he asked.

"Nothing until you get the fire going."

Once more, they entered into a distant conversation. Ben knelt beside the log burner and began building the form of kindling and small logs, while the sounds of pots and pans came from the kitchen, followed by a whirring food blender.

"Did you get to the art class?"

A lull in the whirring left an audible space for him to respond.

"I did. It was shut," he called, and the whirring resumed for a moment then finished. "Next class is tomorrow morning."

"How are your painting skills?"

"Not as good as my fire-lighting skills," he replied, as he struck the long match then dropped it into the nest of kindling he had formed. He sat back on the floor to savour the heat and found Freya standing behind him, a glass of wine in her outstretched hand.

Accepting the wine, and with good grace, he raised the glass in a thanks before taking slightly more than a polite, delicate sip. She stared, as if waiting for him to make a comment. He was sure that in Freya's old world, where he imagined wine bars and finesse were the fashionable places to be, where ladies wore elegant dresses and men wore handmade suits, and where talk of the times and of culture was fluent and articulate, a colleague might offer an educated analysis of the bottle.

Instead, Ben simply swallowed, licked his lips, and nodded.

"That's nice," he said, and as expected, Freya smiled at his simple ways and manners. In his mind, Ben was the contrast to those stuffy wine bars and opinionated folk who peered down their noses at anything less than expensive. He saw himself beside her, rugged and able, however her opinion of him formed. "Just what the doctor ordered. I'm guessing that wasn't a two for the price of one special?"

"That's a Chablis," she replied.

An educated man might have harboured a guess at what dinner might have been. But pairing wine with food was not one of Ben's abilities. Instead, he sniffed the glass and cleared his throat.

"That'll go well with steak," he said.

"Would it? That's a shame. I'm doing a mushroom risotto. I don't much care for pairing. I like what I like, and I would happily nurture a glass of Chablis whatever the meal."

"So, are the rumours true?"

"I don't know how the media found out, but yes. I caught Chapman leaving the pathologist with the report. She managed to get there before the post. It seems our vivacious victim was less than twelve weeks pregnant."

"Can we find out who the father was?"

Shaking her head, Freya dropped to a crouch to benefit from the heat. An orange glow lit the fine down on her cheek. "Scientifically, yes. Realistically, not without significant expense and time. Neither of which are plentiful."

"I want to bring Daniel Blythe in," said Ben.

"Bring him in by all means. But it's not him. Too obvious. He's being too open about his feelings for Jane Blythe."

"I suppose you still think it's the doctor?"

"I do, as it happens. There's more to him than we know. I want to bring him in to answer a few questions."

"I want *you* to interview Blythe," Ben said. "There's something he's not telling us. We need a new approach."

"Ditto," Freya said. "I want you to handle Michael Harris. He's an arrogant arse."

"I also want Blythe's house searched."

"Ditto. Although until we have something on him other than a gut feeling, that won't happen." She stood and moved through to the kitchen. "I learnt something interesting today," she called, then appeared in the doorway stirring the contents of a pan. "Jane Blythe left the surgery on Wednesday the twentieth of October."

"That's roughly when the pathologist report suggested. The same day she sent the text to Harris."

"Yes, but when I asked if anybody looked for her, the doctor became uptight. He's hiding something. He asked Cheryl Butcher to call Jane's house, and she spoke to Daniel Blythe."

"Oh, really?"

"Daniel Blythe told her that Jane wouldn't be going back."

"Well, that suggests he knew where she was."

"But it's not right. If you'd just killed your wife, you would pretend you didn't know where she was. Or at least lie and say she went to her parents' house for a while. You wouldn't just state that she wouldn't be going back."

"But you think the doctor is a more likely suspect?"

"Harris' reaction isn't sitting right with me," Freya said. "I learnt something else today. His wife is wheelchair bound."

"Oh, poor thing."

"Him or her?"

"Both?" Ben suggested. "Can't be easy."

"I have a theory about the doctor. I think he was closer to Jane than he's letting on. I think he's a man that thrives on power. And I think he preys on women like Jane Blythe and Cheryl Butcher."

"As far as I can see, the man has everything. Why would he risk losing that?"

"Because there's one thing he can't get at home."

"What? Are you saying he would cheat on his wife because of her condition? What type of man is he?"

"Wait until you've spoken to him. I'd be interested to hear your opinion then."

"I'll look forward to that," said Ben, and turned to find the doorway where she was standing empty.

She returned less than a minute later with two bowls and two forks. Dropping to her knees, she handed him his bowl and fork, then relaxed into a position that, in Ben's opinion, no man could ever achieve, with her legs folded beneath and behind her.

"He's a snake, Ben. You'll see. But something Chapman said while we were looking at the report got me."

"I see you've found our secret weapon," said Ben, referring to Chapman. "Good, isn't she?"

"Her eye for detail will take her a long way. But it was more her inquisitive nature and empathy that struck me." She took a small mouthful then swallowed. "If you were Jane Blythe, living in a poisonous marriage, and you found yourself pregnant, who would you turn to?"

"I don't really know. I've never missed a month," Ben joked, then his smile faded with Freya's unimpressed glare.

"My doctor?" suggested Ben.

"What if your doctor was also the father of your unborn baby?"

CHAPTER TWENTY-ONE

"That's a disturbing thought," said Ben, as he settled into a more comfortable position. From where he was sitting, he could manage the firewood when needed and lean against the wall while eating his risotto. From where Freya was observing him, she would have his undivided attention. "Is there a chance he and Jane were–"

"Every chance. I overheard him talking to Cheryl Butcher. Let's just say that he gets more from his receptionists than a friendly 'hello, here's your coffee, thank you very much, sir.'"

"And you think he does this because he enjoys the power?" Ben asked, shovelling a huge spoonful of risotto into his mouth.

"It's a possibility," Freya replied. Usually, she would have been disgusted at watching somebody eat that way. But instead, for some reason she found herself pointing to her chin, indicating he had spilled some.

He wiped it off and sucked his finger.

"I know, but he's a doctor?" he explained.

"And apparently an upstanding member of the community. Runs a charity as well, by all accounts. But he's a human being, and from what I've seen on the social media profiles Chapman found, Jane Blythe was an attractive lady. She fits his criteria perfectly."

"His criteria. You make him out to be a–"

"Sociopath. Yes, I know. He is. She was unhappy in her marriage, as is Cheryl Butcher. She was in need of extra cash, as is Cheryl Butcher. And she was impressionable."

"Don't tell me, the same as Cheryl Butcher."

"He has a type. He's calculated, he has money, and he's very manipulative. My guess is that neither Cheryl Butcher nor Jane Blythe were the first girls to fall prey to his manipulation."

"That is interesting. Let me guess. You've set the bloodhound to work?"

"Chapman is on the case. I expect to have answers tomorrow morning. If I'm right and a previous employee is out there, Chapman will find her."

"Do you think a character reference will stand up in court against him?"

"I'm not hedging my bets, Ben. What I want is for him to admit he and Jane had an affair, and that Daniel Blythe knew about it. He might be a sociopath but Michael Harris does not strike me as a killer. The difficulty lies in what he stands to lose if the news of his infidelity gets out."

"His practice?"

"And his marriage. While I was talking to Cheryl, she mentioned that Mrs Harris was working the front desk before either Jane or Cheryl were hired. I'm wondering why a lady of luxury such as Mrs Harris would feel the need to step into such a role."

"I guess we'll find out," said Ben, placing his empty bowl on the floor.

Eyeing the waning flames, he pulled a fat log from the little pile and nestled it into the glowing embers. All the while, his mind was racing with the possibilities.

"What else did you find?" Freya asked, as she adopted a similar position to him, hugging her knees and leaning against the armchair. "I can see you're waiting to tell me something."

"How much of an art lover are you?"

"If you mean, do I appreciate a nice painting? Then, yes. Under the right circumstances. Caravaggio being one of my favourites."

"Who?"

"He was an impressionist. Very dark. And you? Do you have a preference?"

"For art?" said Ben. "I liked Quentin Blake when I was younger."

"Quentin Blake?" said Freya, and she racked her mind for the name. "I can't say I've ever heard of him. What did he do?"

"You've never heard of Quentin Blake? He did all the illustrations in Roald Dahl's books."

"Roald Dahl?" Freya said slowly, in case she had misheard him. "The children's books, you mean?"

"Yeah. Brilliant, they were. The pictures really brought them to life. Really great stuff."

"Do you remember, once, I told you I'd like to bring a little refinement to the station?"

"You mean some of that hoity-toity culture stuff?"

"It's not going to be as easy as I had thought, is it?" she said, still unable to comprehend that he had just aligned Caravaggio with a cartoonist. "Go on. What did you find?"

"While I was in the charity shop, I noticed a painting on the wall. It wasn't exceptional. But it caught my eye. It was only when I was reading through the inventory, particularly the inventory for last October, that I noticed a large amount of new stock had arrived. Clothes and stuff."

"Don't tell me, Jane Blythe's belongings."

"He was telling the truth. He dumped everything. Her clothes, her shoes—"

"Her paintings?"

Pulling his phone from his pocket, Ben unlocked it and browsed to a photo, then slid it across the wooden floor to where Freya was sitting. She sipped at her wine, took a cursory glance at Ben's glass to make sure it wasn't empty, then picked up the phone.

It showed a painting high up on the wall of a shop. Ben had been accurate, despite his lack of artistic credibility. It was not an exceptional painting, mediocre at best.

"What do you think?" Ben asked.

"It looks like trees," she replied.

"Is that all?"

She studied the painting some more, zooming in on areas, looking for an element she hadn't yet seen.

"You don't see it, do you?" he said, pleased with himself.

"Are you going to explain the allegorical significance of the trees?" she asked.

"The what?"

"Nothing," she said with a smile. "Go on."

"Right. Do you see how the trees are central to the frame?"

"Yes, but that doesn't mean anything."

"It doesn't look right, does it? Typically, an artist or a photographer would follow the rule of thirds. The subject should lie on the line of the thirds to please the human eye."

She stared at him. What he had just said was a direct confliction of his earlier statement.

"I might have studied art a bit," he said sheepishly.

"Quentin Blake?"

"Well, you think I'm just a dumb farm boy, might as well act like one."

"I do not think you're..." she began defensively. Then she saw the smile creeping onto his face. "Okay," she said. "So she's an amateur."

"It's central. I think that's her subconscious speaking."

"Oh, come on. This is all just speculation. It's a painting. A minute ago, you were an artistic reprobate. Now you're Bob Ross without the hair."

"This is me getting into Jane Blythe's head, Freya. Do you see how the trees are bright compared to the area around the forest?"

"It has a dark vignette. That's to draw attention to the focal point. Even I know that. You'll see that on thousands of paintings. It's by design."

"Or is it because Jane's world outside of the forest was dark, and she was only truly happy inside the forest?" asked Ben.

"Where she met her lover? You got all that from a painting? And might I add, a sub-par painting at that."

"It could all be speculation. You're quite right. But what if the forest was where she met Doctor Harris—"

"Then it's quite likely that the forest is his little escape," Freya said. "Where he takes all his women."

"We need to talk to his previous receptionist," said Ben. "You find her and talk to her in the morning. I'll go to the art class and talk to the tutor. I want to see if he or she agrees with my analysis, and I want to know what kind of mental state Jane Blythe was in when she painted that painting. It won't stand up for evidence, but if ever we needed a sign we were on the right path, it's this."

"I want you back at the station for midday, Ben," said Freya, with a renewed admiration for the man. The analysis of the painting had shown a softer side to him that she hadn't witnessed until now, and the idea of obtaining an interpretation of Jane Blythe's mental state would add a string to their bow. "Make a plan. I want Blythe brought in."

Ben nodded his agreement.

"Under arrest?"

"Do we have enough to arrest Blythe?" she asked.

"To arrest him on suspicion of murder? Yes. To hold him or charge him? No."

"Then we need to find something to hold him."

"And Harris?" asked Ben.

"I've asked him to come in for a chat, and if I'm right, we can make the media work for us and not against us."

"You'll need Granger on your side."

"Granger will be convinced once I get Harris in that meeting room. I just need to get him there."

"He gave strict instructions, Freya. Harris is not a suspect."

"That's why he's going to volunteer his time. Granger said nothing about the almighty Doctor Harris volunteering." Freya watched Ben. There was doubt written all over his face, and its confliction with his loyalty was evident in the creases on his brow. "It's okay. You focus on Blythe. I'll focus on Harris. And when I'm proved right, you can cook me dinner."

Ben pondered his part of tomorrow's plan. He fingered a huge drop of risotto from his shirt and sucked his finger dry. But that was okay. It was Ben. A self-proclaimed simpleton with more layers to him than an onion.

"What?" he said, when he caught her staring. "Have I got food on my face?"

She smiled briefly.

"There's something I've been meaning to tell you."

CHAPTER TWENTY-TWO

A Brush With Life was a weekly art class held in an outbuilding of a smallholding on the east side of Woodhall Spa. When Ben arrived, there was only one car parked outside – a three-year-old, white Fiat. Situated one hundred yards from the main house and barns, the little building had a red, pantile roof and brick walls that looked as if they'd seen one hundred years or more. Whereas the main house, nestled in a copse of trees a few hundred feet away, had a modern facade that was sympathetic to the vernacular of an old farmhouse. It was an impressive property.

The barn entrance – a pair of double doors large enough to drive a tractor through – was at one end of the building, and the south-facing wall boasted four large windows.

Ben knocked on the door and peered into the space. There were six easels erected to form a fifteen-foot circle around a chair. Each of the easels held a blank canvass, and six small stools accompanied them.

The sound of running water came from the far end of the room, where a man with long, wavy hair was standing with his back to the doors beneath a mounted frame that would not have been out of place on the wall of a manor house or a museum. The painting was clearly somebody's showpiece and depicted horse-mounted soldiers in British red uniforms charging the French amidst cannon fire and raging flames, and the entire scene was awash with thick, grey smoke.

The painting was the central piece in a range of paintings mounted ten feet high along the highest part of the walls. Ben studied them one by one. From exquisite portraits to surreal land-scapes, the paintings were of the finest quality. Ben surmised that only the finest paintings earned a spot high on the exhibition wall. To his right, mounted in a decadent, gold frame, was an image of a forest. The detail was fine, the colours in the fields and trees were of a summer sunset, warm and amber, and the likeness of the forest to the scene depicted in the charity shop was uncanny.

"I'm afraid class doesn't start for another forty-five minutes. You're a tad early," the man called.

Collecting a little clipboard from a small desk in the corner, he turned a few pages then looked up with blue, marble-like eyes.

"Did you call to book a space?" he asked.

"No, apologies. I'm not here for the art class."

"Oh, well, that will be why you're not on the list then."

He took two steps forward to stand in the light from one of the large windows. Stopping with his hands on his hips to assess Ben, he was an impressive looking man, tanned, lithe, and lean, and with his long hair resting on his shoulders and his oversized, white shirt open at the collar, he reminded Ben of the nineteen eighties. Nobody in particular, just the eighties style.

"So," he said, shrugging and gesturing with his hands, "why *are* you here? Can I help at all?"

"Yes, sorry," said Ben, aware that he had been staring at the man in both awe and wonder, more than anything else. He reached for his ID and flashed his warrant card in the man's direction. "DS Savage. I wondered if I might ask a few questions?"

"Oh, I had a feeling today would be one of surprises."

"How so?" asked Ben, as he pocketed his ID.

"No reason in particular. It was just a feeling, that's all. Don't you ever get that?"

"Every day is full of surprises..." He stopped, leaving a pause for the man to introduce himself.

"Tom," he said. "Tom Hendry."

"I was wondering if you could help us with our enquiries."

"Me?" he said. "If I can, I will. It's the woman's body, isn't it?"

Ben nodded, surprised that Hendry knew why he was there.

"Terrible, isn't it?" Hendry added, with a shake of his head.

"Yes," Ben replied. "It's a tragedy."

"Was it anyone local?" he asked, keeping his voice low, as if somebody might hear, even though there wasn't another person in sight.

"You run the art classes, do you, Tom?" Ben said, preferring to talk a little more before he cast his judgement on the man.

"I do. It's more of a passion project than a retirement fund. But I enjoy it. I get to meet all sorts."

"I was wondering if you could tell me who did that painting?" Ben pointed to the forest of warm hues and rich golds.

"Ah, I see," said Tom. "The artist was a lady called Jane Blythe. But I'm sure you knew that."

"Yes. How did you—"

"There's a piece on her in the *Lincoln Today*. But I knew it, deep down, you know? It's strange. All this time, we thought she had just run away. How sad."

The sound of car tyres on gravel came from outside and, peering through the window, Ben saw a middle-aged woman climbing from a black Range Rover.

"Shall we go for a little walk?" said Tom, foreseeing the inevitable disruption. "There's a lovely little path through the gardens. It's wonderful in the summertime, but it also has a certain winter charm."

Leading the way, Tom stepped past Ben and out through the double doors.

"Good morning, Mary. Get yourself set up, I'll be back shortly. The kettle has just boiled and there's milk in the fridge."

"Thanks, Tom," the lady replied, as she retrieved what Ben assumed to be her painting equipment from the back of the car.

Stepping through a small gap in a well-established hedgerow, they emerged in a space that had clearly been cultivated over many years. Flower beds lay on either side of a small, gravel footpath and foreign palms were dotted between them.

"Do you drive, Tom?" Ben asked.

"Me? No," he replied. "I haven't the stomach for it. My sister says I'm away with the fairies most of the time. A daydreamer."

"Probably for the best then?"

"Probably," he replied, admiring the roses. "It always amazes me how the roses manage to hold on so late in the season."

He held a rosebud between two fingers to enjoy the scent as if he were assessing the quality of a fine red wine.

"Hardy, aren't they?" said Ben.

"They have to be around here." Tom gave him a look that suggested there was an underlying meaning to what he had said.

Ben glanced back at the large house and the expanse of gardens and paddocks beyond. "Is this place yours?"

"My sister's. She lets me use the barn," he replied. Then with a mischievous grin, he leaned in closer to Ben. "She says it keeps me out of trouble." And he winked.

"So Jane was a student of yours, was she?"

"For want of a better term, yes. Although, I think I learnt more from her. She was very talented," he explained, in case Ben hadn't caught on to his meaning.

"I've seen her work. Well, one of her paintings, at least."

"Paint wasn't her only medium. She was good with clay too. She could throw anything on a wheel." He stopped and turned back to face Ben. "She was one of those rare people who just

understood art. Her fingers and her mind were so well connected." He glanced over Ben's shoulder. "Not everyone is as blessed
as Jane was."

"Did you know her well?"

"Quite," said Tom, resuming his slow amble. "She was always
first to arrive and last to leave, and she always listened to the
brief. I find that many of my *students*, as you call them, have a
penchant for nodding and agreeing with an instruction, but then
venturing off in their own direction."

"Isn't that what art is all about?"

"Once you have mastered the basics, maybe."

"How was Jane Blythe's mental state? Would you say she was
happy? The last time you saw her alive, I mean."

A grave look spread across Tom's face, as a black cloud might
loom on the horizon.

"Jane was troubled. A sad soul, some might say."

"Do you think that came across in her art?"

"Most certainly. Are you an artist?"

"Most certainly not, I'm afraid."

"You'd be surprised at how passionate a person can be about
something. Not just art. I've seen it in singers, performers of all
sorts. Expression is therapeutic. Jane's paintings could vary from
explosive, bright and surreal, to the dark corners of her mind.
They were sensual, complex, and although they didn't always
conform to standard, she had a particular style. A way of seeing
things and conveying how she felt."

They rounded a corner that led back to the opening in the
hedgerow.

"I'd like to show you something," said Ben, retrieving his
phone from his pocket. He found the photo of Jane Blythe's
painting and held it up for Tom to see.

Taking the phone from Ben's hand, Tom held it into the light
and smiled with fondness.

"Ah," he said. "The forest."

He handed Ben his phone back, glanced up at the sky as if assessing the weather, then turned and walked away.

"I'd like to show you something too," he called over his shoulder.

"Mr Hendry?" said Ben, stopping the man in his tracks. "I hope I can count on your discretion?"

"Certainly. It's no secret that Jane lived in her own world, like a little lost lamb."

"I'm exploring the possibility that Jane might have been meeting somebody," said Ben, waving the phone. "In the forest."

"Ah, well. That, I wouldn't know about," said Tom. "We didn't discuss such matters, I'm afraid."

"Of course. I wasn't insinuating that you were –"

"Jane Blythe was like no other. On the surface, she was a simple girl. A housewife. An artist. She was quiet and soft. But scratch that surface, and you'll reveal a dark, dark world. Let me show you," he said, and turned on his heels.

Back in the studio, two more ladies and a gentleman had arrived, each preparing for the class by setting out their paints. The hum of idle chatter fell away when Ben and Tom entered.

"Morning all," Tom said to nobody in particular, and he led Ben through to the back of the room. Beside the sink there was a doorway which opened into what Ben could only describe as a large stationery cupboard. One of the walls had been dedicated to storing canvasses so that they resembled a bookshelf with paint-splattered spines bearing no text.

"Let me see," Tom muttered to himself, as he fingered the line of paintings.

"I'm sorry to ask, Mr Hendry, but were you and Jane ever–"

"Lovers?" Hendry replied with a laugh.

"For want of a more suitable term, yes."

Hendry leaned in close, dropping his voice to a whisper. "She's not my type, if you know what I mean?" he said with an accompanying wink, then returned to searching through the paintings. "Ah, yes. Here we are."

"You said earlier that you thought Jane had run away. Why would she do that?" asked Ben.

"Because she didn't belong. There was no place for her here," said Tom with a smile that gave Ben the impression he was remembering her fondly. He bit down on his lower lip. "Except one, of course."

He withdrew a painting from the rack, and turned it for Ben to see.

It was of the same forest, only the sky was blue and the detail was incredible, almost like a photo. While Ben was admiring Jane's work, Tom pulled several more from the rack and placed them in a line on the floor leaning against the shelves. There were seven in total. Each painting represented the forest in varying shades and tones of emotion.

"The forest, you see," Tom began, presenting Jane Blythe's art with an exaggerated sweep of his hand, "consumed her."

———

It was while Freya was driving along a narrow lane, admiring the views across the fens, that her phone began to vibrate for the first time that morning. The shrill ring tone followed, something she had been meaning to change for as long as she had owned the phone.

"Bloom," she said, as she directed the connection to the little rental's Bluetooth speaker system.

"Ma'am, it's Chapman."

"Morning, Chapman. I hope you're ready for today. It's going to be a big one."

"I am, ma'am. I've got some news from Sergeant Priest," she said, her tone despondent.

"And I imagine it's not good news?" Freya asked.

"Nothing. They didn't find a single thing."

"Well, that doesn't surprise me. It's been a year."

"I'm sorry, ma'am."

"Not to worry," she said, and was about to end the call when she thought of something. "Chapman?"

"Ma'am?"

"Before you go, run through the facts for me again, will you?"

"The facts, ma'am? There's not much."

"Whatever we have."

"Okay then," she replied, and Freya heard her flicking through her notebook.

"Jane Blythe finished work on the twentieth of October. She left work and didn't return. It was a Wednesday, so they didn't know she was missing until the following Monday. Doctor Harris had the receptionist call Daniel Blythe."

"Cheryl Butcher," Freya added.

"That's it, ma'am. She called Blythe, and he told her Jane wouldn't be going back."

"That's convenient for Doctor Harris, isn't it?" Freya said. "Talk me through the research you've done on Jane Blythe."

"Erm, let me see. Last social media post was in October, before she went missing. No financial transactions since October before she went missing. And just a single text to Doctor Harris."

"And this woman, the old receptionist."

"Fiona Grey? What about her, ma'am?"

"I'm on my way to her house now. Is there anything suspicious there? Anything I can use?"

"I can't get her employment details, so I don't know why she left the surgery. But she had worked there for more than five years, and when she left, she received a lump sum. I'm trying to work out who it's from. Looks like she came into money, bought her house, then retired. Alright for some, eh?"

"Indeed," Freya said. "Anything else?"

"It looks like somebody reported domestic abuse, stating Fiona Grey as the victim."

"Domestic abuse?"

"It says here that she was covered in bruises. Her arms mostly. The caller was anonymous. Doesn't say who. She dropped the charges against her husband. Other than that, she has a clean record."

"Okay, thanks, Chapman. Good work. Call me if you find anything else."

Freya ended the call, sighed, and slowed, searching for the house. She drove at a crawl, trying to see the house numbers. But the houses were set so far back, she only found one or two. Then, by process of elimination, she stopped at the house she thought was the one she needed.

She peered along the driveway nestled into the fen behind a veil of Leylandii. Parking the car, Freya sat for a moment, the car rocking gently with the wind. It was a big day. Harris was being brought in to make a statement in the hope that he would incriminate either himself or Blythe, who was being arrested. A statement from the previous receptionist, Fiona Grey, would be nice. Freya hoped it might encourage Harris to talk. And of course, looming over it all like an ever-darkening cloud was the call Freya had to make to the therapist.

The palms of her hands became clammy at the thought of opening up to a stranger. To talk about the things she had apparently endured but could not recollect, the times that had scarred her and shaped the woman she had become, was unthinkable.

A knock on her window startled her. She found a quizzical face peering in, and Freya knew in that instant it was Fiona Grey. The lines around her eyes suggested long periods of sleepless nights, and her sour expression was the bitter fruit of a deep-rooted seed. It was clear she was middle-aged, but life had not been kind to her.

Hitting the button to lower the window, Freya offered a smile. "Fiona Grey?"

"Yes," she said, a little taken aback by the mention of her name.

"Detective Inspector Bloom, I wondered if I might have a word?" Freya said, flashing her warrant card. She waited for Fiona's hesitancy to fade. "You're not in any trouble."

"What is it?" Fiona asked, holding the collars of her jacket together, a defensive posture.

"I was wondering if you could help us with our enquiries."

"It's about that woman, isn't it? The one that was found?"

"Can we go inside?"

Fiona nodded. Her reluctance was evident, as was the story she had to tell.

It was a pleasant change to enter a warm house. The carpet was soft underfoot and Freya slid from her boots.

"Tea?" Fiona said, as she hung her coat in a small cupboard under the stairs.

"That would be nice. I like your home. Have you been here long?" called Freya, as she peered into the living room. The floor was solid wood, polished and well-kept. The furniture was mostly pine, and the soft furnishings added warmth to an otherwise sparse room. Scatter cushions were placed neatly on the couch and the curtains were thick. A blackout roller blind was in place behind the curtains, an addition that somebody might make to increase their privacy.

She joined Fiona in the kitchen.

"How do you like it?"

"White, no sugar, please," said Freya, as the kettle kicked into action.

"Have you been here long?" Freya asked for the second time.

"No. A couple of years."

"It's peaceful. I like it."

"Thank you."

An uncomfortable lull ensued while the kettle came to the peak of its boil. Then they both began to fill the space at the same time.

"You first," said Freya, encouraging Fiona to talk.

"Was it suicide?"

And there it was. With little to no intervention or guidance, Fiona had opened a new path. Her statement said so much more than those three simple words.

"I can't really discuss the specifics," she replied softly. "What makes you ask that?"

"She worked at the surgery, didn't she?"

"She did, yes."

A knowing nod and tightening of her mouth was enough for Freya to understand.

"I need to try and get inside Jane's head, Fiona. I need to know what it was like to work there."

"I'm not sure if I can describe it in one word."

"Use as many as you need."

"Brilliant. Empowering. Rewarding," she said. "I was left to my own devices most of the time. As long the practice ran like clockwork, nobody interfered. Not even Beatrice."

"Beatrice?"

"Beatrice Harris. Michael Harris' wife," she explained. "The pay was good. Great, in fact. Higher than the average admin role. *And* I was helping people. It was perfect."

"People tend not to leave jobs that they describe as brilliant, empowering, and rewarding."

"It was. But like I said, that was most of the time," she muttered.

"And the rest of the time?"

"Dark. Claustrophobic. Crushing," said Fiona, clearly and without hesitation. The memory enticed a tear to form in the corner of her eye.

"I get the picture."

Sliding Freya's tea toward her, Fiona turned her face away.

"It's okay," said Freya.

"I'm sorry. It's been so long. I should be able to talk about it."

"Don't put pressure on yourself. Take your time. Was it Doctor Harris?"

But Fiona said nothing, suddenly appearing frightened, and her breathing grew heavy.

"Doctor Harris?" Fiona repeated.

"Did he do anything to make you feel uncomfortable?"

"No," she said, this time with indignation. "He most certainly did not. Michael Harris is a good man. If it weren't for him..."

She paused.

"If it wasn't for him?" Freya said, coaxing her on to finish the sentence.

"I'm sorry. I can't do it."

"I need to know, Fiona. I need to know what happened."

"It's none of your business," she said, suddenly closing up. She wrapped her arms around herself, hugging herself. Another defence posture. "He helped me. That's all. He helped me get away. He helped me escape."

"Escape?" Freya said. "Get away from what?"

Fiona Grey leaned against the kitchen counter, unable to meet Freya's stare. The house was immaculate. It could have been a show home. For all its tidiness and cleanliness, there were no memories. It was sterile, devoid of photographs, lacking in evidence of family times.

"Did your husband beat you?" Freya said, throwing the worst possible scenario out there.

Fiona shook her head. "Please, just go. I'm sorry. I've wasted your time."

"We're making arrests, Fiona. What you say could help us. Was it your husband that beat you? Or somebody else?"

But Freya's words went unanswered. Hidden behind chewed

fingernails and gnarled fingers, Fiona's face was screwed into an expression of hatred. She sobbed.

"Just go. I can't help you. This was a mistake. I knew what you wanted the minute I saw you. I can't do it. I can't talk about it."

Moving to be beside her, Freya reached out to put her arm around her shoulder. But, in a flash of anger, Fiona lashed out and slapped her arm away.

"Get away. I want you to leave."

"Fiona—"

"Get out," she screamed. "Get out of my house."

Turning away, Fiona backed into the corner of the room.

"You're not alone, Fiona. He paid you off, didn't he? He controlled you. You can help put a stop to this. Jane Blythe was pregnant when she died. This has to stop."

But Fiona was in another world, shutting Freya and everything she said out.

Retrieving her wallet from her pocket, Freya slid a card out and placed it on the kitchen counter, face-up.

"If you want to talk," she said, and Fiona's reddened face emerged from behind her shield of gnarled fingers.

"Please, just get out of my house."

CHAPTER TWENTY-THREE

"How did you get on?" Freya asked. Even over the speakers on his car, her voice carried her charm, and all the airs and graces of a pleasant memory.

"Nothing concrete. Just a few old paintings and the musings of a man who didn't really know her. Nothing that will stand up in court, that's for sure," said Ben, as he flicked on the heater and directed the heat to his feet.

"What does nothing concrete look like?"

"Seven creepy paintings of a creepy forest painted by a woman who was, by all accounts, severely depressed."

"So your little art theory was correct. Perhaps you're in the wrong job?"

There was something in the way she made the comment that told him she wasn't expecting a direct response. There was humour there, but it was forced. Like her mind was elsewhere.

"Seven paintings, each one painted in a different mood. Some bright, some dark, some neither. But all of the forest."

"Was she bipolar, perhaps?"

"She clearly had her ups and downs, but then don't we all? I know I do. I don't think *I'm* bipolar."

"You don't paint the same place over and over," Freya said.

"I don't paint. Whatever the paintings suggest, that's all they are. Suggestions. How about you? How did you get on with Fiona Grey?"

"I blew it," said Freya. "I moved too fast and she broke."

"But she worked there?"

"Yes. But she won't speak of it. She threw me out," said Freya, and a single laugh came across the line, like she had blown into the phone.

"Well, if she threw you out, you must have got in, and I'm assuming you had some kind of conversation."

"Brilliant, empowering, and rewarding," said Freya. "Those were her words, not mine. Brilliant and empowering, due to her having the freedom to manage her work and run the reception as she saw fit."

"And rewarding?"

"Because she could help people. She could make a difference. She's a kind soul, but she's suffered something awful. Something she clearly doesn't want to talk about."

"It doesn't sound like a very brilliant or empowering place to work."

"Those were the good days. She then used three different words. Dark, claustrophobic, and crushing."

"Crushing?"

"I wasn't fortuned the opportunity to delve any deeper."

"Happy and sad," said Ben.

"Remind you of anything?" asked Freya.

"Seven paintings."

"What's your theory?"

"My theory? Isn't it time you told me yours?"

"My theory is that the dirty Doctor Harris preys on his younger receptionists. He pays well above the average rate, I'm told. He likes them to be younger than him, but not too young."

"But he's in his fifties. Why would three youngish women be attracted to him?"

"I'll give you one reason."

"He's pays them?"

"Oh, for god's sake, Ben. No. He's an influential man. He makes them feel special. Women like that. Hell, everybody likes to feel special."

"There's nothing illegal about an affair," said Ben.

"He controls them. He's manipulative."

"It's not illegal though. Fiona Grey, Jane Blythe, and Cheryl Butcher are all consenting adults."

"Consenting the first time, and probably the second too. He tells them what they want to hear, gives them what they need, and in return he gets what he wants."

"And if they open their mouth–"

"They lose their jobs. A man like Harris can be quite threatening to an impressionable woman. So they carry on pleasing him."

"That doesn't make sense," said Ben. "If he's blackmailing them, then why aren't Jane Blythe's paintings all dark? Why are there bright colours on some of them? Why does the one I found in the charity shop clearly show the forest as being her happy place?"

"Perhaps she fell for him? Perhaps there's more to him than meets the eye? Perhaps he convinced her to leave her husband? Perhaps when she left the house that night, she knew she would never return, because her new life waited for her?"

"Perhaps Daniel Blythe followed her?"

"That's my theory," Freya said. "Are you ready to bring him in?"

"I have uniforms prepped. I just don't think we have anything to hold him. All we have right now are these bloody theories. We know they weren't getting on. We know their marriage was in tatters. We even know he has a temper. But we can't prove that he knew about the affair or the baby. We can't even prove there was an affair. What are we going to bring him in for?"

"Routine questioning," Freya said. "He's the husband of a murder victim. Standard protocol. And given his attitude, I don't think we'll get any pushback from Granger. Have you spoken to Chapman?"

"Chapman? No. Should I?"

"I asked her to check out the scrapyard your friend suggested," said Freya.

"And?" he replied. "What did she find?"

"Nothing," Freya said flatly. "So much for your mate's local knowledge. What a waste of time going to that crummy little pub was."

"Not really. I did learn one thing."

"Go on," she said.

"Not to bring you curry. Next time it'll be Chinese."

"That's more like it," Freya replied, then brought the conversation back to the investigation. "Meanwhile, we stick to the plan. We bring Blythe in under suspicion of murder. I bring Harris in for a friendly chat and a statement."

"Granger is going to flip."

"We need Harris to confirm the affair. If we put some pressure on him in all the right places, he might be able to shed some light on whether or not Blythe knew about the affair. If we can prove Blythe knew about the affair, then we might have a case."

"How do we get him to do that? Harris is married. He's not going to roll over and let us tickle his belly."

"Can I be honest?"

"I would hope so," Ben replied.

"I don't know. The more I talk to him, the more I think he's guilty of something. I just can't prove it. I'm even starting to doubt myself. But I've come too far to let it go now."

"Tell that to Granger," Ben said. "When he holds the door open for you."

"Can you see another way?" said Freya. Her tone and confidence hadn't slipped once. "So, when you say that we don't have anything concrete, you're right. But there are ways and means of getting concrete evidence and I am by no means breaking any of Granger's rules. Harris is volunteering."

"Concrete," said Ben, and he slapped his hand against the steering wheel. "Damn it. Blythe."

"What about him?"

"You weren't there. When I went to see him, both times, he was digging up his patio. Said he had a broken drain or something."

"So?"

"So, that's what he does. He's a builder. It's a bit of a bloody coincidence that he's doing his own patio now when we just found his wife's body."

"Are you suggesting he buried something? The case?"

"It's a possibility," said Ben. "He might have panicked and taken it home."

"If he is the killer, then he's had ample opportunity to get rid of the case."

"That's if there was a case."

"We have to assume there was one for now," Freya said. "At least until we can prove otherwise."

"He's not stupid enough to bury it under his own patio, surely? But how many patios has he done for customers in the past year? If we bring him in, how long can we realistically keep him?"

"We can apply for an extension. Start with Blythe's patio. If he's already digging it up, it'll be quicker. While you're at it, have the place turned upside down. He might not have buried it yet. Then get the bloodhound to go through his company files. We need to know all the jobs he's worked on in the past eleven months."

"Yep, I'm on it," said Ben, as he scribbled his notes in his pad, smiling at her reference to Chapman.

"We have a very small window to link Daniel Blythe to the murder. I've asked Chapman to bring in all her research on bank accounts, phone records, and anything else. We'll take whatever we can get and run it by Crown Prosecution to get the case over the line. We need CPS to agree with our investigation to buy us more time."

"Understood," Ben said. "And one more thing."

"Yep, go," she said, feeling the buzz she felt when things were coming together.

"What you told me last night," Ben said, and the rush faded to a dull ache in the pit of her gut.

"Now?" she said. "Can we go through this later?"

"You need someone to shove you in the right direction. A friend. I'm that friend."

"I can't go and see a therapist, Ben. I've been through it all before. I've literally got nothing to say to them. How are they going to sign me off?"

"Then you'll always be unstable," he said, as if he was describing the weather.

"You think I'm unstable?"

"No. Well, sometimes. But mostly, no. But it doesn't matter what I think. It matters what Granger thinks. He wants the all-clear from a therapist. How do you get that?"

"By convincing them I'm okay?"

"How?" Ben asked. "How do we do that? Can't you lie? Surely you can work a therapist?"

"Are you kidding? They're like bloody living lie detectors. Especially the ones the Met sent me to. They're used to their clients telling them what they want to hear so they can carry on working. They can see through all that. Trust me. I've tried."

"So how? How do you convince them you're okay?"

"You make it sound so simple."

"Well, isn't it?" Ben asked.

"By being okay. By actually being right in the head. That's how

I convince them. By getting over it, and by remembering those three days, and by not doubting myself when I say Harris is a part of this."

She thought about the previous night, alone in the forest. How she had invoked the memory. How she had felt a sense of possibility. And how it had terrified the hell out of her.

"So how do we get there, Freya?"

"Well, first of all, I need to prove I'm right about Harris."

"And if you still have a job?" Ben said. "Then what?"

She paused. Hanging on the words. He made it sound so simple, and at times it was. But when it boiled down to it, the nitty gritty of it, it just wasn't.

"It's something I have to do alone," she said.

"Well, what then? How do you remember? How do you remember what happened? Just enough to convince a bloody therapist you're okay in the head."

"By facing my demons, Ben," she said quietly, but he didn't reply. "I'm not ready to do that. Not yet."

"You can't just give up, Freya," Ben said, as Freya let her head fall back onto the head rest. "Freya? Freya, if you don't finish this, Granger will let you go. Freya? Answer me."

"Bring Blythe in," she said, her finger hovering over the button to end the call. "Do whatever it takes. He's your man, Ben. Prove me wrong."

CHAPTER TWENTY-FOUR

Mill Lane was a residential street at one end of Woodhall Spa. The houses were mostly detached, secluded, and well maintained. Searching for the house number, Ben drove slowly, thinking more about Freya than the task at hand. It was one of those times when, try as he might, he was powerless to help. Yet her reluctance to even help herself was infuriating. She didn't know Will Granger as he did. She didn't know how true to his word he was, and that he'd sooner see a good Detective leave the team than lose face.

Ben considered what life would be like without Freya. He would no doubt be asked to step up again, and perhaps the team would be backfilled from uniform. But that wasn't the point. That was a compromise. That was just unthinkable. She was good for them, and they were good for her. Of that he was certain. She was far better than she had been just a month ago. He hadn't seen her have one of, what he called, her little moments for weeks now. Where before she would disappear into a daydream, or nightmare as the case may be, now she just soldiered on. But he knew that wasn't a sign she was better. *Getting* better, maybe, but not *better* better. Not fixed. Not solid.

Not unbroken. And Will wanted unbroken. He wanted fixed. He wanted the Freya Bloom that was described in her profile – a strong, fearless, smart, career Detective Inspector who could lead the team when he moved on or up, or wherever his own career took him. He wanted solidarity. Ben understood that. It was like preparing to harvest with unreliable machinery, knowing that at any moment the combine might come to a standstill, and the window of opportunity would pass. The entire year's crop wilting, wasted.

There had to be a way to fix her. Or to help her fix herself, at least. But right then, the answer was masked by fog. Blurred by the weather. By the investigation. By the ticking clock. He knew it was there; he just had to let the fog clear and pray there would be time to fix the machinery, and harvest the crop.

There was something he could do, something his father would do if the machinery failed. He would resort to hard labour. He would go out and salvage what he could. He would work his fingers until they bled, and then some.

So that was what Ben should do. He would assume the inevitable demise of the machinery, and he would lead the effort to salvage the crop, with one eye on the task at hand and one eye in the distance, praying for the bright lights of the harvester to emerge from the fog.

He stopped the car, blinked away his thoughts, and considered how he might begin. He would need to lead. He would need to drive the team, giving Freya the space she needed to do whatever it was she needed to do.

With renewed enthusiasm, he climbed from the car and strode up the driveway to the bungalow. A silver Volkswagen van sat on the driveway. It was the type he often saw at the beach, with a few seats in the back, a cooker, and a fridge, with space for some camping gear. Beside it, smaller in comparison, was a Volvo. The family car with space in the back for the dog.

It was that dog that announced Ben's arrival before he even

rang the doorbell, and a young girl in her early teens ran to the door, opening it while holding the collar of an excited spaniel.

"Hello?" she said, not recognising Ben.

"Hello, is your dad about?"

"Yeah," she replied. "Who should I say it is?"

Holding his warrant card out for her to see, Ben introduced himself. "I'm Detective Sergeant Savage. I'm with Lincoln MIT."

"What's it about?"

"I should probably talk to your dad, if that's okay?"

She gave him an distrusting look, then turned and called out, "Dad?"

"What?" a man's voice called from somewhere deeper in the sprawling property.

"It's for you. It's a policeman."

It took less than five seconds for the man to come to the door.

"What's it about, Dad?" she asked with genuine concern on her face, while straining to keep the excited dog from jumping up.

"Nothing, sweetheart. Go inside. I'll deal with it."

"No, Dad. I want to know—"

"I said, go inside," he snapped, then softened. "Please. It's okay. It's just something that happened at work."

Experience had taught Ben not to interfere, although he was a little unsure if the father realised the purpose of Ben's visit. The man watched his daughter go back into the living room, then glanced at Ben.

"Lee Charlton?" Ben asked.

He nodded, a concerned expression set into his brow. "That's me, yeah."

"I wondered if I might ask you a few questions regarding the other night?"

Reaching inside the house, Lee Charlton grabbed a jacket and slid into it. "Back in a bit," he called out. Then he slammed the front door and led Ben back up the driveway, muttering, "Not here. Let's take a walk."

"It's just a few questions. It won't take long," Ben argued.

He turned, aggressive in his stance. "I said, not here." He glanced at the house to make sure none of his family were watching from the windows. A curtain twitched, and he offered somebody a reassuring smile, holding two fingers up as if to say, "I'll just be two minutes."

They walked along the footpath, and it was only when they were a few houses away that Charlton began to relax.

"They don't know," he said finally. "Sorry. It's not always this cloak and dagger."

"It's fine. I get it," Ben replied. "You haven't told your wife what you found?"

"God, no. She'd have a hissy fit. Nobody would be able to walk the dog again if she knew."

"Right," Ben said. "But you're okay, are you? I mean, it hasn't affected you?"

"I'm fine with it. It's not the first time I've seen one. A body, I mean."

Ben raised an eyebrow. It wasn't too common for people just come out with a statement like that.

"I served," Charlton explained. "Saw far worse in Afghanistan."

"I'm sure. Must have been horrendous."

"Did you find out who it was?" Charlton asked, moving the subject on from his own experiences.

"We did, yes."

"I've told you what I know. I'm guessing this visit is just to see how I'm getting on?"

"Kind of. It's a box-ticking exercise really. To make sure we haven't missed anything. Sometimes people remember more about an event a few days after. They don't always think straight."

"I get it," he said, and he stopped at a bench by a small patch of grass and took a seat. Wrapping his jacket around him, he pocketed his hands.

"What were you doing there?" Ben asked, taking the place beside him. "Plenty of places around here to walk the dog. Why drive all the way out there?"

"You're not accusing me, are you, Sergeant?"

"No. Just curious."

"I see. It's a nice spot. Lots of variety. He gets bored, you see."

"The dog?"

"Yeah. It's good to mix the walks up. New smells. New places to investigate. New things to find."

"He certainly did that," Ben said.

Charlton gave a little laugh. "Yes. He did. Took me by surprise, that's for sure."

"The report said you had to go in and get him?"

"Yeah. Thought I'd lost him at one point. Then we heard him."

"Heard him?"

"Yeah, you know. Scratching around. Snuffling. That's the thing about spaniels. They say Labradors are born half-trained and spaniels die half-trained. Have you heard that?"

Ben studied the man, watching how he seemed to feign an interest in the passing cars. He must have felt Ben's gaze. His expression stiffened, and slowly, he turned to him.

"What?" he said.

"We?" Ben replied, to which Charlton raised an eyebrow but said nothing. "You said, we, Lee. Who were you with?"

At least he had the decency not to lie or become indignant. He swallowed, then in lieu of any passing cars, he feigned interest in the sky. A grey, featureless canvass.

"Did you meet somebody, Lee?" Ben asked. "Is that why we came for a walk?"

Charlton smiled then laughed, both weak, and both faded almost instantly.

"It's none of my business," Ben added. "But if whoever you were with saw something, then I'll need to talk to them."

"How confidential is this?"

"You're not under caution, if that's what you mean."

"Are you married, Sergeant?"

"No. But listen, if you're going to talk to me about infidelity, honestly, what you do is nothing to do with me. It's interesting you chose that spot to meet. Why there?"

"It's out of the way. Private," Charlton said thoughtfully. Then he seemed to take a deep breath. "We always meet there. We don't... you know? Nothing illegal."

"I get it," Ben said, trying to move the topic on. "She can't come to your place, and you can't go to hers. I get it."

"He," Charlton said, and he seemed to inflate as he spoke the word. "It's a he."

"Well, like I said, I'm not here to judge you on your relationships."

"It's his favourite spot," Charlton added, and the conversation had gone from a quick chat about what he had found that night to a therapy session. An opportunity for the man to talk openly about his sexuality. Probably something he had never been able to do before. Not with a third party. "He called me during the day. He sounded upset. Said he wanted me to pick him up that night. So I did. We went there to talk, and... well, you know."

"Can you tell me who he is?"

Charlton shrugged. "Will you go to his house?"

"Probably, if we can't reach him by phone. We can be discreet. I'm not looking to create something out of nothing."

"And if I don't tell you his name?"

"Nothing," Ben replied. "Like I said, I'm not looking to expose you here. If we're being honest, then maybe I can open up too? We don't have a lot to go on. The woman you found was murdered. All I'm interested in is finding her killer."

"Murdered?"

"We don't know much else," Ben said. "Maybe your friend can help us? Maybe he saw something you didn't?"

"And it won't come back to me?"

"If I need to talk to you again, I'll call. I can be discreet. But I'll need to talk to your friend."

Charlton pondered the statement, then nodded slowly.

"He runs a little art workshop about a mile from here."

"Art workshop? Tom Hendry?" Ben asked, almost sure there couldn't be too many art workshops nearby.

"You know him?"

"I've met him," Ben said, then realised how the statement may be construed. "I've questioned him. That's all. Have you known him long?"

"No. No, not long at all really. I just got talking to him one day. Over at the forest, you know? Dog stuff."

"Right. Of course."

"I've never done it before."

"Done what?"

"Cheated," Charlton said, without hesitation. "Not with a man anyway."

"You don't need to justify anything to me."

"I wasn't justifying anything," Charlton explained. "It feels good to talk about it. Aloud, I mean. Outside of my head."

"I didn't even know he had a partner," Ben said.

Charlton looked away again, finding interest in a man walking his dog at least two hundred metres away.

"Lee?" Ben said, prompting him to go on.

"I've said too much," Charlton said quietly. Then he stood, raised his collar, and looked down at Ben, steeling himself to return to his family and continue the lies where he'd left them. "Are we done here?"

CHAPTER TWENTY-FIVE

"Right, listen up," Ben called out from where he was standing beside the white board. He clapped three times and waited for a smart comment from Standing. Nothing came, although that end of the room had become very quiet. "Let's have a round-up of where we are, shall we? Cruz, tell us what you found out while you were door knocking."

"Me? I told DI Bloom already."

"What is it, a secret?"

"Well, no. I just–"

"You spoke to the neighbours," Ben said, starting him off. "What did they say?"

"It was number thirty-five. An old couple. They said they saw Jane Blythe leave with her case. Said the case was noisy."

"They heard her? It was definitely Jane Blythe?"

"Certain of it."

"Good, that proves there was a case. When was this?"

"About a year ago. They couldn't be sure of the date. But they did say it was about eight o'clock-ish. They were watching Corrie, and it was just after that. Said they'd been rowing."

"Who had been rowing?"

"The Blythes. They said they were always rowing about something or other."

"Jackie said the same, Ben," Chapman added. "She called a little while ago. She's on her way back."

"How did they take the news?" Ben asked.

"As well as can be expected, apparently. They said her and Daniel argued a lot. Her mum told Jackie they even reported him once. To the local police, I mean."

"Anything come of it?"

"Apparently not. They suspected him of hitting her, but she denied it. Dropped the charges."

"Cruz?" Ben said.

"Boss?"

"Did the neighbours hear anything?" he asked. "And by that, I mean anything specific? Any context to the arguments?"

"No," Cruz said, rolling his eyes. "They don't like to poke their noses in, if you know what I mean."

"No, of course not. For an old couple who don't like to poke their noses in, they've at least confirmed that Jane Blythe did in fact leave on foot, and that she had a case," Ben said, energised. "Anything else?"

"Not really," Cruz muttered, then, unable to restrain the smile that was just itching to spread across his face, he cleared his throat. If he was going to have the floor, he'd make the most of it. "Only that Daniel Blythe went out shortly after Jane had left."

"They said what?"

"Yep," Cruz said, his chest swelling with pride. "They thought he'd gone after her, but he came back alone."

"He went after her?" Ben said, amazed that Cruz was only just delivering this jet piece of information.

"He went out," Cruz said. "They heard his van."

"It was definitely him?"

"Yeah. They heard the van. It's a diesel, right? A builder's van?"

"Yes. It's a Transit."

"Went out right after she left," Cruz said. "It's all in the report I sent the team."

"I haven't read it yet," Ben said. "Are there any other key points in there I might need to know? Like Daniel Blythe returning covered in blood?"

"No, but that'd be a turn up though, eh?" he said.

Ben shook his head at the young DC, amazed how he'd survived working with an impatient taskmaster like Standing these past few years.

"Right, so we have Jane Blythe confirmed as leaving the surgery on the twentieth of October then leaving her house later that night with a case. And thanks to wonder boy, we now know that Daniel Blythe went out shortly after. Regarding his wife, we have a text sent to Doctor Harris at just after eight p.m., but we don't know what it said. We also now know that Jane Blythe was in fact in the early stages of pregnancy, and very likely depressed."

"Depressed?" Cruz said, and he flicked through his files, searching for the reference.

"I went to the art workshop this morning. Spoke to the man who runs it. A man named Tom Hendry. He seems to be the only one who actually had any time for Jane. According to him, she was obsessed with the forest where she was found. In fact, it's quite eerie that all of her paintings were of the forest and that was where she died."

"You don't think..." Cruz began, then quietened, as if he was rubbishing his own idea before he'd finished verbalising it.

"Think what, Cruz?" Ben said.

"Well, you don't think she knew, do you?" he replied. "You know? You hear about stuff like that. Like some kind of subconscious premonition?"

"No, I don't think she knew. But I do think there's a strong link between her fascination with the forest and her death there. Hendry said she was consumed by it, whatever that means. Which leads me nicely onto my next point. Tom Hendry."

He left the name hanging there, hoping somebody would recognise it and chip in an idea. But none did.

"It turns out that our friend Tom Hendry was with Lee Charlton when he discovered Jane's body."

"That's not in the records, Ben," Chapman said, and she began sifting through her records to support her comment.

"You're right. There's no mention of Hendry in there. I paid a visit to Charlton at lunchtime. Turns out he and Hendry meet up there quite regularly."

"Tom Hendry?" Cruz said. "Why was *he* in the forest? It was pitch bloody black, wasn't it?"

"I think that's why they were there," Chapman said, giving Cruz a clue that flew straight over his head.

"Eh?" he said. "Why would they be in a dark forest? I thought Charlton was walking his dog?"

"He was," Ben said, slowly, giving Cruz a few more seconds to fall in.

Sadly, Cruz was not falling in anywhere fast.

"In the dark?" he repeated.

"Oh, for god's sake, Cruz," Standing called from the far end of the room. "You know what happens in that forest, don't you?"

"People walk their dogs?"

"And?"

It was clear by the look on Cruz's face that he didn't know a single other reason for anybody being in the forest at night time, and Ben was growing tired of the charade.

"The little track in the forest is where people meet up," he said. "It's where people go to, you know? Enjoy each other's company. Out of sight."

"Eh? Why?"

"So they can't be seen or recognised," Ben said, then called up to Standing and his team. "Can someone please explain the birds and the bees to Cruz?"

It was DC Nillson who spoke up, a young female detective who, like the rest of Standing's team, operated in his shadow.

"They usually get in the back seat," she added, then reddened. "Apparently. I caught a few of them while I was in uniform. Never did it myself."

"Oh, like a lovers lane?" Cruz said.

"If it was nineteen fifty, then maybe," Chapman said. "Nowadays it's more like an outdoor brothel. You get all sorts over there."

"Is that right?" Cruz said, smiling. "Is that from experience?"

She rolled her eyes and smoothed her hair back over her ear. "It's just one of those places. Ask uniform. They'll tell you."

"Like a dogging hot spot?" Cruz asked.

"No, not dogging. I don't think the people of Woodhall Spa would tolerate that. It's just a place where people go. Boyfriends and girlfriends," she said, then widened her eyes conspiratorially. "Lovers."

"An affair?" Cruz said. "There's got to be easier ways than that."

"There are easier ways. Hotels. Or an Airbnb or something," Nillson, the only female member of Standing's team, explained. "There's a load of places people can go if they don't want to be caught."

"So why go there?" Cruz said.

"Because some people enjoy the thrill of nearly being caught."

"Oh," he said, clearly not understanding. Then it dawned on him. "Hang on. So why would Lee Charlton and Tom Hendry..."

He stopped mid-sentence.

"There we go," Chapman said, checking her watch. "What was that? A full five minutes explaining the mechanics of an affair?"

"So, Tom Hendry is..."

"Yes," Ben said.

"And Lee Charlton?"

"Secretly. Highly confidential."

"Aye, it's a popular spot," Gillespie called out. "You should get yourself down there, Cruz. Might lose your virginity."

"I am not a virgin," he called back.

"How about we bring Tom Hendry in?" Chapman suggested. "He seems to be the one linking all this together."

"Alright, alright," Ben said, regaining control of the room. "DI Bloom thinks Daniel Blythe is a lost cause. I disagree. I'm bringing him in. DCI Granger is working on my warrants as we speak."

"Ben?" Nillson said, raising her pen in the air a little.

"Anna?"

"Where's DI Bloom?"

"DI Bloom is otherwise occupied right now," Ben replied. "She's following up on another lead. So let's give her the support she needs."

"I heard she's having some issues," Standing called down. He twirled his index finger beside his temple. "Something about seeing a shrink. Makes sense to me. She's obviously a nut job."

The comment raised a rumble of muffled laughter from Standing's end of the room. But Freya's team, to Ben's relief, found nothing amusing in the comment.

"And where did you hear that?" Ben asked.

"Oh, you know. I like to keep my ear close to the ground, as it were, Ben. Keep your friends close and your enemies closer. That's what they say, isn't it?"

"Is she an enemy, Steve?" Ben said, snapping the lid back on the white board marker and tossing it onto the desk. "I was under the impression she was on our side. One of us."

"Oh, make no bones about it, Ben. I've got nothing to fear from her," Standing said leaning back in his chair and linking his fingers behind his head. He stared at Ben wistfully. "It's you that should be worried, sunshine. You remember that promotion you worked so hard for? Gone. You can kiss it goodbye. If she stays, Ben, you'll never make DI. You'll never run a team. You'll spend the best part of your career as a Sergeant. You know? That big bloke that works for Bloom. Her sidekick. Or, as I like to call it, her bitch. You mark my words, Ben. She's nothing but trouble."

CHAPTER TWENTY-SIX

"Does everyone know what they're doing?" Ben said, when Standing had finished his monologue. He clapped his hands three times, the way Freya did. "Right, let's get to it. We're bringing Blythe in."

Freya watched him from the window. She saw how well he led the briefing, how he'd held his own against Standing, and how the team listened when he spoke. He was a leader. He was what they needed.

She had planned on walking in just to see if Ben would relinquish control to her. She would have let the squeaky incident room door announce her presence, but to observe had been far more enlightening, if not discouraging.

Slowly, she backed away, walking faster with every passing thought, until she burst through the fire escape doors, bumped into a uniform, and then ran down the stairs. She stopped at the door to the car park.

He was bringing Blythe in. He was wrong. He had to be. He was wasting time. There was something in Harris, and to see Ben so obsessed with a dead end was infuriating.

She turned, marched through the doors to the custody desk, and caught Sergeant Priest's friendly smile.

"Afternoon, ma'am," he said, using one finger to type while he spoke. "What can I do for you?"

"I could do with some help," she said, hearing the door open behind her. "I need a couple of men."

"Just a couple, Bloom?" a voice said from behind her. "What, are you just warming up?"

"Bugger off, Standing."

"Watch this one, Sergeant. She'll chew them up and spit out the bones."

Ignoring Standing, Freya addressed Priest. "And a car, please. I'm bringing someone in."

"I can spare one unit. Ben has everyone else booked out. Should I prepare a room?" he asked, referring to the suite of cells behind him.

"No need. It's voluntary. It's just a precaution more than anything."

"Who you going for, Bloom? Not the dirty doctor, surely?" Standing said, and this time Freya turned to face him. "Not after what Granger said?"

"What is it, Steve?" she said. "What's your problem?"

"Problem?" he said, staring down at her. "I'm just making conversation, that's all. No need to get your knickers in a twist."

"Ever since I arrived here, you've been nothing but a..." She stopped herself from saying too much.

"A what?" he teased, smiling. "An arse? A bastard? Come on. We're all friends here."

"Come on, Steve," Priest said, defending Freya.

"It's okay, Sergeant. I've handled far worse than him," she said, then turned her attention back to Standing, pointing at him. "You've got a problem with me. What is it? Because I'm new? Because Granger gave me the Jane Blythe case and left you picking up the pieces? Is that it? Or maybe you're worried I'll make DCI and make you work for a living?"

"No. Even if you do make DCI, it won't be here. Not under Granger," he said with a smile.

"Or is it because I'm a woman?" she said. "That's it, isn't it? You don't like being outdone by a woman."

"Oh, you won't outdo me, sweetheart," he said, and he closed the gap. "In fact, I'll go as far as to say that you'll never get the chance. I'll give you a week."

"A week?"

"Until you're out," Standing replied. He leaned in close, so that Freya could smell the tuna he'd had in his sandwich on his breath. He tapped his head. "I know all about your little problem."

"Well, maybe you could enlighten me. I seem to have misplaced my memory. Part of it, at least. The gory bits."

"Don't be smart. Granger is going to send you packing, and when he does, I want to be sure you look up to the first-floor windows on your way out. Why? Because I'll be up there with my team, popping the corks on our champagne." He leaned in even closer to whisper in her ear. "Waving you goodbye."

It wasn't the first time she'd been threatened by a man, and it certainly wouldn't be her last. He'd walked right into her trap, blinded by his own bravado. All she had to do was open her hand, find his genitals in his loose-fitting trousers, and squeeze.

He gasped in her ear, but stilled, unable to move without causing more pain.

"Have I got your attention?" she said. "I hope so, because I'll say this only once."

He gasped again and swallowed loudly in her ear.

"I said, are you listening, Steve?"

"Yeah," he whispered, and she squeezed harder.

"Granger might very well kick me out. You're right. I don't

know how you know, and I don't care, but I won't lie. Just remember this. If I go, I'll be free. I'll be free to walk the streets and not have to deal with arrogant, chauvinistic men like you anymore. You, on the other hand, will spend the rest of your life looking over your shoulder. You'll always be wondering, what if somebody finds out? What if Freya Bloom, that bitch, exposes me?"

"Exposes me for what?" he said, his voice rising in pitch.

"Shh," she whispered. "Let's face it, I could open the flood gates on a whole investigation into how you run your team, the way you treat suspects, the corners you cut. Do I need to go on?"

"No," he croaked.

"So, from now on, you keep your opinions to yourself and we'll go our separate ways. And if Granger does let me go, I'll go quietly. I'll even look up to the first-floor window when I leave. Will I see you there, Steve, popping champagne corks?"

"No," he whispered. "You're hurting."

"And as for this moment, I doubt very much you'll be telling anyone, will you? You wouldn't want the whole station to know a woman hurt you, would you?"

"No," he said, breathless now.

"Your car is outside, ma'am," Priest said from behind her, clearly not at all fazed by the little interaction on the other side of the custody desk.

She let go then patted Standing on the shoulder. "Run along now," she said. "There's a good boy."

CHAPTER TWENTY-SEVEN

The Harris house occupied just a fraction of the acre plot, yet it took the centre stage in all its architectural glory. Two large dormer windows gave the old building height and appeared like eyes, ever-watchful for those who dare tread the gravel driveway.

And as if the sentiment was true, a pale face, partially obscured by the leaded glass, peered down at Freya from the left-hand dormer as they pulled in and parked.

"Stop here, please," said Freya to the uniformed driver she now knew only as Anderson. Only as he applied the handbrake did Freya experience a pang of slight regret. Realising she hadn't said a single word to Anderson during the drive after their initial introduction, she offered him a few words, not wanting to be like those plain-clothes officers she had worked with while she had still been in uniform. "Thanks, Anderson. I'm sorry. I've got a lot to think about right now. I hope you don't think me impolite."

"Not at all, ma'am," he replied, but said no more, choosing instead to stare out of the window.

The doorbell was encased in a brass housing and its classic ring was still fading when the door opened. A young face appeared. It was the girl who had been pushing Mrs Harris' wheelchair when Freya had first been to the practice. Her eyes widened when she saw Freya's warrant card.

"I'm looking for Michael Harris," Freya said. Then, to ease the girl's panic, she added, "He's expecting me."

"Who is it, Rita?" It was the doctor's voice, and the girl turned then opened the door fully for him to see.

"Good morning, Doctor Harris," said Freya, not needing to give any further explanation.

"I said I'd give a statement. I didn't expect the cavalry," he said, and he peered past Freya to see if the neighbours were watching.

"Just in case you changed your mind," said Freya, and she smiled inwardly.

"Who is it, Michael?" a shrill voice called from upstairs.

"It's a police officer, dear," he replied, his scathing eyes never leaving Freya. "The one I told you about. She just wants to ask me a few questions."

"What about? What have you done?"

"We can talk in my office," Harris growled, then turned, clicked his fingers at the girl, and waved for her to see to his wife. Then he made his way toward an oak-panelled door at the end of the hallway.

"I'd prefer if we could talk at the station," said Freya, loud enough for his wife to hear. "We could be some time."

Before the girl could reach the stairs, a set of double doors slid open, retracting into the walls and finishing with a muted *ping*. To Freya's surprise, it was an elevator, and with a firm shove of the wheels, Mrs Harris rolled herself into the hallway. The rubber wheels squeaked slightly as she turned on the parquet floor, and she came to a stop beside her husband.

"Good morning, Mrs Harris," said Freya. "We just need to borrow your husband for a few hours."

"A few hours?" said Harris, and then, following a nervous

glance at his wife, his confidence resumed. "I must be home by four," he explained. "My wife needs her medication."

"But I can—" the girl started.

"Not now, Marie," the doctor cut in, without moving his gaze from Freya's.

"We'll make it as fast as we can. But you do understand this is a murder investigation?"

"A murder, you say?" Mrs Harris said. "Oh, Michael, what have you been up to?"

"Well, I haven't bloody killed anyone if that's what you think."

"Nobody is suggesting you have," Freya said, then looked past him to his wife. "He's just going to answer a few questions, Mrs Harris. To help us, that's all."

As his wife's curiosity grew, so did Harris' willingness to attend the station for the questioning.

"Let's make it fast," he grumbled, then stopped at the front door and turned back to his wife. "I shan't be long, dear. It's just a formality."

He left, and at the sound of the gravel drive beneath his feet, his wife caught Freya as she was leaving.

"I didn't catch your name," she said.

"Detective Inspector Bloom. I'm leading the investigation." She retrieved a card from her ID wallet and took the few steps to hand it to the lady. But Mrs Harris was faster than Freya was bargaining for. She grabbed Freya's wrist and held her close.

"It's that little Blythe cow, isn't it? You found her, haven't you?"

"I'm afraid I can't divulge any information at this point."

Mrs Harris nodded knowingly.

"I know it's her."

Gently, Freya freed her hand.

"Is there something you wish to add to your husband's statement, Mrs Harris?" Freya asked, then peered outside to see Mr

Harris being helped into the waiting car. "Perhaps we could invite you in to give a statement?"

Scoffing at the idea, Mrs Harris wheeled herself back toward the elevator, where the carer stood uneasily holding the door.

"How well did you know Jane Blythe, Mrs Harris?"

The lady in the wheelchair came to a rolling stop, but didn't turn.

"I knew her well enough to know she was trouble. Nothing good was ever going to come of her. I told him we should have got shot of her. I told him long before any of this happened."

"Any of what happened?"

"This," she said, slowly turning in her chair. "Her disappearance. Who do you think had to step in and pick up the pieces? Who had to manage the other one?"

"Cheryl Butcher, you mean?"

"Yes. Me. That's who. Another one with her head in the clouds. Play on my husband's good nature. That's what they do. Blood suckers."

"So you knew Jane Blythe quite well then?" Freya asked.

"Oh, I knew her alright. Knew her well enough to know she was a lost soul. A daydreamer."

"Would you say she had problems, Mrs Harris?" Freya asked, hoping for some real insight into Jane Blythe's mind.

"Oh, she had problems alright."

"Did she confide in you at all?"

"Me? No. I would have been the last person she talked to."

"So you didn't see eye to eye?"

The lady in the chair cocked her head at the question, and pondered her response.

"What are you suggesting?" she asked.

"I'm not suggesting anything, Mrs Harris. I'm investigating the murder of a woman who, by all accounts, had no friends and nobody to turn to. I guess I was hoping I'd found somebody who really knew her and liked her."

"Well, that isn't me," she replied. "And you'll be hard pushed to find somebody who fits the bill."

"So you won't mind me asking where you all were the night Jane Blythe went missing?"

Mrs Harris beckoned the girl over to her, gesturing for her to turn her around and wheel her into the elevator.

"Twentieth of October?" she asked, and seeing the conversation was continuing, the girl held the doors again. Mrs Harris peered out from inside. "Is that right?"

"You have a good memory," Freya said.

"My husband was out somewhere. I don't know where."

"And you, Mrs Harris? Do you remember where you were?"

"Vaguely. I was in hospital," she began. Then her voice lowered to a bitter rumble. "Having the stroke that put me in this bloody thing."

CHAPTER TWENTY-EIGHT

A convoy of flashing blues snaked its way toward the peaceful town of Woodhall Spa. On either side of the road, the sprawling fens glowed in the early morning sun. A kestrel hovered in the air, eyeing its prey, and further on, a kite stood among the tall grass beside a deep dyke, against a background of fine winter mist.

At Ben's request, the sirens were switched off. Four liveried cars, a transporter, and the trailing forensics van carried enough of a presence, in Ben's opinion.

Using the dashboard radio, Ben addressed the team. It was down to him to make the operation a success, and he suddenly felt a space that Jackie should have filled.

"All units," he began. "We're here to arrest Daniel Blythe on suspicion of murder. I need units in position at the rear of the premises before we go in. I want his van secured and black lighted. There may be traces of Jane Blythe's blood inside. When we have Daniel Blythe under arrest, I want him taken back to the station under escort, and then I want his house flipped. Lastly, forensics are to undertake GPR in the back garden, specifically the patio area. He may have buried the weapon. We can expect a media presence at some stage and we can expect Daniel Blythe to be a flight risk, therefore, I need a unit to drop back and bring up the rear. Close the street off. Nobody in or out until we're done."

A flurry of chat from the other vehicles began, and in Ben's side mirror, one of the police Astras pulled to one side of the road then fell in at the rear of the convoy.

He grabbed the radio handset as the convoy entered Woodhall Spa.

"One minute out," he said, then let go of the push-to-talk button and addressed Griffiths, who was driving. "When you turn into the street, pull to one side and let the others through, please."

"Will do," was the only response he got.

Griffiths was a good officer. Ben had worked with him before and deemed him a safe pair of hands with a promising future in the force. He could also, according to Gillespie who often arranged drinks in the local pub, open his gullet and sink a pint in under three seconds. Ben would have bet that particular skill wasn't on his CV.

An increase in heart rate was not unfamiliar for Ben during moments like these. A trickle of adrenalin began to seep into his bloodstream and his palms became clammy. Acacia Drive came up on their left. Griffiths slowed, turned, and rolled to a crawl while the drivers of the vehicles behind gunned their engines and fanned out surrounding number thirty-three.

"Go, go, go," Ben called, his last command over the radio.

Checking his mirror, he saw the driver of the tail unit positioning the liveried car across the entrance to the road. Ahead of him, eight uniformed officers adorned in protective vests and helmets stormed the small residential property, splitting up to take the front, rear, and both sides. By the time Ben had reached the end of the driveway, more than one curtain was twitching and one elderly gentleman had even ventured out to his driveway to see what was happening.

"Go back inside, sir," Ben called.

"What's happening?" the man replied.

But before Ben could reply, movement at the end of the driveway caught Ben's attention. Two uniforms shouted commands, and all Ben's planning hung in the air. He turned just in time to find Daniel Blythe in full flight, pelting down the driveway with a look of panic in his eyes.

There was no time to react. Ben reached out to stop him, but the fleeing man was on top of him in moments, knocking him to the ground before Ben could grab hold. Barely was Ben back on his knees and regaining his senses when all hell seemed to break loose. Two officers gave chase as Blythe ran hell for leather toward the end of the road. Ben followed, but was already well behind the chase. With a clear view of the road ahead of him, Ben could see a route through the uniforms.

Radios chattered and hissed, and men's shouts filled the tiny cul-de-sac. Grabbing his radio from his pocket, Ben began issuing commands from behind.

"We've got a runner. White IC-1 male. Wearing blue jeans and a red sweater."

He lowered the radio to watch as Blythe made his escape.

"Back up," he screamed at the driver of the tail unit. But it was too late. Blythe's speed and power ploughed through two uniforms, bowling them down as he had done with Ben. One officer's spent Taser fell to the ground having missed its target. One of the lead cars roared into life from behind Ben. A fast-thinking Griffiths, having seen as much of the action as Ben had, was at the wheel. But Griffiths' quick thinking was undone when the unit Ben had asked to block the street prevented him from getting any further.

"Damn it," Ben screamed at himself, and he tossed the radio away in anger. He turned and kicked at the wheel of one of the squad cars, placed his hand on its bonnet, and tried to control his anger. But the situation was out of his hands. He turned and leaned on the car, dropping his face into his hands, thinking of how exactly he was going to explain this to Granger and Freya.

A screech of car tyres cut through the din of voices and radio murmur. Glass shattered and fell to the street, followed by a lull in activity. With his head in his hands, Ben peered up through his fingers and couldn't believe his eyes.

A blue Vauxhall had come off the main road and buried itself into a roadside tree. Three uniforms were grappling with Blythe who, Ben presumed, had caused the accident in his attempt to escape. Ben ran at the melee of activity, praying that this luck had turned. Verbal abuse was being hurled at all parties by the time Ben reached him, and with his hands cuffed behind his back, Blythe saved the most offensive for him.

"Daniel Blythe, I'm arresting you under suspicion of the murder of Jane Blythe. You are under arrest on suspicion of murder. You do not have to say anything, but it may harm your defence if you do not mention when questioned something which you later rely on in court. Anything you do say may be given in evidence," said Ben, and he could barely remember a time when he had felt so pleased to say the words, as the officers half-walked and half-dragged Blythe towards the nearest police vehicle.

One person, who had been hidden from sight by the scuffle, remained beside the crashed car. She wore an anorak, her hair was tied back as it nearly always was, and she hugged herself, slightly shaken by the accident.

"That was some arrival," he said.

"Granger is going to kill me."

"Will Granger will be patting you on the back. Trust me."

"I heard you on the radio and got here as quick as I could. I was on my way back from seeing Jane Blythe's mum and dad. But he just came out of nowhere. I didn't hit him, did I?"

"No, but you stopped him from getting away."

"I've got so much to tell you."

"I'm glad you're here, Jackie."

"I couldn't let you have all the fun, could I?" she said, as she leaned on the ruined Vauxhall. "It was nice to be away. I know it was only work. But the time to think was nice."

"A long drive will do that for you," Ben said. "Do you need to get going and see Charlie?"

"I've got to take him back to the doctor's," she said, checking her watch. "But I've got an hour."

"How's he doing?"

"I called my mum on the way home. She said he's much better. Still coughing, but he's got his colour back and he slept through. She thinks he's on the mend, but Doctor Harris said he'd see him and decide."

"That must be a weight off your mind?" Ben said.

"Yeah. That and the night in a hotel. I feel a bit guilty for leaving him with my mum. Especially while he's sick. But I think I just couldn't concentrate. I was so tired. I mean, it wasn't a flash room or anything. But just to have a night to myself did wonders, Ben. Thank you."

"Don't thank me. Thank Freya," Ben replied. "She's the one who calls the shots, remember?"

"Am I still alright to come in?" Jackie asked. "I can't stay long, but I'd love to be a part of the case. I feel a bit left out."

"We can't win with you, can we?" Ben said, admiring her sheepish smile and waving his arm by way of an invitation. "Come on, let's get inside, shall we?"

CHAPTER TWENTY-NINE

"I must admit, an unmarked car would have been my preferred choice," remarked Harris from the back seat of the police Astra.

They were just two miles from the station, and Freya watched him discreetly in the rear-view mirror. For an influential member of the community, he was a restless and nervous man, shifting in his seat, scratching at his neck, and biting an apparently irritating fingernail.

"We'll have you done as quick as we can," said Freya, as she reached inside her coat for her phone. She found Ben's number and hit dial.

"I was wondering where you were," he said without a greeting. "You okay?"

"I'm fine."

The pause that followed signified that Ben didn't entirely believe her.

"Did you pick up Harris?" he asked.

"We're on our way back to the station now," said Freya, with one eye on the mirror.

They turned into the high street. The station was at the far end of the town, another five minute drive.

"How did it go?" she asked.

"It was touch and go at one point. Blythe bolted."

"You had enough uniforms, though. Priest said you wiped him out."

"He got through most of them. It was Jackie that stopped him."

"Jackie Gold?"

"She was on her way home and heard us on the radio. She arrived just in time and blocked his path. I think Arthur will have something to say about the cost of repairs to the car, but it all ended well."

"But he ran. There's a guilty sign if ever I saw one."

"That's what I thought. He's on his way back to the station now," said Ben. "I've got a team in the garden with the GPR now while the house is being flipped."

"How long until you're back? I'd like to start the interviews."

"Jackie and I are about to join in the search. I'm hoping to have some kind of report from the GPR by the time we're done here. Give me two hours."

"Have you spoken to Granger?"

"He's not happy, Freya. Seeing as he asked you not to bring Harris in."

"Well," Freya said, "I never was one to listen to good advice."

They approached the station, and as if on cue, the pedestrian crossing turned red to allow a group of people to cross. Two of them carried cameras with professional ring flashes mounted to the top.

"What's going on here?" Freya asked Anderson, with her hand over the phone's microphone.

"Not sure, ma'am. Looks like the press."

Removing her hand from the phone, she addressed Ben again, "Keep me posted, Ben. I think we have a problem here." She hit the button to disconnect the call.

"What's happening?" asked Harris from the back, and then

Freya saw the small group of people that crossed the road join a larger group of people standing outside the station.

"Your guess is as good as mine," she replied, and watched him lean back to keep his face from view. "The Jane Blythe investigation is big news. People want to know what happened."

"Well, can we go?" Harris said, with slight panic in his voice. "I don't particularly want to be seen in the back of this bloody thing."

"As soon as we can," Anderson replied, motioning at the red light.

"Can't we just go?" Harris asked, as two more members of the public took the opportunity to cross the street in front of the car. "You lot have done enough bloody damage as it is."

A large group of children between two adults were ambling toward the crossing. They eyed the green man signalling it was safe to cross, then coaxed the kids onto the crossing. There must have been nearly fifty of them.

"I'm sure we'll move on soon," said Freya, adding a purposeful dose of nonchalance to her remark.

"Well, tell them to hurry up, will you?"

"There are children in the road," Freya said, turning in her seat to watch him. "Do you know why I asked you in today, Doctor Harris?"

"You want me to give a statement. Although, I don't fully understand my part in this. I've told you everything I know."

"I need to document everything you've told me. It's a murder enquiry, Doctor Harris. And I'm going to need you to tell me all about your relationship with Jane Blythe."

"Relationship?"

"That's right. I want to hear about the affair you were having."

"I wasn't having an affair," he said, becoming agitated. "Let me out, will you?" Trying the doors, which had the child-locks enabled so they could only be opened from the outside, Harris slammed his hand against the door. "This is outrageous."

"You were having an affair with Jane Blythe. You used to meet her in the woods where we found her body. You used your position to manipulate her, and she wasn't the first."

He stopped trying the doors. "I don't know what you think you're playing at, Inspector Bloom. But I am not the one you're looking for," he growled, his baritone voice grumbling with spite.

"See if you can gee them up a bit, Constable," she said to the driver, who in response, honked the horn and waved for the children to hurry up.

A few heads in the small crowd of media folk turned to see what the commotion was.

"You bitch," Harris snarled.

"Did Daniel Blythe know about the affair, Doctor Harris?"

Two members of the press were inquisitive enough to start towards the car. Looking from the approaching reporters to Freya and back again, Harris squirmed in his seat. The line Freya walked was as fine as a baby's hair. She needed Harris to confess to the affair, and fast. If the media saw him and a photo of him in the back seat of a squad car made the papers, the repercussions could be horrific.

"This could ruin me," he said.

"I'm sure we'll be moving in no time," she said, struggling to keep her voice calm and soft.

The two reporters were just fifty yards away at the edge of the police station car park.

"Do you understand the significance of your statement, Doctor Harris? We have Daniel Blythe in custody and what you say could help us put him away."

Forty yards.

Their heads lowered as they tried to peer into the car from a distance. The photographer raised his camera, and Harris shielded his face with his hands.

"It's time to tell the truth," said Freya, eyeing the driver as he prepared to move away as soon as the children had crossed.

Thirty yards.

"Did you, or did you not, have an affair with Jane Blythe?"

Knock knock.

The taps on the rear window had come from the other side of the car, the side that nobody had been monitoring.

"Doctor Harris?" a muted voice said, one that Freya recognised, and she cursed herself for pushing her luck. "Molly Fox from Lincoln Today. Can you tell me your involvement in the Jane Blythe investigation?"

There was a flash from the photographer on the other side of the car as he caught Harris' rage in a perfect profile.

"Go, go, go," said Freya, and the driver lurched the car around the last of the children and the second of the adults into the oncoming traffic, and then accelerated into the police station car park, leaving the reporters with enough to destroy one, if not two, careers.

They came to stop, and as the lead car entered behind them, the gates closed.

Freya sighed, letting her head fall back onto the headrest.

"You bloody idiot," Harris scowled. "Do you realise what you've done? This could ruin me. I could lose everything. If my photo ends up in the paper, I'll sue you. You're finished. Do you hear me? You'll get nothing from me now. I didn't bloody kill her. I have a life, you know?"

"And that's more than what Jane Blythe has, isn't it?" she snapped, and regretted it the moment the words left her lips.

CHAPTER THIRTY

With the excitement at an end, Ben surveyed the small cul-de-sac. The neighbours were huddled in small groups within the safety of their driveways. Forensics were unloading equipment from their van, and the remaining uniforms were turning the house upside down.

It wasn't the exact result Ben had been looking for, but Blythe was in custody and the search was under way.

"So what's been happening?" asked Jackie, as they walked toward number thirty-three. "Bring me up to speed."

"Harris is on his way to the station," said Ben.

"Under arrest?"

"No, voluntarily. Freya is adamant he's involved somehow."

"But you're not certain?" Jackie said. "What about DCI Granger?"

Ben shook his head. "She doesn't know him like we do."

"Do you think he's got something to do with it?"

"All the evidence points to Blythe. He doesn't exactly hide how he felt about his wife. He gave all her belongings away the week she left. He got rid of her car, which we still don't understand why. He even told Cheryl Butcher when she called to ask after her that she wouldn't be back."

"No?"

"Yeah," Ben said. "Who does that?"

He stopped at the top of the driveway to thirty-three and gestured to the house behind him. "Do you remember he was digging up his patio?"

"Oh, come on," Jackie said. "He's not stupid enough to bury anything there?"

"Maybe not here. But he's done a few patios and construction jobs since Jane Blythe went missing."

"Hence the forensics?"

"I've got a team black lighting everything they can and another using GPR in the garden."

"GPR?" said Jackie. "Ground radar? Christ, Ben. You've gone all out."

"He was digging up his patio, wasn't he?" Ben said, as he led them down the drive.

"Yes, but a year after the murder took place?" said Jackie.

"I know, but we have to come at this from every angle. There's something he's not telling us, and we need to know what it is. He might even have buried the case."

He stopped beside the front door to allow Jackie to enter. They had both been inside the house before, but with uniforms and the white-suited forensics team working alongside each other, the scene was very different. The kitchen had been sealed off with clear plastic sheeting and two uniformed officers were meticulously working through the open-plan living room. Investigating every drawer, cupboard, and box they found.

Looking beyond the mess of the search, the walls were white and the soft furnishings were natural and light. Shaded areas on the walls marked where photos might have once hung. Wedding photos perhaps? Or just memories that Daniel Blythe no longer cared for? All that remained were the scars of what used to be.

The only dark tones in the room were embedded in a painting above the fireplace. It was of a man's silhouette beneath a streetlight. A fog was rolling in and the road was cobbled. The painting was more dark than light, and in such earthy surroundings, it took centre stage.

It was a similar scene upstairs. Only the master bedroom was free of activity.

"We figured you'd want to do this one," said Griffiths, standing in the doorway. He didn't wait for a response, so Ben and Jackie moved into the room.

It was clear that Daniel Blythe had slept on the side closest to the door. Although both bedside tables had lamps, his side had a book, a pair of reading glasses, and a glass of water, whereas, aside from the lamp, the far bedside table was empty and the sheets had barely been disturbed.

"I'll take her side," said Jackie, reading the same into the set up as Ben.

From inside his jacket pocket, Ben pulled out a handful of disposable gloves. He selected two then tossed them to Jackie before donning a second pair and pocketing the spares. He crouched in front of Blythe's bedside table. The first drawer contained exactly what Ben had seen in a dozen or more property searches – coins, keys, half-empty packs of chewing gum, with the addition of Blythe's laminated RAF ID on a branded lanyard and a pocket multi-tool, which Ben dropped into a clear evidence bag. He then gathered the remaining items into a second bag. The second drawer was a little more fruitful. Beneath a stack of *Blythe Construction* calling cards was a handful of photographs held together with a rubber band. He sat back against the bed and snapped the band off, being careful not to disturb any fingerprints that the glossy surface might have retained.

The first image was of Daniel Blythe in his service uniform, and the following few looked to be of the same day but with him standing in a group in front of a fighter jet at a ceremony. Among the pile of miscellaneous photos from various events were images of him with a much younger Jane Blythe at his side, and another of her lying on a beach somewhere hot. At the back of the pack were images of Daniel Blythe and his van, which Ben assumed to have been a proud moment as he had started his own construction business while working his way towards retirement from the air force. The final few images were of the rear of several houses, and judging by the cleanliness of the gardens, Ben assumed they were jobs he had done. It was the beginning of his construction portfolio.

He wrapped the images in the band again and bagged them, tossing them into a pile with the other two bags.

"Anything?" he asked Jackie, not realising that she had finished with her bedside table and was rummaging through the wardrobes.

"The bedside table was empty," she explained. "And this side of the wardrobe is just empty boxes."

"Nothing at all?"

"Not much. Nothing female anyway. I found a few of his old service shirts and there's a set of his number ones in the suit carrier, but nothing of Jane's. He really must have taken everything to the charity shop."

"Ruthless."

"Or was he just hurt?"

"Or was he getting rid of something?" said Ben.

"Ben?" a voice called from downstairs.

"Up here."

One of the white-suited forensics team climbed the stairs and spoke through the balustrade.

"The patio is clean," he said. "Nothing down there."

"I didn't think we'd be that lucky, but it was worth a shot," said Ben, as he left the bedroom with Jackie in tow and descended the stairs. "Jackie, can you get the next address off Chapman and escort the GPR team over there? Use your charm. Hopefully they'll let us in."

"I'll call her now," Jackie replied, and Ben heard the muted beeps as Jackie navigated her phone, searching for Chapman's number.

The living room had been searched and restored to how it had been – sparse but tidy, exactly as Ben imagined an ex-military man would like it.

The man beneath the streetlight remained. Although it was hard to tell if he was walking towards the viewer or away. Stepping closer, Ben examined the strokes of oil. There was a texture to the finish. The raised mounds of paint and brush strokes added to the overall composition. It gave the piece life.

It was as his phone began to ring that Ben noticed the fine, white signature in the bottom right-hand corner.

CHAPTER THIRTY-ONE

Standing in the corridor that linked the custody desk to the interview rooms and the front desk, Freya watched through the window in the door as Priest finished processing Blythe.

"I've got cell three ear-marked for him," Priest finished, looking up at Ben, his deep Yorkshire accent booming out. "Want me to take him through?"

Blythe gave him a look of absolute disgust, then turned to Ben as if he was expecting a long wait on an uncomfortable blue mattress.

"No, thanks, Sergeant. I'll take him straight through to the interview room."

On hearing those words, Freya darted the length of the corridor as fast as she could. She passed the stairwell and, using her security access card, opened another set of doors to the waiting room. A few seats were occupied by a mother with her toddler, and a teenager who, like a thousand others Freya had seen, appeared scared of what might happen to him. Impatient and thoroughly annoyed, Harris looked up from the corner seat he had chosen, as far from the public entrance door as possible.

"Thank you for your patience, Doctor Harris. This way, please," she announced.

He stood and followed, choosing not to wait for the interview to begin voicing his opinion.

"Is it not bad enough that I had my bloody photo taken? Did you really need to announce my name in there?" he said, as the doors slammed closed and the electro-magnetic lock clicked on.

Choosing to ignore the doctor's complaints, and with one eye on the door to the custody desk, Freya lingered, inwardly telling Ben to hurry the bloody hell up.

"What are you waiting for?" Harris asked.

She peered inside the interview room, then glanced back at the door to the custody desk.

"A bit of organisation wouldn't go amiss," Harris mumbled just as the doors opened and Ben led Daniel Blythe into the corridor.

"Detective Sergeant Savage," Freya said, loud and clear. "This must be Mr Blythe?"

"It is indeed," he replied.

Harris, who had been pacing the corridor, passing the delay by reading the dozen or so posters that were pinned to the walls, turned at the disruption. Then with almost cartoon-like animation, he did a double-take as he saw Blythe and clearly recognised him. His mouth hung ajar and he caught Freya's eye with a look of sheer terror on his face.

Blythe walked beside Ben, apparently not even noticing Harris existed. At the door to interview room one, Ben turned and looked across at Freya.

"I'll let you know how it goes," he said.

"Ditto," said Freya, and they both led their interviewees into their respective rooms.

She closed the door behind her, inviting Harris to take a seat.

"Is this going to take much longer? I have patients this afternoon. A few questions. That's what I agreed to. So far, all I've bloody well seen is a circus."

"A few questions is all it will be, Doctor Harris," Freya said, marking the tape and preparing the recording. She hit the button to begin the recording. "Interview with Doctor Michael Harris, employer of the deceased, Jane Blythe," Freya announced, before stating the date and time. "Present is myself, Detective Inspector Bloom, and Doctor Michael Harris."

"Do I need legal representation?" he asked.

"I don't know, do you?" Freya replied. "This is a voluntary interview to help us with our investigation into the murder of one of your employees. If you have nothing to hide, then you have nothing to worry about."

"That's what I thought. Come on then, let's get this over with. There'll be a bloody pandemic by the time I get back to the surgery."

"Just for the record, Doctor, can you state the position Jane Blythe held at your surgery, please?"

"Her position? You know where she worked. She managed the front desk."

"The reception?" Freya asked, for clarity.

"Yes, yes," he replied, with a wave of his hand. "She managed the appointments, queries, and whatnot."

"And made you coffee?"

"What?"

"You said before, she made you coffee."

"So?"

"I'm just stating it for the record that her role was perhaps a little looser than what might have been stated in her job description."

"Yes, she made me coffee."

"Just you, or did she make it for the other doctors?"

"How the bloody hell should I know? I barely get a chance to come up for air. I don't have time to see who she made coffee for."

Freya eyed him, enjoying the sight of him getting worked up. She raised an eyebrow.

"Yes, probably," he said. "She probably made coffee for my staff. Anything else? Or can we get to the details?"

"The details would be nice," Freya said. "Can you tell me when you last saw Jane Blythe alive?"

"Yes, it was the twentieth of October. Last year."

"You're sure about that?"

"Yes. Why?"

"Because when I asked you two days ago, you weren't so sure."

"I asked Cheryl. I didn't have the answer then, but I do now."

"Cheryl Butcher?" Freya said, again for clarity.

"Well how many Cheryls do you think I know?"

"I'm just trying to be clear. For the recording, you understand?"

"Yes, Cheryl Butcher, who, I might as well state now, currently holds the position of receptionist at my surgery."

"And coffee maker?" Freya added.

"What?"

"She also makes you coffee?"

"Yes, she does. And before you ask, yes, she probably also makes coffee for my staff too. Next question."

"Can you tell me about when you last saw Jane? What was her mood like?"

"Her what?"

"Her mood. Was she upset? Angry? Had she argued with anybody?"

"I don't know. Jane was Jane. She was always miserable."

"You said that before. Why do you think that was?"

"How the bloody hell do I know? Probably because of her husband?" he said, gesturing to the next room.

"For the recording, Doctor Harris has indicated to the next interview room where my colleague is currently interviewing Daniel Blythe, Jane's husband."

"What?" Harris said. "Why is that important?"

"It's not," Freya said. "But it might be."

His anger abated momentarily, long enough for a suspicious look to sprawl across his ageing features.

"What's your game?" he asked. "What is this? You're trying to make me slip up, aren't you?"

"I'm doing no such thing, Doctor Harris. I'm investigating the murder of a young woman who, as far as we can tell, interacted with a very small number of people. What you tell us might very well lead us to find her killer. I'm sure a man of your position can appreciate the significance of the words of a doctor such as yourself. Not only a doctor, but a man of repute. You have a charity, am I right?"

"Yes," Harris said slowly, suspicious, still hanging on every word.

"For the children?" Freya added.

"Yes."

"Do you have children of your own?"

"Why?"

Freya gave him another of her disparaging looks. She wouldn't rise to his refusal to answer her question directly. Instead, she would wait for him to grow even more impatient.

He sucked in a breath, then sighed.

"Yes. A daughter. She's no longer a child, though."

"Where is she? Do you see her often?"

"As it happens no. Would you like a full rundown of my family affairs, or shall we keep this strictly business?"

"I was just wondering," Freya said, sensing tension at the mention of his daughter. "Building a picture, as it were."

"Well, you can keep her out of your bloody picture. She's been out of mine for long enough."

"I see," Freya said, doing her best to maintain her neutral expression. "And you mentioned before that you didn't really know Jane well. Is that right?"

"Yes. She was an employee. That's all."

"Just an employee?" Freya asked. "Not a friend?"

"No, of course not—"

"How about a patient?"

He stilled. His eyes darted left to the door, then slowly worked their way back to Freya.

"Yes. She registered at the surgery, I believe—"

"You believe?" Freya said, and he paused before answering.

"She was a registered patient."

"And you were her GP?" Freya said. "Or did you hand that responsibility to one of your staff?"

"No. I dealt with her myself for the most part," he said. "Where are you going with this, Inspector Bloom? My patience is growing extremely thin."

"I was just wondering, that's all," Freya said.

"About what?"

"Well, you see, when somebody dies in suspicious circumstances, we perform an autopsy. A post-mortem. It helps us establish the actual cause of death, gives us an insight into the weapon, if there was a weapon, and also gives us a little look at the type of life the victim lived. Did they smoke? Were they a heavy drinker?" Freya said, as casually as she could. "Were they pregnant?"

His eyes narrowed, and his tongue darted out to wet his lips.

"And?" he said.

"Jane Blythe was pregnant, wasn't she?" said Freya.

"I'm not here to discuss the personal details of a patient—"

"She was pregnant and it was yours, wasn't it, Doctor Harris?"

"Right, that's it. I've tolerated as much as I can possibly tolerate," he said, and he pushed his chair back, collected his jacket, and made toward the door.

"Just be honest with me," Freya said, staying exactly where she was. "Were you having an affair with Jane Blythe?"

Refusing to answer, Doctor Harris placed his hand on the door handle.

"Are you arresting me?"

"No," Freya said, shaking her head slowly.

"Am I free to go?"

"Be my guest," she said.

Slowly, he opened the door, keeping a watchful eye on Freya.

"You haven't heard the last of this, Bloom. And those media people. If my picture appears in the papers–"

"Is there a problem here?" a voice said from outside. The door open further, and looming in the doorway was DCI Granger, doing his best not to explode in front of the doctor.

"No problem, guv," Freya said. "Doctor Harris was just helping us out with our enquiries."

"Doctor Harris," Granger said, looking at the man and not hiding the surprise in his tone.

"And you are?"

"DCI Granger," Granger said slowly, not liking the doctor's tone, but not enough to get Freya out of the hole she was in. "We met at one of your charity gigs a few years ago."

"Ah, well then, perhaps you should know a few things about your lead detective."

Granger cocked his head, inviting the doctor to continue.

"I have volunteered my time to help your investigation. She's been rude. Intrusive. And above all else, thanks to the media frenzy out there, I'll most likely be on the front page of the local rag in the morning. And if I am..." He paused, waiting for Granger to repeat his name.

"Detective Chief Inspector Granger."

"Well, if my photo is in the paper tomorrow, you'll be hearing from my lawyers. And I'll be holding her personally responsible," Harris said, seeming to grow even more agitated as he spoke. "Am I free to go?"

"You volunteered to come," Freya said, knowing full well what was coming next.

"Good," he said, and brushed past Granger before storming up the corridor. He returned a few seconds later, more indignant than ever. "I can't seem to open the door."

Granger stared at Freya, like he was trying to peer directly into her mind, his anger boring holes in her.

"I'll walk you out," he said finally, without looking at Harris. He raised his finger to Freya. "I'll be advising your team that DS Savage is running this investigation as of this moment. They are to take no instructions from you whatsoever. You'd better bloody well stay here until I get back."

CHAPTER THIRTY-TWO

Ben took the seat opposite Blythe, while DC Cruz, who had prepared the recording, was already waiting opposite Blythe's solicitor. The legal representative leaned in close to Blythe and asked a whispered question, to which Blythe shook his head. He was of Asian descent, well-dressed and groomed, and he sat forward in his chair like he was waiting for something to happen.

After announcing the time and date, Ben closed his file, leaned on the table, and prepared himself to listen to a pack of lies.

"I'm Detective Sergeant Ben Savage," he began, then gestured for Cruz to take over.

"Detective Constable Cruz."

"Duty solicitor, Satish Manoharan."

All eyes fell on Blythe.

"Daniel James Blythe," he said, sounding bored already.

"Now that we know who everybody is, I should remind you why we're here," Ben said, staring across the table at Blythe. "Daniel Blythe, you have been arrested under suspicion of murder. You do not have to say anything, but it may harm your defence if you fail to mention when questioned something you later rely on in court. Anything you do say may be given in evidence. Do you understand?"

Blythe stared back at him, an eyebrow raised. Ben returned the gesture, with the addition of a smile. He was confident Blythe was going to be leaving the room and going straight to the custody desk to be charged. The only question was how long that process took.

"Yes," Blythe said eventually. "I understand why I'm here. What I fail to understand is why you think I would kill my wife."

"Well, maybe we can get to that a bit later," Ben replied. "First of all, I'd like you tell me about the days leading up to Jane leaving."

"What about them? You don't honestly expect me to tell you what I did?"

"No, but perhaps you can tell us how the mood was between you both?"

"The mood?" he replied, shaking his head. But when he saw Ben's straight face and abhorrent expression, he stilled. "Fractious. Frosty. Awful."

"And that was normal, was it?"

"Walking up my driveway every night was like coming home late from school when I was a kid. I knew the moment I walked through the door, my mum was going to pounce on me. Getting married was no different, except it wasn't my mother giving me grief, it was my wife."

"Yet you kept on going home. That has to mean something," Ben said.

"Yes, I kept on going home. Everything I have ever earned is invested in that house. I was never going to be the one to walk away from it."

"And what was the reason for the atmosphere?" Ben asked.

"A hundred things. No, a thousand. A thousand minuscule things that weren't worth arguing over. So we didn't. We bottled them up instead."

"Such as?"

"Not cleaning up behind her. Leaving her drawers on the floor. Leaving the fridge open. Married stuff. It happens."

"And if the roles were reversed, what would Jane be saying about you? What little things used to get on her nerves?"

"I'm a picture of perfection. How the bloody hell would I know? Always tidying up behind her, maybe? Maybe I moaned too much about her leaving a mess? Or maybe I just huffed and puffed because I couldn't be bothered with an argument? Do you get the picture? We weren't compatible. We thought we were. But as it turns out, we weren't."

"I get it," Ben said, making a note of what Blythe had said. "How about her last evening?"

"What about it?"

"Talk me through it. We know she left work in the evening. Around five o'clock. We know she came home to you. And we know she left around eight o'clock. What happened in those three hours?"

Blythe shrugged. "Same old, same old. She came home. Left her shoes by the door. Had a shower and left her clothes on the floor. She made something to eat, left her dishes by the sink, then went off to watch telly in bed. Me? I followed her around. Picked up the shoes. Tossed them in the bin. Picked up her clothes. Binned them as well. Dishes in the bin. Anything I could find of hers, in the bin."

"That doesn't sound very much like you avoiding an argument."

"No. I guess by that point I was ready to talk about it."

"So, you talked?" Ben asked. "Seems an odd way to instigate a conversation."

"You didn't know her. I had to do stuff like that to get her attention."

"Right. So where did you talk?"

"Upstairs. In the bedroom. Where she always was."

"There's no TV in your bedroom," Ben said. "I was in there."

"I broke it," Blythe said, sighing.

"And I'm guessing you threw that away as well?"

"I guess I did, yes."

"You seem to throw a lot away."

Blythe shrugged again. "Not anymore I don't."

"So, you had the argument. How did that go?"

Blythe laughed. He actually laughed out loud, like Ben had told a one-liner.

"Are you kidding? Is that actually a question you want me to answer?"

"Of course," Ben said. "I want to know all the gory details."

"Okay, then. We rowed about me picking up her stuff. She said some things that hurt me, I said things that hurt her. I packed her case and told her to get out. She got out. That's all there is to it."

"Was there any violence?"

"None whatsoever," Blythe replied. "She went downstairs, fished her shoes out of the bin, put her coat on, and left. I went down and threw her case at her."

"You did actually throw it at her?"

"Well, yeah–"

"Why?"

"To hurt her. I wanted to hurt her. I'm sorry if I'm not getting this across, but we're talking about the end of our marriage here. It's a big thing. I was hurting, and that's what you do, isn't it? When someone hurts you, you want to hurt them back."

"But you didn't actually harm her at all?"

"It's a suitcase. It landed at her feet."

"And this was at eight o'clock, was it?"

"I have no idea. I slammed the door and left her to it."

He spoke as if it was perfectly normal. As if leaving your wife in the cold with nowhere to go was acceptable.

"What did you do then?"

"Tidied up," Blythe said proudly. "I cleansed."

"And where did you think Jane was going to go? Bearing in mind it was eight p.m. and she, by your own admission, had no friends."

"I honestly couldn't have cared less. As long as she was out of my life. It was like a dark cloud had lifted. Have you ever been in a relationship like that? When splitting up is uplifting? Motivating, even?" He shook his head, reliving the moment in his mind. "I could be who I wanted to be."

"And who was that, Daniel? Who did you want to be?"

"I just wanted the mess out of my head. The clutter. I needed it gone. I needed to find myself. To be myself."

"We've got witnesses supporting what you said," Ben said. "You and Jane argued. She left on foot at eight p.m."

Blythe smiled and rolled his eyes. "Don't tell me. My neighbours."

"But where the stories don't add up," Ben continued, ignoring his comment, "and perhaps you can help me here, is that our witness states that you left shortly after Jane. They heard your van. They watched you go after her. Yet, you say you spent some time cleansing. Decluttering. Which of you are wrong?"

"They are," Blythe said. "There's a million vans like mine. It's a white Transit, for god's sake."

"There aren't a million that are parked down your road. In fact, yours is the only one," Ben said. "The other thing that is bothering me, and again, I'd appreciate your input on this, is her car. You said you got rid of it, yet there's no DVLA record of you selling it, or scrapping it."

"I told you. I gave it to some travellers. Rag and bone men. They came by in their truck, you know, ringing their bell. I told them to take it and they came back and got it the next day."

"And this was on the twentieth, was it?" Ben asked. "The day Jane left?"

"No this was later. A few days afterwards. I didn't really know what I was going to do with it. It wasn't worth anything. I saw them and figured they could get rid of it for me."

"Decluttering?" Ben said.

"That's right."

"You're aware, of course, that we found Jane's car?"

"My car. It was in my name."

"Well, we found it recently. Burned out. We had to use the chassis number to confirm who it belonged to."

Blythe shrugged again, but his confidence waned a little, his eyes narrowing as he considered what he might say.

"Maybe the travellers sold it on?" he suggested.

"Maybe. But highly unlikely. I don't like to generalise, but the type of traveller you're talking about wants hard cash, and as you said, it wasn't worth anything to anybody."

"Are you going to provide any evidence to support your accusation, Detective Sergeant Savage?" Mr Manoharan said, speaking up for the first time. "All my client has heard so far is an account of what may or may not have happened, with two minor discrepancies, which I'm sure can be straightened out."

"Your client, sir, has just admitted to arguing with his wife. To wanting to hurt his wife. To getting rid of her belongings as soon as she had left. And I have a witness placing your client in his van going after Jane shortly after she left. That's not really a discrepancy. And as for straightening them out, that's why we're here. May I continue?"

"You may," Manoharan said, making a note of everything Ben had said.

"Good, thank you," replied Ben. He turned back to Blythe. "Now then, Mr Blythe, I'm going to give you one more opportunity to tell me the truth, and then I'm going to give you my account of what happened. If there's anything I've missed so far, then now is the time to get it out there."

Blythe leaned in closer to his legal rep and whispered something, then, when Manoharan nodded his agreement, he sat back in his seat, folding his arms. It was the start of what Ben knew to be a long series of no comment responses. It was the response that achieved nothing, helped nobody, and only prolonged an interview.

"Did anybody call you a few days later, Daniel? Somebody looking for Jane, perhaps?"

"No comment."

"Her employer, for instance? Did anybody from the surgery call to see where she was?"

"No comment."

"You see, we spoke to Doctor Harris. And his receptionist, in fact. They both said that somebody called to see where Jane was. She didn't turn up for work the following Monday. They were worried about her."

"No comment."

"They said, you told them quite specifically that Jane wasn't coming back. What did you mean by that, Daniel?"

"No comment."

"And at what point in the next year did you think it was odd that you hadn't heard from Jane? There's no records of you splitting any money. No settlement on the house. Nothing."

"No comment."

"You see, usually, when a married couple split up, the house is either sold off, or one buys the other out. But that doesn't seem to have happened. In fact, Jane hasn't made a single transaction since the time she left your house."

"Is that a question?" Blythe asked.

"No, but feel free to add anything," Ben replied.

"No comment."

"Do you want to know what I think?"

"No."

"That was rhetorical. I'm going to tell you anyway," Ben said. "I think Jane left work that evening. She went home, and things played out as you said. She dropped things on the floor. You picked them up. You argued. She left. You threw her case at her. All that is totally fine. Makes sense. And we have evidence and statements to back that up. But when Jane left, moments after leaving the family home, she sent a text message. Do you want to know who to?"

Blythe stared across at him, apparently out of no comments, and patience.

"Her lover," Ben continued. "I think she sent a text message to her lover. To arrange to meet. She was in trouble. She needed somewhere to go. Money maybe? I think you went back into your house. I think you tried to tidy up, but the thought of her with him was too much. The thought of her in his arms. So, you went after them. You knew where they met up, because you'd seen her paintings. You'd seen how obsessed she was with the forest. The forest was her way out of the relationship. The forest was her light, and you, Daniel, were the darkness."

"You're wrong," Blythe mumbled, his eyes softening.

"You followed her. Or maybe you drove ahead of her? Maybe you were waiting in the forest for her."

"No."

"And when she appeared, you stepped out of the shadows. You stepped out of the shadows and hit her with the first thing you could find. You killed her, Daniel," Ben said, his voice a whisper now. Watching every little facial movement, Ben went in with the last card up his sleeve. "You killed her and her unborn baby, and you left them for dead."

CHAPTER THIRTY-THREE

Not a single muscle moved, flexed, or even twitched in Blythe's face at the mention of the baby. He knew.

"You knew she was pregnant, didn't you?" Ben asked.

Blythe said nothing. He stared down at his hands, habitually picking at the dead skin on his callouses.

"In light of your responses, Daniel, and in light of the evidence against you and your unwillingness to cooperate fully, you're going to be formally charged. Perhaps a trial will jog your memory some more? Either way, it's out of my hands now," Ben said, and he glanced across to Cruz, giving him the nod.

"Daniel Blythe, I'm arresting you for the murder of Jane Blythe. You do not have to say anything but it may harm your defence if you do not mention when questioned something you later rely on in court. Anything you do say may be given in evidence."

Perhaps it was those words. That slight alteration of Cruz's statement. Omitting the part that states Blythe was under suspicion of. There were not suspicions now. There was solid ground for CPS to proceed. Perhaps it was all that that sparked a single tear to begin its journey along Blythe's face. To form on his eyelid and run for freedom. And as Ben watched him, studying his body language, it wouldn't have surprised him if that tear was the first he had produced since before Jane had walked out of his life.

"Take him to the custody desk and charge him," Ben said to Cruz, then turned back to Blythe, gathering his file from the desk. "Is there somebody you'd like us to call on your behalf?"

Blythe shook his head and didn't raise it.

Nodding his farewell to the duty solicitor, Ben opened the door to the corridor. He loved those moments, but it should have been Freya by his side. She should have been sharing his glory. He peered into the next meeting room, finding it empty. Just faintly, he could smell her perfume lingering in the usually stale air.

He checked his phone while he walked. If Harris had given her anything to work with, she would have messaged him, or even called. But there was nothing.

Her number was in his recently dialled numbers, so he hit dial, checked he was alone, and leaned against the wall waiting for the call to connect. But it didn't. A recorded message told him that his call could not be connected at this time.

Thinking that she might be in the incident room, he was about to go through to the fire escape stairwell when the door to the front desk opened. A uniform called out.

"DS Savage?"

"That's me," he replied, not recognising the individual. But to be fair to himself, he was in a world of his own.

"There's a man waiting to see you. Shall I send him through?"

Curious, Ben closed the stairwell door and approached the door to the public waiting room, peering through the narrow, reinforced glass as he approached.

Uniform buzzed him through and he stepped into the room, feeling the cold from the open front door.

Tom Hendry looked up from the end of a row of four hard, plastic chairs. He was the only person in the room.

"Tom?" Ben said. "Tom Hendry?"

"Hi," he replied, standing and walking over to Ben. He was as tall as Ben, if not taller, and good looking too, with all the charm and confidence of a public schoolboy. "I was hoping to find you here."

"It's a police station. It's a good start when you're looking for a police officer."

"I hear you arrested somebody. Daniel Blythe?"

"I'm afraid, I can't really–"

"It wasn't him."

"Sorry?" Ben said, sensing something big was coming.

"It wasn't Daniel," Hendry replied, and checked around the room to make sure they were still alone. "He was with me."

"Daniel Blythe was with you the night Jane left?" Ben repeated for clarity.

"He came to me. He was upset. He needed to talk."

"Why you?"

Biting his lower lip, Hendry gave some thought to how he might respond. Although Ben had an idea why Blythe might go to him, it was a large leap to make, unaided, on the basis of the single painting that was hanging in Daniel Blythe's living room.

"We were lovers," Hendry said, just as a middle-aged lady entered the waiting room. She eyed them, then stepped over to the desk and gave a knock for the duty officer to tend to her. "Is there somewhere we can talk?"

Flashing his ID card at the little receiver, the door clicked open and Ben peered through, seeing Blythe being led towards the custody desk at the far end of the corridor. He waited a moment for Cruz to close the door, then turned to Hendry and ushered him inside. He used the interview room they had just finished with, closing the door behind him and leaning against it, still unsure of what was about to unfold.

"You and Daniel?" Ben said, and Tom nodded. "Do you want to tell me about it?"

"What's to say? Daniel and I, we... That is..." He seemed to falter with his words. Unlike when Ben had spoken to him before, when he had been full of confidence.

"You were in a relationship?" Ben suggested.

"Yes. He came to the studio once. A long time ago. When Jane had first started coming. He was looking for her, but she wasn't there. I was just cleaning up. We'd had a good evening. My students and me. Anyway, they'd all gone home, and I was just doing what I always do. Cleaning brushes and palettes. It's part of the job, I guess. I saw the headlights of his van, and he came in. He was upset. I think he found me easy to talk to."

"He opened up to you? Just like that?" Ben asked.

"Not just like that. I had to calm him down. But I couldn't let him leave. Not in that state. I gave him a drink. I always keep a bottle to hand, and it was just the one. He was driving, after all."

"Go on," Ben said, sure it had been more than just the one, but the details at that point were insignificant.

"Well, one thing led to another. He told me they were unhappy. Said he thought she was having an affair. I think that's why he did it. You know? With me. The first time, anyway."

"There were more times?"

"Oh yes. Many more. It became a regular thing. Not at my studio, you understand? My sister wouldn't allow it. No. No, we used to go to this spot. Private. Secluded."

"The forest?"

"Yes," he said, unsurprised that Ben had worked that part out for himself.

"What about Jane?" Ben asked. "Was she faithful?"

"Well, that's where it gets a little muddled," Hendry said, and he met Ben's stare, making a point of looking him in the eye. "She caught us."

"In the forest?"

"In his van. One moment we were, well... you know? Then the door opened. I guess she wasn't expecting to see him with another man." Taking a seat, Hendry leaned forward, elbows on his knees, and took a deep breath. "I should never have got involved. He was married. I should have just left it alone."

"What happened?" Ben asked. "What happened then?"

"She left. He drove me home then went back to his house to face the music. Do you remember her paintings?" he asked.

"Of course."

"Do you remember I told you she was consumed by the forest?"

"Yes."

"Now you know why. The marriage was already in tatters before Daniel and I got together. That forest destroyed her life."

"Why didn't you tell me about any of this before?"

"It wasn't my place to."

"You didn't want to announce that Daniel is gay? You thought that should be up to him?"

"It's a big thing, to some anyway. Not for me. For me it was obvious. When I came out, people just laughed and said they already knew. But for a man like Daniel, it's a big thing. It's a big step."

"And how about now? Do you still see him?"

"No. No, we parted company shortly afterwards. He went a bit... well, inside himself."

Ben digested the news. Part of him knew he should go and stop Blythe being processed. But he would need to see evidence first of all. The word of a man who had openly admitted to being dishonest from the start would count for nothing in a legal battle. But there was something else. A question that needed answering. A question that might shed some light on Jane's death.

"Tell me, Tom," Ben began. "What was Jane Blythe doing out there in the forest to begin with?"

He smiled at the question. Of all the responses Ben had imagined, a smile was not one of them. Confusion maybe? Or even ignorance. But the smile was something else.

"She followed us," Hendry said, stating the obvious.

"What time did Daniel arrive at your house on the evening of the twentieth? The night Jane left?"

"Not long after eight," Hendry said, confident in his answer.

"What makes you so sure? Could it have been later?"

"No. I'd been looking after my sister's kids. Her and her husband had been out. They got back at eight, just like they always do."

"Did they see Daniel? Can they support your statement?"

"No. Like I said before, my sister doesn't approve of me bringing my *friends* home," Hendry said, gesturing the inverted commas around the word friends. "But I'd be happy to stand up in court."

"That brings me to my next point. If you aren't with him anymore, why are you doing this?"

Hendry stood, tucking his chair in under the desk. Then he leaned on the chair back and sighed.

"Daniel Blythe is a good man. Jane Blythe was a good woman. They were just..."

"Incompatible?" Ben suggested.

"Yes," Hendry said. "I didn't drive them apart. You have to know that. They both deserved to be happy. Daniel sought happiness with me. Jane? Well, I doubt she could ever have been happy."

CHAPTER THIRTY-FOUR

"I told you we wouldn't have to go to the hospital," Jackie's mother said.

"You did not," Jackie replied, holding the door to the surgery open for Charlie and her mother to enter before her. "You said he needed to lie on his side and get plenty of fluids. It was me who said he needed something stronger."

"Well, I knew he wouldn't have to go into hospital. You can't beat a bit of love and attention in the comfort of your own home," her mother said, as they approached the front desk.

Ignoring her mother, Jackie waited for Cheryl to finish what she was doing and look up.

"Good afternoon," she said, her smile forced.

"Hello, Cheryl. We've got an appointment with Doctor Harris."

"I'm afraid Doctor Harris isn't in, so Doctor Greaves will see you. Is that okay?"

"I'm sure that'll be fine," Jackie said.

"Doctor Greaves?" her mother said, leaning onto the counter. "He's good, is he?"

"I don't think we'd have him if he wasn't," Cheryl said, unsure of the question.

"As good as Harris?"

"Erm–"

"It's okay, Cheryl," Jackie intervened, eyeing her mother to back down. "I'm sure Doctor Greaves will be fine."

"Has Charlie's files, does he?" her mother added.

"Yes. Everything is digital, so all the doctors can access the patient records."

"Even the notes?"

"Mum?" Jackie said, feeling herself blushing with embarrassment.

"It's okay," Cheryl assured Jackie, then turned to her mother. "Everything Doctor Greaves needs will be on the system. He'll be able to pick up right where Doctor Harris left off."

"It's just that Doctor Harris made some notes last time we were here. On his pad, you know?" Jackie's mother continued.

"Come on, Mother," Jackie said, coaxing her from the desk. "Leave the poor woman to do her job."

She turned and stepped to one side as a lady in a wheelchair was wheeled past. The girl who was doing the pushing stopped beside the front desk so that the lady in the chair could lean around the side and talk to Cheryl. While Jackie's mother pursued the little bookshelf with Charlie, Jackie turned and cast her eye over the advertising board, recognising it as the one DI Bloom had taken a photo of. In the top right-hand corner was a small, black card featuring the name of a therapist. A Prof. D. Ford. The contact details were below, and Jackie made a note of the number, hatching a plan. When she was done, she glanced across at her mother to make sure she hadn't seen her. Not that there was any problem with that, but she was bound to ask questions.

'What are you writing down?' she would say. To which Jackie would have to lie, just as DI Bloom had done. 'You don't need yoga. We didn't have yoga in my day. We just walked everywhere. We were fit and strong. We carried bags home and walked ten miles to school, through snow and sleet and god knows what,' Jackie imagined her mother saying.

It just wasn't worth the effort.

The lady in the wheelchair was behind the desk now, and Cheryl was crouching beside a filing cabinet, her expression a stark contrast to the smiling and welcoming face she had shown Jackie. The old woman in the chair was dishing out hissed orders, too quiet for Jackie to hear. Then it dawned on her that she was Mrs Harris. The report had said she was wheelchair bound.

"Charlie Gold?" a voice said from behind her.

Jackie turned to find a very handsome-looking man, around six foot something, the same as Ben. He had a light beard, groomed and trimmed, and his eyes were like the blue marbles Charlie had somewhere in his toy collection. The doctor was in his early to mid-thirties, the same as Ben. And he ushered them in with a wave of his hand, just as Ben had done earlier.

"Are you Charlie's mum?" he asked, catching Jackie staring.

"Me? Oh, yes," she said, becoming flustered in a heartbeat.

"Get yourself together, Jackie dear," her mother muttered under her breath as she led Charlie past her. "All you ever bloody think about, isn't it?"

There was no time to argue. Her mother and Charlie were already entering the doctor's room. He waited for her to catch up, beaming down at her.

"Now then," he said, as he closed the door behind him and worked his way between everyone to get to his seat. "What can I do for young Charlie? Bronchiolitis, isn't it?"

"Yes–" Jackie began.

"It's a lot better since Doctor Harris gave him the stronger pills," her mother intervened.

"He's sleeping through now, at least," Jackie added.

"I've been keeping an eye on him," her mother said proudly, emphasising the word *I've*.

"His cough is a lot better, too," Jackie said.

"I've been keeping him well hydrated," her mother finished. "Making him sleep on his side. You know? The old ways still work, don't they?"

The doctor tick-tocked between the women, then made a point of stopping on Charlie who was standing between them.

"How are you feeling, Charlie?" he asked, his tone soft and calming, and one that Jackie could grow used to.

"Erm..." Charlie began.

"Tell him, Charlie," his grandmother urged.

"Leave him be, Mum," Jackie said. "Go on, Charlie. In your own time."

"I was just giving him a gentle nudge. The boy takes after you. Dithering about nothing and everything. He just needs some confidence–"

"Charlie?" the doctor said, cutting her mother off, at which Jackie smiled inwardly.

Charlie nodded. "I feel better. My throat isn't so sore, and it's easier to breathe."

"That'll be the higher dosage Doctor Harris prescribed," Doctor Greaves suggested. "I'll just have a listen to your breathing, and we'll go from there."

He collected his stethoscope from a drawer then made his way around to Charlie, crouching beside him and accidentally bumping into Jackie's leg. "I'm ever so sorry," he began.

"No, not at all," Jackie said.

"She was probably standing in the way," her mother said, seeing the opportunity to get a sly dig in.

"I can be a little clumsy," the doctor admitted, seeing Jackie blush. "And the room is small. But I like the view."

"No, it's my pleasure," Jackie said, then heard what she said replayed in her mind. Her *pleasure?*

Her mother's wide-eyed and knowing expression pretty much summed up all Jackie was thinking, only with the addition of an eye roll.

It took just a few moments for Doctor Greaves to finish listening to Charlie's breathing and carefully edge his way around to his seat.

"Right then, it seems young Charlie here is on the mend," he said. "I'll issue another week's worth of antibiotics, and that should be that. Any problems, feel free to drop by again, but I'm very happy with his progress."

"Thank you, Doctor," Jackie's mother said. "That's ever so kind of you."

"My pleasure," he replied.

"One more thing," Jackie said. "Was that Mrs Harris I saw outside?"

He looked a little taken aback by the question, glancing at the door then back at Jackie.

"The lady in the wheelchair," Jackie explained.

"Yes. Yes, that's her. She comes in from time to time. I think she likes to crack the whip. You know? Keep Cheryl on track."

"Ah, I see," Jackie said.

"Why's that?"

"Oh, no reason. It's just that Cheryl said Doctor Harris isn't here. I just wasn't expecting to see her, that's all."

"We don't see much of her anymore. You know? Since the stroke. But she likes to keep on top of things while she can."

"Do you get on with her?" Jackie asked.

"Jackie, is this really necessary?" her mother interjected. "Here? Now?"

"I'm just curious, that's all."

"It's fine," Doctor Greaves said, laughing off the sudden turn of topic. "She's lovely. I've never had a problem with her. But to be honest, I don't see much of anyone outside this room. It's a busy time of year."

"Plenty of flu going about, no doubt," her mother said.

"Yes. That's right. Have you had your jab?"

"Yes. Yes, I have thank you," she replied, before the doctor could comment or allude to her age.

"We'll be seeing you," Jackie said, closing the appointment off. She opened the door, stepped out into the corridor, and held her hand out for Charlie to take. "Thank you, Doctor."

The three of them walked towards the exit, calling out their thanks to Cheryl, who was still rummaging through the filing cabinets. The receptionist closed the cabinet drawer, stood, and avoided Jackie's gaze.

"He seemed nice," her mother said, in that tone that suggested she knew she was pushing her luck.

But Jackie wasn't paying attention. There was something about the way in which Mrs Harris was watching Cheryl, with the occasional furtive glance towards Jackie, that wasn't sitting right.

"Sorry?" she said.

"Oh, come on, dear. You're in a world of your own sometimes," her mother said. "I said, he seemed nice. The doctor."

"Leave it, Mum. Please."

"I'm just saying. You clearly made an impression on him–"

"Mum!"

"You could do worse. A young doctor. Good money. Clean."

"Mum, do you have to list the qualities of every man you think is a suitable husband?" Jackie said, a little louder than she had hoped. Of the remaining few people in the waiting area, two looked up, both with raised eyebrows.

"Let's just get out of here," Jackie said.

She held the door open for her mother and Charlie, and was about to follow when she saw Mrs Harris being wheeled towards her. She held the door open a little longer, and the young girl that was pushing her smiled her gratitude, though it was clearly an effort.

"Thank you, dear," Mrs Harris said as they approached.

"Oh, I'm sorry," Jackie said, noticing the younger girl was struggling to get the chair through the doorway. She pulled the door open a little further.

"In a world of her own, that one," she heard her mother say from outside, when Mrs Harris was wheeled into the biting cold.

Jackie followed, her hand clutching her phone inside her pocket, and as her mother made her way towards her car, Jackie stopped, unlocked her phone, and dialled a number.

"Jackie, dear. Come on. It's late."

"Do you mind taking him, Mum?"

"What? You've just got back. Don't tell me you have to go in?"

Peering down at Charlie and seeing his disappointed expression, Jackie caved.

"No. No, it's okay. I can pop in later. Let's get home, shall we? What do you want for dinner tonight, Charlie?"

"Chips," he said enthusiastically. "And chicken dinosaurs."

"You'll have vegetables," Jackie's mother stated. "You need vitamins. I've got a casserole in the slow cooker. That'll keep you warm, lad."

Charlie rolled his eyes at Jackie, who smiled at him and ruffled his hair.

"Come on. Dinner, bath, and bed for you. And if you're good, I'll read you your favourite story."

CHAPTER THIRTY-FIVE

The scene reminded Freya of Jane Blythe's paintings. Stars shone like jewels and the moon was full and bright, despite streaks of winter sun still clinging to the eastern sky. It was one of those rare moments in nature. The perfect timing where solar and lunar light cast their combined glory to the landscape below in surreal hues of pale blue. In contrast to the painting, the forest was a dark stain on an otherwise bright, open space, and the vignette was of sheer natural beauty.

The track that led into the trees was bumpy, but Freya's little rental handled it well. She took it slow, steering around the potholes and divots when she saw them, until she entered that dark stain and rolled to a stop where she and Ben had parked. She killed the engine and sat in silence. From the outside, the forest had seemed impenetrable, but beneath the leafless winter oaks and elms, the power of the moon graced the forest floor and lit the fat, gnarled trunks of ancient trees, casting shadows, deep and dark.

Fingering her phone, she hit the power button and navigated to the recently dialled numbers. It wasn't a conscious decision.

But some sick part of her savoured the torment that arose as her thumb poised above the name.

Diane.

'Get help,' he had said, and Freya laughed a single stab of laughter at the incomprehensibility of the idea.

"Help," she muttered to herself, and gazed out of the window to where, close to a year ago, Jane Blythe had been fatally wounded. She could picture the scene, her attacker's face masked by shadow. Jane would have fallen to the ground from shock more than pain. Freya saw her in her mind's eye. She was clear – her eyes wide, her mouth open, gasping for air. Blood ran down her face then dropped onto the ground. Her fingers clasped around dead leaves and dirt encrusted her nails. Broken sticks and twigs dug deep into her body and she pulled herself into the safety of the brambles, where thorns pierced and scratched her cold skin with blind malice.

Jane stopped.

A cold shiver ran through her body and her blood-wet clothes clung to her skin.

Only her breathing could be heard. There were no birds chattering in the trees. There was no scurrying of rodents and mammals in the dead leaves. Just her laboured breath and the fine mist it produced.

Somewhere close by, a car started. The engine roared and wheels splashed through puddles in the driver's haste to get away. Then, amidst the new silence, adrenaline spiked and the fight for survival kicked in. The journey through one hundred feet of torturous brambles must have been hell.

And Freya knew.

There was a clarity. A time that she had long forgotten. A monumental moment in her existence that her mind had tucked away in a dark corner, never to be retrieved.

She climbed from the car and stared at the forest floor, and at her hands. It wasn't her imagination that brought Jane Blythe's last moments to life. It was a memory, vivid and clear. They were not Jane's hands that had clutched at the debris. It was not Jane's face that had been shredded by thorns, or her skin that was cold with fear. And it was not Jane Blythe's adrenaline that had coursed through her body when Freya had pictured the scene.

Breathless, Freya fought her mind for Jane's story. For her nightmare. But when she roused herself from her imagination, the nightmare was Freya's. The forest that surrounded James Marley's house in the woods was lit by the moon alone. There was a lake behind it and a strong wind blew the tall trees so they swayed in unison around it, like sentries, uniform and in time.

A crack of a branch close by.

A cloud of Freya's breath. Her hands had shaken; she remembered how her hands had shaken uncontrollably, just as they shook now. Then a scream.

"Yes," she said aloud.

A scream from inside the house. A female voice, hoarse with fright and pain.

Pain.

And she saw it.

She felt him behind her. Darker than the deepest shadows the moon could muster.

There was no time to turn. No time to defend herself. And there was no time to save the girl.

And then his hands, firm and strong, had gripped her legs. She hadn't crawled. She was being dragged backwards through the forest.

The memory was clear enough that a sheen of sweat had developed on her back, and she shuddered.

She was dragged from the forest to the little, wooden house. It was little more than a large hut with a wooden porch and deck. His heavy boots were like drums on the planks. She felt the bite of the wood and the ripping of flesh as it tore off a fingernail. The door crashed open and light spilt into the night, offering her a final view of the normal world. The world where Freya Bloom was a strong, independent woman with a promising career. The light, sparse though it was, revealed nothing. An empty forest. A glimpse of nothing but the terrible truth.

She was alone.

The door closed behind her. A hood was pulled over her face, and all hope of rescue was as dead as the light.

She clung to a tree, breathless, waiting for the nightmare to end. It was now. It was always now. The fingernail, the door, the hood, and then nothing.

"Well, well," the voice said, and she froze, eyes wide. Her knees ready to give way beneath the weight of the memory. "Detective Inspector Freya Bloom. You're almost as pretty in real life as you are on the TV."

"Let me go, Marley," she breathed, the hood offering little in the way of fresh air. "I'm alone. You don't need to do this."

"Run, you mean?" he rasped, lowering himself down so that he straddled her, holding her flailing arms at bay with ease. He forced her arms up over her head, pressing her face into the hard, wooden floor. With his free hand, he traced the outline of her spine through her shirt, stopping at that spot between her shoulder blades, that spot only Greg knew existed. That spot that, once ignited, would send her wild with lust.

He'd been watching her. Watching them. Greg and her. The weekend away. The campsite. It had just been them. And Greg had taken advantage. He'd kissed her there, just as Marley kissed her now.

But her reaction was not one of lust, and she doubted from that moment on it ever would be. Just a cold, dead place on her back, where nerves ended, and nothing more.

He moved up, countering Freya's attempts to throw him off-balance by gripping his thighs around her. Until he was there again. At her nape. Breathing. Smelling. Kissing.

"You can get away," she whispered, settling down to regain some strength. Her body tensed at his touch. His body hardened at hers, pressing into her, reminding her of Greg.

"It's too late for that," he whispered, with a delicate nibble of her ear. "You've seen me. Nobody gets to see me."

CHAPTER THIRTY-SIX

Ben's Ford had handled the bumpy track with ease on previous visits to the forest, when he hadn't been in third gear clearing fifty miles per hour, when the suspension hadn't been pushed to its limits, and when the bottom of the car hadn't been slamming into the ground at every single bump.

He slowed for the corners, then buried the accelerator into the carpet as he emerged onto the straights, the full-beam headlights carving a path through the night.

It was only as he approached the forest that he slowed, seeing the glint of Freya's rear window in the moonlight. His seatbelt was off before he had stopped, as was the engine. He pushed open the door and wrenched open Freya's passenger door, only to find the car empty.

The forest around him was in pitch darkness. She could have walked in any direction. Pulling his phone from his pocket, he dialled her number but cursed when her phone flashed on the passenger seat of her car.

"Freya?" he called out. "Freya, it's me."

There was no reply.

Cautiously, he stepped off the track onto the well-trodden

path they had taken the first time they had come to the place. But there had been lights to follow then. And if there hadn't been lights, there had been men's voices, and the reassurance of a handful of uniforms to guide them.

But there was nobody now. Not a soul. Not a single light save for the moon, which may have lit the track behind him but was blocked by the tree canopy this far into the trees.

"Freya, are you here?" he called, then stopped to listen for movement. Although he couldn't be sure in the dark, he thought he had made it to the spot where the light had been set up. The place where they had left the well-trodden path and ducked beneath the bushes to find the body of Jane Blythe lying face down in the mud.

He pushed his way through, sure he was in the right spot. Sure that if she was in the forest, then she would be there. She had to be.

And she was.

Although the Freya Bloom he had known was *not* there. The witty, smart, powerful, and confident woman he was growing to adore in more ways than one was gone. Only the carcass remained. A shell. A pitiful, sullen, weak, and miserable wretch. Like the fragile skin a snake leaves behind after grinding itself against a rock.

But in this instance, the forest was the rock. The shadows and fear were the sharp edges. And it was memories she was shedding. He knew even before he had seen her. He knew she wasn't there for Jane Blythe. She was there to remember. She was there to prove them all wrong – Granger, Standing, all of them. She was there, suffering memories Ben could barely imagine, torturing herself to the realms of madness. So that she could be reborn. So that she could start again. So that she could forget – no – choose to forget at her own whim, all over again.

But the process of shedding the skin that had been throttling her, restraining her, and devouring her from the inside, it was destroying her.

She was sitting on the wet ground, her knees drawn up to her chest in perfect silence, save for the irregular breaths of a woman at the end of her limit.

He crouched, as quietly as he could, and leaned into her, preparing to wrap his arm around her, to hold her, as she needed to be held.

"I thought I'd find you here."

The moment the words left his lips, she sat bolt upright, eyes wide with terror. He grabbed hold of her arm.

"Freya. It's me," he said, trying not to alarm her.

But she lashed out, catching him clean across his face, and she scrambled to her feet, shoving him out of the way and then disappearing into the tangle of bushes.

"Freya, stop. It's me. Ben."

He tore after her, breaking through the first bush only to be confronted by another, guided only by the sounds of her somewhere ahead, scrambling through the undergrowth. He burst through a patch of dense thorns and stumbled onto the track, where the moonlight lit the two cars a hundred metres away. But in the centre of the road, lit by the bright moonlight, Freya stared at him, frightened and spent.

She dropped to her knees, making no effort to run as Ben closed in. He stopped six feet from her, not wanting to scare her, and she peered up at him, her eyes black holes on pale, white skin.

"I'm not here to hurt you," he said. "It's me."

He offered her a hand, to which she did not flinch. Her sagging shoulders looked as if they had carried all they could carry.

"Ben?" she said finally. "Ben, is that you?"

"It's me, Freya. Yes, it's me. You weren't at home and, well, I figured you'd be on the case still," he said.

"You know me too well already," she replied.

He held out both arms, slowly, to reassure her, and she reached for him, her arms feeble. It was only when he had touched her, and she had not baulked or ran, that he dropped to his knees before her. He smoothed the hair from her face, tucking it behind her ear, and then wiped the tears from her eye.

But it wasn't consolation she needed. He knew her. Even only knowing her for such a short period of time, he knew she needed to hear the truth.

"You were right," he said, holding her tight against him, hoping that single embrace would convey everything in his mind. All the things he dared not say, wanted to say, but couldn't.

"I know," she replied, her voice hoarse and whispered.

Her response was one he hadn't been expecting, and after a moment of rehearing it, repeating it his head over and over like an echo, he held her at arm's length.

"What did you say?"

"I said, I know, Ben," she cried, her voice as strained as her expression. "I remembered."

"Jane?"

"No. Me. Marley. I remembered it. I remembered it all, Ben. Every detail. Every smell. Every word."

"I don't understand," he said, thinking she was clearly delusional. He pulled her into him again, holding her tight. Burying her face in the crook of his neck. "You're safe now."

"She was watching him," she said. "She came here to watch Daniel."

"But she saw something," Ben finished for her, the way she always did to him. "Daniel didn't kill her."

"I know," she whispered, and it was her turn to push him to arm's length. The skin had been shed. The lies and memories cast away. Her new skin shone with tears and was marred with scars, but she could heal. She would heal. In time. "Jane Blythe saw Harris with somebody. He couldn't let her get away."

CHAPTER THIRTY-SEVEN

Jackie closed Charlie's favourite book quietly. It was a collection of stories and tales, and included those that Jackie had been read when she was a child. She could hear her mother cleaning up the dinner things downstairs. A saucepan clanged and two plates clashed together. But Charlie didn't move. His mouth hung open, and every so often, his fingers twitched.

Slowly and carefully, Jackie stood up from the chair, bent, and kissed him on the forehead. Now was the most dangerous time, leaving his bedroom without the floor creaking or the door squeaking. A few well-placed steps got her to the door, where she turned to make sure Charlie was still asleep. Then, her door strategy. Slowly was no good. In fact, slowly was bad. Slowly seemed to make the door squeak even louder. But too fast and she would be in danger of the clothes hangers on the back of the door rattling and waking him up.

She gave it a tug. Just enough for her to slip through the gap and onto the landing, where she breathed a sigh of relief. It didn't seem a lot, but should Charlie wake and want another story, that would be another twenty minutes, when she really needed to get out. An idea had been forming in her mind ever since they had left the doctor's.

"Mummy?"

Her shoulders sagged with the call and she closed her eyes at the thought of another story.

"You okay, Charlie?" she asked.

He said nothing until she popped her head through the gap and found his bright eyes in the darkness.

"What's the matter, mate?"

"Welcome home, Mummy," he said. "I missed you."

It was moments like this that tore at Jackie's heart. Moments that made the sleepless nights worthwhile. That made dealing with her mother tolerable. And moments when being a single mum and not having to share his love was the best thing in the world.

"I missed you too," she said. "I love you."

"I love you too, Mummy."

"Do you need another story?"

"No. It's okay. You must be tired as well."

She smiled at his answer, and as much as she was glad not to have to read another story, suddenly she wanted to. She wanted him to want another story. He was growing up. Something she always knew would happen.

"You okay, Mummy?" he asked, and she realised she was staring at him.

"I am now," she replied. "Sweet dreams."

Downstairs, her mother was dousing the kitchen surface with a cleaning spray and going at it with the rough side of a sponge. Whichever way she addressed it, the kitchen always looked better when her mother had cleaned it, and Charlie always ate more healthily. Jackie stepped over to her, wrapped her arms around her, and rested her head on her mother's shoulder.

"Thank you, Mum," she said.

"Oh, you don't have to thank me, dear," her mother assured

her.

"I know. I just wanted to. I love you. You do know that, don't you?"

"Is this your way of telling me you need to pop to the office?"

"No. Can't I just tell you from time to time?"

"You can tell me as often as you like, but I'll see through it every time," her mother said.

"I love you, Mum. I just want you to know I appreciate what you do."

"So you don't need to go to the office?"

"Well, I do need to pop out and see someone–"

"Right," her mother said, pulling away and dousing the surface again, in case a microscopic particle had survived the first dousing. "Go on, then."

"I didn't hug you to get you to stay."

"I know."

"I'll be quick."

"You'll have to be. I'm leaving in an hour. I've got my own house to look after, you know."

Jackie said nothing. Not until her mother had stopped scrubbing the counter top and stared at her. Then she smiled.

"Go on," she said. "The clock's ticking."

Grabbing her keys and her jacket, Jackie was in her car within a few moments and waiting for the engine to warm up. She found Ben's number and was about to hit dial when she considered what she was about to do. The difference she could make. If she pulled it off, they'd have to take her seriously. DI Bloom would be forced to recognise how valuable she was.

She locked her phone and set it down on the passenger seat, then, after a quick check in her mirrors, she was off. The streets were dark with intermittent lighting, but she didn't have to go far. Woodhall Spa was just a few miles away, and the journey was just three lanes that cut through the fields, as straight as arrows. Easy enough that her mind could wander and relive that moment over and over. Charlie telling her he loved her. Welcoming her home. It meant the world to her. It meant so much, in fact, that she had to force herself to think of the task at hand. Charlie's affection would have to take a back burner.

But the task at hand was mundane, and she soon found her mind wandering again, this time thinking about how Ben had made it possible for her to have a night away. Yes, sure, her mother would no doubt remind her of the huge favour Jackie owed her, over and over, but it had been worth it. The hotel had been one of those Travel Lodges. A cheap, clean room identical to the other thousands of cheap, clean rooms the chain of hotels offered. That had been fine. The bed had been fresh and comfortable and once she had finished with Jane Blythe's parents, she had watched a movie and slept like a log. She'd woken to find the TV still on, but that didn't matter. It was a hotel. That kind of thing was allowed. It was expected, almost. As was the mess she'd made by the little kettle. The sachets of coffee never seemed to all go into the mug. But again, that didn't matter.

The sleep had been glorious, and to top it off, she had arrived back in to Lincolnshire in style – swerving her car off the road to block Daniel Blythe's escape. They'd be talking about that for weeks at the station. And combined with what she was about to do, her name would be on everybody's lips, including DCI Granger's. If they had employee of the month, like they did in the supermarkets, then this month would be hers. People would walk into the station and see her face on the wall, with a plaque below stating her reputation. It would, of course, be beside the posters on drink driving, drug abuse, and signs your child is suffering from bullying, but that was okay. It was a step.

The Butcher house was situated on a quiet street on the far side of Woodhall Spa, and in the late evening, the street was quiet.

Popping open the door, Jackie climbed out and glanced up and down the road. There was nobody about.

The doorbell rang inside the house. Following a few seconds of silence, Jackie used the brass knocker – three heavy raps, just like Ben did. Finally, a light came on at the top of the stairs, and a man appeared behind the frosted glass.

"Who is it?" he asked, his voice groggy from being awoken.

"DC Gold," Jackie replied. "I'm with Lincoln Police. Can you open the door, please?"

The door opened to reveal Mr Butcher in his dressing gown. He frowned and cast his eye over Jackie, squinting against her car headlights that washed over the street.

"What the bloody hell–"

"Mr Butcher, is your wife home? I need to speak to her urgently."

"Cheryl? No, she–"

He didn't seem to know exactly where she was.

"Do you know where?"

"She had..." Still dazed from sleep, Mr Butcher tried to string a sentence together. "She got a text. Said she had to go out. She does it all the time. It's that boss of hers. Doctor Harris. Works her to the bone, he does. What's all this about?"

"She's meeting Doctor Harris? Do you know where she's gone?"

"The surgery, probably. They've been working on a project. Compliance or something. I don't know. What's this about anyway?"

Turning back to the driveway, Jackie noted Cheryl's car was missing. And despite her hopes of making a difference, of bringing in crucial evidence, Jackie was forced to make a decision.

"Thank you, Mr Butcher," she said. "I'm sorry to have bothered you."

"Eh?" he complained. "Aren't you going to tell me what this is about? Bleeding woke me up, you did."

Without issuing a response, she walked to the end of the driveway, retrieved her phone, and dialled Ben's number.

CHAPTER THIRTY-EIGHT

"Jackie?" Ben said, over the Bluetooth system in his car. He signalled to Freya that they should hear what she had to say. "Are you okay?"

"Where are you, Ben? I think I've made a mistake."

"I'm about to go into Harris' house. We've pieced it together."

"You what?" Jackie said, sounding disappointed.

"Daniel Blythe was in another relationship," Ben explained, as he pulled up on the road outside the huge, detached house. The property was impressive, even when only the up lights lit the front. A pale light shone from the bonnet of Harris' Jaguar, and the stripes on his lawn could just be made out.

"With who?"

"Tom Hendry."

"What? No?"

"Yep. And guess where they used to meet."

"Not the forest?"

"Got it in one. Seems like the forest wasn't just Jane's favourite place. Tom Hendry seems to enjoy it there too."

"I don't get it. Why was she there then?"

"She followed him. Caught them in the act, as it were. I spoke to Hendry. He said she used to go there often. They knew she was there somewhere, hiding in the bushes."

"But what does that have to do with Harris?"

"We think she saw something she shouldn't have. Something Doctor Harris would rather keep quiet, if you know what I mean."

"An affair," Jackie said.

"Yes. Seems like the forest is the place to go if you're into all that."

"With Cheryl Butcher?"

"Maybe," Ben said, but before he could embellish his answer, Jackie continued.

"Definitely," she said. "I'm outside her house."

"You're what?"

"I saw her, Ben. I had to take Charlie back. You know, for his bronchiolitis? She was acting weird. Hunting through filing cabinets for something."

"So why are you there?"

"I don't know. A hunch, I guess. I was going to ask her if she was okay. I was going to tell her she looked like she was under pressure, and, well, ask her if it was to do with us finding Jane Blythe, and if she needed any support."

"And what did she have to say?" Freya asked, speaking up for the first time. "Sorry Jackie, it's me, Freya. I'm with Ben. What did Cheryl Butcher have to say for herself?"

"That's just it, ma'am," Jackie replied. "She wasn't there. I spoke to her husband. He said she'd been called into work."

"Work? You mean the surgery?"

"That's what he said."

"No prizes for guessing why. Okay. His car is still here. Head to the surgery. Call me when you're there," Ben said.

"Gold?" Freya said, before the call was ended.

"Ma'am?" Jackie replied.

"Call Priest. Have him send somebody to go in with you. I don't want you going in alone. Is that clear?"

"Yes, ma'am," Jackie replied, and the call ended.

CHAPTER THIRTY-NINE

The music was soft and light and rhythmic, yet a sinister atmosphere was carried on the building intro of Vivaldi's Winter. The ground floor was dark, save for a single lamp that burned and the flickering orange hues from the wood burner.

A trio of strings led the masterpiece into full flow. Freya and Ben were motionless at the foot of the few steps that led up to the front door.

Freya pictured the scene in the house. The music was Harris' choice, of that she was certain. He had arrived home, perhaps anticipating his evening with Cheryl Butcher. The ground floor would be void of life. It was his time. His disabled wife would be upstairs in a space that had been designed for her needs, leaving him alone to think about his sordid night ahead. She imagined him pouring a drink. A brandy perhaps? From a crystal decanter. The man had taste. That, she couldn't deny him. He would be staring through the window, enjoying the light of the moon on his trees. The music would calm his nerves.

This was his time.

"What are you thinking?" Ben asked, his voice a whisper in the night.

"This is his time to be master. To enjoy the fruits of his labour," she replied, then looked up at him, admiring the moonlight on one side of his perfectly imperfect face. "Because all other times, he isn't the master."

Vivaldi's Winter developed into its racing conclusion, and her thoughts kept pace with the strings and horns.

"He isn't the master. He is the slave. She is the master," she said, as if she was somehow reaffirming her thoughts aloud. She glanced at the stairs then back at Ben. "That's why he does what he does."

"You mean, it isn't just sex he gets elsewhere?" Ben asked.

"No. It's a chance for him to be in charge. To dominate," Freya replied.

She took a step forward onto the first of the few steps.

"Are we sure about this?" Ben asked. "We can't prove anything. We've still got nothing on him."

Turning back, she found Ben's face masked in total shadow. Only the moisture in his eyes shone.

"You don't have to come in, Ben. I'll understand if you don't. You have a career and–"

"Oh, shut up, Freya. We're here. We just need to be certain."

To that, she laughed. It was loud in the night, followed by an inevitable silence.

"Nothing is certain in this life, Ben," she said, and she climbed the remaining steps.

The front door was unlocked. She pushed it open and waited in the doorway, greeted only by the building crescendo of Vivaldi's Spring. The light of the single floor lamp was joined by the orange hues that emanated from the fireplace. The heat from the fire had yet to reach the spot where Freya stood, but an old, leather armchair before it was crowned with the top of Harris' head. He hadn't been standing at the window as she had imagined him; he had been savouring the heat of the flame. She took a step inside, mindful of her heels on the wooden floor, and caught sight of the tumbler of brandy on a small coffee table beside him.

He was still, and hadn't yet heard or felt presence. Venturing forward, Freya moved into the heat.

"It's over, Michael," she said, announcing herself. She moved forward, taking a wide arc around until she could see the side of his face. He stared at the fire. Tears glistened on his cheeks and his eyes were glazed. "We know about you and Cheryl. We know Jane saw you."

Harris didn't move and uttered not a sound. With his arms relaxed on the plush leather arms, his expression was one of calm regret.

Taking one step closer, then another, Freya stood in front of the fire. That was when she saw it. A blue file resting on the hot embers. It had been placed there just moments ago. A page had slipped from inside and was curling with the heat, yet to be consumed. A series of photos. Baby scans.

"Your wife, Michael. Is she upstairs? She'll be cared for. There are places for a woman like her," said Freya, her tone soft.

But still, the doctor didn't move or react in any way.

She took a step forward and touched his shoulder. He was warm, but offered no resistance, save for his head, which fell limp to one side and caused his body to slump, revealing the fatal wound in his neck.

"Ben?" she called softly and without urgency.

He entered the room and stared across at her, like he knew what she had found. She shook her head to indicate it was over for Harris. In five large strides, Ben came to Harris' side and dropped to a crouch.

"Who did this?"

Freya glanced once at the fire. "Jane Blythe's medical records," she said.

"The baby was his?"

Freya shook her head. "No. The baby was Daniel Blythe's. Of

that I'm certain. A last ditch attempt at fixing their marriage, maybe?"

"What's this?" Ben asked, unfurling Harris' limp fingers. "His phone."

Watching him open the phone and browse the messages, Freya knew what he would find.

"He's messaged Cheryl. He's told her to meet him. But it doesn't say where."

Just then, the sound of the Harris' car roaring into life cut through the silence. Bright headlights lit the driveway. They ran to the front door in time to see the car tearing up the driveway, gravel spraying across the lawn.

"Who was that?" Ben asked, just as the sound of splashing water came from upstairs.

He stared at her, wide-eyed, uncertain. Everything had changed in that single moment.

"Harris didn't send that message. Warn Jackie," she said, glancing at the staircase. "And get an ambulance here."

———

Like the space downstairs, the upstairs was open-plan. Designed with wheelchair access in mind, the entire floor was a single suite comprising everything a disabled person might need, including the little elevator beside the staircase. The floor was solid wood and the furniture was sparse yet expensive. There was just one door, which was ajar, and the light inside revealed a bright white, tiled floor. A gentle splashing sound came from inside and Freya placed the scent of lavender.

Moving forward, slowly and very aware that she was both alone and uninvited, Freya moved toward the door. Peering through the gap, she saw a white marble counter top and two wash basins side by side. His and hers. The mirror above them was partially steamed, but the vague shape of what waited inside was just about discernible.

She pushed the door a little further, expecting a squeak of hinges, or a squeal of fright.

But nothing came.

She pushed a little further and stepped inside.

Beneath a large window, with heavy, cream drapes fashioned to form an archway, was a free-standing bath. Its brass feet were claw-shaped and the taps were ornate, mimicking a classic design. The bath was nearly full and a thick layer of bubbles threatened to overflow and wet the floor, on which an empty wheelchair was waiting.

Mrs Harris was lying inside, her bare arms outstretched along the flanks of the tub.

"Is that you?" she said without looking. "Can't I have five minutes of peace?"

Freya said nothing. She took a step closer and her heel clicked on the tiled floor. The lady in the bath said nothing. Nor did she move. Yet something in the air altered. Recognition.

"I expect you'll want me to get out," Mrs Harris said with a slurred voice. "I'm afraid that won't be possible."

"Your husband is dead," said Freya, expecting the sound of her voice to startle the woman.

But she wasn't startled. She barely reacted at all, save to glance up in Freya's direction, and, in a cold and chilling tone with only a hint of sadness, she muttered, "I know, Detective Inspector Bloom."

"You nearly got away with it, Mrs Harris."

"Beatrice, please," she said, and her soapy hand slipped into the water causing a splash. "I always hated the name Harris."

"How do you live with yourself?"

"How do you think you would cope? Confined to a chair all day every day?"

"I can't say. I think I'd be more concerned with the guilt."

"What would you know about guilt?"

"You're right. What would I know? All I have are my thoughts and theories."

"Your theories?" She sneered like an old drunk.

"You killed Jane Blythe, Mrs Harris. I think you were jealous and angry. I think you drove your husband to get his kicks elsewhere."

"My husband was a sick—"

"Do you want to know what I think happened the night Jane Blythe died?"

"Do I have a choice?"

"No," Freya replied. "I think your husband left to meet Cheryl Butcher. I believe you found his phone and saw the message from Jane Blythe. You went to the forest, where you knew he would be. You waited for her. I think you waited in the forest for her to arrive, then, like a coward, you hit her with the first thing you found."

She didn't argue and she didn't agree. Instead, she stared at the little table beside the bath. There was a glass of water and a book. And lying on its side on the polished wood was a pill bottle. It was empty. Beatrice Harris smiled up at her weakly.

"You coward," said Freya, and she reached for the bottle. A handful of pills remained, but not many.

"They say it's like slipping into a hot bath." Laughing at her own joke, the old woman sank further into the bath until the water touched her chin.

"Don't you dare think you're getting away with this."

"It's too late," she slurred. "What's done is done."

Moving behind the woman, Freya held her beneath her arms, keeping her face from slipping into the water.

There was no fight left in the woman. Her body was too weak to resist.

"Get off me," she slurred.

"I'm right, aren't I? It was too much for you, wasn't it? Your mind couldn't handle what you had done. That's when you suffered a stroke. It happened shortly after you killed Jane Blythe." Freya pulled her up further. "Don't you die and leave that poor girl's memory hanging."

It was over and she knew it. Mrs Harris' expression dropped into one of acceptance, and she smiled as best she could.

"Talk to me, or I'll make damn sure the world knows what you did."

"It happened in the forest. Right there beside Jane." She spoke as if it was all a dream. Then she laughed, but it wasn't really a laugh, more of a breath. "She was screaming. She was weak. She fell to the ground beside me. I remember that much. But it was just noise. It was like I wasn't really there. There wasn't any pain. Not for me. Just an immobility. I'm one of the lucky ones, they say. I can still use my arms and talk. But I'm not lucky. None of us are, really."

She slipped away again, her voice fading with her life.

"Talk to me, Beatrice," Freya called, but she was losing her grip on the old woman's loose skin. "I need to know about Jane. Don't you leave me—"

"It was a bright evening. Surreal, I guess some would call it. She fell to the ground beside me. I heard her crying. I heard the little slut scream. I wanted to reach out to her. To finish it. I couldn't, of course. She dragged herself away. I never saw her again. I thought it was over. But of course, deep down I knew it never would be. Not until now, that is."

The sound of the dying woman's cackle was a sound that Freya was sure she would never forget.

"Talk to me, Beatrice. Don't you die on me."

But Beatrice Harris didn't respond. Her heavy eyes were closed and her body hung limp in Freya's arms.

CHAPTER FORTY

"She what?" said Ben, holding the phone to his ear and covering his other to hear her over the chaos inside the bathroom. Freya stared at him as the paramedics took over from her resuscitation efforts. He mouthed Jackie's name and returned his attention to the call.

"She's not here," Jackie said, her voice muffled by the wind. "I've got uniform here now. The surgery is locked, and there's no sign of Cheryl. The husband said Cheryl got a text message. He said she'd be here."

"She's not going there," Ben said. "She's going to the forest."

"The forest? But why?"

"I'll explain later," Ben said. "Call Chapman have her set up an ANPR alert for Harris' Jaguar just in case. And we might need another ambulance."

Freya tapped his arm and gestured she wanted to hear.

"Another ambulance?" said Jackie. "Ben, for crying out loud, what's happening?"

"Harris is dead," he said, putting the call on loudspeaker so that Freya could listen in.

"Dead?" she replied. "Doctor Harris, you mean?"

"His throat was slit," Ben said.

Jackie was silent for moment, and when she spoke, it was with a heavy heart.

"His wife? Was it his wife?"

"I don't think so, Jackie. His wife attempted suicide shortly after."

"Oh my god. Is she—"

"Alive?" Ben finished for her. "The paramedics are working on her as we speak."

"That leaves just one person," Freya said, causing both Ben and Jackie to wait for an explanation.

"Who?" Ben asked.

"Jackie, Doctor Harris was your doctor. Is that right?" Freya called out.

"Well, yes, but—"

"Think back to when you were in his office. His desk. There was a photo in a wooden frame."

"Right?" Jackie said, slowly, trying her hardest to follow. "Yeah. It was on his desk. He was a family man."

"Who was in the photo?"

"Who was in it?" Jackie replied, buying time to think. "Erm, Doctor Harris, of course, and his family. That must have been before the accident though. They were at some kind of event."

"A charity fundraiser. For his own charity," Freya explained to Ben. "Who else?"

"Jane Blythe was there. Her and Cheryl, in fact. They were standing beside each other."

"Our killer is in that photo," Freya said. "Somebody none of us have even considered."

"Cheryl Butcher?" Jackie said, just like Freya knew she would. "You don't think—"

"Jackie, get everyone to the forest. As many uniforms as you can," she said, and looked across at Ben. "We'll meet you there."

Leaving the paramedics to work, Ben and Freya put uniforms in charge of the house and told them to wait for CSI, and they were now speeding toward the forest in Ben's Ford. Ben's imagination ran amok, trying to piece together the motives of everyone involved.

"I told you it wasn't Harris," Ben said. "And the worst part is, Granger did too."

"He's not as innocent as you make out."

"He's not the bloody killer, Freya," Ben spat.

"It's always the quiet ones," Freya said, and she smiled at Ben, who hadn't been at the surgery to see the photo on Harris' desk. "Contrary to belief, Jane Blythe was not sleeping with Michael Harris."

"You're changing tack," Ben said, but Freya ignored his comment and continued her summary. "Are you going to tell me what's going on in your head?"

"Michael Harris was accused of sleeping with Fiona Grey when, in fact, all he did was help her out. He helped her escape a violent relationship. Helped her start over."

"You think Jane texted him for help?" Ben asked. "When she left Daniel that night, you think she texted him for some money or something?"

"She had nowhere else to turn," Freya replied. "He was all she had. The forest was the middle ground. Somewhere she could tell him what had happened without fear of somebody seeing."

"But Beatrice Harris intercepted the call," Ben said, seeing where Freya was heading.

"She saw everything. I think she went there to see Jane, in just the same way Jane had been there to see Tom and Daniel. Nothing more."

"But she didn't kill her?"

"I think she saw Jane's killer and she's protecting her. She told me she was already on the ground when Jane landed beside her. She knew who killed Jane. And she knew we were getting close. Beatrice Harris is not the type of woman to go down without a fight. And if she does go down, it'll be on her terms."

"Hence the suicide."

Ben slowed the car and turned onto the track that led to the forest. The moon still lit the fields, and the stars were visible in abundance. But the forest was an impenetrable mass of darkness.

"Looks like a Jane Blythe painting, doesn't it?" said Ben, but the quip was met with a deep sigh and a tired look from Freya. "How do you want to play this? We can park up and go in quietly, or we can try a less subtle approach."

"Let's walk in," Freya said. "I'd like to see how things play out."

Dropping the car down into second gear, Ben guided them around a long bend and accelerated on the long straight. A trail of mud flew from the rear wheels and the underside of the car came under a barrage of stones and rocks. It was only when they were a hundred yards from the forest that Ben eased off and coasted towards the gap between the trees.

"This is far enough," said Freya, peering across to Ben. "Stop the car."

The door was open before Ben had stopped, and Freya leaped out, glancing up the track, peering into the gloom. The track was well lit by the moon, though there were parts of the forest that even the brightest moonlight could not reach. Looking back at Ben, she hissed, "There's nobody here."

Through the windscreen, Ben searched the forest for movement, but saw nothing. He climbed out, easing his door closed so as not to break the deadly silence.

Freya stared at him, as if questioning her own theories and conclusions, doubt written all over her face. Entering the forest was like walking into another world. Surreal and peaceful. Private and secluded.

Two hundred yards away, a pair of headlights shone in the gloom.

"That's the Jaguar," Ben said confidently.

"Then we might be too late," Freya replied.

They walked on, keeping to the sides of the track, out of the moonlight where possible, closing the distance on the parked car just as Jane would have done to spy on her husband's affair.

Then came the sound of a footstep on gravel and Freya stared wide-eyed at Ben, her doubt quenched. She turned as somebody stepped from the trees and out into the middle of the track some twenty metres from Freya. The shape stopped in the bright head-lights, as though on some kind of stage. Then she waved once at the car, and the driver flashed the lights once in response.

"Cheryl?" Freya called. "Cheryl, stay where you are."

Surprised by the voice, Cheryl stopped, spun around, and glared into the shadows.

"Who's there?" Cheryl called back, and she glanced behind her like she was checking nobody was sneaking up on her. "What do you want?"

"I want to talk about the evening Jane died," Freya said, as she too stepped out of the shadows into the beams of the headlights. Their shadows seemed to stretch on and on, thin and tall.

Cheryl stiffened at the mere mention of Jane's name.

"I don't know anything," she said, holding the collars of her blouse together. "I don't know what you're talking about."

"Then why are you here?"

A guilty expression washed over her face. "It's not what you think. I–"

"Here's what I think," Freya continued. "I think Jane Blythe and her husband split up. She left the house and had nobody to turn to except Doctor Harris. Am I right, Cheryl?"

Cheryl said nothing but took a step backward, putting distance between them.

"I think the text message was intercepted by his wife. I think it was Beatrice who came to meet Jane that night."

A tear rolled down Cheryl's cheek. But she did nothing to stop it or wipe it away.

"But Beatrice Harris suffered a stroke, didn't she, Cheryl?"

Cheryl shrugged, shaking her head from side to side.

"That's where things get a bit hazy. Maybe you can help me out?"

"Me?"

"You were here, Cheryl, weren't you?" Freya said. "That night."

As if in complete resignation, Cheryl simply stared at her. The truth was out.

"I came to finish it," she muttered, with a glance back over her shoulder at the waiting Jaguar. "I came to end it. I couldn't live with the lies."

"The truth had to come out some time," Freya said, taking another step closer.

"It wasn't Michael," Cheryl muttered. "He's a good man."

"That's not Michael Harris in the car, Cheryl."

"It's what?" Cheryl replied, with another of the furtive glances over her shoulder, as if she was checking the car was still there.

"He's dead," Freya called out. "Michael Harris is dead."

"No," Cheryl exclaimed, her jaw hanging free. Her eyes widened and she battled with the idea. "Dead?"

Her voice was drowned out by the sound of Michael Harris' Jaguar roaring into life, and Cheryl turned just as the car launched from where it lurked and bore down on her.

Mud sprayed from the back of the roaring Jag as its tyres sought solid ground. A cloud of exhaust fumes rolled across the scene like a winter fog, and as the car began to move, its rear wheels leaving fresh soil in its wake, it was clear to Freya what the driver had in mind.

It was a split-second decision based on instinct alone. The front end of the Jaguar rose, driven by torque. Wide-eyed and frozen with shock, Cheryl Butcher looked back over her shoulder to find the car gaining speed along the narrow track.

With no time to consider alternative options, Freya dived at the woman, driving her shoulder into Cheryl's side and pushing with everything her legs could give. The pair landed in the debris-covered forest floor at the edge of the brambles that, only a year before, Jane Blythe had crawled under to die.

Glass shattered and steel twisted as the Jaguar ploughed into a tree, the driver wedged into the wreckage with their foot planted on the accelerator.

Beneath Freya, Cheryl Butcher was clearly bewildered and overcome. She scrambled backwards away from Freya, backing onto the track to get away.

"What the bloody hell is going on?" she screamed at Freya, then looked up at the crashed Jaguar. "Michael? Michael, what are you doing? Are you okay?"

Ben had sped over and now tugged at the Jaguar driver's door handle, shouting for the driver to open it. "Open the door," he screamed, pounding on the glass with little effect.

Except for the engine, which quietened.

The reverse lights flicked on, and as Cheryl squinted to peer through the rear window at the driver, the engine revved once more. The ruined car lurched into life and drove back onto the track. But it didn't stop. In fact, to Freya's horror, once the car had straightened, it began to accelerate in reverse. This time, Freya's reactions were too slow. She tried to dive for cover. But there was no telling which direction the wayward vehicle was going to turn.

It came straight for her, and all she could do was peer up at Ben, who in the chaos screamed for her to move.

She rolled onto the low boot, raising her legs into the air, then smashed into the rear windscreen, from which she was launched into the brush. She didn't fly through the air like the movies portray. Instead, she was hurtled into the forest like a bullet. She landed in a heap, her entire right hand side numb with pain. The car powered on, now out of control, and came to a hard stop at the base of an old oak tree. Freya watched, drunk with agony and semi-conscious, as the engine fluttered to a stall. Then, like a dying breath, it gave off a final hiss of steam.

CHAPTER FORTY-ONE

Ben watched with horror as Freya was hurtled into the forest. He ran to her side, skidding to a halt beside her.

"Freya?" he yelled. "Freya, talk to me."

She groaned and clutched her ribs. Feeling all around her body, Ben found no sharp fragments of bone protruding from her torso or her legs, and there was no blood on his hands. She was dazed, but conscious.

"Ben?" she whispered. "Ben, it's not her. It's not Cheryl."

"What do you mean?"

"Help me up."

"No, Freya, stay there."

"Ben, help me stand, damn it. I'm okay. I'm just bruised."

But it was too late. There was a muffled scream from behind Ben, followed by the sound of feet scrambling across the track.

"Don't move," a voice called out. It was a new voice. One that Ben hadn't heard before, but one he wouldn't forget for a long time. "Your car keys. Throw them to me."

"You knew?" Ben whispered to Freya.

"I had an idea," Freya whispered sheepishly, but none of it was making sense. "Help me up."

"I said give me your car keys."

With his arm around Freya, Ben heaved her up to her feet then held her for balance. Turning to face the track, he found the driver's door of the Jaguar open and a young woman with her arm around Cheryl's neck, hand covering her mouth. In her free hand, she held a kitchen knife to Cheryl's throat.

"You're the carer," Ben said, confused but recognising her from the photo in Michael Harris' report.

"Not just the carer, Ben," Freya said. "This is Michael Harris' daughter."

"Daughter?" he repeated, and looked between them. "But you said she left. You said she'd run away–"

"I'm right, aren't I, Rita?" Freya said, her eyes never leaving the woman with the knife.

The girl stiffened at the words, like Freya had touched a nerve.

"Somebody none of us even thought about," Freya continued. "And why would we? You're just the carer, right? Rita Harris left Woodhall Spa a year ago. When her mother suffered her stroke. In fact, when Cheryl here told me about the tragic accident, she told me the stroke was because you ran away. But that was a lie, wasn't it, Cheryl?"

Cheryl struggled a little, but her weak attempts were stilled with a hushed threat from Rita Harris.

"Rita, it's over. You don't have to do this," Freya said. "We know you killed Jane Blythe. This place will be surrounded in a few minutes. It's over."

"You know nothing," she spat, tightening her grip on Cheryl and repositioning the blade against her throat. "It's gone on too long for me to give up now. I've had to bloody hide for a year. A year out of my life. All because of that little layabout."

"At least you have a life," Freya said. "At least you're still breathing. Unlike Jane Blythe. Tell me what happened, Rita. Tell me how it played out. Tell me how you came to hit Jane with a rock."

"I'm not telling you anything."

"Well then, I'll tell you, shall I?" Freya said, her top lip curling into a look of disgust. Ben felt her body tense beside him, and heard the tone of her voice deepen, as if she spoke from the very pit of her stomach. It was the closest Ben had seen to Freya losing her temper, and he held her no longer just for her own safety, but for that of Rita Harris' too.

She took a deep breath and eased her bruised leg into a more comfortable position, grimacing as she did so.

"Your mother intercepted the message from Jane, didn't she?" Freya said. "Or was it you? Was it really you who found your father's phone and read the text message? What did it say, Rita?"

The woman with the knife sneered at Freya's tone.

"It said, I need to see you. You know where. Please."

"Ah," Freya said. The aggression dropped from her tone and she adopted that calm and casual, all-seeing tone that Ben had come to adore. "And in your mistrusting mind, you thought that was Jane arranging a secret rendezvous with your father. You read it. You showed your mother. And you convinced her to go and put a stop to it. You knew he was having an affair. You knew he'd been cheating for years. And now was your chance to stop him. Now was your chance to make everything okay."

"You bitch."

"So you came to the forest. You knew that was where your father met his lover. You knew because you accused Fiona Grey of the exact same thing. In fact, you've been trying to catch your father at it for years. You saw what it was doing to your mother, didn't you? You saw the anguish she went through, even before her stroke. And you were her rock. Who else could she turn to, with an upstanding member of society as a husband? Who else could she confide in, but you?"

Rita said nothing, only sneered back at Freya, a sign she was striking a few chords.

"It was killing her. The not knowing. The threat of an affair.

The threat of her life coming tumbling down around her. It was killing her. Wasn't it, Rita? Answer me, damn it."

"Yes," she said, suddenly, like an explosion of frustration. "Yes, it was."

Freya bit her lower lip, restraining a torrent of verbal abuse that threatened to break loose.

"And do you want to know the funny part?" Freya said, when she had restrained the words that conveyed how she truly felt. "You got it wrong twice. The girl your father has been sleeping with all these years is right there. You've got a knife to her throat."

Cheryl gave a scream, which was soon quenched by Rita pressing the blade harder against her skin.

"Your mother came here in search of Jane Blythe. But you waited in the car. Your mother wanted to have it out with Jane, woman to woman. Face to face."

Rita's silence spoke volumes, and panic began to set in. She shuffled nervously, adjusting her grip on the knife.

"Tell me I'm right, Rita. Tell me I'm right," Freya urged her. "They spoke, didn't they? Maybe they argued. But your mother didn't strike her, did she? No. No, that was you. The moment you saw your mother fall to the ground, you saw red."

"I didn't mean to," Rita snapped. "I thought she'd hit my mother. What would you have done?"

"The same, maybe?" Freya said calmly. "Perhaps worse. But we're not talking about me. We're talking about you. We're talking about you hitting her. Jane fell down beside your mother. They were face to face for a while. Until she crawled off. Fight or flight, they call it. Adrenalin takes over," Freya explained, gesturing carelessly with her free hand while the other gripped Ben's shoulder. "She crawled into the shadows to die, and you let her. After all, you had your poor mother to tend to."

"So?" Rita yelled. "So what? You worked it out. Good for you. But what's the point you're trying to make?"

"Oh, I'm not trying to make a point. I just like to reiterate the facts. It's kind of like gloating, but not really. Gloating to myself doesn't count. It just reaffirms I was right. It reinstates my confidence, because, trust me, I nearly gave up. I was this close," she said, holding her finger and thumb half an inch apart. "But I knew your father had something to do with Jane's death."

She leaned away from Ben, closer to Rita and Cheryl, and did a little stage whispering for effect.

"You nearly won, Rita. You nearly got away."

She winked to complete her act, and Rita's top lip drew back as she prepared to launch into a scathing tirade.

"How are you so sure?" she spat, to which Freya smiled her best winning smile.

"Oh, the cherry on the cake, you mean? When I'd worked out who you were, there was one thing that didn't quite make sense."

"Go on," Rita encouraged her.

"Look at you. You're five foot five and built like a ballerina, no doubt a result of your father's lifelong health advice. But there's no way you could have carried your mother to the car and loaded her in the back. Not on your own. No, you needed help. Luckily, help was to hand, wasn't it, Cheryl?"

Cheryl tried to speak but the blade was digging into her throat. A tiny bead of blood had been drawn already. A little more pressure and the skin would be torn.

"Let her speak," Freya said. "I want to hear it from her."

Cautiously, Rita glanced back to the forest entrance. Three or more police cars had stopped by Ben's car, and behind them, an ambulance waited.

Ben held his hand up, signalling that they should stay where they are, and Rita relaxed her grip on the blade.

"You saw it all, didn't you, Cheryl?" Freya said, pointing further up the track to where Rita had been waiting in her father's Jaguar. "You were parked up there, no doubt making love to Michael on the backseat of his car."

"We weren't," Cheryl said, her voice croaky and hoarse. She glanced fearfully at Rita, who still clutched the back of her neck. "We hadn't. Not that time, at least."

It was then that two things happened. Freya let go of Ben's shoulder, a signal for him to move. And Rita, enraged by Cheryl's admission, drew her arm back, preparing to lunge.

Freya hit the deck at the same time as the full force of Ben's weight collided with Rita in a rugby tackle, tearing Rita's grip from Cheryl. His hand groped for hers to bring the knife under control, and he pinned her wrist to the ground, avoiding the knee she aimed at his groin, and her free hand, which clawed at his face. Twice he slammed her hand into the ground to no effect, but on the third time, with all his weight behind him, the knife fell from her grip, and he tossed it away before forcing her onto her front and holding her down with his knee.

Cheryl Butcher staggered back and nearly fell to the ground. She stood there shaking, not knowing if she should run or drop to the ground as well.

With the knife well and truly out of harm's way, Ben tugged Rita's hands behind her back, cuffed her, and left her face down in the dirt. Then he rushed back to Freya's side, helping her to her feet once more.

"Rita Harris," said Freya. "I'm arresting you on suspicion of murdering Jane Blythe and Michael Harris. You do not have to say anything, but it may harm your defence if you do not mention when questioned something you later rely on in court. Anything you do say may be given in evidence."

As if she had spent her energy reserve, Rita Harris let her head drop to the muddy track in resignation. With the aid of Ben's shoulder, Freya hobbled over to her. If her body would have allowed it, she would have crouched, if only to get a glimpse of her victory. But as it happens, her body would not allow it. Her entire right side felt battered and bruised. So she said what she had to say from high above.

"You're going to prison for a very long time, Rita. But before you go, there's something I want to tell you. A week ago, I was in a very different place. Mentally. I had a memory problem. Long story," she said with a dismissive wave of her hands. "Anyway, if it wasn't for you, I'd still have those problems. I'd still be harbouring all that negative energy. All the hate that was building up inside me. It's all gone. I've got you to thank for that."

Freya waited a few seconds for her message to sink in, and Rita rolled onto her side to stare up at her.

"Thank you, Rita," Freya said, gesturing to Ben that they should make their way out of the forest and let uniform take over. She called back over shoulder, "It's just a shame Jane Blythe had to die in the process. I would have liked to meet her."

CHAPTER FORTY-TWO

On the eastern edge of Lincoln city, in the *Accident and Emergency* waiting room of the hospital, Freya sat with her head in her good hand, her other arm in a sling provided by the paramedics. The night's events played out. Her ideas of who and why had been way off. Doubt crept into her mind like a shadow, so that any reasoning with her own mind was void of evidence.

It was his aftershave that she smelled first. It was the type a man might receive as a gift from a wife, thereafter, becoming his scent, marking him as taken, or unobtainable into middle age and beyond. He sat beside her, well-mannered enough to leave an empty seat between them.

The home screen of Freya's mobile phone displayed two missed calls from an unknown number. Remembering that she had asked the paramedic to call her if Beatrice Harris passed away, Freya sneered inwardly before pocketing the phone. A silent invitation for him to commence.

"How are you doing?" he asked, his tone more genuine and empathetic than Freya bid him due.

She sat back but didn't look his way. Letting her hand fall to her lap, she glanced at her near-broken body then studied the empty room, choosing a distraction rather than the truth.

"In London, this place would be full on a Thursday night. Drunks, kids, mothers, and all manner of reprobates."

"Reprobates? You mean, the general public?"

"Some of them," she replied.

"I never asked you if you miss it? London? The buzz and the pace of life."

"Is this the precursor to you sending me back there?"

"You missed your deadline."

"My deadline? Guv, I–"

"I asked you to seek help, Freya. I asked you politely. You ignored me. I gave you formal notice, and you ignored that too. I asked for a confirmed appointment with a therapist and I gave you until the end of the week to get it. It's not the end of it all, I know that. It takes more than talking to a therapist to recover from what you experienced. But talking about it is the starting point."

"I remembered, Will. I remembered the night–"

"So? What does that even mean? I'm not trying to be a bastard here. Honestly, I think you're a great detective. But you're a loose cannon. What happens if something serious occurs as a result of your mindset? Where would I stand? Negligence. That's where I'd stand."

"Nothing is going to happen as a result of my mind."

"Ben told me you jumped in front of a moving vehicle this evening."

"To stop Cheryl Butcher being run down."

"What the bloody hell do you think this is? The wild west? Where do I go from here? You can't tell me I haven't been fair."

He was right and Freya knew it.

"I'll be writing my recommendation to terminate the secondment tomorrow morning. If you can make an appointment before then, let's talk. Otherwise, I expect a full report of the Blythe investigation before midday. CPS are scheduled to arrive at two p.m. The least you can do is arm Ben with the facts."

"Will you make him DI when I go?"

"Probably. He deserves it, don't you think?"

Nodding, she smiled at the thought of DI Ben Savage.

"That softens the blow a little," she said.

"You two have become quite close."

"It's a professional relationship."

"I wasn't suggesting otherwise. But it's noticeable. I used to be close to David."

"Ah. The legendary, DI Foster. My predecessor."

"Yes. We worked well together. I think you know when you have a bond. I know Ben thinks a lot of you."

"Hopefully I left my mark on him."

"And the team," said Granger. "Ben told me a while ago that you're a leader. In some ways more so than David was, and more than I ever could be. I hope you manage to channel that into yourself. If anybody needs a leader right now, it's you, Freya."

"Understood, guv," was all Freya could say. Arguing was pointless, and she lacked the energy for any kind of debate. But more so, she agreed with him.

"You said you remembered what happened."

She nodded.

"Strike while the memory is warm. Go and see somebody. I'm sure London is full of people who can help. You have to get over this. I offered you a chance, but like I said–"

"Understood, guv," she said again, choosing to cut him off rather than be lectured all over again.

"It's not personal," he added, and leaned into her, as a father might offer his daughter encouragement. "It's business."

She nodded, and for the first time in too long, she thought about the life she had left behind. Going back to Greg and Billy was out of the question. It would be a new start, or it would be a dramatic ending.

"Will you do me a favour?" he asked.

"You're still my line manager."

"Will you debrief the team tomorrow? Shall we say ten a.m.? It would be good to attend one of your briefings one last time. I do enjoy your approach."

She gave a laugh that wasn't really a laugh. It was the laugh of defeat. Of acceptance, or worse.

"Ten a.m.?" she said, just as her phone began to ring.

Nodding in agreement, he smiled at her. "No theories this time, though, eh?"

She studied the caller ID on her phone and a glimmer of hope shone like a beacon.

"No theories," she agreed, trying her best to maintain the sombre mood. "Mind if I take this? It's CSI."

He nodded again, clearly unsure how genuine she had been. But that was of little concern right now. She hit the green button to answer the call and took a breath.

"Michaela, talk to me," she said, by way of a greeting. "I need some good news. Something to send me off with a bang."

———

"Sorry I'm late," Jackie said, letting the incident room door close behind her with an ear-splitting squeal and a slam. Many heads turned to see her. In addition to Ben, Jackie, Chapman, Freya, Granger, and Duty Sergeant Michael Priest, several uniforms had joined the debrief at Freya's request.

"It's okay," said Freya, who in Ben's opinion, despite her tired eyes, was dressed even smarter than usual. And although she stood in some discomfort, probably heavily bruised from the accident last night, her smart skirt suit was pressed and she wore heels that he hadn't seen her wearing before. Plus she had done something different to her hair. Was he the only one to know that beneath that immaculate facade was an ugly bruise that ran the length of her body?

Allowing Jackie time to take her seat under Granger's watchful gaze, Freya sipped at her water with her left hand, being careful not to smudge her lipstick. "I'm used to debriefing a room full of people," she began, and seemed to reflect on a memory while holding Ben's stare. "I'm used to working with large teams, more than a dozen people on a single case, and that's not including the wider effort." She gave Priest a nod in recognition of his team's work. "So before I start, I think I need to say what's on my mind."

"Bloom?" said Granger, but she fended him off with a slight raise of her hand.

"There's only a handful of us here. Quite possibly the smallest team I've ever worked with. But I don't think I've ever been so proud. Every single one of us pulled our weight. Every single one of you has a unique skill set, which, when combined with the rest of you, forms something quite wonderful. It's truly remarkable what a small team can do."

"This sounds like the beginning of a wedding speech," Gillespie joked from the far end of the room. Ben laughed out loud, along with all the others, but not because he found it funny. It was to hide his own sense that it was a goodbye speech more than any other reason.

"No wedding, Gillespie," Freya said. "I was raised to be grateful. That's all."

"I think the sentiment is shared, Freya," said Granger, steering the debrief back on track. "Let's get this wrapped up. CPS will be here at two p.m."

"Yeah, get on with it," DI Standing called down, seeing an opportunity to belittle her. But she paid no heed to Standing. Instead, she smiled up at him with what looked like sympathy in her eyes.

"Okay." Freya took another careful sip of water, then cleared her throat. She paused for a moment to enjoy the look on each of their faces, then began. "This may get a little complex, but bear with me. There's a neat little bow on top when we're done. On the twentieth of October, last year, Jane Blythe had her final argument with her husband, Daniel Blythe. We now know that Jane was *not* having extra-marital affairs with Michael Harris, and that was *not* the cause of the argument that ended their marriage."

"So what was the cause?" Granger asked.

"The cause of the argument was Daniel Blythe's own infidelity. He was in a relationship with Tom Hendry, the owner of the art class which Jane attended. However, Daniel Blythe is not as innocent as I thought."

"You sound like you're going to drop a bombshell, DI Bloom," Granger said. "Let's get it out there then, if you will."

"You'll remember, guv, I took a call at the hospital last night?"

Granger nodded.

"It was CSI. GPR undertaken at one of Blythe's construction projects, as requested by DS Savage, showed an anomaly in the ground. The owners of the house consented to CSI digging up their patio late last night, in which a jerry can was found, along with a pair of overalls. He finished that job the day before his wife's body was discovered."

"So," Granger said with a shrug.

"So, the overalls have been examined by CSI. They are RAF issue and covered in red diesel."

"Red what?" Standing said from the far end of the room.

"Red diesel, DI Standing," Freya said, pleased to have roused him. "We can now link these two items to the death of Andrew Summers, who you should all remember as the victim of the barn fire, and who was, until now, thought to have committed suicide."

"You what?" Standing said, the humour gone from his voice. He marched down to Freya's end of the room, his face aghast. "Andrew Summers? That's my investigation."

"That's right," Freya said. "Don't thank me. Thank Ben. He solved it for you."

Standing glared at Ben, who held his hands up in defence.

"How was I to know?"

"Daniel Blythe was stealing red diesel from the RAF. But he couldn't get rid of it. He's too easy to trace and he has too much to lose. So, he enlisted the help of Andrew Summers, a man who we all know to be well-connected."

"And the jerry can and overalls prove that, do they?" Standing growled.

"They will. I'm quite sure. If you have a look at the photographs that were found in Daniel Blythe's house, you'll find one of him with the rest of his squadron in front of a fighter jet."

"So?" Standing said, coining Granger's question in an equally aggressive tone.

"Andrew Summers is in the photo. They served together. Do the maths, Standing. You can have that one on me," Freya said. "Oh, and I suggest you talk to Michaela Fell at CSI as nicely as you can. Ask her to take a look at the remains of a little, blue hatchback in Andrew Summers' burned-out barn."

"The car. I've seen it. Why do they need to look at it? It's just an old junker."

"Because, when Tom Hendry discovered Jane Blythe's body, he did what anybody would do if you were a little embarrassed to be there, that is."

"He ran?" Ben suggested.

"Yes. But in his haste, Hendry had a little accident."

Standing gave her a quizzical look. "What are you getting at, Bloom?" he growled.

"Your hit and run. The one you haven't been able to solve yet. I just solved it for you. You're welcome," Freya said. "Again."

"What the..." Standing began, and looked at Granger for support.

But Granger shrugged once more. All he cared about was the trio of results. Who got them was of little consequence to him.

"Tom Hendry told DS Savage that he doesn't drive," Freya explained. "Yet how could he get to the forest to meet his boyfriends?"

"Maybe he has a bike?"

"With a dog?" Freya said. "Lee Charlton discovered the body while he was out supposedly walking his dog."

"Supposedly?" Granger said.

"It was an excuse to get out and meet his lover, Tom Hendry. However, I believe Tom Hendry discovered Jane Blythe's body before then. The night before, to be exact."

"Why the night before?" Cruz asked. "And why didn't he call it in then?"

Freya turned to find the young DC at the back of the room, a confused look on his face.

"Cruz, you've been working with DI Standing on the hit and run case, yes?"

"Yes, boss."

"Where did the hit and run take place?"

"Just outside Woodhall Spa," he replied, a few cogs beginning to fall into place. "About half a mile from the forest where Jane Blythe was found."

"Exactly," Freya said. "I believe Tom Hendry was so upset at finding Jane's body that he had an accident in his haste to get away."

"An accident which left a woman dead," Standing finished.

"So what does he do? He calls the only man he knows who can help him. The man who actually owns the car he drives."

"Daniel Blythe," Cruz said, smiling at the sheer beauty of all the pieces coming together.

Freya nodded, a little disappointed that she wouldn't be around long enough to bring the young DC on. He would have been a good mentoring project. "Daniel called in a favour from

Andrew Summers, who agreed to let them hide the car in his barn."

"The same barn where the diesel was being stored," Ben added, smiling at the brilliance of it.

"Exactly," Freya said.

"So, Daniel Blythe burned the car?" Cruz said. "And Andrew Summers died trying to stop his barn going up?"

"Exactly. And then Tom Hendry asked Lee Charlton to meet him the following night, knowing he would lead Charlton to the body and have him believe he discovered it. That way, Tom Hendry was in the clear," Freya said, then turned her attention to Standing. "You need to have CSI match the skid marks at the hit and run to Jane Blythe's car, but I think it's a goer. That one's on me, DI Standing, and again, you're welcome."

"We should at least get a manslaughter charge on that," said Granger. "I'll talk to CPS when they get here later, but for now, let's bring everyone in for questioning."

"That's what I call a result," said Freya. "Up until today, a family were coming to terms with the fact that their dad committed suicide. Whilst it doesn't bring Andrew Summers back, it does at least provide some closure for his wife and children. If CSI can place Tom Hendry in that car, and if the skid marks match it, the family of the hit and run victim will have some closure too."

Granger nodded his approval.

"Moving back to Jane Blythe," Freya continued. "She left the house with just a suitcase and she walked two miles to the forest where she regularly met with Doctor Michael Harris, now deceased."

She glanced up at Jackie and Chapman before moving on.

"After last night's events, I can confirm the following proceedings took place. Jane Blythe messaged Michael Harris, presumably once she had left the house. But Michael Harris was with Cheryl Butcher. It was Rita Harris who intercepted the message."

"Rita Harris?" Granger said, pulling a bemused expression.

"The daughter, guv. Rita reportedly ran away a year ago and was the cause of Mrs Harris' stroke. But that's lie. Beatrice Harris and her daughter, Rita, took it upon themselves to meet Jane. Jane Blythe arrived in the forest on foot expecting to meet Michael, and after what can only be described as an argument, Beatrice suffered her stroke. Rita thought Jane had struck her."

"So she hit Jane with a rock?" Jackie Gold asked, shaking her head. "It takes all sorts, don't it?"

"Mr and Mrs Harris then agreed to hide Rita away. They made up a story about her leaving to work abroad, and so Mrs Harris' carer was brought in. And because Jane Blythe's death was not reported, and no body was found, nobody suspected anything. Rita took on a new identity as her mother's carer. She hadn't been out of university for long, so nobody really knew her well enough to realise, certainly not in the surgery. In the photo on Harris' desk, she had long, blonde hair. But all that took was a little makeover, a haircut, and a pair of glasses. Nobody was any the wiser. The new carer, a pretty French girl who rarely spoke in public, arrived and nobody batted an eyelid."

"So how did you know it was her?" Jackie asked. "We all thought it was the husband."

"By that point, my credibility was all used up. I knew Michael Harris was part of it somehow, but I couldn't prove it. If I had pushed any harder, DCI Granger would have locked *me* up."

"True," Granger said, nodding.

"It was something that Beatrice Harris said to me, just before she died, that made me think. It raised a doubt in my mind. But one thing I did know for sure," Freya said. "On that evening, on the twentieth of October, Cheryl Butcher and Michael Harris were sitting in his car not two hundred yards away. They saw the entire thing. Cheryl Butcher was the only surviving witness to Rita Harris murdering Jane Blythe. We have Rita Harris in custody, and following the CPS interview later today, she'll be charged with a minimum of two accounts of murder and one attempted murder. If we can get her for aiding her mother's suicide, then we will. That should see Rita Harris behind bars for at least thirty years."

The applause was subtle but genuine, and not one individual directed their thanks to any singular person. It had been a team effort, and the success was astonishing.

"There is one thing," Jackie said, and the volume of chatter in the room dropped once more. "How can Rita Harris be charged for aiding suicide?"

"Because although it is no longer illegal for an individual to commit suicide, it is illegal to help, or convince another–"

"But she's not dead. She's alive. Didn't you see the reports from the hospital? Beatrice Harris is stable. She survived, ma'am."

There was a silence, during which time a multitude of expressions passed across Freya's face.

"Well, that is good news," said Freya, unconvincingly pleased. She stared at the floor like she was figuring something out. "What a nice way to end it all."

———

"Well done," said Ben, while the team chatted and the noise in the room was loud enough for them to have a quiet word.

"Like I said, Ben, it wasn't just me. You did well, you all did well," Freya said, shuffling her paperwork into one big pile for somebody else to sort out.

"You got it wrong, didn't you?"

From where he was standing, Freya was able to analyse Ben's profile. His forehead was flatter than most, and his nose was straight like a Roman's. But with his square jaw and two days of growth, Ben Savage was a particularly handsome man. He would make somebody a good husband one day, and it amazed Freya that he hadn't been snapped up already.

"Got what wrong, Ben?"

"Beatrice Harris. You thought she was dead. That was a bit of a clanger."

"It was a mistake. I've been making lots of them lately, some too blatant to hide. It's just..." She paused and scratched at her forehead with a fingernail that was in dire need of some attention. The thought distracted her for a moment, an all-too-often occurrence for her liking. "Do you remember when we left the paramedics with Beatrice Harris?"

"Yes. It was only last night."

"I gave them my card. I said to call me if they lose her. I remember saying it."

"Yeah, I remember it. But she survived. I don't see what you're getting at."

"I had some missed calls last night. That's all. I thought it was the paramedic. I presumed she had passed away."

"It's been a long week. Get some rest. I don't know what Will has in store for us next week, but this'll take some beating."

"Yes," she said, but didn't have the heart to enter into a conversation about her leaving. "Yes indeed."

"Freya?" called Will Granger, and she turned to see Jackie and Chapman smiling at whatever he had just said to them. He pointed at the corridor. "A word in private?"

The squeaky door squealed and slammed.

"I won't miss that door," she said, following Will to his office along the corridor. He waited at the door. Ever the gentleman, he held it open for her.

"Some say that DSI Harper asked facilities to make it squeak so he can hear people working. A noisy door is a sign of activity."

"Do you hold any value to that claim?" she said, and sat when he offered her a seat.

"I think it's like everything else around here – old and in need of some freshening up. You did well in there. I enjoy your briefings."

"No theories," she said. "Well, not too many anyway."

"No. You're a good leader, Freya. The team admire you. They respect you. That's half the battle."

"They're a good team. I respect them. Maybe that's why? I have the reports you asked for. Everything Ben needs to get through the CPS interview is in the files."

Offering the beginnings of a smile, he looked sad.

"Can I ask you why?" he said.

"Why what, guv?"

"Why you didn't just make an appointment somewhere? I don't understand it. There really is no official procedure for this. Your secondment came highly recommended."

"So why did you ask me to see somebody?"

"Because you're a damn fine detective, Freya. Because like you said, we're a small team. But in a small team, the little things are noticeable. The mistakes. The attitude. The distant stares."

"Distant stares?"

"Ask Ben, when you see him. You disappear somewhere some-times. Nobody knows where. My guess is that you were trying to remember what happened. But I can't get inside your head."

"I wouldn't recommend attempting to."

"I'm sure. You see, when I asked you to make an appointment to see somebody, I was of course hoping that talking to somebody might help, but more than that, I was looking for some kind of commitment from you. An appointment means nothing. A trauma like that which you suffered, I'm sorry to say but I'm sure you know, can take months or years to come to terms with. All I wanted was for you to show me you were serious about staying. But you didn't or you couldn't. I'm not sure which."

There was nothing for Freya to say. At least, nothing that would have made a difference. She had tried. But her reasons for hanging up the calls were unclear, even to her.

"I guess it wasn't meant to be," he said. "Have you said your goodbyes?"

"Where I needed to, yes. I think so."

His old-school sense of professionalism and manners were admirable. He stood, straightened his tunic, and offered Freya his hand.

"I'll let you slip out the back door, if you'd rather a fuss wasn't made."

"I'd appreciate that," she replied, standing and shaking his hand.

He held her there and made eye contact.

"I hope this isn't the last we see of you, DI Bloom."

"Likewise," she said, and swallowed at the sound of her breaking voice. "I'd like to come back and celebrate Ben's promotion."

Just then, there was a knock at the open door. They both turned to see Jackie in the doorway, breathless and holding a folded piece of notepaper.

"I'm sorry for interrupting. Should I come back?"

Blushing at her careless intrusion, Jackie shuffled her feet and bit her lower lip.

"It's fine," said Granger. "DI Bloom and I were just finishing up. How can I help?"

"It's actually for DI Bloom, guv. A message."

"For me?" Freya said, surprised at the time and the place. "What is it, Gold?"

Holding out the notepaper for Freya, Jackie's nervousness rang alarm bells.

"I'm sorry, ma'am," Jackie said. "I'm so sorry."

CHAPTER FORTY-THREE

"One word," Ben said, before Freya even had a chance to open the door fully. She peered out at him standing there in the dark, grinning like a schoolboy.

"Suitcase," she said dismissively.

"How did you know I was going to say that?"

"Lucky guess, I imagine," she said, to which he cocked his head in disbelief. "It's the only loose end. And it's neither here nor there, is it?"

"It might be. We don't know, do we?"

She stepped aside to offer him a view of her own suitcase at the foot of the stairs.

"Besides, it's hard not to think of a suitcase when everything you own fits inside one," she said.

He said nothing. He didn't have to. His expression spoke volumes, and he pushed past her, entering the house that belonged to his father.

By the time she had followed him into the lounge, he was already loading logs and kindling into the burner thing. Freya resumed her position in her armchair, collected her glass of wine from the floor, and settled back to watch him.

He was a handsome man. Larger than average in nearly every way. Probably something to do with being farming stock. She wondered what his brothers were like, and his father. Maybe they were just as broad and heavy set?

"So?" he said, unable to look at her.

"Suitcase?"

He nodded.

"I'd like to think that when Jane Blythe was hit and she fell to the ground, she let go of her suitcase. In my mind, Rita Harris, Michael Harris, and Cheryl Butcher were all too focused on Beatrice to worry about the little suitcase lying there. I hope somebody found it and made use of it," she mused, sipping at her wine. "Better than it sitting in an evidence locker until the time comes for it to be burned."

"You're a romantic at heart, aren't you?" he said, the side of his face glowing orange from the flames he was nurturing.

"Not really. But too many good things happen to those who don't deserve it. Not enough happen to those that do," she replied cryptically. "Maybe the person who found it needed it? Maybe it helped them? That would be nice."

Ben sat back on his haunches and studied her.

"It's not the only loose end though, is it?"

He was smarter than she had given him credit for.

"The press?" she asked, and his face dropped into a bemused expression. "Somebody called the press."

"How do you do that?"

"The same way you do," she replied. "I think of every angle. That's what makes us good detectives."

She tipped her glass to see how much was left, dreading the idea of limping back into the kitchen to top it up.

"Jane Blythe was pregnant," she said, resting the near-empty glass on the arm of the chair. "Who knew?"

It was obvious they were going to talk about the elephant in the room, or the suitcase at the foot of the stairs, but there was still time to watch him squirm.

"Daniel, probably. They were trying, after all."

"And?"

"Doctor Harris. Her GP."

"Yes, and...?"

He shook his head. "Mrs Harris? Or Cheryl? But they would've both had to have read her notes."

She withdrew some of the credit she had given him earlier. But then his face lit up, and his mouth opened at the idea.

"Tom Hendry?"

"Daniel Blythe's lover. His confidante."

"Why would he call the press?" Ben said, a question to himself, not to Freya, and one he answered well enough for Freya to mentally return some of the withdrawn credit. "Because he wanted to shift our attention from the hit and run, and away from Andrew Summers."

"You'll make a good DI," she said, and this time his expression didn't just drop. It plummeted.

"It's true then?" he said, glancing back at the stairs.

She turned away from him to stare out the window. It was pitch dark outside, so she could see almost nothing of the sky. But still, she often found herself looking at it, her imagination filling in the blanks.

"The night I sent you and Jackie home," she began, avoiding his direct question. "You stacked the wood. Am I right?"

He nodded, sullen and withdrawn.

"And you thought that by letting Jackie Gold light my fire so the house was warm when I got home, I'd somehow forgive her for the way she acted?"

He nodded again and stared at the floor. Maybe in shame?

"Jackie found something, didn't she?"

"She wasn't snooping, Freya."

"I didn't say she was. But she found something, yes?"

He nodded, this time taking the rap like a man. He stared at her now, shoulders back. Ready to accept whatever criticism she offered.

"Do you realise there was sensitive information among my paperwork?"

"Yes, but–"

"Do you realise there were things in there that even you shouldn't see. Reports, personal files–"

"Listen, Freya–"

"Do you realise that what she saw could have destroyed whatever is left of my career?"

He closed his eyes and stared at the floor again.

"Yes," he said, sucking in a breath.

"I should feel betrayed."

"And do you?"

"A little," she replied.

"Can I make up for it?"

She weighed the choices in her mind, then settled on one that seemed the most fun. "Yes. Yes, you can."

"How?"

"Fetch me the bottle of wine from the fridge. Bring another glass. I feel like getting drunk."

"Drunk? Now?"

"Are you making amends, or do I have to drink alone?" she asked. "I want to know who the real Ben Savage is. I want to know what goes on in that mind of yours. The best way to do that is to drink. So drink with me, Savage."

For a man of over six foot and at least sixteen stone, Ben was lithe. He sprang to his feet and was back from the kitchen in no time, brandishing the bottle and a glass for himself.

"So?" he said.

"So what?"

"What will you do?"

She sighed and sipped her drink, then rested the glass on the arm again.

"So Jackie told you, did she?"

"A little," he replied. "But I wouldn't let her go into detail. I told her to drop it."

"Noble of you," she replied, admiring the way he held himself, despite knowing he was in the wrong. There was a strength to him, and it was in those moments of tension between them that she could really imagine what he was like. What it must feel like to be with him, close to him, or part of him, even.

"Thanks to you and DC Gold, with her inquisitive nature–" she began.

"Oh god, Freya..."

Unable to hide the smirk that was tightening her lips, she filled the glass he was holding, although it was more of a distraction technique than her desire to share the wine.

"Granger gave me a week to get myself an appointment."

"You told me," he said.

"But you already knew."

Deeming the fire established enough for a larger log, Ben placed one strategically then closed the burner door.

"Did you make the appointment?"

"No, I didn't. I couldn't," she explained. "How could I talk to somebody about something I can't remember? How can I grieve for something I can only imagine?"

"But you said you remembered. You told me–"

"It was all too little too late, Ben," she said. "Granger did all he could. And I agree with him. He can't be seen to go back on a decision. It wouldn't look good on him."

"Freya–"

"He was good enough to let me slip out of the office unseen. He's a good man," she said.

"I don't believe this."

"And I was all set to go."

"Freya, I'm so sorry. I had no idea Jackie would read your thing," he said, opening the burner door to distract himself with the fire.

"Well, it's a bloody good job she did," Freya said.

A few moments passed, during which time Ben prodded and poked and rearranged the logs the way men like to do. It took a few moments more for what Freya had said to permeate.

"Eh?" he said, his face suddenly filled with hope.

She set the grin free.

"Jackie Gold, the nosiest police officer I have ever known, booked me an appointment with the therapist."

"And you can talk to her now," Ben said, excited. "You remembered."

"She came in at the eleventh hour. Handed me the appointment right in front of Granger."

"What did he say? Was he pleased?"

"Well," she said, sucking in a breath and enjoying the sensation of the smile on her face. "You're now looking at the latest permanent Detective Inspector on the team. Watch out Steve Standing, that's what I say."

She raised her glass, and Ben nearly clinked his against hers, until he remembered what she had once told him, about clinking glasses to be poor etiquette.

"To Jackie Gold," he said.

"The nosiest, and loveliest, Detective I've ever met," Freya added, and they drank.

Resting the glass on the arm again, Freya mused over something Ben had said.

"You said her."

"Eh?" Ben said, once more finding distraction in managing the logs.

"You said I can talk to *her* now. The therapist. How did you know the therapist is a she?"

"Oh," Ben replied, taking a much larger sip of his wine, this time to conceal his own grin. "Lucky guess, I imagine."

The End.

IN COLD BLOOD - PROLOGUE

Emma Jackson's boot crunched through the crispy layer of frost, then sank into the few inches of mud beneath. The surrounding fields were obscured by a thick fog that rolled in off the fens. Occasionally, a break in the clouds revealed the sky above, laden with stars so close she could almost reach out and grab them. Though they would simply slip through her fingers like everything else she cherished.

She found him staring out into their field, watching the mist as they had done together on many occasions. She slipped her arms around him to nuzzle into his back.

She said nothing. Not at first anyway. Enough had been said already, and nothing had changed. She was still leaving.

His body tensed at her touch and did not relax when she squeezed. Not the way it used to. Not before the old man had died.

"I'm sorry," she offered, and heard how feeble it sounded. "I've ruined everything."

Somewhere out in the field, beyond the blanket of fine mist, a neighbour's dog barked at something. There was nothing unusual there. Almost every household in Wasps Nest had a dog, and one of them would always find an excuse to bark, even in the early hours.

"Will you call when you get there, at least?" he asked. "Wherever *there* happens to be."

"No," she replied without hesitation. "It's better if I don't."

"How will I know you're safe?"

"You won't. You don't need to anymore," she said, though it pained her to say the words.

"Emma–"

"I've made up my mind, Jason. Don't try to change it. Please."

He turned in her arms before she could stop him, and he held her by her shoulders, searching her eyes for a weakness to exploit. That was his way.

"You don't have to leave," he said. "Who cares what people think?"

"Don't. Please."

"No. I won't let you go. What about our dream? The farm. The bed and breakfast. Kids even–"

"Oh, come on. We both know you never wanted–"

"I do. I do. If that's what it takes, then I do want them."

"It's too late for that."

"Then we'll both go. We'll sell up. It's nearly Christmas for crying out loud."

"I see the way you look at me."

"What?" he said, and pulled away, turning to stare out at their field.

"There's doubt, isn't there?" she said. "In your mind, there's doubt. You're not sure if I did it or not."

"Of course I'm sure," he said, and reached to stroke her hair.

"Really? So look me in the eye and tell me you believe me."

He turned away to gaze into the fog once more.

"Jason? Come on. Look at me and tell me there's not a shred of doubt that I'm innocent."

"You're being stupid, Emma."

"And you're lying. How am I supposed to live with this? How am I supposed to run a bed and breakfast? Who's going to want to stay at a place run by a killer? A loser."

"You're not a killer, or a loser."

"As good as," she said. "In their eyes, I'm as good as."

"You were found not guilty. The jury said so. It's all in your head. You're being stupid and–"

"And what, Jason?" she said, and her temper flashed red, like a pulse of blood behind her eyes. She exhaled, and softened her tone. "And what?"

"Selfish," he said flatly. "You always were selfish. I should have known you'd do something like this."

"No–"

"I should have known you'd bail on me as soon as it got hard. It was never going to be easy, Emma. I told you there'd be times when we had no money. When we'd scrape a living doing whatever we could. That's what you have to endure. That's the price you pay to get what you want. Suffering."

"To get what *you* want, you mean."

"Oh come on, this was your dream as much as mine. Now you're going to leave me to run a bed and breakfast. What am I supposed to do out here on my own? We're in the middle of nowhere, Emma."

"You chose it–"

"I *found* it. We chose it. We chose the place where we could both be together away from everyone. We – just you and me, we don't need anybody else. Now you're bailing on me, and I'm stuck out here."

"A man died in my care, Jason," she snapped. "I'm plagued by death. I've lost the game."

Her words carried across the field, startled some birds, and that dog began barking again. A dark shape flashed then was lost to the mist once again. A trick of the light maybe?

"I have to live with that," she said. "Regardless if people think I did it or not. Regardless if even you think I did it–"

"Which I don't–"

"I have to live with it. I have to live knowing that, had I done something differently, he might be alive. Had I not left him alone for a few minutes, he might still be alive. I have to live knowing that had we chosen someplace else, we might have had more money behind us. I wouldn't have had to clean up after old men, and heat up their rancid dinners, or wipe their bloody arses. And you know what? I might even sleep at night. I might even enjoy being with you, being here. But I don't."

"Sleep at night?"

"Neither, Jason. I see it in your eyes. I see the doubt. It's bad enough that I can't step foot in the local shop anymore–"

"Of course you can. People take time, that's all."

"They hate me, Jason. They bloody hate me. A car nearly knocked me down yesterday when I was walking up the lane."

"Oh, come on, it's a narrow lane."

"The driver sped up when he saw me."

"It was a man, was it?"

"No. I don't know. It doesn't matter. You don't bloody get it, do you? I'm scared to leave the house, and when I see the doubt in your eyes, I'm scared to be here with you. I can't go on like this. I need to go."

"Go where? You have nowhere else to go."

"Anywhere. I need to go where nobody knows me," she said softly. "I need to start over."

"Then we'll both go."

"No," she said, as she stepped out of arm's reach. "No, I have to do this alone. I dream there's somebody standing over me when I sleep. It's so real. Like, I can feel a sharp point on my throat."

"It's all in your mind, Emma. You've been through a lot."

"Three months on remand. Three months locked up with

bitter women with nothing to lose. But you know what, I felt safe there. I felt like I belonged. Like I deserved it. I slept too," she said, hearing the fondness in her voice. "There was no man standing over me while I slept. Nobody tried to run me down on the lane. I'm going, Jason. This is no life for me, and it's no life for you either."

"Shh," he said, and he half-turned, holding his finger to his pursed lips. "Did you hear that?"

"Hear what?" Emma said. "I didn't hear anything."

"Who's there?" he called. He hurdled the fence to run out into the field where the long fingers of mist seemed to envelop him.

"Jason, wait," Emma called, and she unstuck her boot to climb onto the fence, then swung a leg over just as she heard two footsteps in the mud.

But her loving boyfriend did not run out of the mist, and the footsteps ceased.

"Jason? Where are you?" she called, stumbling into the field. She tripped once on the rough terrain, then dropped into a divot their little tractor had created, and fell to her knees. "Jason?"

And then she saw him. Through the fog just twenty feet ahead. A dark and lifeless form lying in the frost. A wave of mist formed, then passed, but the spot where he had been lying was empty.

"Jason?"

And then she smelled it. The chemical scent of oil.

And then she felt it. The rough, gloved hand that clamped over her mouth, and the cold bite of a steel blade against her throat.

ALSO BY JACK CARTWRIGHT

The DCI Cook Murder Mysteries

A Winter of Blood

A Secret to Die For

The Wild Fens Murder Mysteries

Secrets In Blood

One For Sorrow

In Cold Blood

Suffer In Silence

Dying To Tell

Never To Return

Lie Beside Me

Dance With Death

In Dead Water

One Deadly Night

Her Dying Mind

Into Death's Arms

No More Blood

Join my VIP reader group to be among the first to hear about new release dates, discounts, and get a free Wild Fens novella.

Visit www.jackcartwrightbooks.com for details.

COPYRIGHT

Copyright © 2023 by JackCartwright.

First published in 2022.

All rights reserved.

The moral right of Jack Cartwright to be identified as the author of this work has been asserted by him in accordance with the Copyright, Designs and Patents act 1988.

All the characters in this book are fictitious, and any resemblance to actual persons living or dead is purely coincidental.